Exposed to You

Exposed to You

Beth Kery

HEAT I NEW YORK

THE BERKLEY PUBLISHING GROUP
Published by the Penguin Group
Penguin Group (USA) Inc.
375 Hudson Street, New York, New York 10014, USA

Penguin Group (Canada), 90 Eglinton Avenue East, Suite 700, Toronto, Ontario M4P 2Y3, Canada
(a division of Pearson Penguin Canada Inc.) • Penguin Books Ltd., 80 Strand, London WC2R 0RL,
England • Penguin Group Ireland, 25 St. Stephen's Green, Dublin 2, Ireland (a division of Penguin
Books Ltd.) • Penguin Group (Australia), 707 Collins Street, Melbourne, Victoria 3008, Australia
(a division of Pearson Australia Group Pty. Ltd.) • Penguin Books India Pvt. Ltd., 11 Community
Centre, Panchsheel Park, New Delhi—110 017, India • Penguin Group (NZ), 67 Apollo Drive,
Rosedale, Auckland 0632, New Zealand (a division of Pearson New Zealand Ltd.) • Penguin Books
(South Africa) (Pty.) Ltd., Rosebank Office Park, 181 Jan Smuts Avenue, Parktown North 2193,
South Africa • Penguin China, B7 Jaiming Center, 27 East Third Ring Road North,
Chaoyang District, Beijing 10020, China

Penguin Books Ltd., Registered Offices: 80 Strand, London WC2R 0RL, England

This book is an original publication of The Berkley Publishing Group.

PUBLISHING HISTORY
Heat trade paperback edition / November 2012

Library of Congress Cataloging-in-Publication Data

Kery, Beth.
Exposed to you : a one night of passion novel / Beth Kery. — Heat trade paperback ed.
p.   cm.
ISBN 978-0-425-25915-3
1. Motion picture actors and actresses—Fiction.   2. Art teachers—Fiction.
3. Man-woman relationships—Fiction.   I. Title.
PS3611.E79E98   2012
813'.6—dc23
2012011832

PRINTED IN THE UNITED STATES OF AMERICA

10   9   8   7   6   5   4   3   2   1

Exposed to You

One

If someone had told her when her alarm clock went off that morning that in a few hours she'd be calmly given the odds of her continued survival, Joy would have rolled her eyes and laughed her fears into the corners of her consciousness.

If someone had warned her that later that afternoon she'd be going down on a gorgeous stranger, she'd have told that person they were certifiably insane.

Wilkie shouted her name as she raced through the din of the makeup room. A photo shoot for movie posters and other promotional materials was scheduled today. The special effects makeup department was roaring in high gear. Wilkie James looked too busy to chat, so Joy merely slowed her rapid pace. Her friend held an airbrush and was staring intently at a female's right breast as he turned it pale green, his shaggy, dark brown hair just inches away from a nipple.

"He's in his lab, angsting for your talent. 'I need Joy,' he keeps moaning," Wilkie imitated, adding a tremble to Seth Hightower's gruff baritone for comic effect. "He's been trying to reach you for hours. Where've you been, beautiful?"

"Don't I have a life, or was that all my imagination?" Joy asked, grinning.

"You may have had a life before we began production on *Maritime*, but that's all just a dream now, honey," Wilkie drawled as he moved to the left breast, and his model yawned widely.

That's all just a dream now.

Wilkie's careless words struck her with frightening precision. She shrugged off the shadow of dread that hovered at the corners of her consciousness and walked on, willing the energy from her surroundings to distract her . . .

Numb her.

The drama and excitement of a Hollywood film set wasn't Joy's typical work world. As an art teacher for gifted high school students and a painter, she preferred the atmosphere of the classroom or her quiet, sunlit studio at home. Even the clamor and bustle of a Hollywood makeup department couldn't fully penetrate her dread, however.

Not today.

She felt as if she were moving through a dream . . . something like the brilliant, surreal underwater world film director Joshua Cabot was creating for United Studios's latest blockbuster, *Maritime*.

She willfully ignored the uncomfortable pounding in her chest and flung open the door to Seth Hightower's office-studio. She needed to see the familiar, loved, bold-featured face of her uncle; he was the only true family member she still possessed. Seth glanced around at the sound of her tool kit rolling over the threshold behind her.

"There you are!"

"I didn't get the messages until a half an hour ago. I was at the doctor. I came as quickly as I could."

Seth looked contrite. "I know. Ignore me. I'm in a bear of a mood."

Joy smiled. Her uncle was a bear of a man in stature, perhaps, but hardly in temperament. At least not with Joy, he wasn't. He tossed a few tubes of paint and glue into his kit before he straightened, swept down on her from his great height and gave her a quick, affectionate kiss, his shoulder-length dark hair flicking against her cheek. "You're not even officially part of my staff and I snap at you like an intern. Your mother would have my hide." Seth focused on her face, his brows drawing together in a V shape, giving him an expression that anyone besides Joy would have found intimidating. "I know you had to take off school a few days last week. Is that why you were at the doctor? How's the cough?"

"Better," Joy said as she glanced around the meticulously organized room. As the makeup department head, Seth claimed the right to privacy. His office-studio was like the still eye of a storm. "I don't have pneumonia," she reported honestly. "What's the emergency?"

"It's coming at me from all directions. Our leading lady decided to drink some Coke spiked with vodka without a straw. The latex is lifting around her mouth," Seth said, referring to the actress's prosthetic mask. "She's throwing a fit and holing up in her trailer, refusing to let anyone touch her up but me. Meantime, I'm running behind on the tattoos."

Joy gave her uncle a humorous glance of sympathy. "There's a cost to being the best."

"Anybody on my staff could reglue Ellie, you know that. She's just throwing her weight around by asking for me personally."

"She must think you're the best at a few things."

"As if I'd ever give that little shrew the chance to find out," Seth muttered with a disgusted, distracted air. Joy's heart went out to him. This had to be one of the most hectic days of his life. "Anyway, that only leaves you who can do the last tattoo—"

Seth paused when someone rapped and the door opened several inches. Her breath caught at what she saw.

Joy had helped Seth with projects for Hightower Special Effects on several occasions, and she'd assisted him with the illustrations for his initial proposal to win the contract from United Studios and director Joshua Cabot for *Maritime*. As such, she was used to Seth's fantastical art concept for the film. She wasn't so immune, however, that she didn't stare in wonder at the bizarrely beautiful head of the part man, part exotic sea creature that appeared around the edge of the door.

Her uncle was going to have an Academy Award sitting on his mantel for sure, she thought with a mixture of admiration and pride.

"Hey, Tommy told me I should stop by," the walking piece of art said.

"Perfect timing," Seth mumbled. He pointed at an illustration and some scribbled notes on the table. "Here's what I need, Joy. You're the only one I trust to do it. Go ahead and touch him up after you finish the tattoo. I won't have time before the photo shoot. Wish me luck," he said, glancing at both of them.

"Luck. You'll need it," the marine man said, his lips twitching subtly.

Seth snorted in agreement and rolled his kit behind him toward the door. The man, who was probably one of dozens of extras, stepped into the room so that Seth could pass. Joy noticed distractedly that her uncle and the aqua-colored male were nearly the same height—an oddity, as her uncle was usually the tallest man in the room. The two men nodded to each other before Seth shut the door behind him. Joy lifted her kit to the table and began to extract her paints, brushes and tattoo pens.

"Give me just a minute, and I'll be right with you," she said as she checked Seth's notes and began to mix her colors.

He didn't respond, but Joy was too focused on her preparation to mind. Actors and extras reacted to prosthetic and makeup application across a spectrum that ran from stoicism to whining to outright acting out. Hours and hours of sitting or standing motionless were often required while an artist created his magic. *Maritime* was a particular challenge. Over a hundred actors and extras required waterproof prosthetics and full-body makeup in order to transform them into exotic sea creatures. Only dozens might be required to be in full makeup and costume during a given day of shooting, but Cabot had decided he wanted the entire cast in full regalia to give the grand scope of the movie for the photo shoot.

Joy was working up a sweat as she mixed her paints. She walked over to the unit air conditioner and turned it on high, the sound of the fan muting the cacophony of voices, music and movement just feet away from Seth's office-studio.

"So you're Seth's niece?"

She paused in the action of removing her hoodie. His deep, resonant voice had taken her by surprise. She met his gaze for the first time and blinked. His eyes were a clear aquamarine. The elaborate foam latex prosthetic he wore on the upper half of his face and the sublime makeup application only added to their brilliance. His gaze struck her as startlingly alert. Compared to this man, other people's stares were those of sleepwalkers.

She had the strangest sensation seeing his eyes peering through the elaborate costume he wore, as if she'd caught a glimpse of his soul through the beautiful artifice. Seth's makeup, which subtly alluded to the emerging humanity of the sea creature, only added to the impression. The body paints included brilliant blues and greens, but flesh colors rippled and swirled over chiseled muscle and bone as well, creating a stunning living landscape. He was beyond beautiful, the subtle shadowing wrought by the air- and paintbrushes highlighting every ridge and smooth, hard plane of his long body.

His gaze flicked downward.

She became aware that she was holding both sides of her cotton
hoodie wide open in preparation to remove it. Her breasts felt tight
suddenly, straining against the fabric of her bra and a thin layer of
her cotton tank top. Her nipples beaded, as if he'd reached out and
brushed a finger over the sensitive flesh instead of just glancing
at her.

She blushed, her reaction surprising her. Joy was an artist, and
she'd long ago grown accustomed to partial and full nudity. She
didn't work full-time in the movie industry, but she'd had sufficient
experience, thanks to Seth. Gorgeous models and want-to-be actors were the norm in Hollywood, as commonly found as a corn-
stalk on a July day in Indiana.

She whipped off her hoodie and tossed it on the table.

"Yes. I'm Joy." She nodded to a spot in front of the table and
reached for a chair, all brisk business.

"You're the art teacher."

She met his stare and was once again snared.

"Seth told me," he said quietly, shapely blue-and-white tinted
lips barely moving.

"We better get started or you'll miss the shoot," she murmured,
discomfited for some reason by the idea of Seth sharing even the
smallest details of her life with this stranger.

He walked to the spot she'd indicated. Joy sat and rolled her
chair directly in front of him, her face situated in front of his abdomen. Without another word, she picked up a tattoo marker and
began to outline the design in Seth's illustration on her human
canvas. Seth had altered the tattoo art somewhat from his original
proposal. The brilliant starburst through rippling water was bolder
and much more intricate than his original design. Joy liked the
change.

She never looked at his face once while she worked, but she was
highly aware of him. Her knuckles brushed occasionally against

warm, dense flesh. Her nose was just inches from his body. The alcohol base from the body paint filtered into her nose. Beneath it, she smelled the musk of his skin like a subtle, living thread twining through the chemical artifice. The fragrance was potent somehow, sending a loud, clear message of male virility to some ancient part of her brain.

Only a stretchy, seaweed-like boxer-brief costume covered his genitals. Joy couldn't help but be conscious of the fact that her chin was mere inches from the fullness behind the flimsy material. She worked steadily, but a dull, pleasurable ache began to grow at her core.

A light glaze of perspiration had dampened her brow and upper lip by the time she leaned back. She glanced up at him, a calm— entirely fake—expression plastered on her face.

"You'll have to lower your briefs enough for me to make the transition look natural," she said.

The air conditioner made a loud, chugging sound and then resumed its typical hum. She saw his throat convulse. Was he as uncomfortable with this situation as she was? He held her stare with those striking eyes and moved his hands, folding down the seaweed brief and exposing the stretch of skin just above his genitals.

She lifted her tattoo pen and paused.

Seth had used the airbrush below the brief, but not in a thorough manner. Joy could see several patches of naked, golden skin along with a smattering of light brown hair. Pubic hair was usually several shades darker than hair on the head, which meant he must be blond beneath the beautiful headpiece affixed to his head.

Below that strip of skin, the flimsy material barely contained a virile package. The vision was nearly as striking as that of the man's eyes peering through the elaborate mask. What was it about that stretch of skin below the belly and just above a man's cock that spoke of sensitivity . . . vulnerability?

His arm muscles clenched tight. He kept his hands on the material of the briefs, as if he wanted to be prepared to jerk the garment back into place at the slightest provocation. Joy didn't know
whether to feel compassion for him or annoyance. He was the six-
foot-four-inch tower of brawn here, not her. She was hardly going
to attack him. She disliked this intimate aspect of her work, but the
human body wasn't something that could be ignored when it came
to art. He was just a backdrop, not any different from the canvases
in her studio.

Her expression hardened at the thought. She leaned forward
and continued her design, the tip of her marker slipping across firm
flesh. She was doing fine for the next minute or so until she noticed
the brief was stretching and expanding to contain his erection. His
cock rode along his left thigh. The column of it was clearly delin-
eated beneath the insubstantial garment.

Shit.

She glanced up at him anxiously. He was looking down at her.
She'd known he would be. She'd sensed his stare on the crown of
her head the entire time. He closed his eyes briefly. She sensed his
regret even through his half mask.

"I'm sorry," he said in a gruff voice. "Just . . . just ignore it."

Heat flooded her cheeks and she looked away.

How mortifying.

It wasn't uncommon for a model to occasionally experience an
unwanted erection during a makeup application, but the evidence
had never been so . . . *close* to her before. Nor had it ever been so
appealing.

For a few dreadful seconds, she felt like she couldn't expand her
lungs. They finally released, however, and she reached for a pot of
paint.

"Do you want to take a quick break?" she asked, striving to
keep her voice even.

"No. Go ahead." His voice sounded so strained, she glanced up at him in concern. She saw the rigidness of his angular jaw. His eyes blazed through the prosthetic mask.

"I'm not sure that's such a good idea," she said.

"I can take it if you can."

She wasn't quite sure she *could* take it. Things had gotten warm and wet between her thighs. She looked down at her lap and used her forearm to wipe at the thin layer of perspiration on her upper lip. Her heartbeat segued from a throb to a roar in her ears. She swirled her paint—twice right, once left, twice right, once left—the familiar task of moving the brush through the thick liquid striking her as rich for some reason . . . sensual.

She lifted the brush to his skin and began to paint. It was a little like working while a ravenous lion raced toward you in the periphery of your vision. She was acutely aware of the power in him, the incipient energy, like a giant spring that was being held down tight with effort. She worked steadily for the next half hour or so in the area of his lower abdomen, creating the impossible—a flare of fire in water.

The realization hit her as she moved to the lower left quadrant of her design that she should have told him he could release the garment until she began to work in that area again. He'd kept his hands on the sides of the brief the whole time, however, exposing that strip of sensitive skin. Something about his pose excited her for some reason. It was as if he were frozen in the moment of offering himself to her . . .

Giving her a taste.

Her cheeks burned at the uncontrollable thought. She leaned away from him, feeling the loss of his subtle, radiant body heat on her cheeks and lips. She exchanged her paints and went back to work.

What was wrong with her? She'd never had this reaction before while she'd been working. Her skin felt flushed and prickly with awareness. There seemed to be some strange, inexplicable connection between where her paintbrush stroked his taut skin and her clit.

Why did she want to hold on to that brilliant flare of lust that the stranger's fierce eyes and hard cock promised? *Maybe because you were told today that life and a future aren't a certainty, that both of those things were as ephemeral, as difficult to hold on to as an unexpected lightning strike of desire?*

Joy didn't want to let go. She wanted . . . no, she *needed* to hang on.

The air around them seemed to have taken on a weight. She forced her lungs to move as she exchanged brushes and reached for a paint she'd deposited at the far end of the table. When she touched him with the wet tip just below his hip bone, his taut abdomen muscle twitched. She glanced up and saw a small smile on his mouth.

"It's colder than the other ones," he said.

"I'm sorry. The paint was sitting right in front of the air conditioner."

"It's okay."

His mouth moved again, but no sound came from his throat. Some instinct inside her told her this man didn't typically become speechless.

She felt a surge of liquid heat at her sex.

She swallowed with difficulty and resumed painting, the feeling of moving in a dream only amplifying. How long would this surreal sensation last? When would the reality of her diagnosis of cancer really set in? Her grim future seemed impossible to grasp as she sat there, flushed with arousal, painting a brilliant tattoo on a beautiful, virile male she'd never seen before that moment, and would probably never see again.

"It's finished," she murmured minutes later as she placed the solvent that set the paint on the table. From the corner of her vision, she saw that he didn't move his hands, keeping his briefs lowered. The fullness behind the seaweed design hadn't dissipated during the past forty-five minutes.

"Joy."

She glanced up slowly, both hesitant and anticipatory at once at the sound of his hoarse voice.

"I hope you don't think I'm a complete jackass for saying this, but that had to be the most erotic thing I've experienced since Peggy Barton let me touch her breasts when I was fourteen years old."

She just stared at him in amazement for a second before she laughed. The strangling sexual tension fractured slightly, letting her breathe. He smiled, full-out and brilliant.

Her laughter ceased.

Oh my God, she thought, stunned. Her sunburst tattoo would be considered dim next to that smile.

Suddenly, unaccountably, fear broke over her. She stared at the very image of vibrant life. What would it *be* like to be snuffed out of existence, no longer able to see, to hear . . . to feel?

Her gaze sunk over him. She absorbed his image hungrily, drinking it like an elixir that vanquished terror. His cock jerked in the briefs when her glance landed on it.

The realization struck her that if she wanted to touch him, if she wanted to stretch this strange, powerful moment, she was going to have to make the move. Who knew? Maybe she wouldn't even be here this time next year.

It felt nowhere near as anxiety-provoking as she would have thought it would to touch him. In fact, it seemed like the most natural thing in the world to do.

She thrilled to the heaviness of his cock beneath the cloth. Arousal spiked through her, and those life-altering words—*primary mediastinal B-cell lymphoma*—scattered to the periphery of her consciousness like frightened moths.

"Do you mind?" she asked, looking up at him, her voice vibrating with barely restrained emotion.

His nostrils flared slightly. "Are you kidding?" He sounded downright incredulous at her question. Their gazes held as she felt his heartbeat thrum against her palm. He reached up and ever so gently, careful of his paint-covered skin, touched her jaw. A strange, strangled sound escaped her throat at his caress.

She carefully, deliberately reached inside the pocket of the costume boxer-briefs, intent on not ruining the makeup application on his thighs. She bit her lower lip when her hand closed around the circumference of his cock. She drew out his length.

For a moment, she just stared.

It was like holding life in her hand.

His naked penis stood in stark contrast to the elaborate makeup applied to his body. The long, straight length of it running from root to fleshy cap struck her as sublime. She held him up before her face, the tip slanting toward the ceiling. She ran the tip of her tongue from the ridge beneath the head all the way to the base, flicking a firm testicle experimentally.

He made a muffled gasping noise like his lungs had deflated in an instant. His male scent filled her nose. She twitched her fingers on the shaft, relishing his sheer virility, his weight and firmness.

Yes. This is what she needed.

She tightened her grip, closed her eyes and arrowed his cock between her lips. She abandoned herself to the voluptuous, eternal moment, escaping into it like a fugitive from a harsh, meaningless world.

Everett Hughes became distantly aware that his muscles were so tense, they felt like they'd break given one more ounce of pressure. He ached.

Everywhere.

He studied the crown of her head like he thought his stare could bore down into her brain and read her thoughts. It would probably do him good to read her mind, he thought with grim amusement. Her thoughts were undoubtedly mundane and matter-of-fact. Nowhere near as X-rated as his had become ever since he'd walked into the room and seen Seth Hightower's niece standing there, looking like a fresh wild flower amidst a field of artificial and hothouse blooms.

She'd been about as aware of him as she was the paint on the wall as she prepared to work. It was an unusual feeling for Everett, to be overlooked. He relished the opportunity to study her openly.

If he'd gone by her face alone, he might have guessed her age in her midtwenties. Only her swift, sure movements as she prepared her paints and the feminine curves accenting a slender, toned body hinted to him that she was likely nearer to thirty than twenty. He knew that Seth was part Pueblo Indian. He saw some evidence of Native American heritage in Joy, but to a lesser extent than in her uncle. Mostly her still, calm expression and smooth, apricot and copper-hued skin called that strain of her heritage to mind.

Everett had become disenchanted with the term *beautiful* long ago, feeling the hollowness of the term as it was applied to every second woman he met. But this woman—Seth Hightower's niece— she didn't just deserve the descriptor. She epitomized it without trying.

He found himself staring at the top of her long mane of chestnut brown hair as he endured the erotic sensation of her felt-tip marker sliding across his skin. His cock was thickening. He couldn't seem to help it. He closed his eyes and breathed through his nose, trying to envision the mechanics of a particularly challenging scene with Ellie Granolith, the leading lady in *Maritime*. Every scene with Ellie was a trial to get through, but this one was particularly difficult.

His half-assed attempts to distract himself fractured when Joy's marker stimulated a patch of sensitive skin just below his hip bone.

He looked down into a pair of large hazel eyes.

You'll have to lower your briefs enough for me to make the transition look natural.

His heart had lurched next to his breastbone when she'd said that. Everett was not unfamiliar with recognizing a spark of desire in a woman's eyes. If he was seeing it in Joy Hightower's solemn gaze, it *had* to be the result of wishful thinking, though.

His throat felt tight when he swallowed. He reached for the side of his briefs and lowered them. It felt very vulnerable for him, to expose himself in this way. He typically preferred being the dominant during sex, and something about this situation seemed to speak of the opposite of control. First off, this wasn't a sexual situation. It was inappropriate for him to be aroused. He couldn't control his sexual response, however, and that made him both uncomfortable and, paradoxically, more aroused. When she paused for a moment, staring at him while she clutched her marker, he felt sweat bead on his upper lip.

Seth was going to slug him if he ruined his makeup. The makeup department head was formidable, not the sort of man Everett would choose to piss off.

Seth would likely skip punching and go straight to killing him if he knew what Everett was thinking about doing with his gorgeous, wholesome niece at that moment.

Seeing her lovely face so close to the midportion of his body, studying the outlines of her full, thrusting breasts from above, feeling the whisper of her breath on his skin while the tattoo pen rolled over supersensitive nerves; all of it had been titillating. But when Joy transferred to using her paints, Everett entered the realms of torture. His cock swelled so large, he didn't think there was room in his skin anymore. His jaw hurt from clamping it shut. He was going to explode, and all he could do was tell himself to stand still. It was like telling a lit fuse to be calm.

He couldn't hide his arousal. How could he? Regret sliced through him when she glanced up, and he saw the anxiety in her eyes. His baser nature had prevailed, however. He'd told her he could handle his discomfort. How could he possibly move away from the temptation of Joy and her slippery, cool brush sliding just inches away from his straining, hurting cock?

Why was he having the most debauched fantasies about taking advantage of her, of wrecking her smooth, calm exterior . . . of making Snow White so hot, she begged for it?

He suppressed a laugh at his idiocy. He really was losing it.

He wasn't young anymore. A man in his position in Hollywood learned quickly enough that casual sex often didn't end up being as casual or as sexy as a novice might expect. He'd become extremely particular about whom he associated with in the past several years. So particular, in fact, that his sister, Katie, had taken to calling him jaded. Maybe Katie was right, because in the past few months, he'd been choosy to the point of abstinence.

Maybe that was what made this unexpected experience feel so sharp, so imperative.

Seth could come in at any moment. Dozens of people moved and talked and shouted just feet away from the still room where he stood and Joy sat, etching her magic on his flesh. More importantly, Everett didn't pull stupid, crazy stunts. Not anymore, he didn't.

But a moment later, when her laughter had morphed into that still, sublime expression, he would have dared much, much worse than to explore the promise of her inner fires.

Then she'd spoken . . . and he'd almost had a heart attack at age thirty-six.

"Do you mind?" she'd asked.

He minded, all right. If he didn't get the opportunity to feel her touch where it counted, he was going to boil and cook in his own sweat.

It'd felt like he was balancing on a narrow, straining wire the entire time Joy had sat before him and caressed him with her marker and tickled him deliciously with her paintbrush. When she so carefully reached into the briefs and extricated his cock, he fell right off that thin line of enforced rationality straight into a vat of need.

His cock felt like it was steaming when she wrapped her cool fingers around it. The image of her removing his length from the stupid seaweed pants was so exciting, he nearly came then and there. Her tongue was surprisingly red when she delicately licked him. Energy arced between them at the direct contact, their naked flesh becoming a conduit. She dragged the tip of it from head to pulsing root. Ripples of pleasure shot up his spine.

He bit his tongue hard enough to make him wince in pain. He'd be damned if he was going to ruin the richest erotic experience he'd had in . . . he couldn't remember how long by exploding before he truly got to enjoy it.

The metallic flavor of blood spread in his mouth before he allowed himself to pry open his eyes. He groaned upon seeing her spreading her lips wide and angling his cock into her warm, wet mouth.

Christ, his cock was iron hard, so how was it that he felt like he was melting on her tongue?

She may look fresh as a wild rose, but she knew how to suck. She pulled at him. He winced in pleasure as he slid across her tongue, going deeper into the humid, hot glory of her. How could he have thought she was so contained, so cool?

She was a raging fever on the inside.

His hand moved, seemingly of its own accord. He cradled the

side of her head. He withdrew and flexed forward again, suppressing a groan.

"God, that's good," he mumbled.

She ducked her head, sucking and sliding his cock between tightly pursed lips, taking him on a thrill ride of a lifetime. With every pass, she took him deeper. Her hunger was a palpable thing, the strength of it shocking him, a force that drove her farther and farther down onto the shaft of his cock. He watched her with a tight, feral stare, taking in every nuance of her—the way his erection strained her lips wide and stained them a dark, vivid pink as she pumped at his cock with a furious focus.

The sight of her consuming him like she thought it was her last meal was so powerful, he shut his eyelids to protect himself. Sensation still bombarded him: the feeling of her firm, sweet suck; the slippery sounds of his cock moving so forcefully in wet flesh reaching his ears even through the hum of the air conditioner. She continued to pulse him in and out, her unceasing suction assuring him he wasn't going to continue this little side trip into fantasyland for very long.

"Fuck," he muttered under his breath, unable to hold back any longer from the singular power of the experience and his own demanding nature.

He tightened his hold on the back of her head, stabilizing her, and began to thrust between her lips, his ass flexing tight. It was like plunging straight into the essence of pleasure. It surged through him in bursts, spiking through his flesh.

Ah, Jesus. This is what he'd stooped to—face-fucking Snow White while only a few feet and very thin walls separated him from dozens of coworkers.

His face collapsed in regret when he sensed her recoil slightly at his demanding possession, but then she was back—fiercer than before, sucking him until his eyes crossed.

He felt his balls pinch in delicious pain when the muscles of her throat closed around the tip of his cock. If he hadn't been holding it in, his shout of pleasure would have made him hoarse. As it was, it scalded his throat as he strangled it.

Pleasure ripped through him. He held her head steady as he erupted, not because of his dominant nature, but because his body had been paralyzed in a rictus of sensation. As the second wave rocked him, he recognized the discomfort he caused her. He released her with a slight jerk, rocking them both. She made a sound in her throat—God, he hoped it wasn't of dismay—but then his body tightened again in release. He came on her tongue, and his worries were buried by flooding pleasure.

He groaned gutturally, feeling like he was being emptied and filled all at once.

The need for a long, full breath overcame her at last. She slid his softening—but still formidable—penis out of her mouth. The slick, fleshy cockhead pressed against her cheek as she gasped for air, filling her lungs. His hold on her gentled. He stroked her hair as she desperately tried to catch her breath.

It was as if she'd just been caught up in the furious twist of a cyclone, only to be suddenly tossed out again into a motionless, hard world. Her mind struggled to make sense of what had just occurred. Fragments of vision and sensation bombarded her awareness.

"Are you okay?"

She froze on an inhale at the sound of his voice.

She felt a slight pressure from his hand, as if he were willing her to look at him.

Her cheeks burned. Dear God, what had she just done?

"Joy?" he prompted when she didn't move.

Keeping her head lowered, she leaned back, separating herself from him. She carefully raised his boxer-briefs and covered him, keeping her gaze averted from his glistening cock.

He was just as beautiful to her satiated as he had been rigid with need . . . so naked, so vulnerable. She began to anxiously search for damage to his makeup.

"What the—"

His bewildered-sounding voice stopped abruptly when someone shouted in the distance.

"Seth!"

"What?" Seth Hightower barked impatiently, his voice sounding as if it came from twenty or thirty feet away.

"I need you to take a look at this."

Joy stood so abruptly, the chair she'd been sitting in rolled backward several feet. She met the man's startled gaze.

She didn't even know his name.

"He'll be here any second," she said. She immediately picked up her paints as the first wave of panic started to flow through her. He caught her wrist.

"Hold on. It's going to be okay, Joy."

She was mortified to realize tears had sprung to her eyes.

"No. No, it's not." *Not for me, it's not.* He looked taken aback. For a second or two, the silence swelled.

"Of course it is," he said, smiling even though puzzlement shadowed what she could see of his features.

She swallowed and looked away from his smile. "I need to touch you up," she said, realizing for the first time that her voice was hoarse from taking his cock so deep. Another wave of heat flooded her cheeks. She tried to move to gather her paints—to gather herself—but he continued to hold her wrist.

"Joy."

She glanced up at him doubtfully, her heartbeat pounding in her ears.

"Meet me later. After the shoot. Please?" he added when she just continued to stare in the vicinity of his collarbone.

"I . . . I don't know what . . . why . . ."

"I understand," he said quietly. He released her wrist and touched her cheek until she looked at him. "I'm not sure I know, either. But I want to figure it out. Meet me at the statue? The studio statue? After this craziness is done? Just give me enough time to get out of this getup and shower, and I'll be there. I just want to talk to you. Please, Joy."

Something squeezed at her heart a little when he entreated her. In the distance, she heard her uncle's voice as he approached.

"I haven't got time right now. You'll have to handle it," Seth called out, as if he was walking away from whomever had interrupted him.

"Joy?" the stranger said sharply.

She looked into his clear aquamarine eyes and nodded once.

"Say it. Say you'll be there."

"I'll be there," she whispered.

Six hours later, she checked her watch yet again.

He wasn't coming.

She should have known better than to come herself.

The photo shoot had been completed now for almost three hours. She'd kept herself busy in Seth's studio during the shoot itself. Seth had returned after a while in order to oversee prosthetic removal. Joy had helped him, but she hadn't caught sight of the man she'd promised to meet.

She'd been waiting by the United Studios' statue of the seven muses for long enough. There was no way the man was still occupied. Not when almost everyone else on the set had long since showered and left. He'd stood her up, plain and simple.

She stood from one of the benches that lined the little park at the north studio entrance. One of the bronze muses caught her eye.

Joy lowered her head and walked toward the gate. She didn't need the muse's somber stare to know it was time for her to leave the whimsy of fantasyland and deal with the reality of a harsh world.

Two

FOURTEEN MONTHS LATER

Joy leaned back in a booth at Harry's Brew and Bake and let the air-conditioning do its thing. Being a native Southern Californian, she'd had no idea that Chicago summers sweltered. Wasn't this supposed to be the land of frigid lake winds and blizzards that brought the city of broad shoulders to a halt? The mixture of heat and humidity in the air this afternoon had her wilting by the time she hit the second step outside her front door.

"Oh, look," Sarah Weisman, a fellow teacher at the Steadman School, exclaimed, pointing out the window. Outside on North Avenue, a bus paused at a light. An advertisement for the movie *Maritime* looked oddly colorful and surreal on the mundane city bus, the bored profiles of passengers in the windows above the poster only adding to the impression. "I read in the *Tribune* this morning that the Midwest premiere of *Maritime* is going on in Streeterville tomorrow," Sarah continued excitedly. "You're going, right, Joy?"

"No." Joy laughed. She fingered her short tresses. Her hair was growing back after her cancer treatment, and she was almost back to her usual weight. She'd been fastidious about taking care of herself—regular diet, exercise, vitamins and supplements out the wazoo. Still, she was hardly up for attending a high-profile, gilded event.

"Why not? Don't tell me you didn't get a ticket?" Max Weisman, Sarah's husband, asked, his brow bunched in consternation.

"No, I could go with my uncle if I wanted," Joy said quickly. She thought she understood Max's confusion. Sarah and Max both taught with her at an art school for gifted high school students. The entire staff had been involved in the hiring process, so they'd all seen Joy's résumé, including her mention of having done makeup on several high-profile movies, including *Maritime*. "A movie premiere isn't really my scene, that's all," Joy said, taking a sip of her iced chai tea.

"You're crazy," Sarah said with typical bluntness. "I'd give my right butt cheek to attend that premiere."

"I'd give my left one to make sure your buttocks stay exactly the way they are," Max said drolly to a smirking Sarah. He leaned toward Joy, suddenly intent. "You're not going doesn't have anything to do with how you're feeling, does it?"

Joy's cheeks heated. She hated the fact—despised it, actually—that the teachers and administration at her new job knew about her cancer diagnosis. It'd been necessary to reveal the basics of that information since she'd chosen to take a half semester off from the school where she'd taught in Los Angeles while she'd undergone six cycles of chemotherapy followed by radiation. After her treatment and recovery, she'd decided to move. Start anew. People asked questions about a missing chunk of time in a résumé, though, and Joy had felt compelled to tell the truth, even if she kept her explanation to the bare minimum. It made her feel guilty, knowing that her good friends in L.A. knew less about her illness than near strangers at her present school. Not that Max and Sarah were near strangers, but still . . .

"Max, you have the finesse of a dull ax," Sarah mumbled, obviously noticing Joy's discomfort.

"No, it's okay," Joy assured. "My health is perfect, aside from the fact that I melt every time I go outside in this humidity. I can't believe you two grew up in summer saunas like this."

"She changes the subject to the weather," Max said archly to Sarah, sipping his coffee.

"I am not changing the subject," Joy said, laughing. "Look, if you like, I could ask Seth to get you two tickets. He's staying at the Elysian Hotel over on Walton. If he has a couple tickets, you could pick them up after we finish here. I'll call him right now," Joy said, extricating her cell phone from her pocket.

"Hold the phone," Sarah said in an odd, tense tone that made Joy glance up. She'd thought Sarah had been referring to the call she'd been about to make, but Sarah's turned head told her that her friend wasn't even aware of Joy's actions. Instead, she stared fixedly at the entrance. Sarah jerked her hand down, slapping Joy's thigh. She squeezed convulsively at the same time she placed her other hand over her heart. Joy glanced around her shoulder, curious as to what had transfixed a usually practical, down-to-earth woman. She saw a tall man wearing a newsboy cap and a gorgeous woman with long golden hair tumbling around her shoulders entering the coffee house.

"It's Everett Hughes," Sarah said in a strangled voice. *"Everett Hughes* just walked into Harry's Brew and Bake."

"You're losing it," Max told his wife as he scowled at the couple. "You've got *Maritime* on the brain."

"It *is* Everett Hughes," Sarah hissed at her husband as if she were a poked snake.

Joy craned to see around Sarah. The man who was the focus of Sarah's undivided attention had a tall, lean frame and filled out his jeans in an eye-catching manner. He was nice to look at, but she suspected Max was right in thinking Sarah had Hollywood on the brain—until the man tilted his head back to study the blackboard menu. Beneath the bill of a newsboy cap that had seen better days, Joy glimpsed the profile of one of the most famous faces in the country. He sported a short, golden brown goatee. Besides the newsboy cap and well-worn jeans, he wore what looked like a vintage bowling shirt. It was awful. The fact that the man made the shirt look like the height of careless-sexy said a lot about him.

"It *is* him, Max," Joy said, sitting back in the booth and smiling. She'd grown up in the land of movie stars and was used to occasionally glimpsing a celebrity. It was strange how her heart had lurched upon seeing Hughes's profile. Perhaps it was because he was one of the most super of the superstars she'd ever witnessed combined with the strangeness of it happening in an innocuous coffee shop in Chicago. "Er . . . Sarah, can you release the death grip on my thigh?"

"Oh sure, sorry," Sarah said distractedly, still watching Hughes, but now straining to do so in a less obvious manner. Even though she'd consented to releasing Joy, she continued to grip her leg until Joy manually removed her hand.

"He's here for the premiere. Is that his wife?" Max asked in a hushed tone.

"He's not married." Sarah scowled, her gaze still trained sideways, her entire attention seemingly focused on the single point of Hughes. "How could you *not* know Everett Hughes is single?"

"What do I care if he's single or not? What's so great about Everett Hughes? The guy dresses like a bum," Max mumbled under his breath. "His friend there—now she's a different story."

Joy chuckled at the same moment that Sarah whispered, "Be quiet. He's coming this way." Joy glanced in the direction where Sarah was staring and suddenly found herself looking into shadowed, gleaming eyes that were trained directly on her.

A memory flickered in Joy's brain and faded elusively. Something inside her quickened.

She looked away. It must be true what they said about Everett Hughes: His insouciant good looks and easygoing charm reputedly had the power to stun a woman. His sex appeal was utterly effortless, but that didn't make it any less potent. She was vaguely aware that Sarah went stiff as a board next to her.

"Oh my God," her friend whispered shakily.

"Joy?"

Joy blinked at the sound of the deep, resonant voice. Everett stood right next to their table, an expectant look on his face, his gaze fixed on Joy. Sarah was looking at her, aghast.

"Uh . . . yes, I'm Joy," she said, her feeling of disorientation only escalating. She crushed the napkin in her fist.

"Hi. I'm Everett. Everett Hughes?"

"I know who you are," said Joy, blushing at the stupidity of her statement. Everybody in the coffee shop knew who he was. Everyone in the *country* did. Why was he looking at her that way? "I'm sorry . . . I'm a little . . ."

Confused, shocked, breathless.

He straightened. "You don't remember me, do you?"

"Well, I've seen several of your films."

"No. We met," he said significantly. When she just stared at him with blank incredulity, he glanced first at Max, then at Sarah. He must have decided he wasn't going to get any help from that department, because he returned to Joy. "On the set of *Maritime*? Remember? Your uncle was busy, so you gave me the starburst tattoo."

The napkin she'd been clutching dropped heedlessly to the table.

"Joy, you didn't tell us you did Everett Hughes's tattoo for *Maritime*," Max said. "I'm Max Weisman, and this is my wife, Sarah." He held out his hand and Everett shook it. "We work with Joy at the Steadman School. On Joy's résumé, she said she did body paint and tattoos for some of *Maritime*'s extras, but she never mentioned she did *your* tattoo. Modest," Max said, giving Everett a significant glance, which Everett didn't see. He was too busy studying Joy, his brow creased in consternation.

"No. I wasn't being modest. I didn't know," Joy said in a strangled voice. "I . . . I thought he *was* an extra."

"Hi." Everett's companion approached their table carrying two cups. Sunlight turned her hair into a golden cascade of waves and curls. She gave everyone a friendly, frank appraisal and smile, and then nudged Everett with one of the cups. "Here's your coffee. Who are your friends?"

"This is Max and Sarah Weisman and Joy Hightower. Remember, I told you about Joy?" The blond woman's green eyes widened and she stared at Joy with increased interest. Joy wanted to slither beneath the table, she was so mortified. She couldn't believe this was happening to her. The man she'd shared that impulsive, crazy, steaming sexual encounter with on the set of *Maritime* had been *him*?

She'd gone down on *Everett Hughes*?

"I'm Everett's sister, Katie. I've heard all about you from Everett."

A wave of panic flashed through her.

"I just mentioned how talented I thought you were. As an artist," Everett added quickly. She met his stare. His eyelids narrowed. Joy couldn't decide if he seemed confused or concerned as he observed her.

"And of course I know all about Hightower Special Effects," Katie continued. "Your uncle is very well respected in the business. Rill would do cartwheels to get Seth Hightower for *Razor Pass*," she murmured as an aside to her brother, then smiled at Joy. "You might even see him do a couple tomorrow at the premiere to get your uncle's attention," she said, her grin widening as if she found the prospect amusing.

Joy inhaled slowly, commanding herself to focus. She'd been

doing nothing but gaping like an idiot and blushing the entire time. "Are you referring to Rill Pierce?" she managed to ask.

Katie nodded. "He's my husband. Do you know him?"

Joy shook her head. She'd never met the renowned Irish director, but she'd read somewhere that he'd done a screenplay adaptation of the postapocalyptic classic biker novel *Razor Pass* and planned to direct the film. Everett himself had been slated to play the lead role of Slader.

"You'll get to meet Rill at the premiere tomorrow, then," Katie said brightly.

"Oh . . . I'm not going."

Katie's smile faltered. "No? Isn't that why you're in Chicago?"

"She works here," Everett said gruffly. He'd been standing there wearing a slight frown for the past minute, his gaze never leaving Joy.

"I teach at a high school near here," Joy said.

"She teaches drawing and painting," Sarah said in a rapid, pressured fashion, as if she'd just found her voice and couldn't wait to use it. "It's an art school for gifted students."

"That's interesting," Katie said warmly. "I must have misunderstood Everett when he spoke of you. I thought you lived and worked in the Los Angeles area."

"I did. I moved here last winter."

"Well, how come you're not coming to the premiere? It seems a shame, since you worked on the movie and all. Can't your uncle get tickets? Why don't you ask her, Everett?" Katie said, sipping her coffee and glancing at her brother casually.

Joy's cheeks went from hot to scalding. "Oh no, that's not it—"

"Do you have other plans?" Everett asked.

"No, I just hadn't planned to go."

"Well, why don't you? We can all sit together," Katie said.

"*Katie,*" Everett warned under his breath.

"Well, I just meant—"

Everett jerked his arm abruptly, waving toward an empty corner of the café. "Can I talk to you for a second? In private?" Everett asked Joy pointedly.

A bomb going off would have startled Joy less. Four sets of eyes pinned her to the spot.

"I . . . well, yes, of course."

Sarah shot out of the booth, making way for her. Joy stood and glanced at Everett warily. He gestured for her to pass in front of him. She led him to an empty corner and turned to face him, her forearms crossed beneath her breasts, and stared at the second button on his shirt. Her heart began to beat uncomfortably.

"You cut your hair. I like it."

She blinked and glanced up into his face. This close, she could make out the bluish-green color of his eyes beneath the shadow of the bill of his cap.

"Thank you," she murmured, studying his shirt again.

"I didn't mean to make you uncomfortable," he said.

"It's okay. You're not making me uncomfortable."

He gave a soft bark of sarcastic laughter. Her gaze shot up to meet his, and this time it stuck. No wonder he was a movie star. Those eyes were like sensual laser beams.

"When you didn't come to the statue after that . . . that time, I asked your uncle for your phone number. Seth and I always got along pretty well, but after that day, he got pretty tight-mouthed when it came to you. I guess I shouldn't have bothered him about it. You must have told him not to tell me anything about you."

"I never said anything to Seth about it," she blurted out. Tell her uncle she'd impulsively gone down on a stranger? *Not likely*. But that wasn't the most significant thing Everett had said. "And I *did* go to the statue," she said, anger filtering into her voice for the first time. How dare he claim *she'd* stood *him* up, when it happened the other way around?

His expression shifted. "I waited for hours and hours for you by the statue after the shoot. I thought maybe you were held up, helping Seth, but when I went back inside, the studio was empty. Everyone, including Seth, was gone."

"That's not true," she said, irritation melting away the haze of mortification and shock that had settled on her since Everett had greeted her like an old friend earlier. "Why would you bother to say that when you know perfectly well that I'll know you're lying?"

His expression stiffened. "Yeah, why would I? It would be stupid to lie about it. I was *at* that statue."

"*I* was at that statue."

Something flickered across his face. "How long were you there?"

"More than an hour," she muttered after a pause, hating to have to admit the truth to him. "I thought maybe you'd been held up."

"You're serious, aren't you?"

"Of course I'm serious. Why would I lie about . . ." She faded off as something struck her. "The statue of the seven muses, right? At the entrance of the studio?"

He shook his head mutely.

"There's more than one statue at United Studios?" she asked, understanding dawning.

"If there is, I didn't know it until now. I was talking about the statue of Leon Schuster," he said, referring to the founder of United Studios. "The one in that little park area by the café?"

"I was at the statue of the seven muses. By the front entrance."

"I've never seen it." Something about the flat incredulity of his tone told her he was telling the absolute truth. She exhaled shakily. *Of course.* Superstar Everett Hughes wouldn't use the visitor's entrance to the large studio.

"But you were there," he murmured. "You went to meet me."

"Yes," she whispered. "And you went to meet me."

Joy swallowed thickly. She'd been more affected by that heated encounter with a stranger than she cared to admit. Her behavior on that afternoon had bothered her deeply, as had being stood up in the aftermath. But in the weeks and months that followed, she'd been too caught up with treatment, too focused on survival to dwell on an uncharacteristic moment of sexual promiscuity for long.

Now all of it came back to her in a rush. Her embarrassment. Her attraction. The mesmerizing quality of Everett Hughes's eyes.

"It was a misunderstanding," Everett said, his nostrils flaring slightly.

She lowered her head. "All of it was."

He touched her elbow and waited for her to meet his stare. "Not all of it."

She swallowed thickly.

"Will you go with me to the premiere tomorrow night?" he asked.

She grimaced. "Everett, I can't."

"Why not?"

"I don't have anything to wear." It'd been the lame excuse she used with her uncle because she didn't feel up to a huge public spectacle, but it was technically the truth, as well.

He glanced down at her figure appraisingly. "Katie and you are about the same size, even if you are a little taller. I'm sure she brought more than one dress—she usually takes the contents of a walk-in closet with her for an overnight stay."

"Don't be ridiculous. I don't even know her."

"Wear what you've got on then. We'll make a pact. I won't change clothes, either. I hate dressing up for these stupid things."

She studied him for signs that he was joking, but no . . . he was completely serious. She even got the impression he was hoping she'd agree with his proposal.

"If I go, I'm not going like this," she assured him, thinking how out of place she'd feel going to such a high-profile event on Everett's arm. She'd melt in embarrassment if she appeared under the microscope of the world wearing jean shorts and a T-shirt.

"Whatever you want. Just say you'll go."

"I don't know," she hedged, her thoughts swirling around her head like a jerky Tilt-A-Whirl ride. His fingers tightened ever so slightly on her arm.

"Please?" he murmured.

Her mouth dropped open. She knew it was foolish, but it was difficult to deny an entreating Everett Hughes. She dared any straight woman on the planet to try.

"Okay," she whispered.

His mouth tilted into a grin. Warmth flooded her. She'd forgotten the impact of seeing that smile up close and personal. She found herself smiling back. He pulled his cell phone out of his pocket.

"First things first," he murmured, tapping his thumb. "Give me your phone number. There's no way in hell I'm going to take the chance of your disappearing for another fourteen months."

Forty-five minutes later, Everett stood in the shadowed entryway of a brownstone that was up for sale. He watched the entrance of Harry's Brew and Bake unblinkingly. Katie and he had left with their coffees almost immediately after he'd won Joy's consent to go out with him tomorrow night. He'd walked Katie to the Wicker Park townhome where Rill and she were staying with a friend this weekend. He'd told himself he'd catch a cab over to his hotel, but found himself retracing his steps back to the coffee shop. One surreptitious glance in the window told him that Joy was still in there with her friends.

After the hot, oppressive day, a storm brewed. Dark gray clouds on the southwestern horizon rushed toward the city. Thunder rumbled ominously. He took a step back in the entryway when a hot wind rushed down the street, bending some of the young saplings lining the sidewalk until he wondered if they'd snap. The air—his very blood—felt charged with electricity.

Joy walked out of the café with her friends when the dry squall remitted slightly. She planted her long, bare legs as she shouted a cursory good-bye. The Weismans did the same, clearly as intent on getting home before the storm hit as Joy appeared to be. He heard Max's deep voice before it was carried away by another gust of wind. Joy's short hair whipped around her head, and the T-shirt she wore plastered against her breasts. She nodded, waved and hurried in the opposite direction from the couple.

He sprang out of the entryway. He ran down the street holding his hat in his hand, hurling himself against the wind like a running back against a monster defensive line, keeping Joy's pale T-shirt in the center of his vision the entire time.

He was behaving purely on instinct.

It started to rain when he got halfway down the block. Thunder cracked, and a second later it started to pour so heavily he was blinded. He flopped on his hat, the bill providing his eyes the chance to blink out the water so he could see. Joy opened a wrought iron fence gate and dashed between it, her head ducked against the torrent.

"Joy!"

The rain pounded on the pavement so hard, she couldn't hear him. She raced toward the front steps of a brownstone. He was about to lose her . . . again.

"*Joy,*" he bellowed, running down the wet sidewalk, holding his hat in place.

She still didn't appear to hear him. She opened the heavy wooden door and ducked her head out of the downpour. His heart dived. He opened his mouth to give one last desperate shout, but she paused suddenly on the threshold and hesitated. She turned and looked back. The wind whipped water into his eyes, but even in his half-blinded state, he felt her stare on him. For a second as he ran, he held his breath.

Would she turn away?

She backed into the doorframe, her front facing him, waiting. Electricity made the hair on his forearms stand on end. Lightning split the gray sky, and thunder boomed. He raced up the front steps, squinting to see her. Her exquisite face gleamed with moisture. Water dripped from her lips. Her hair spiked onto her cheeks and clung to her head. Her new haircut emphasized her elegant neck and the graceful shape of her skull. Earlier, when he'd been talking to her at the café, he'd felt an urge to cup the back of her head in his palm.

"Come in," he thought he heard her say when he stomped up the last step.

He entered a stuffy foyer with a hallway to the right and a flight of stairs to the left. Joy shut the door behind him, and the roar of the rain became a muffled hum. He took off his hat and wiped his face of dripping water before he turned to her. She was watching him, her arms crossed loosely beneath her breasts. He read the question in her large eyes.

"I'm not usually so impatient," he explained, swiping his hand over his wet hair. "But tomorrow night started to seem like an awfully long time when I've been waiting since last year."

Her lips quivered. He found himself longing to witness her full-out smile. There was something a little sad about her . . . poignant. Lovely. Looking at her was like glimpsing a crack in the matrix of the universe. The world really was a larger, more incredible place than he'd ever considered. He couldn't take his eyes off her. She dropped her arms, and his gaze dropped to her breasts outlined in clinging, wet fabric. He felt his body stir.

"I'm upstairs," she said, pointing, her voice tickling in his right ear. She had a low, melodic voice that reminded him a little of the actress Kate Winslet's, whom he admired greatly. But Joy's voice was even sultrier . . . sexier.

"You're sure it's okay?"

"Yes."

She walked in front of him and headed up the stairs. Her legs looked smooth and damp, well-muscled and slender. When she got to the landing, she dug in the pocket of her jean shorts, the action tugging wet fabric against the juncture of her thighs. He stared at the numeral 3 on the front of her door and made himself consider the Dodgers-Mets series opening in New York today.

The door swung open and he followed her inside. Cool air hit his wet body.

"Oh . . . I'm sorry," she said, kicking off her sandals and rushing through the foyer. "I left the air-conditioning on high. It was so stifling when I left this morning."

He stood there, dripping. He could see Joy straight ahead of him, standing in a hallway, fiddling with a thermostat. She turned to him, shivering.

"Come in," she said, beckoning.

"I'm going to get your floors all wet," he said, nodding at the gleaming hardwood.

"I already did. It's nothing a towel won't dry up."

He entered a large expanse, consisting of a living area to the right and a kitchen and dining area to the left. Three windows at the end of the living space had a long, cushioned window seat beneath them and were bracketed by two well-stocked, built-in bookshelves. Water pounded against the windowpanes and on the roof above them.

"Come on," she said with a wave, sounding breathless. She led him down a dark hallway and took a left. She flipped on a light. He poked his head through the doorframe and saw her pulling out towels from beneath a bathroom sink. When she stood, towels in hand, her gaze ran over him dubiously.

"I'm not sure I have any dry clothes that would fit you," she said.

"That's okay," he assured her, wringing his soaked hat out in the sink. He took one of the towels and started to wipe off. "I'll be fine. You get into something dry. Get in the shower. You're shivering," he said, gesturing toward the tub while he rubbed the towel over his wet head. "I'll go to the kitchen and drip on the tile there."

She laughed, and he paused in his toweling motions. She really did shine brightly in his eyes.

"No, I'll find something for you. That was some downpour. We're both soaked. Hold on."

She disappeared down the hallway. He continued to dry himself off, feeling the cotton chafe against his oversensitive skin. He glanced around her tidy bathroom. The fragrance from Joy's earlier shower still hovered in the air, teasing his nose.

"What about this? I think it's the best I can do," she said apologetically from behind him a moment later. She held up a dark blue bathrobe. "It was large on me, so I never wore it. It'll be small on you, but it'll . . . cover you up."

"Sure. It's great, thanks."

She seemed relieved that he hadn't turned down her offering. "Feel free to jump in the shower, if you need to."

"You should get in the shower. You're freezing," he said quietly, noticing the pebbled skin on her upper arms.

She shook her head and took a step back, but lingered in the doorway. "I'm fine. I'll just go dry off and change."

He supposed you would call her eyes hazel. He didn't know what else to call them. They were singular. A cobalt blue ring enclosed brown, blue-green and amber shards of color. Similar to when he'd looked down at her while she gave him the tattoo, he saw a mixture of desire and wariness in her eyes.

"Sorry to be such a pain. All because I couldn't be a little more patient at the idea of finally being able to talk to you."

"Talk about a buildup. I haven't got much interesting to say, Everett. I'm bound to disappoint you," she said, donning a rueful smile.

He chuckled. "I'm very easy to please."

She gave him a half-incredulous, half-amused glance. "Everett Hughes—easy to please?"

"When it comes to you, it'll be easy as breathing."

A delicate pink color spread in her cheeks. He watched the puffy flesh of her lips part. A vivid image popped into his mind's eye—unwanted, but uncontrollable—of arrowing his cock between her lips while she was restrained and her cheeks were flushed with desire. A tingling sensation flickered across his cock and segued into an ache. He blinked and glanced away.

"The washer and dryer are in there," she said, pointing to a double folded door a few feet down the hallway. "Go ahead and put your clothes in to dry them off. I'll meet you out there in a minute," she said, waving vaguely to the living area.

He nodded and closed the door. He accepted her offer and took a minute-long shower, waiting for his unwanted erection to dissipate. How was it that Joy Hightower managed to remind him of a living, sacred poem and raw, elemental sex all at once?

So much for the existential not being sexy.

Three

She changed into a cotton, floral print summer dress that was pretty without being overtly sexy. Joy didn't want to send the wrong impression, although she was so confused about Everett being in her apartment, she wasn't precisely sure what impression she *wanted* to give.

She passed the hall bathroom quickly. The sound of the shower curtain being whipped back struck her pitched ears. She came to an abrupt halt.

She couldn't believe Everett Hughes was standing in her bathtub at this very moment, stark naked. The graphic memory of holding his heavy, shapely penis in her hand exploded into her mind's eye.

Had it really happened? It seemed so unlikely and strange . . . so compelling.

She entered her kitchen and filled the tea kettle. A moment later she heard the bathroom door open over the sound of her heart beating loudly in her ears.

"Would you like some hot tea?" she asked without removing her gaze from an opened cabinet when the wooden floor creaked behind her a moment later.

"I'll have whatever you're having," he said. She glanced around and did a double take when she saw him in the robe. He grinned and double-pumped his eyebrows.

"Sexy, no?" he said. The robe was gender neutral enough, but his shoulders were too broad for the fabric, leaving a V shape of his chest exposed.

She suppressed a laugh and turned away to fill the teapot. "I understand you're known for a . . . *colorful* style of dressing," she said tactfully after a pause, "but I don't know how well this getup would go over with your adoring public."

"Colorful, huh? I thought the magazines said I dressed like a slob," he said distractedly as he noticed some of the artwork she had displayed in the dining and living room.

She smiled to herself as she opened a box of tea. "Those same magazines also seem to name you the sexiest man of the year for I don't know how many years running, so I guess dressing like a slob works."

"Do you mind if I have a look at your paintings?" he asked, pointing at a collection of three canvases arranged in her dining room.

"No, of course not," she said, her torso twisted so she could look at him. Had she offended him with the sexiest man of the year comment? No, it wasn't that, she realized as she watched him wander away. He just hadn't considered the topic vaguely worthwhile. His entire focus had shifted to her paintings.

"They're yours," she heard him say once he stood before them.

"Yes."

She approached him a few minutes later in the living room, carrying two steaming cups. He now studied the oil mounted above the fireplace, his focused attention almost tangible. Her gaze ran over him from behind. How could he possibly appear so comfortable— so masculine—while wearing a woman's bathrobe? His strong-looking calves were dusted with light brown hair. The fabric outlined muscular buttocks. The artist in her wanted to remove the robe and memorize every inch of him with her brush. The woman in her longed to make the study using lips and fingertips.

He turned as she approached and blinked.

"I love your stuff. Reminds me a little of Rousseau—meticulous, primitive, yet dreamlike—but your femininity civilizes it," he reflected, taking the cup she offered him. "What?" he asked, pausing when he noticed her small smile.

"Do you ever do or say anything without total confidence?" she wondered aloud, taking a step back and setting her own tea on the table behind her couch. She walked around the couch and sat down.

"Does that mean I sounded like a pompous ass just now?" he asked, a grin twitching his mouth as he followed her around the couch.

"No, not at all," she assured him. She stiffened slightly when he sat down on the cushion next to her. She swore he noticed—did he miss anything?—but he said nothing. "I wasn't being sarcastic. I studied Rousseau extensively while I was at art school in Paris."

"Did you study undergraduate there?" he asked, taking a sip. His wet hair waved around his temples and on his forehead, a glorious mess.

"Just my junior and senior years."

"I studied art history for undergrad at UCLA," he said, surprising her.

"Really? I would have thought acting."

"Nah, I just fell into that by accident. I needed some cash for Christmas presents for my family senior year, and did a walk-in audition for a commercial."

"And your fate was sealed," she murmured, picking up her tea to take a sip. He glanced at her and they shared a smile. "What did you plan to do with your art history degree?"

"I thought I'd travel the world, collecting art for a gallery or museum. Turned out, the part that appealed to me the most was the travel, not the art collection. No offense."

"None taken." She set down her cup and settled back on the couch. Did one ever become accustomed to his sexuality? It was like a third person in the room, a guest Joy wasn't sure if she should ignore or welcome. Her gaze skittered over the opened portion of the robe he wore. The hair on his chest wasn't a pelt, by any means, but it emphasized his potent masculinity. Hollywood golden boy Everett may be, but he was the polar opposite of an effeminate fop. He seemed about as aware of his looks as he was his own skin.

She noticed his stare on her. Her gaze bounced off him and landed on her coffee table.

"Why did you move to Chicago?" he asked.

She paused before answering. She'd moved to Chicago because she'd been haunted by the idea of seeing all the old places she'd used to visit with her mother following her own bout with cancer. She'd been haunted by the idea of her only family member—her uncle, Seth—being forced to witness another round of chemo or radiation, or another excruciating wait for a doctor to give them results.

Joy's physician had declared her completely healthy on her last several visits, but the fear of the cancer returning—of inflicting further misery on Seth—had been what had instigated her move across the country. She didn't want to put Seth through what her father had been through when her mother had been diagnosed with cancer.

She didn't want Seth to suffer like she had when she'd been a child, watching as the cruel disease stole away a loved one bit by bit until there was nothing left but insubstantial memories.

"I needed a change of pace," she said quietly. "The Steadman School is one of the finest preparatory schools in the country for art."

"Davis is considered the same," he pointed out, referring to the prestigious high school where she'd taught gifted students in Hollywood. He noticed her expression of surprise. "Oh—Seth told me the name of the school where you taught. That was before I . . . we . . ." He cleared his throat. "Met. Like I told you earlier, Seth pretty much clammed up whenever I asked about you after that."

A strained silence ensued. She couldn't tell him that after their electrical, impulsive tryst, she'd informed her uncle about her cancer diagnosis. Seth had become as anxious and protective as a mother bear after that. She hadn't told him specifically about her sexual encounter with Everett, because she hadn't even known it *was* Everett at the time. Apparently, Seth had taken it upon himself to deflect Everett's interest in his niece because he'd been aware that Joy had more crucial things to focus on for the next several months than an affair with America's heartthrob.

"So . . . why the desire to transfer schools?" he persisted after a moment.

He knew she'd sidestepped the original question, she realized. She sighed. "Sometimes we just need to wipe the slate clean. Start somewhere new."

He nodded. "Begin a new chapter. I get that. I'm jealous," he added after a moment.

"Why would *you* want to wipe your slate clean?" she asked. He glanced at her calmly. Joy realized she'd just asked him the question she'd hoped he wouldn't ask her. She reached for her mug of tea. "Never mind. You don't have to answer that. It's just that you seem to be at the height of a very successful career. I would have thought . . ."

"What?" he asked, when she faded off.

"I would have thought you would be one of the last people in the world to want to make a fresh start. You have a pretty impressive body of work on your slate to consider erasing it all," she said with a smile.

His brow creased into a slight frown as he stared at her mouth. Joy dropped her chin and studied the surface of her tea. "Thanks," she heard him say. "But sometimes, success can lock you into a certain pattern. You can't help but wonder if things would be different if you just knocked over the whole house of cards and started from scratch."

I can tell you what it's like: it's lonely, she thought before she had the opportunity to censor herself.

"Joy?"

It felt like all the tiny hairs in her ears and on her neck stood on end at the sound of his quiet voice.

"Yes?"

"You asked me earlier if I ever wasn't confident. I'm not right now. You don't want me here, do you?"

Her gaze zoomed to his face. "No. I mean, I *do* want you . . . here," she added quickly.

"Then why are you so skittish?" In the distance, she heard the drone of the dryer spinning. The tightness she'd been experiencing in her chest rose to her throat.

"You don't know?"

"You're embarrassed?" he asked slowly, as if he'd seen the answer with those sharp eyes of his and plucked it right out of her consciousness. "About what happened at the studio?"

"I've never done anything like that before. I didn't know who you were. I didn't even know your name."

His facial muscles convulsed slightly. He set down his cup on the coffee table and suddenly he was touching her cheek with one hand while the other cradled her neck. A silent spasm of emotion went through her when she felt his fingers slide into her hair and rub her scalp. Her lungs seemed to have locked up.

"It shocked me, too," he admitted. "Maybe not in the same way it did you, but still. I couldn't stop thinking about you, Joy."

She just stared at him, mute, all those old feelings flooding into her awareness, a wave of fear for her own life, a lightening flash of lust . . . Everett's eyes watching it all, a bright beacon she couldn't quite interpret, but couldn't help seeking.

She was healthy now, at least the doctors said so . . . alive to face another day, another moment. Who could possibly not relish *this* one?

His head dipped toward hers.

"I don't want to make you feel strange or guilty about this." She inhaled him, her floral-scented soap transformed by his male essence. "Is it okay?"

Her gaze came unglued from his moving lips and glided over his nose, meeting his stare. Maybe he read her bewilderment . . . her enthrallment.

"Is it okay that I'm so attracted to you?" he clarified somberly.

Her mouth dropped open in amazement. She nodded.

"So you're not going to back out of going out with me tomorrow night?"

Uncertainty reared its head, breaking through the surface of her lust-addled awareness. This was her chance to back down. Everett may understand what was happening here—he probably had this effect on every woman he encountered. For her own part, she was quite sure this whole thing was a bizarre mistake. His fingers found a sensitive spot on her scalp. She stopped herself from purring in pleasure when he rubbed it.

"No. I'm not changing my mind," she whispered.

His smile stunned her—a quick, unabashed flash of distilled

happiness. He leaned down and brushed his mouth against hers before she'd recovered. She felt a shock go through her at the unexpected contact. His mouth caressed hers like his fingertips had her skin earlier, a tender exploration. She closed her eyes and trembled. His kiss wasn't a ravishment to trigger lust and make her forget everything else.

It was better. Much better.

He lifted his head a moment later. She cracked open her eyelids and saw that he was watching her.

"If you had any idea about the things I'm fantasizing about doing to you right now, you might change your mind about tomorrow night."

"I don't think so," she said slowly, surprising herself.

His nostrils flared slightly. Joy had the thrilling thought that she was about to be sexually consumed.

"I hated the fact that I wasn't able to touch you that first time," he said in a hushed tone. His hands spread along the sides of her rib cage, distracting her. "I hated the fact that you probably were left thinking I was single-minded and selfish—"

"I didn't think that," she interrupted him.

He brushed her lower lip with the tip of his thumb, his features tightening. "I *was* selfish. I *was* single-minded. That's not the part I regret. I just regretted not being able to give you the same unselfish pleasure you gave me in return. Let me do that now, Joy. Let me show you I can give as well as get."

Her brain stalled. It took her a moment to realize he was watching her expectantly, his face tense, his eyes reminding her of the starburst tattoo—fire in water.

"Okay," she whispered.

His hands moved gently to her back. He found her zipper and lowered it, his gaze remaining on her the whole time. His hands brushed over her shoulders, lowering her dress below her breasts.

He removed her bra and tossed it aside so quickly, one second she possessed meager protection, and the next her breasts were bared to the cool air and Everett's hot stare.

"So lovely. So perfect. I knew you would be," he murmured, touching a peaking nipple with the tip of his forefinger. Her breath stuck in her lungs as she watched him detail both crests at once, looking fascinated by the changes he wrought in her flesh with his drawing, plucking fingertips. Prickles of pleasure spiked along the surface of her chilled, pebbled skin. She gasped softly when he pinched at her lightly and seemingly pulled an invisible cord of sensation that led all the way to her womb.

"You're cold?" he asked, running his hand along the tiny goose bumps rising along her chest and breasts.

"No," she managed to say. "Well, maybe a little."

He smiled and covered her breasts with his large, warm palms. The next thing she knew, he'd seized her mouth with his own. For a few seconds, she was stunned at the onslaught of his kiss. His former nibbling at her mouth was a mere tiny sampling of his passion. He gave it to her now in full force, his lips molding hers hungrily, his tongue plunging between her lips, searching and probing. Liquid heat surged between her thighs. God, he knew how to kiss. Joy had never considered her mouth to be a sexual organ on par with her pussy, but when Everett kissed her, it suddenly felt like it was. She moaned shakily beneath his heat, her tongue sliding against his, joining in a sensual duel. His hands moved on her breasts, shaping her flesh to his palms.

It was like dipping her chilled flesh into a heated bath. She melted against him. Had he known his kiss would have that effect on her?

He came up for air an untold period of time later, but his mouth was immediately on her neck, one hand spreading at the back of her skull. Joy panted as he ravished her skin, her eyelids opened into slits, staring sightlessly at the light fixture on the ceiling. Shivers of sensation rippled through her as he rained kisses on her bare shoulders and paused to take a gentle bite out of the muscle.

She realized she was just sitting there, dazed beneath the tsunami of sensation caused by Everett. She reached into the opening of his robe as he continued to ravish her, a thrill of excitement going through her as she touched warm skin and dense muscle. He went still when her fingertips brushed against a small, erect nipple. He grunted softly and wrapped his hands around her wrists.

She looked into his face, surprised, when he pulled her hands away from his body.

"Let me touch you right now," he said, his voice slightly gruff from arousal, his face tense and somber.

"Okay," she said uncertainly.

A small smile flickered across his lips. He gently moved her wrists to the small of her back. "Arch your back," he said. "Present your breasts to me."

Confusion and alarm went through her at his words, but the sharp pang of arousal that tightened her sex trumped them. Her breath coming in shallow pants, she arched her back, causing her breasts to rise toward him. She saw his cock leap against the fabric of the robe. It was as if invisible fingers pinched at her clit.

She moaned raggedly when he squeezed one breast gently while he slipped a nipple between his lips. He drew on her with his mouth and she shifted restlessly on the couch. She pulled on her wrist, intuitively needing to hold his head against her, to rake her fingers through his hair, but he held her hands firmly at her middle back.

"Shh, it's okay," he soothed, lifting his head momentarily. "Keep still for a moment while I taste you."

He lowered his head again and took a love bite out of the flesh he held cupped in his hand. Joy gasped. He continued to maraud the captive breast, using lips, teeth and tongue to stimulate her until Joy wiggled helplessly on the couch, desperate for friction on her sex.

"Everett," she pleaded softly when he finally enclosed the nipple with his warm, sucking mouth. She made a choking noise, and he laved the crest with a warm, slightly raspy tongue as if to soothe her.

He lifted his head, spearing her with his stare. He smiled.

"You're very beautiful," he said, glancing at her flushed breasts. He placed his hand matter-of-factly between her thighs and pressed.

Joy gasped.

"It's okay," he assured, using his hand to gather the fabric of her dress, sliding it over her thighs. "Lean back," he instructed. "Keep your hands behind your back, please."

She followed his instructions, watching him mutely as he temporarily released her wrists and knelt on the floor. He raised her dress to her belly and let it drop. He deftly lowered her panties to her thighs, then spread her legs so that the fabric stretched tight. Joy moaned in anticipation when he firmed his hold on her wrists again with one hand, restraining her, and leaned into her lap. It embarrassed her a little, how aroused she became by the fact that he held her captive to what was to come.

He dipped his tongue downward between her labia. "Aw, Jesus, you're so wet. You taste so *good*."

She convulsed in a distilled spasm of pleasure as he laved her clit. She jerked in his hold, shocked by the sharp sensation. He held her in place with a spread hand at her waist and continued to press his tongue against her, his movements concentrated and eye-crossingly precise. She whimpered helplessly, Everett's head in her lap, his tongue shooting her straight to heaven.

The pleasure he wrought was hot, forbidden and completely, utterly inescapable. He lapped at her, pressed her clit like it was a magic button, and before she knew it, she was riding the crest of the wave of climax.

Her muscles clenching tight, she thrust her hips against his warm, wet tongue and came in a delicious, pounding rush of release.

She gasped in the aftermath, her brain still spinning in the vortex of pleasure, her flesh still vibrating and singing in the aftermath of bliss.

She opened her eyes at the sensation of Everett's open, warm mouth kissing her thigh.

Holy shit, she thought dazedly as she gasped for air. It'd felt like he'd plunged her straight into the center of passion . . . the heady, intoxicating experience of being alive. Had she been so dead—or so afraid of death?—for so long now that she'd forgotten the experience?

Had she ever *known* what it was to feel alive to this degree?

It took her a few seconds to fully comprehend that Everett had stood and was walking toward the hallway.

"Where are you going?" she asked, disoriented.

"I should leave," he said shortly.

"Everett?"

He paused and turned toward her. Joy lowered her dress and raised the fabric over her breasts. Her confusion altered to bewilderment when she saw how rigid his face was with arousal, how regret flickered across his features when he saw her hurriedly cover herself from his gaze.

"I really *did* just come here to talk to you," he said hollowly.

"Oh," Joy said stupidly. She stood and watched as he stalked out of her living room. She heard the sound of the dryer door opening and closing, and then the bathroom door shutting behind him. Disappointment smacked into her like a physical blow.

Of course it would be better to cool off a little, to take things slower. Joy wasn't even sure what was happening here. Whatever was going on between her and Everett was extremely powerful and potentially volatile. Better not to go so fast that she was utterly consumed.

Of course she was lying to herself. How could she not long to leap into the blazing flames with Everett?

She pulled herself together and was in the kitchen rinsing out their mugs when he returned a minute or two later, completely dressed. She set the cups in the drainer and turned to face him. His hair was starting to dry, turning the color of it to a mélange of dark gold, pale blond and burnished light brown. He often was photographed wearing hats. Joy had a flash of understanding as to why. His hair was truly his crowning glory. He would draw attention and stares from quite a distance if he didn't routinely cover it.

She wiped her hands on a dish towel and glanced toward the windows. "It's still raining outside," she said shakily.

He grinned and glanced significantly down at his clothes. "It's okay, I'm already wet."

So was she. She could feel the wetness between her thighs, the tingling sensation in her pussy from his masterful lovemaking.

"So, we're definitely on for tomorrow night, right?" he asked.

She blinked in amazement at what she was seeing. Everett Hughes? Looking uncertain? Worried, even? Did he think she wasn't going to agree to go out with him because he'd taken her on a mind-blowing afternoon ride to heaven?

"Absolutely," she said with a tone of conviction.

He looked relieved. "I'll come by and pick you up—say at around six o'clock? We'll have a late dinner after the premiere," he said.

"Sounds great."

She followed him as he headed toward her front door and watched him step into his shoes. She was a little bewildered by the contrast between his raw sexual intensity just moments ago and his slightly uncomfortable, practical manner at present.

He slapped his wet cap on his head and turned to her. He opened his mouth as if to speak, then shoved one hand into his jeans pocket and reached for the doorknob with the other.

"See you tomorrow night," he said.

Her front door shut with a click. Joy just stood there for a stretched minute, wondering what the hell had just happened to her.

Four

❧

She spent a good portion of the time she was supposed to be sleeping enumerating all the things she needed to do the following day in preparation for the premiere. How did one go about getting ready for a date with the most eligible bachelor in the country? She'd have to get a manicure and pedicure and get her hair trimmed. She'd have to dip into her savings account and buy a dress.

In the moments she wasn't having those anxious thoughts, she was busy replaying every second she'd spent with Everett in vivid detail. What had he meant when he'd said she'd be shocked by his sexual fantasies in regard to her? What specifically had he been thinking about? Joy had had several long-term boyfriends and one or two intense sexual affairs that hadn't lasted long. Still, none of those experiences called to mind the experience she'd had with Everett out there in her living room . . . the way he'd restrained her gently, forcing her to face her pleasure head-on.

Excitement tingled in her flesh, sending teasing tendrils all the way to her clit. She slid her fingers beneath her panties and found herself wet. Eyes clamped tight, she imagined Everett looking down at her while his cock pounded high inside of her. He was telling her to take it all—all he had to offer, all she could take . . . and then more. She was powerless, a quaking bundle of clamoring nerves and naked flesh. He was ruthless, demanding more, fucking her like he planned to start a fire with the friction of their straining bodies and was close to ignition . . . so close.

She cried out shakily as orgasm shuddered through her, a hot, delicious rush that temporarily crowded out her anxieties and uncertainties about getting involved—no matter how briefly—with a man like Everett Hughes.

She woke up with so much stiffness in her muscles, she knew she needed to add some vigorous exercise to her to-do list. Otherwise, she'd grow tense and rigid as a board from all this nervous anticipation.

After her morning jog and yoga routine, she showered and stood before the mirror, nude. She ran her hand along her chest, neck, armpits and groin area, searching for swollen lymph glands, experiencing the daily dread of what she might find, but determined nonetheless. Then she quickly, efficiently completed a breast exam. She'd been diagnosed with a type of B-cell lymphoma and was now in complete remission. She'd seen how cancer could spread, however. Her mother had been riddled with it by the time she died. That fear was what motivated her daily obsessive checking.

She was taking her vitamins when she heard her buzzer ring. It must be Seth, she thought as she hurried toward the foyer, tightening her robe around her. Her uncle had been busy with a few publicity interviews and a demonstration of his craft at a local college yesterday, but maybe he'd decided to stop by and see if she wanted to do breakfast.

"Hello?" she said into the intercom.

"Hello, Joy?" came a bright female voice. "It's Katie Pierce. I met you yesterday at the coffee shop?"

"Oh, yes . . . hello," Joy said, amazed. What could Everett's sister be doing here?

"I hope I'm not stopping by too early. Rill and I are staying with a friend who lives just around the block."

"Not at all. Come right up the stairs. I'm in number three," Joy said, pushing the button to release the lock on the front door. A few seconds later, Katie swept into her foyer wearing shorts and a tank top, her hair in a ponytail.

"I did catch you at a bad time. You were showering. I'm sorry," Katie said, her green eyes flickering over Joy.

"No, I don't mind if you don't," Joy assured her, waving vaguely at her robe. "I went out for a jog this morning and it was already stifling outside. I would have thought that storm we had yesterday would have washed away the humidity, but it seems to have made it worse. I was drenched by the time I got home, so I hopped in the shower." She paused, noticing the garment bag Katie was holding in one hand. Katie looked where she was staring.

"Oh . . . I brought these for you," she said, holding up the bag. She must have noticed Joy's dumbfounded expression. "A few dresses? For the premiere tonight? Everett called me early this morning before he went for a round of publicity interviews at the Four Seasons Hotel. He was very grouchy. He can't stand those things. Anyway, he asked me to bring by some dresses for you. I hope one of them works."

Embarrassment swept through her when she recalled Everett's and her terse, charged conversation on the previous day in the coffee shop. He had taken her initial excuse for why she couldn't attend the premiere literally. In her shock over the unlikely unfolding of events, she'd completely forgotten about his suggestion that she borrow a dress from his sister.

"I'm sorry, Katie. Everett mentioned something about borrowing a dress, but I didn't think he was serious," she said, flustered.

"It's sort of hard to know when to take him seriously, isn't it?" Katie replied airily as she glanced behind Joy into her apartment. "I'm one of the few people on the planet he can't BS, though."

"Is that right?" Joy asked warily.

"*Bullshitting* is just another word for *acting*, isn't it?" Katie asked, meeting Joy's gaze and grinning. Her brow creased as if she'd just evaluated what she'd said and found it wanting. Her smile faded and she rolled her eyes. "Oh . . . that sounded all wrong. Everett is going to kill me. I just meant brothers tend to BS their sisters as a matter of course, and sisters tend to see straight through it. So you can take it from me. He's serious about you." She tilted her head and studied Joy with interest.

Joy cleared her throat. "I can't imagine why. We hardly know each other."

"Everett's a creature of instinct. It's why he's such a great actor. Most people live by reason. Everett lives by his wits, and there is a difference." She shrugged. "I could tell he was interested in you when he talked about you last year. It doesn't happen often, that I sense he's interested—*really* interested—in a woman, so it stuck in my head. I could also tell he was disappointed when I asked him about you a few months later and he said you'd disappeared from his radar, despite the fact that he'd been sending out signals that he wanted the opposite."

I'd disappeared into the grim, day-to-day battle of fighting cancer, Joy thought. She took a step back, disconcerted not by Katie's frankness, but by what she'd implied. Everett had suggested he was interested in Joy to his sister, and that wasn't his normal MO? Frankly, she didn't know how to make sense of that.

She was reading in to Katie's comment. That must be it.

"Please, come in. Would you like a cup of coffee?" she asked, waving Katie into her apartment.

"I'd love one. I like your place," Katie said as she followed her.

"Thanks. It's coming along. I'm doing a little here and there, decorating on a budget. Here . . . let me take that," Joy said when she turned around and realized Katie still carried the garment bag.

"Why don't I show them to you while you get the coffee?" Katie suggested.

"Everett really did misunderstand. I didn't expect you to bring over dresses—"

"Do you have a dress to wear?"

"No, but I'm going shopping later this afternoon."

"See if one of these doesn't work for you first, then."

Joy opened her mouth to protest, but Katie was so natural and down-to-earth, it seemed churlish to continue to contradict her. Katie and Everett not only had the golden good looks in common, Joy realized; they also were both sublimely comfortable in their own skin.

Joy poured them both a cup of coffee while Katie draped the garment bag over one of her counter stools and unzipped it.

"These gowns are from my days in Hollywood working as a tax attorney. I used to represent a lot of old-school movie stars—or old *coot* movie stars, as Rill would put it. I'd have to attend a lot of boring soirees and fund-raisers."

"You don't practice law anymore?"

"Oh, yes . . . well, in a manner of speaking. I'm now a county employee, and only part-time at that. No more designer gowns for me, at least not on the scale I used to buy them," Katie said ruefully as she tossed the garment bag on another stool. "You know, I'm excited for Everett's new movie, but I can't wait for this premiere to be over and done so Rill and I can get back home."

"Where's home?" Joy asked at the same time she held up a sugar bowl and creamer, her brows raised in a query.

"Just the cream, thanks. Vulture's Canyon, Illinois. Pretty odd name for a town, isn't it? It's entirely fitting, trust me. Smack dab in the middle of the Shawnee National Forest. Wacky artists, isolationists and weird characters abounding. I'm proud to call it home. When I'm away from Daisy for too long, I start to feel like I'm missing a vital organ. I even miss Barnyard," Katie murmured under her breath as she whisked several dresses into the air. She noticed Joy's confused expression.

"Daisy is our little girl. She's only five months. Barnyard is our dog, even though Barnyard thinks the entire town is his family. This is my first overnight stay away from Daisy. She's staying with a good friend in Vulture's Canyon—Olive Fanatoon. Olive takes excellent care of her, but . . . well, it's hard being away. I miss her like sin. Thank you," she said, accepting the cup Joy offered her. She took a sip and set it on the counter. "Okay, see if any of these appeal. Candidate number one—a little strapless chiffon number."

Joy eyed the gown that featured a ruched sweetheart bodice, a metallic floral print and a pink sash. It was fun, flirtatious and very sexy—gypsy haute couture.

"It's darling. It's also made just for you, Katie," Joy said honestly.

Katie peered at the dress as if she were seeing it for the first time. "Do you think so?"

"You'd look great in it with your hair down and a pair of dangly earrings."

"Hmm, maybe you're right," Katie said, giving her a bright smile. "Guess I bought it for a reason. Okay, bachelorette number two—she may look simple, but once you get her on, she packs a punch."

Joy made a sound of admiration when she saw the elegant, sleeveless white gown with layers of white beads and sequins and a graceful scooped neck. One thing was for certain: Katie's gowns were far and away beyond what Joy could have afforded. Could she really borrow something so exquisite?

"It's stunning," Joy murmured.

"It is nice, but I'm leaning toward candidate number three. Perfect for a hot summer evening. With your coloring and figure, it'd be a showstopper," Katie said, whipping around another gown. Joy gasped.

"Oh, it's beautiful," she said, instinctively reaching across the counter to touch the gown. The delicious fabric descended from a single twisted shoulder strap, falling in lustrous folds of tangerine fluid satin.

"It'd set off your tan and skin, and here's the kicker," Katie said walking around the counter and turning the gown. "It looks sedate, but it has a slit in the back that shows major leg action. I should have known you were a runner when I saw your legs yesterday in the coffee shop. The crowd will be left ogling in your wake."

Joy laughed. "I'd rather do without any ogling."

Katie waved her free hand. "They'll be stunned speechless. You'll never know it happened. What do you think? Everett will love it."

"He will?"

"He loves color on a woman. Hates a washed-out palette." She nodded toward Joy's paintings mounted in the dining room. "I'm assuming those are your work?" Joy nodded. "Then I see you agree with Everett about color."

"It is incredibly vibrant and rich-looking," Joy murmured, sliding her hand along the decadently soft folds.

"Try it on?" Katie asked, twitching the dress temptingly in her hand.

Joy hesitated. She wasn't much for glitz and glamour. But something about the dress—something about the idea of Everett seeing her in it—appealed to her. Maybe it was because, like Everett, the dress didn't speak to her of pageantry and drama, but of vibrancy, sensuality . . . the risks and rewards of living.

She met Katie's sparkling eyes.

"Are you sure, Katie? What if I spill something on it?"

"I'm not worried. I have a crack dry cleaner. Please say yes. I'm dying to see you in it."

Joy bit her lip uncertainly and again touched the fabric, allowing it to seduce her. Katie grinned triumphantly when she took the hanger from her hand.

At ten to six that evening, Joy suspected she was on the verge of a panic attack.

She pushed a button on the remote control and the television in her bedroom switched off. It had been a mistake to turn it on. A local news station was doing red-carpet coverage of the *Maritime* premiere. Hundreds of people were congregated on Illinois Avenue. Guests were already arriving, flashing glittering smiles at the cameras and fans crowding behind waist-high barriers.

She felt like Cinderella on the night of the ball. A woman used to clipping coupons, doing her own sewing, and scouring her own floors didn't wander into the world of the golden people without some major anxiety. It would have been bad enough for Joy to attend the premiere with her uncle and a few friends she knew from his special effects makeup company, but Joy had gone and made it worse. She'd agreed to attend the high-profile event with Prince Charming himself.

She placed her hand on her chest and forced herself to take a long, slow breath. The feeling of her breast draped in rich satin sent the alarming reminder through her that she wasn't wearing a bra. Katie had insisted she didn't need one—the fabric was ruched around her breasts, hiding the contours of her nipples. No one could tell that the only thing she wore under the gown was a tiny thong.

But *Joy* knew.

She felt naked—no, *worse*. The rich fabric slid and caressed her skin every time she moved, creating a sensual friction, a hyper-awareness of her sensitive body.

She inspected herself in the full-length mirror. It was difficult to find flaws in her image. Her insecurities were just beneath the surface. The dress fit her to perfection, its flowing lines seeming to make love to her feminine curves, skimming and suggesting as she moved versus clinging obviously. She'd been fortunate in being left with a relatively innocuous reminder of her chemotherapy. The single strap that tied at her left shoulder covered her small port scar. She rarely wore much makeup, but knew the dress called for some dramatics. She'd focused on her eyes. The result was a smoky, seductive look.

Her one criticism of her appearance was the lack of her long mane of chestnut brown hair. It would have looked perfect with the dress. She'd combed back her short hair for a sophisticated, simple look. She touched the strands on her neck, hating them, longing for her tumbling tresses . . . wishing for the confidence she'd possessed before her cancer diagnosis.

The loss of her hair had brought back so much to her—shaving her mom's head as a mother and daughter ritual on three different occasions, putting on the act that shopping for a wig was fun. No wonder Samson's hair had meant life and vitality in the myth. She suspected every cancer patient and survivor understood the analogy.

The buzzer going off made her jump.

"Hi," she said into the intercom in her foyer a few seconds later.

"Hi."

Reality shuddered through her at the sound of his deep voice.

"I just have to grab my purse. Do you want to come up, or should I come down?"

"I'll come up."

She pushed the release on the downstairs lock. A few seconds later she swung open the door.

"Wow."

He'd said it, but he'd stolen the word straight from her mouth.

"You look wonderful," she murmured, her gaze gliding over him. It fascinated her how he could epitomize shabby insouciance one moment and elegant male sophistication the next. Maybe it was just because he possessed an amazing body that he could wear anything; apparel was just a negligently donned accessory to the man beneath it. He wore a classic black tux, white dress shirt with wing collar, points tucked behind a black bow tie. His hair looked neat for once, combed back in glossy waves. The overall look was immaculate and utterly masculine.

His eyes gleamed as they moved over her, making her self-conscious in an entirely different way than she'd felt just moments ago.

"I'm glad you chose the tux over the bowling shirt," she said, grinning.

"I'm still partial to your jean shorts," he murmured as his gaze roved over her belly and breasts, "but this dress has its charms. At least it does on you." He met her stare, his eyes warm. "You're beautiful."

She didn't know what to say. If it'd sounded like flattery, it would have been one thing. It hadn't, though. The compliment had sounded candid and a little amazed.

She turned, anxious to hide her embarrassment. "I'll just get my purse."

She returned a moment later carrying the gold clutch that matched her high-heeled sandals. She noticed his raised eyebrows.

"What?" she asked, approaching him. He cupped her hip in his palm. She focused on his small, teasing smile and the way her heart raced at his touch, letting his charm and her excitement silence her anxiety.

"Have you seen what you look like from the back? Are you trying to kill me or what?" he murmured.

She laughed, and then shocked herself by drawing nearer, letting the front of her body brush lightly against him. She craned up and pressed her lips to his. By the time she took a step back, he looked like she'd slugged him instead of kissed him.

He also looked pleased . . . and aroused.

"You'll just have to stay beside me all night and never fall behind. I have no malicious intent in mind," she murmured.

"Are you kidding? And let all the other guys have the pleasure of seeing the best pair of legs this side of the Atlantic?" he asked with a look of mock scandal. He took her hand and opened the door wider, urging her to walk ahead of him. "I don't think so. Not when those legs belong to my date."

Maybe it was something in the way he'd said it, but remembering those words gave her a sense of newfound security. No matter how crazy and temporary this thing with Everett was, he clearly wanted to be with her tonight. Even when their limousine passed the security check and proceeded down Illinois Avenue—people were packed like sardines on either side of the street—the spell lingered. It was Everett and the other artists who had created *Maritime*'s night. She knew—better than many—how much meticulous detail and hard work went into such a gargantuan production. She was proud to be there as his guest.

Besides, if you think for a second anyone is going to pay attention to you when you're with Everett Hughes, you're so flattering yourself.

Despite her self-assurances, her heart lurched when the limousine came to a halt in front of the red carpet and canopy that had been set up in the entrance of the AMC East 21 Theatres. She heard a muffled cheer go up in the crowd. She peered out the window and had the brief, flashing vision of several teenagers and a middle-aged couple staring at the limo with rapt excitement.

"They're all usually really nice people," he said. "Not what you'd think."

She stared back at him, eyes wide. The driver didn't immediately exit. Everett took her hand. For a few seconds, they seemed to exist in some kind of surreal bubble of invisibility in the very midst of a clamoring crowd.

"You okay?" he murmured.

She nodded, taking heart from his warm gaze on her face.

"It wasn't a great first date idea. I see that now. But again—I was selfish."

"It's a wonderful first date. I'm really looking forward to seeing the film."

"Yeah. You probably tell your dentist the same thing about your next appointment. We could have seen this at a matinee in a few days," he said, his mouth twitching in a combination of regret and amusement.

"No. It's your special night."

"And Seth's, too," he reminded her.

Joy nodded. "I'm *glad* you asked me to share it."

His grin vanished. He leaned over and kissed her. His lips almost immediately parted hers, his tongue sliding between them. He tasted like he'd sucked on a peppermint just minutes ago. He tasted like sex.

He tasted like heaven.

Joy made a muffled sound in her throat and returned the kiss, going from warm to a low simmer in a matter of seconds. It was strange to feel her body awaken so immediately after what she'd been through in the last year, sense her flesh flooding with new life. He applied a slight suction as their tongues dueled and tangled sensually. She felt that sweet pull all the way to her sex. He swept his hand along her bare shoulder and cupped the side of her neck, his thumb beneath her chin, holding her steady for his ravishment of her mouth.

Someone let out a shrill shriek of excitement that penetrated the cocoon of the limo. Everett sealed the kiss, but his head remained bent over hers. He studied her somberly, his eyelids narrowed.

"God, Joy. Why do I want you so much?"

Five

She swallowed thickly when she heard his muted incredulity. He must have read the confusion on her face.

"Don't say anything. I know you don't have the answer any more than I do. I only think it's fair to warn you, that's all," he muttered. He glanced out the door into the sunny, hot summer evening before he turned back to her. "I usually sign a few autographs before I go in, but I won't if you don't want me to. Then I'm going to do a couple really quick interviews, but I won't be long. My agent planned it so that I did most of them earlier today."

"I'll be fine," she assured him. "And of course you should sign some autographs. I can just imagine how long those people have been waiting."

He nodded once and lifted his hand as if to knock on the glass that separated them from the front seat. "Kenny can take you in to the reception. I told Katie to look out for you, and you might see your uncle at the preparty they have going on upstairs. I won't take long, I swear."

"Okay. Wait!"

He turned back to her and she wiped her lipstick off his mouth. Fortunately, she'd chosen a fairly neutral shade. He grinned, did the same for her smudged mouth.

"Perfect," he said, inspecting her. He tapped on the window between them and the driver, Kenny, and another man who had been introduced to her earlier by the name of Roger. Both men acted in the capacity of driver and security for Everett. The pane lowered.

"Ready?" Kenny asked.

"As we'll ever be. Can you please escort Joy inside once we get near the doors?"

"My pleasure," Kenny replied.

The next thing she knew, the door was opening. A shockingly loud cheer went up before Everett ever put his foot on the pavement. Once the crowd caught a glimpse of who the limousine held, the clamor increased several decibels, female shrieks spiking through it. Joy didn't have an opportunity to be nervous between the cacophonous cheering and shouts for Everett's attention and the flashing of cameras. Everett leaned into the limo and took her hand, helping her alight. He squeezed it slightly once they both stood on the carpeted sidewalk, and she instinctively paused next to him. She made random eye contact with a girl of about ten with dark bangs and a ponytail, who was looking at her with huge eyes. She smiled.

Lights flashed and people screamed Everett's name and she was walking by his side toward the doors. Distantly, she realized he was calling hello to the people closest to the fence as if they were his neighbors, asking casually how they were. His manner had a civilizing effect on those nearest to him. They ceased their screaming and just grinned at him from ear to ear, like he was a hero son or brother making his triumphant return home.

He halted a few feet from the glass doors and pulled lightly on Joy's hand. He swept down and kissed her briefly. The crowd cat-called, and suddenly Joy was being escorted up an escalator by Kenny, the burly driver. Everett had told her that Kenny had worked for him for years now.

"Do you ever get used to it?" Joy asked him, stunned by being in the proximity of so much potent adulation.

"Not really. I thought I'd seen it all being Britney Spears's bodyguard. But working for Everett trumped that experience—in the most interesting ways," he said with a rueful smile.

Joy chuckled and followed him off the escalator. She could just imagine. They stepped into a crowd of well-heeled guests sipping champagne. She caught sight of Seth's head at the far side of the lobby. There was a definite advantage to having a six-foot-four-inch-tall uncle—she could typically spot him in the largest crowds.

Kenny snagged a glass of champagne from a wandering waiter and handed it to her.

"Oh, thank you. I think I see my uncle over there," she told Kenny.

"Will you be all right if I leave you?"

"I'll be fine. Thank you."

Kenny nodded politely and turned to leave. Wilkie James saw her approaching first. He called out excitedly to her and ran over to give her a hug.

"I haven't seen you in ages," he enthused, stepping back to inspect her. "Look at you—Ellie Granolith is going to be furious that a high school teacher has stolen her thunder on the night of her screening."

Joy laughed at the reference to the reputedly spoiled, difficult star of the film. She'd never met Ellie personally, but her uncle had been forced to work with her last year repeatedly and had told Joy point-blank that the rumors were 100 percent accurate, if not generous in favor of Ellie.

"Quiet, Wilkie. With your luck, she's around here lurking behind the ferns or something. That's the last thing we need to do, insult Ellie Granolith. You look fantastic," she said, tweaking his bow tie.

"You're the one who looks fantastic. But why did you cut your hair?" Wilkie asked in his typical candid, irrepressible manner.

She took a sip of champagne to cover her discomfort. None of her L.A. friends knew about her cancer diagnosis. She hadn't wanted to burden them. Worry and fear were not feelings she cherished passing on to her friends. Joy knew all too well from her experience with her mother that there was nothing they could have done but sit by and watch helplessly.

"Shut it, Wilkie. I think her hair looks stunning," Seth said, suddenly standing next to both of them. She grinned as Seth swept down to kiss her. "You're glowing. I'd like to think it's from excellent health."

"And aren't you the handsome devil in your tux?" she complimented, sidestepping his reference to her health.

Seth had been born fourteen years after Joy's father, making him only ten years older than Joy. She'd adored her uncle Seth for as long as she could recall. As a child, she'd worshipped him like a girl might her affectionate, protective, cool older brother. Even after Joy's father had left them during Joy's mom's protracted illness, Seth had never wavered as the immovable, solid pillar of her life. She suspected she wouldn't be alive today if Seth hadn't been there.

"Where's Everett?" Seth asked her, glancing around. Was that a hint of worry she caught on Seth's face? She recalled what he'd said yesterday when they spoke on the phone and she'd told him about her date with Everett: At first he'd been silent, but then he'd said, "Everett is one of the nicest guys I've ever met—movie star or normal guy. But be careful, Joy. I don't really know him all that well. And their kind really is a different breed."

Joy had gotten what Seth meant. Everett belonged in the highest realms, that narrow band where the stars burned most brilliant. Yet she innately understood that Everett Hughes would resent being confined to such a shallow sphere.

"He's doing a few interviews. He said he'd be right up," she answered her uncle.

"Everett who?" Wilkie asked, his youthful face tightening with incredulity, as if he was sure he must have been mistaken in what he'd heard.

"The man himself—Everett Hughes," Seth said with dry amusement. He nodded toward the direction of the escalators, where everyone's attention seemed to be turning. Joy caught a glimpse of Everett's golden head. Like her uncle, he rose above the crowd.

Wilkie blanched. "What? You go crazy and abandon us by moving to Chicago, and the next thing I know, you start looking like you were born on the red carpet and dating Everett Hughes? What is going on? Someone has got some storytelling to do."

Joy was laughing at the thought of offering a highly edited explanation of how she'd ended up as Everett's date when she heard her named called.

"Katie," she greeted her warmly. Katie breezed up to her, looking lovely in the floral chiffon, her hair spilling around her shoulders. She gave Joy a quick hug.

"You look fantastic. I knew you would," she told Joy confidentially under her breath. "Joy Hightower, this is my husband, Rill."

"Hello. It's such a pleasure to meet you," Joy greeted him breathlessly, shaking hands with Rill Pierce. Katie's husband looked ruggedly handsome in his tux, but he seemed tense.

"Don't pay any attention to him," Katie told Joy in a subdued voice that managed to carry. "He's just grouchy because Ellie Granolith was badgering him a moment ago about putting her in *Razor Pass*, Rill's latest project. When he told her he'd already chosen Jennifer Turner for the part, she told him Irish whiskey must have killed his sense of taste. Rill told her vodka must have done the same for her sense of reality if she really thought there was a chance he'd cast her."

They all glanced at Seth when he made a snorting sound.

"Oh, this is my uncle, Seth Hightower, and Wilkie James, one of Hightower Special Effects artists," Joy said. "Rill and Katie Pierce."

"I'm sorry," Seth said, trying to hide his laughter. "It's just . . . I worked with Ellie. The comment about the vodka was dead-on." Seth shook Rill's hand. Joy blinked at the sudden appearance of Rill's brilliant smile. Katie certainly was a lucky woman.

"I've been wanting to meet you for a long time," Rill told Seth. "I would have tried to contact you sooner, but Katie suggested I might meet you in person tonight. Would you consider working on my next film?" Joy heard Rill ask Seth.

A thrill of excitement went through her for Seth. Working for Rill Pierce was something he'd always hoped to do. Someone touched her bare shoulder. The shiver that went through her told her who it was. She turned.

"Have I missed anything?" Everett asked, his gaze on her face. She shook her head, struck momentarily speechless by the sight of him. Her heart throbbed against her breastbone when he put his arm around her and caressed the bare skin of her upper arm.

"No. We were just waiting for you. Should we go up?" Katie asked, glancing from Everett to Joy over to Rill, who was too busy conversing with Seth and gesturing broadly to notice her question. She cupped her husband's elbow and tapped Seth. Both men blinked distractedly and glanced down at her.

"Come on, you can talk business on the way up to the theater. It's showtime, folks."

Everett's hand slid down Joy's arm and he took her hand. For once, she didn't have the wherewithal to hide her excitement—or her attraction—when he glanced back at her and gave a slow smile.

* * *

Several hours later, Joy slid into a circular leather booth, highly conscious of Everett following her. The premiere had been a huge success, the audience's approval of the groundbreaking film evident in the ebullient mood of the crowd and the standing ovation after the final scene. Seth's makeup had been stunning. Everett's performance had been riveting. She'd lost herself in the film, her rapt focus only breaking when Everett caressed her hand or shifted slightly in his seat, his trousers brushing against her thigh.

It was a little like waking up from one fantasy to find herself in another, even more compelling one.

Joy couldn't believe she'd survived the difficult part. The glitter and manic energy of the premiere were over. Now Everett and she were alone in a private, draped-off room at the Capital Grille, and the euphoria of the evening mingled with a heart-racing sense of anticipation.

Everett touched her neck. She turned, only to find that he was close. He kissed her, his lips firm and hungry.

"I like you like this," he said a moment later, his mouth hovering near hers.

"Like what?"

"You seem happy . . . Available."

She laughed. *"Available?* I think I've made it pretty clear I'm available, haven't I?"

He didn't reply immediately, just studied her closely while he caressed the juncture between her neck and shoulder, his hand moving seductively over the single strap of her dress.

"I suppose," he murmured after a second. He leaned back. "But your guard is up at times."

Joy opened her mouth to ask him what he meant, but the waiter entered the curtained-off area of the private room. After they'd placed their orders and were alone again, Joy spoke.

"What did you mean, my 'guard is up at times'?"

He shrugged and took a sip of his ice water. "It is, isn't it? You're not too certain about the idea of getting involved with me." He set his glass down and met her stare levelly. His eyes gleamed in the candlelight. "I'm not one of those people who lets Hollywood go to their head, Joy. I know reality from fantasy."

She glanced away from his piercing gaze. "It's heady stuff—the crowds, the adulation, the praise from millions. If you can tell the difference between reality and fantasy, my hat goes off to you. I wasn't even the focus of it tonight, but I was affected by it," she admitted, considering the golden glow of excitement that surrounded her. Was that the type of experience her father had craved, both as a race car driver and a manager for a high-profile Formula 1 racing team?

She glanced at Everett. "I don't think you can't tell the difference between reality and fantasy. You're very down-to-earth—shockingly so, considering your job."

"Then why the hesitance about going out with me?" he challenged quietly.

She inhaled slowly. "Maybe it's me I'm concerned about. I'm worried I might give in to the lure of it all."

His brow crinkled in confusion. "You don't strike me as the fame-starved type, Joy."

She laughed. "I'm far from wanting attention. If anything, I'd rather avoid it."

"That's what I thought. So what did you mean, 'the lure of it all'?"

Her gaze flickered across his handsome, sober face. "I meant the lure of you."

His mouth tightened. "That's a nice thing to say. I think."

She smiled. "I haven't been dating much recently. To suddenly be on a date again—and not with just anyone or on any date, but one with Everett Hughes on the night of a premiere—well, it's a little overwhelming," she admitted, taking a sip of her water.

She'd put dating and men on the back burner since she'd learned of her cancer diagnosis. She'd been declared cancer free, but the threat still lingered like a toxic cloud. To Joy, the whole experience of doing battle with death had been a highly personal experience. She'd even kept Seth at the periphery, never allowing her uncle into the central arena where her fears and anguish resided.

"How come you haven't been dating? Bad breakup?" he added when she didn't immediately respond. She was spared having to answer when the waiter entered the private dining room with their drinks. While they were served, she had the opportunity to come up with an answer for Everett. She turned to him once the waiter had left.

"Like I said, I find you to be very down-to-earth and grounded. It's myself I question. You must know that I'm attracted to you," she said. "It's a little hard to figure out how much of that is real, though. Almost every woman in the country has at least a minor crush on Everett Hughes."

"They don't know me."

"I realize that. But neither do I, Everett."

His nostrils flared slightly. He took a sip of his drink and set it down before he turned in the booth and faced her. She stilled when he placed his opened hand on the side of her neck and brushed her cheek with his thumb. The gesture struck her as cherishing and highly sexually possessive at once.

"Maybe that's true. But you have to admit, there's some serious chemistry between us."

"I won't even try to deny it. I still can't believe I did what I did at the studio that time."

His gaze roved over her face, intense . . . hungry. His face lowered.

"Serious sexual chemistry is as good a place to start as any."

He seized her mouth with his own. She felt the effect of his lips and tongue from the tips of her breasts to the center of her sex and all the way to her curling toes. He cupped both of her shoulders with his hands and molded the muscle to his palms. One hand trailed down her arm. She shivered.

"You've been driving . . . me crazy all night . . . in this dress," he murmured as he pressed kisses along her jaw and neck. "Your skin is so smooth . . . so soft . . . such a beautiful color." She gasped when he began to nibble at the skin of her neck. He took her hand in his and laced their fingers together. He raised his head and met her stare. "I know you probably think I'm coming on too strong, but I can't seem to stop myself."

He sunk his head, and once again she was made drunk by his kiss. He caressed her along the side of her waist and up her ribs, playing her nerves like a master. He opened his hand when he reached the side of her breast, his fingers lightly massaging her back, the ridge of his thumb cradling the weight of her breast, only the thin satin fabric separating his skin from her own. He groaned quietly and deepened their kiss.

His hand shifted, covering her breast. Warm moisture seeped from her pussy, an answer to the call of his touch. It felt so good feeling her desire flow like sap, reminding her she was alive. Vibrant. Sexually desirable to a man like Everett.

It was heady stuff.

It was also intoxicating, because only distantly did she remember they were in a public place. His hand slid beneath the satin of her dress, her nipple pulling tight and hard against his stroking fingers, and her concern faded to the periphery of her mind.

He lifted his head and murmured something she couldn't hear, but understood—a searing endearment. He untied the satin straps at her left shoulder and lowered her dress. She felt a flicker of uncertainty when his fingertip brushed over the thin, three-quarter-inch scar just beneath her clavicle.

"What happened here?"

She blinked and lowered her head. He must not have noticed her port scar yesterday during the heat of passion. "I had a minor surgery done last year. The scar is fading—slowly," she whispered.

She prayed to God she'd never have to have another port inserted into her chest. She'd hated it—walking around with a hole in her chest so that she could have a bunch of toxic chemicals poured into her with ease.

Everett lowered the fabric farther and his head at the same moment, and her anxiety fractured and scattered. His lips skimmed her chest, brushed across the small scar and kissed the upper slope of the breast that he'd bared. The friction of his goatee sliding over sensitive skin created an arousing contrast to his soft, warm kisses. She glanced down, watching him through a sensual haze.

The image of him opening his mouth and slipping a pink nipple between his lips was burned into her consciousness. She saw his cheeks hollow out slightly, the suction on her breast tugging at her clit and deep inside her. She gasped and clutched at the back of his head, letting her fingers tangle in his hair.

The abrupt cessation of his warm mouth and laving tongue startled her. He covered her damp nipple with the fabric of her dress and draped the strap over her shoulder. He put his arm around her and hugged her to him in a protective gesture.

"Your salads," the waiter said, making Joy blink in disorientation. Everett must have heard his approach. Joy hadn't been aware of anything but his mouth on her breast.

"Thank you," Everett said, catching the middle-aged man's eye. "Can you please give us some privacy for ten minutes or so?"

Heat rushed into Joy's cheeks at Everett's casual request, but the waiter took it all in stride.

"Of course. I'll tell the chef to delay your entrées a few minutes, as well."

"Thank you," Everett said to the man's retreating back.

He turned to her. She opened her mouth to speak, but paused when she saw the heat of his gaze. He held her stare as his hand moved again to the tie at her shoulder.

He lowered the fabric below both her breasts. She just sat there, her breath burning in her lungs, her nipples prickling against the cool, air-conditioned air. His stare lowered. She made a soughing sound as she inhaled with effort. His gaze flickered back up to her face.

"Can't this wait?" she asked desperately. She was aroused—exquisitely so—but why must he do this here? She could hear the murmur of patrons in the main dining room in the distance and the clatter of china in the kitchen. She felt the weight of his stare pressing on her lungs. Her nipples felt tight, like every nerve in them demanded to be touched.

"No," he said. "I want to make you feel like I did that time at the studio. Willing to do something impulsive, willing to take a risk when you know you shouldn't. Do you think I do something like that often?" he asked, his manner intent. Joy's breath flew inward when he touched the side of her breast with a fingertip.

"I . . . I don't know. I hadn't thought about it."

His glance at her was sharp.

"No? Not since you've discovered who I was? You haven't wondered if Everett Hughes wasn't as used to having beautiful strangers go down on him as he was drinking his morning coffee?"

She bit her lip when he touched a nipple. He circled it, detailing its contours gently. Her vagina clenched tight at the caress.

"Joy?"

She gasped when he pinched lightly at her other nipple. Arousal spiked through her body.

"All right. Maybe I've thought about it."

He nodded, his gaze never leaving her face. His eyes had narrowed into gleaming slits. She couldn't look away. She inhaled his scent in short, irregular breaths. His teasing fingertips on her nipples caused excitement to shudder through her.

"In my business, behaving like that on a regular basis is a sure way to have your private life stolen away from you completely. If the press has learned as a general rule that you know not to act like an idiot and how to keep your pants zipped, they start to expect a decent guy instead of a jerk. It's all about managing expectations."

She inhaled sharply when he molded both breasts to his palms and continued to stroke her nipples. "Then why are you doing this now, in a public place?"

"Because. What happened at the studio was a singular experience—one I hadn't expected. Now it's your turn," he murmured. He pinched at both of her nipples, the caress soft and insistent at once. She moaned, her rising desire like a living thing, stealing over her flesh, making her its captive.

He cupped both of her breasts from below and examined them. He'd made the nipples prominent and hard with his stroking fingers, the rose color a stark contrast to the paler flesh. They looked like firm, lush fruit in his cradling hands.

"So beautiful," he murmured before he bent and took a nipple into his warm mouth. Shards of pleasure tore through her. Her pussy tingled in approval of his lashing tongue. She gasped his name when he drew on her nipple and fondled her other breast with a lazy sort of deliberation that she found unbearably exciting. Her fingers raked through his hair. He groaned roughly and lifted his head, finding her mouth with his own. He slid his tongue between her parted lips, caressing her teasingly before he nibbled at her with kisses that struck her as controlled and feverish at once. She was so enthralled by his molding mouth that it took her a moment to realize he'd grabbed both of her wrists. He held her hands down on the leather seat.

"There," he said, his gaze flickering over her face. "Now I have you at my mercy."

"Everett. You told the waiter to come back in ten minutes."

"Plenty of time," he murmured.

He leaned down and began to ravish her breasts, moving back and forth between them, his actions unapologetically hungry. He explored every curve with warm, seeking lips, he took gentle bites out of the tender flesh, he sucked on her nipples until she gave a restrained cry of anguished arousal.

"Stop. Please," she said shakily when he transferred his head from one nipple to another and began a new sensual torture.

He lifted his head, but kept his lips close to her pink, wet nipple. "Do you really want me to? Or would you rather come?"

She glanced down, panting softly. A woman laughed loudly on the other side of the curtain. It was madness, and she knew it was madness, but a thrill tore through her nevertheless.

She arched her back. Her breasts looked flushed, the nipples erect and reddened. The only thing she could consider was the desire to have his mouth back on her. She bit her lower lip.

"I don't want you to stop," she whispered. "But there isn't time to—"

He released one of her hands and sat up slightly, pushing back the table several inches from their seat. He leaned down, reached toward the floor and drew up his hand. Joy realized he'd just pulled up the hem of her dress. She shifted her hips, allowing him to place the bulk of the fabric in her lap. For a breathless second, his hand remained between her parted thighs.

"What's wrong?" she asked in a strangled voice when he didn't immediately move.

"If I touch you now, it would be too much for me. I reached the end of my rope yesterday in your apartment. I won't be able to wait, and I don't want my first time inside of you to be in a public place," he rasped, sounding tense. He reached for her wrist.

"Everett . . . what—"

"Touch yourself while I play with your beautiful breasts. Let me feel you shake in my arms. *Please*," he added tersely when she opened her mouth to protest. It was a ridiculous request. She'd never masturbated in front of a man before, let alone done so in the midst of a crowded restaurant.

"Go on, Joy. Take a risk."

He used his hand to tuck hers between her thighs. Despite his insistence that he shouldn't touch her, he didn't move away immediately. She felt his knuckles through her panties, pressing against her sensitive labia. Her own fingers touched damp silk. His face went rigid. He remained still, his hand entwined with her own as her heat penetrated his skin.

He made a rough sound and slid his hand away. Suddenly, he was ravishing her mouth as he had her breasts earlier, a sweet, savage consumption.

"You're so warm and soft," he murmured before he was kissing her again, and her fingers were moving of their own accord, rubbing and sliding over her clit, feeding her mounting hunger.

He dropped his head and began sucking and licking a nipple until she gritted her teeth in pleasure. She wanted to scream, the tension mounting in her was so imperative. She pressed at the slick button of her clit, agitating and circling. Everett grabbed her free hand, his actions abrupt and tense. He brought it to her left breast, his hand enfolding hers, urging her to fondle the firm, tender flesh. At first she resisted the wantonness of his silent demand, but then he transferred his mouth to the breast she held. He slid the nipple into his warm, suctioning mouth, and she held herself from below, plumping the flesh . . . offering herself to him. She squeezed her breast, the lewdness of her actions somehow liberating her.

He moaned. The sound of his appreciation as he sucked on her voraciously made her a little mad. She pressed hard with the ridge of her finger on her clit. She began to shudder in silent orgasm.

Everett bit down gently on her nipple, the edge of his teeth a tender lash. A desperate, tiny cry broke free of her throat. His arms went around her. He pressed his face against her chest, holding her against him, absorbing her shudders of pleasure.

He raised his head and examined her when her convulsions ebbed. She sagged against the leather booth. She watched him, made mute with disbelief and wonder as he reached between her thighs and brought her hand to his face. He inserted her forefinger into his mouth. He closed his eyes and suckled her juices from her skin. A muscle jumped in his cheek. He slid her finger from his warm, wet mouth.

"Now I've seen you undone. I'm glad."

"Why? Was this a sort of payback for what happened at the studio?"

"No," he said, his expression grim. He smoothed the fabric of her dress over her thighs, letting it fall until it reached the top of her feet. He slid his fingers beneath her bodice and carefully drew it over her breasts. Her nipples ached dully next to the smooth cloth.

"Everett?" she prompted when he didn't offer any further explanation for his statement, just tied the straps at her left shoulder.

He lowered his hands and glanced into her face.

"I'm glad because I wanted you to know how I felt that afternoon at the studio. I don't know if I completely succeeded," he admitted as he slid the table closer to their seat. "But I think maybe now you have some idea."

Understanding trickled into her lust-dulled brain slowly. He hadn't been paying her back, tit for tat. He'd wanted her to know that the way she felt right at this moment—turned inside out, stunned by her own actions—had been how he'd felt.

Someone directly outside the curtain cleared his throat. Everett glanced around calmly when the waiter parted the thick curtains. The man's gaze ran first over her, and then Everett. Joy sat up self-consciously and brushed back her short hair. There was no way she could disguise her recent arousal. She suspected the skin around her mouth was reddened from whisker burn. Her cheeks must be tellingly pink.

"Would you like me to bring your entrées now, Mr. Hughes?" the waiter asked.

"We've had a change of plan. Would you mind packing up our food to go?" He glanced at Joy, his eyebrows raised. "If that's all right with you?"

"Yes, I'm not very hungry anyway," she murmured. She busied herself with unfolding her wrap, keeping her flushed face averted from the waiter. Seeing a total stranger standing there, just feet away from where she'd just been sitting with her breasts exposed, bringing herself to climax, brought it all home to her.

What other shocking things could Everett encourage her to do? She recognized that the answer was *a lot*.

And what does it matter? she asked herself as she took Everett's hand a moment later and he led her out of one of the rear doors of the restaurant. He could be with any woman on the planet, but he chose to be with her—if only for this brief moment of time.

Joy was a realist, that much could be said about her. Life had taught her again and again that escape from an often harsh world was not a possibility. But life could be beautiful, too, and exciting, even if those moments were ephemeral.

She followed Everett into a warm summer night. The long, black limousine glided up to the curb like a magical carriage. Everett glanced back at her. A lock of hair had fallen onto his forehead. He smiled, and she smiled back.

She might as well enjoy the fantasy while it lasted.

Six

"Would you like to eat together, or would you rather just call it a night?" Everett asked when Kenny brought the limousine to a halt in front of her apartment. He'd had his arm around her the entire ride home. She'd been a little stiff at first—did she imagine he was going to try to screw her in the back of the limo? After what he'd done at the restaurant, that may have been precisely what she'd thought.

Still, he couldn't regret it. Seeing Joy so aroused that she'd forgotten caution and wisdom and taken a risk had been important to him for some reason. Only when they were a few blocks away from her brownstone did she lower her head and snuggle against his chest.

She lifted her head now. He tried to make out her expression in the dim light, but once again, he felt as if the gate had been closed. It was hard to believe she could be skittish around him after the way she responded to him sexually. Was she just cautious, or was

Joy reserved to the point of shyness? He thought the answer might be both.

"I'd like to eat, if you would. I mean, if you're not too tired," she said.

He brushed her bangs off her forehead. Her face looked still and mysterious, cast in bluish light from the streetlights and shadow.

"I'm not too tired," he said.

"Then why don't you come up?"

He paused to tell Kenny and Roger he'd take a cab back to the hotel and then exited the limo with Joy. Once they were inside, he set the bag the Capital Grille had packed for them on her dining room table.

"I'll set the table. Where are your plates?" he asked, removing the jacket of his tux and hanging it on the back of a chair.

She glanced around from where she'd been setting her purse down on the counter. She looked surprised. Obviously, she hadn't thought he'd been serious when he asked her if she wanted to eat with him.

"In there," she said, pointing to one of the cabinets.

"The lobster smells fantastic. It should still be hot."

She stood by the counter, her wrap clutched around her waist. Her cheeks still carried the telltale signs of arousal. Her lips still looked swollen from the way he'd ravaged her mouth. He forced his mind onto his task and opened the cabinet she'd indicated.

"Do you want to go change?" he asked as he loosened his bow tie. He opened a couple drawers, looking for silverware. "Might as well get comfortable."

"Okay. I think I will, if you don't mind."

"I'd prefer that you were as comfortable as possible," he replied as he found the silverware and grabbed a couple forks and knives. From the periphery of his vision, he saw her waver for a split second before she headed toward the hallway.

She really couldn't figure him out, he thought wryly as he set the plates and silverware on a couple placemats on the table. He couldn't imagine why. His feelings on the matter seemed a lot more clear-cut and obvious than Joy's.

"Try some of the lobster tail," he told her a while later, holding up a mouthwatering-looking bite of perfectly poached lobster coated in butter. She'd come out of her bedroom a few minutes before looking like a summer day in a simple peach-and-white cotton dress that tied at her shoulders. She parted her lips and he slid the fork between them. He stopped himself just in time from sharing in her groan of appreciation. She smiled as she chewed.

"The kind of thing that really makes you understand the phrase *I could die happy*. I hate to think of what it's doing to my arteries, but it's delicious enough to make me forget," she said after she swallowed. She cut a slice of her salmon and offered it to him. He held her gaze as he accepted her offering.

"Hmmm. I taste fennel in the relish."

She shook her head and took a sip of the chardonnay he'd poured for them. "There really isn't much you don't know, is there?"

He shrugged. "I took a six-week cooking course in Spain once."

"You like to cook?"

"I like to eat," he said, waggling his eyebrows. He cut into his tenderloin, which melted like butter around his knife. "But yeah, I like to cook once in a while, too. Do you?"

She nodded. "Very much. Brings out my creative side."

"It can be a very sensual thing. I took classes from a Spanish master chef at his country home. He had this amazing kitchen, with all these antique etched glass bottles and carafes. It was a feast for the senses, having all this colorful, fragrant food in front of you, the hissing sound the fresh ingredients made when they hit the hot oil, the way the sunlight struck all his beautiful glass containers. Here . . . have a bite of this tenderloin. It's amazing," he said.

"It sounds wonderful," she said, her eyes taking on a dreamy cast as she chewed the bite of juicy meat he'd slipped between her lips. He wondered if she had any idea how sexy he found the dress she was wearing. The ties at her gleaming shoulders were the most remarkable teases. "I'd love something like that. To direct all my attention for six weeks to one task, and to do it in such an evocative place."

He nodded. "That's the main thing—the direction of all your attention into one task, one action, one moment. Very Zen."

"Are you a Buddhist?" she asked as she tore a slice of bread apart.

"No, but I have spent a lot of time in Tibet and Thailand. I admire their spiritual practices. I use a lot of mindfulness to prepare for a role. I don't want to just pick up a hammer and mimic being a blacksmith, for instance. I want to *do* it—feel what it's like to have this extension, this hammer in your hand, to be melding all the elements of fire, air, earth and water into a concrete tool, imagine what it'd be like to have that fire blaze in your face while you forged and branded this something that would serve its purpose and be passed from father to son for a century or more."

She regarded him soberly. "I saw that, where you played the fourteenth-century blacksmith. It was the first movie I ever saw you in," she said quietly. "Afterward, when I learned you were an American, I was shocked. I would have sworn from your accent that you were Welsh."

He shrugged. "I have an ear for accents. It's not a skill, really; more like something I was born with. Some kind of freak gene, as Katie puts it."

"I think you're being modest."

"No. I'm not. A lot of it just comes when you throw yourself wholesale into something. Put on the clothes of the character, live in the landscape, use the tools, eat the food, and do it all mindfully."

"You're right. It is all very Zen."

"I told you I respected the religion. I would, even if their only offering was tantric sex," he said, grinning.

Her eyes widened. He stilled. It was true, what he'd said, but he shouldn't have been so blunt. He rushed in to smooth over his error.

"But in the end, I suppose it's hard to completely wring the Protestant kid from Southern California out of me. Or maybe I'm just too lazy to be a full-fledged Buddhist. Or too hedonistic," he said, eyeing another bite of butter-drenched lobster. "But enough about me. Let's talk about you. I hope you don't think I'm being nosy, but I saw that Formula 1 racecar postcard in your kitchen. Are you a fan of the sport?"

"No, that's from my father. He manages the European Formula 1 team. He used to drive himself and was very successful."

"Are you close to him?" Everett asked.

"No, not especially. His job is his one true love. We're not one of those feuding fathers and daughters or anything. I don't begrudge him the life he's chosen, or the fact that I rarely see him. We don't have a lot in common. I'm much closer to Seth, and always have been. Seth has been my whole family for half my life."

Her comment seemed to ask for a follow-up question, but Everett restrained himself. Joy was such a private person. He respected that, even if he did plan to peel back her layers. Discovering Joy's depths clearly wouldn't be a quick endeavor, or an easy one.

He found himself relishing the challenge.

"Rill asked Seth to do makeup for *Razor Pass* tonight," Everett said.

Her eyes warmed. "I know! I'm so excited for Seth. What a wonderful opportunity—to work with Rill. And Seth *loves* the book," she enthused, referring to the novel Rill was adapting to film.

"Did he give Rill an answer yet?" Everett asked.

Joy shook her head. "Knowing Seth, he's at the hotel right now, drawing feverishly. He'll give Rill an answer when he gets some results."

He smiled. "Rill didn't ask him for any samples. He just offered him the job."

She made a face. "You have to know Seth. He's a perfectionist. He won't accept until he sees the proof in front of him that he's right for the job. He has to draw to find the proof."

"Strange lot, artists," he said, tracing the graceful line of her neck and shoulder with his gaze.

"They say the same about actors," she murmured, her eyes lowered, her voice smoky.

"They say correctly." He touched the back of her hand where it rested on the table. She turned it over, twining her fingers with his.

They talked for a while longer, sipping their wine, Everett drawing her out until she seemed much more comfortable and relaxed. The clock in the kitchen caught his eye. He reluctantly withdrew his hand from hers and wiped his mouth with his napkin.

"I'm being inconsiderate. It's midnight on a Sunday. You have to teach in the morning, don't you?"

She nodded and pushed back her half-eaten plate of salmon. "I do. Although it's only from nine until noon. Summer school has a very relaxed schedule. Besides, it's my last week before the term ends. The kids' final project is tomorrow."

"What are you teaching?" he asked.

"Drawing Three. The students are more advanced, so it's a fun, laid-back summer class."

He nodded slowly, searching her harmonious, calm features. He wanted to stay and make love to her. He wanted that more than anything. His arousal had ebbed since he'd held her and felt her quaking in orgasm, but it'd never fully dissipated. It flared to life nearly every time she smiled or laughed or studied him with that somber stare that cut him down to the quick. He'd probably made a mistake by doing what he'd done at the restaurant, but he'd wanted her to understand how singular this experience was for him, how unique she was.

People often alluded to the fact that he could have any woman, but those people didn't understand that a female body wasn't enough for him. He wanted connection. He wanted something that counted—something like his parents had, or Rill and Katie shared. He didn't know if Joy could be the woman for him or not, but he'd been with enough female companions at this point in his life to know that what he experienced with her was different. Special.

It was rare finding that spark with someone—magical, even— and that was true if you were a truck driver, an accountant or a film actor. He could make a decent argument for the fact that it was *harder* for him to find someone special. On more than one occasion, he'd wondered if fate had blessed him in so many different ways but would deny him the precious gift of a life mate. He dreaded the possibility.

He took a large swallow of his ice water. "I should be going then," he said, setting down his glass. He paused when she put her hand on his forearm. He looked into her face.

"I don't want you to go," she said.

He again took her hand in his and squeezed. Her smile struck him as shy . . . radiant. He felt blood rush to his cock, creating a full, taut feeling of anticipation.

"I can't tell you how happy I am to hear you say that," he murmured. He stood, her hand still in his, and raised her to her feet.

Joy led him to her bedroom, her heart starting to jump and pound against her breastbone. Maybe she should shower? Maybe she should brush her teeth? He drew her hand to his face and kissed her, his mouth warm and reassuring, and her stupid questions scattered to the sidelines of her awareness. She dropped his hand momentarily while she turned the bedside lamp on to a dim setting. She felt a strange mixture of excitement and awkwardness when she joined him where he stood at the side of her bed. He cradled her jaw and turned her face up toward his.

"Nervous?" he asked.

She nodded. "It's the first time . . ."

Her voice trailed off uncertainly, but he nodded. "The first time that we've been deliberate about it all instead of bowled over by lust," he said, a smile pulling at his mouth. She sighed and turned to press a kiss to his palm.

"I actually meant something else."

"What?" he asked.

"The first time we've paused to take off all our clothes?" she murmured, smiling up at him.

He laughed. His hand trailed down her arm. Her flesh tingled beneath his skimming fingertips. There was something about his touch that really did something to her. He leaned down and brushed his lips against hers. "I want to be inside you," he murmured. "It's all I've thought about for the past two days."

"I want the same thing."

"Then let's give each other what we want," he said gruffly, his warm breath striking her upturned lips.

"Yes," she whispered, before his mouth covered hers. She closed her eyes and gave herself to the power of his kiss. His mouth was still cool from drinking ice water, but she felt his heat just beneath it. His taste inundated her—complex, male, intoxicating. Her shyness melted, and the true Joy rose to the surface. She penetrated his mouth with her tongue, eager to taste more of him.

He groaned and took both of her shoulders in his hands. She encircled his waist with her arms. He squeezed her shoulder muscles lightly and brought her closer to him, until her breasts crushed against his ribs and her belly pressed along his zipper. She felt him behind the fabric, hard, warm, teeming with life. He shifted slightly, and she realized the shaft of his penis rode down his left pant leg. She caressed his back muscles, thrilling to the sensation of all that lean, corded power. If he felt this good with his clothes on, what would it be like to feel his naked skin sliding beneath her fingertips? She shifted her hand between their straining bodies, suddenly ravenous to discover firsthand the answer to her question.

Her fingertips slipped between two buttons of his dress shirt. She touched the smooth skin covering his ribs. Her forefinger dipped down to stroke his abdomen. She felt the muscle spasm slightly, and he broke their kiss.

Joy sensed him looking down at her, but she focused on her task of unbuttoning his shirt. If she looked into his eyes, her self-consciousness might dampen her ardor, and she wanted no interference to her desire at the present moment. She parted his shirt and for a few seconds just stared at the expanse of flawless, golden brown skin covering ridged, defined muscle. His small, coppery-tinged nipples nestled in a smattering of light brown hair on his chest. The narrow path of hair that bisected a flat, defined abdomen seemed to beckon Joy . . . tempt her to follow it beneath the waistband of his crisp black trousers.

She looked into his face, feeling overwhelmed. God, he really was something from another world. This felt beyond her.

Perhaps he read the mixed anxiety and longing on her face, because his arms came around her loosely. He opened his palm at the small of her back and kneaded her flesh gently.

"Touch me, Joy. Let me see your hands on me," he rasped, his voice coming from just above the top of her head. She looked straight ahead, her line of sight directly on dense pectoral muscles. She reached. A small sigh leaked past her lips. His skin felt thick and soft, the muscle beneath rigid against her seeking fingertips. She touched the crinkly hair on his chest and then a nipple. His breath hitched. His flesh beaded beneath her stroking finger. His cock lurched next to her belly.

"Joy," he muttered. He bent and covered her mouth with his own. As if his kiss gave her permission, she began to touch him everywhere, sliding her palms along the sides of his ribs, molding his back muscles to her palms, testing to see if the trail of hair down his taut abdomen felt as silky as it appeared.

It did. It also made Everett groan into her mouth and seal their kiss. She glanced up, her first and second fingers dipping beneath his waistband, pausing when she saw the glint in his blue-green eyes.

"Let's get you out of this dress," he murmured. She felt his hand at her shoulder. Instead of immediately pulling on the cotton straps, he toyed with them for a moment, running the cloth between his long fingers. For some reason, his actions made liquid heat surge between her thighs. When he eventually did pull at the material, releasing the bow, he smiled. By the time he'd untied the other strap, she breathed raggedly.

"It's like unwrapping a priceless present," he said, devilish grin in place.

She laughed softly, although his teasing tone couldn't entirely erase the tension inherent to the moment.

His hand shifted to her back and he lowered the zipper on her dress. Instead of allowing the loose fabric to drop, he stepped back a few inches and lowered it deliberately, exposing her chest and the top curves of her breasts, allowing her nipples to peek above the cloth, then the fringe at the neckline to scrape across her ribs and belly.

Joy held her breath. It was almost unbearable, the anticipation, watching his face when he exposed the sensitive strip of flesh above her mons and the tiny triangle of ivory silk that covered her pubic hair. Her dress bunched in his fist. He lowered it farther. She gasped softly when his knuckles brushed against her naked thigh. He dropped it suddenly, the dress fluttering to her ankles. He spread his hand along the front of her thigh.

"God, you're lovely."

She made a strangled sound as his hand coasted upward. He touched her pussy through the meager fabric of her thong, the caress firm and confident.

"Bless it, you're wet," she thought she heard him say. His gaze flickered up to her face. "You're ready."

"Yes," she said shakily.

He placed his hands on her shoulders and guided her back to the bed. She sat and then lay back at his silent urging. Her throat tightened uncomfortably when he carefully removed her thong.

He stood and began to undress. She wanted to undress him as he had her, so sweetly, so seductively, but she felt almost debilitated by her desire. Her limbs felt heavy. Her pussy felt like a living thing between her thighs, tingling with arousal, hungry for stimulation, aching to be filled.

She swallowed with difficulty a moment later as she watched Everett lower his pants. He wore boxer-briefs, the stark whiteness of them a contrast to his gilded skin. His erection strained against the fabric, the outline of his cock clear to see.

She didn't know what to say when he stood before her naked, didn't know what to do. He was so beautiful, it almost hurt her a little to look at him. Something so amazing, so brilliant, couldn't be a lasting thing. It wasn't even conceivable. She lay there, her flesh prickly, needful of the friction of his body against hers. It surprised her a little to see her own arms stretched out, beckoning him. He quickly donned a condom, the strength of his arousal stretching the prophylactic tight.

He knelt between her opened thighs and placed his hands next to her head, his shoulder and arm muscles flexing hard. He leaned down and kissed the nipple of her left breast, flicking his tongue over the tip before he pressed his mouth above her pounding heart.

"Lovely Joy," he whispered next to her skin. She encircled his neck with her hands, delving her fingertips into the corded muscle of his upper back. His hand moved to the back of her thigh. He pushed her knee toward her chest and shifted his hips, the motion fluid and natural. She felt the head of his cock nudge her pussy and met his stare. He slowly began to pierce her. A convulsion of emotion shuddered through her. It'd been so long since she'd been with a man.

"Are you all right?" he whispered.

She bit her lip and nodded. His girth was stretching her, but even as he flexed with his hips, she felt her flesh melt around him . . . welcome him.

"You're very small," he said through a tense jaw.

"I haven't done this for a while," she whispered. She ran her hands down his sides. She placed one hand on a smooth, dense buttock. Another shudder went through her, this one of excitement. Her vagina tightened around him. He groaned and flexed, seating himself farther inside her. She tightened her hand on his ass, cupping him, urging him. A feverish flush went through her.

"Jesus. I can feel your heat," he muttered tensely, sinking inside her several more inches. She lowered her other hand, holding both of his cheeks. She pushed, letting him know with her actions what she wanted.

"Joy," he grated out. He gave in to her wish and pushed into her to the hilt. His ass felt as hard as stone beneath her clutching hands. It hurt a little, to be so filled with him. But her excitement was greater than her discomfort. Not so long ago, she'd felt so broken, so polluted by her illness and by the chemicals running in her veins—the poison to kill the greater evil. Now she was brimming with life, golden and rich, overfilled by Everett's powerful energy. He pulsed against her clamoring nerves, kissing deep, secret flesh with his cock.

She glanced up at him, taking in the gleam of sweat on his rigid stomach muscles, the bunching of his chest and shoulders and the feral gleam in his eyes.

"Fuck me," she whispered.

His nostrils flared. He held her stare and granted her request, drawing out of her several inches before he sank back into her to the hilt. Her breath caught at the sure, firm stroke.

"Am I hurting you?" he asked, pausing, his stomach muscles clenching.

"No. No. It feels so good."

He began to fuck her with slow, thorough strokes that built a delicious friction in her. She admitted the fact that it wasn't enough to Everett before she acknowledged the truth herself. She clutched his ass and tensed her biceps tight.

"Harder. Please."

They might have been a stranger's words flying past her lips. His gaze searched her face. The next moment, he granted her request. Her eyes flew wide. He'd drawn his cock out of her until the thick head licked at her swollen labia in a teasing caress. Then he drove deep again . . . and again. She bobbed her hips, so needy for that delicious stretch of her flesh that sent a pang through her clit, for that moment when he sank his cock completely inside her and gave his hips that slight jerk, grinding his pelvis against her wet, tender tissues.

Distantly, she was aware of her antique brass headboard clacking against the plaster wall. Her eyelids sagged as she became transported by sensation.

"Joy."

His sharp call made her eyelids flutter open. He'd paused, his pelvis pressed tight against her hungry pussy.

"Don't stop," she whispered, hovering on the precipice of orgasm.

His cock jerked inside her womb.

"Keep your eyes open."

He began fucking her again, his eyes like lancing lasers that wouldn't allow her to look away.

"Oh . . . it's . . ."

"Let it happen. Come," he said as he plunged into her and the bed rattled.

Her first cry sounded panicked to her own ears. Then climax ripped through her from root to limb, and she knew nothing but shuddering pleasure.

Through a hot haze of satiation, she became aware of Everett's full, firm cock sliding out of her body.

"No."

"It's okay," he whispered.

She opened her eyelids and watched through a slit as he came to rest next to and above her, on the pillow.

"Come here," she heard him coax, his hands sliding beneath her back, urging her to rise off the mattress. She moved, feeling strange . . . disoriented.

"Straddle my lap," he said.

She blinked and pushed her bangs out of her eyes. He'd sounded so tense. He sat on her mattress, his back a foot away from the brass posts of the headboard, his long legs sprawled before him. She straddled his thighs, her gaze falling to his lap. Awareness snapped through her consciousness like a whip. He was still hard— incredibly so. She was surprised the condom didn't snap around his swollen member.

"I'm sorry," she whispered, clambering closer to him. "I hadn't realized."

"There's nothing to be sorry about. I wanted it that way," he said, putting his hands on her shoulders, guiding her over him. She noticed that the condom glistened with her own juices. "I want to savor you. I want to take you like an animal, too," he admitted under his breath. "But I'm trying to fight the instinct."

He put his hand at the root of his cock—the naked stretch where the condom couldn't reach. Something about the image of him touching himself, his fingers draping down over his large, full testicles, made her clit pinch in renewed arousal. He held himself at a hospitable angle, his hand on her hip. Joy raised herself and caught the bulbous head of his penis between her spread thighs.

He felt so huge as he began to penetrate her vagina, she would have sworn he was entering her for the first time, fresh. She held on to his shoulders, gritting her teeth at the intense pressure as she slid down the shaft several inches. She could feel the defined ridge beneath the head of his cock in this position, feel the tip carving into her while her flesh melted around him, hugged him tight.

"Shh," he murmured, and she realized she'd gasped at the effort of taking him when her body was so open, so vulnerable to him. He caught her bottom, just beneath her buttocks, his strong biceps flexing tight as he held her in place for a moment with his cock half inside of her.

But Joy wiggled her hips in his hold, coaxing his cock farther inside her. He was stretching her, and the friction was sharp. She burned, existing on a delicious edge between pain and intense pleasure. She dropped her weight, bending her knees farther. They both gasped when she fell in his lap, his balls pressing against her damp, delicate tissues.

"Oh, God," he muttered tightly.

For a few seconds, neither of them moved. Everett dropped his head, his chin on his chest. She saw his shoulders and chest rising and falling as he tried to catch his breath. She, too, was having difficulty gathering herself with a large, swollen cock throbbing deep inside her.

After a moment, he looked up, a grim expression on his face. He leaned back slightly on one arm, putting his lean, gilded torso at a backward angle. He caressed her thigh.

"Do you think you can straighten your legs behind me? Lean back, like me," he instructed gruffly.

She moaned, feeling feverish, not entirely understanding what he meant.

"I want to see you while I'm in you. All of you," he muttered, breaking through her disorientation. "Please."

She let out a shaky groan when she attempted to move with him lodged so deeply. Was he on the edge of orgasm? He felt enormous, she thought distractedly as she attempted to do what he'd asked, straightening her knees so that her legs were on either side of him. His cock slid slightly out of her in the process. When she'd settled, her legs spread, her hands behind her, bracing her upper body, she pushed with her hands.

They both clenched their teeth when she slid him back into her to the hilt.

She sat facing him, her lap nailed to his by his erect member, her legs spread, staring at the glorious length of Everett's muscular, sweat-glistening torso.

She'd never felt so aroused in her life.

He reached between her thighs and slid a finger between her labia. She whimpered as he agitated her clit.

She'd never felt so vulnerable.

Her vagina tightened around him as he stimulated her.

"Everett," she whispered desperately.

"You're beautiful," he said, his hot stare running over her flushed face and down over her breasts and heaving belly to her pussy. She glanced down and moaned when she saw how pink her outer sex looked beneath his rubbing finger, how wet. She was completely exposed to him in this position. There was nowhere to hide. She shifted her hips against his ruthless finger and felt his cock jerk inside her.

"Don't move," he ordered abruptly.

She glanced into his face.

"I'm sorry," he said more calmly. "If you move, I'm going to come. I'm right on the edge."

"I want you to come," she moaned when he resumed torturing her clit.

"I want *you* to come."

She bit her lip in an agony of rising friction and bliss.

"I want to move," she pleaded shakily. "Let me move."

"Stay still." She heard the edge to his quiet voice and forced her hips to remain immobile. It was so hard. She didn't want to climax, sprawled out like this, so vulnerable to his watching eyes.

She couldn't stop it from happening, though.

He pressed on her clit in a relentless rhythm, and she felt herself cresting. She clenched her jaw hard and tilted her pelvis down, adding the friction of his thick, penetrating root to the pressure on her clit. She began to shudder in orgasm.

"That's right," she heard him say through waves of pleasure. "Ah, God, that feels good."

Her tremors abated slowly, deliciously. He finally removed his hand from her clit, and she opened her eyes.

He was *still* high and hard inside of her. She couldn't believe it.

"You weren't joking about that tantric sex thing, were you?"

His grin was both mischievous and strained. She blinked her eyes, noticing the tension in his rigid stomach muscles and in his face. His nipples were very erect. It gave her some measure of satisfaction that even if he wasn't as desperate as she was, he wasn't finding this easy.

"Would I kid you about something like that?" he murmured at the same time he put one of his hands beneath her ankle and lifted.

"No, Everett," she said shakily when he lifted her leg so that her calf rested on his shoulder. He'd just increased the pressure of his lodged cock inside of her, and he knew it, she realized.

"No?" he asked, his eyebrows arched in a query.

She gasped for air, her body becoming accustomed to the new position. She gritted her teeth and pushed down on his cock, squeezing her vaginal muscles. It was a complete reflex action.

"Jesus, Joy," he muttered. "Tell me if you want me to stop. Don't do that, though. I don't want to come yet."

"Why are you doing this to me?" she asked him in a spurt of frustration. A tear splashed down her cheek. She felt wholly exposed. She wanted him to fuck her so hard that he joined her in a mindless frenzy of need. Her entire body began to shake; her emotions felt so chaotic, and she was so aroused. Her eyelids clamped shut.

She felt his palm on the back of her thigh, stroking her in a soothing motion from her buttock to the back of her knee. Her vagina once again tightened around his cock. She could feel his heartbeat deep inside her. It was incredibly erotic.

It was almost unbearably intimate.

"Do you want me to pull out?" she heard him ask.

"No. No. Please don't," she begged brokenly.

Emotion shuddered through her when he gently lifted her other leg to his shoulder. If she'd been exposed to him before, now she was raw—a bundle of quaking, unshielded nerves.

"Open your eyes," Everett beckoned.

She couldn't resist the sound of his voice, couldn't deny his quiet command. She unclenched her eyelids and met his gaze. There was so much desire in his glistening eyes, it stunned her . . . confused her.

Every muscle in her abdomen and pelvic region bunched tight. Suddenly, his hand was between her thighs again, demanding . . . insistent.

She detonated at his touch. She mewled as another orgasm thundered through her, this one impossibly more powerful than the previous ones. Through a haze of sensual bliss, she heard his sharp curse. While her orgasm still shook her, he leaned forward and put his hands on her waist. He lifted her off his erection. Joy cried out at the pain of sudden deprivation.

"Shh," he said, although he hardly sounded soothing this time . . . more impatient. Desire had finally sunk its claws deep into him, Joy realized in disorientation. She couldn't help but feel triumphant. He guided her with his hands. She followed his silent, urgent demand until she found herself on her belly, her legs draped over the edge of the bed.

He lifted her ass with his hands. She assisted him, putting her knees on the edge of the bed, raising herself to meet him.

She cried out sharply when he slid the entire length of his cock into her with one powerful stroke. Her eyes went wide. She stared sightlessly at the window on the far side of the room as he began to ram into her, fucking her without pretense or politeness—taking her in just the way she'd craved.

She should be careful what she wished for.

He held on to her hips, completely controlling her actions, serving her pussy to his swollen cock. He was voracious, relentless, so selfish in his erupting need that it left her incapable of thought or movement. In those tense, electric moments where he slammed into her like a locomotive, their skin slapping together with brisk smacking sounds, Joy lost her own will.

She gave herself to him, mind and body, subsumed by Everett's desire.

Seven

~~~

"Joy? Are you all right?"

Regret spiked through him when he saw the damp tracks of tears on her cheeks. He pulled her closer into his arms and used his thumb to dry her skin. "I'm sorry. I know I was rough. I wanted you so much," he said, recalling in graphic detail how he'd just fucked her like a madman, completely abandoning himself to unbridled lust. Even though he'd just had the mother of all orgasms while pressed tight against the limit of Joy's womb, and even though guilt washed through him, he felt his cock stir again at the memory.

Her flushed lips parted. Her wide-eyed gaze struck him as dazed . . . incredulous.

"Joy?" he asked warily, unable to fully interpret her expression.

"Excuse me," she muttered.

Everett stilled an instinctive reflex to pull her back into his arms when she sat up. She slid her slender legs over the edge of the bed. He stared helplessly at her retreating form. A few seconds later, he heard the bathroom door close.

"Fuck," he muttered under his breath, his head hitting the pillow. *"Fuck."*

Self-recriminations paraded across his consciousness. He must have hurt her. He shouldn't have let his arousal build to the breaking point as he had. She'd probably never want to see him again.

But she'd been so exquisite, lying back with his cock lodged so high in her warm, clinging pussy. She'd been so open to him, so vulnerable. It'd driven him a little nuts.

A lot nuts.

He'd made her pay the price by not better regulating his lust.

Now he was going to have to forfeit the price if he'd alienated her completely. His bitter, silent self-lecture continued as he removed and disposed of the condom. He drew on his boxer-briefs and sat at the edge of the bed, his head down.

He was about to go and check on Joy when he heard the bathroom door open. He braced his arms on either side of him, his muscles bunching tight, when he heard her tread in the hallway.

"Are you okay?" he asked when she entered the room wearing a short pink bathrobe. At first he thought she'd splashed her face with water, but then he realized that her hair was damp at her temples and nape from perspiration. He was wet with sweat himself. It'd been like running a marathon, making love to her.

She nodded and silently came and sat next to him on the bed, several inches from his hand. He wanted to touch her. He wondered if he'd lost the right.

"Did I hurt you?" he asked.

"No."

He paused. Her tone had sounded starkly honest.

"Then what's wrong?"

He saw her throat convulse as she swallowed. Her sideways glance struck him as wary . . . bewildered.

"Why did you do that to me?"

He just stared at her. For some reason, even though she'd said *why*, he'd heard *what*. It struck him that she felt wholly vulnerable. He covered her hand with his.

"I didn't just want to have sex with you. I wanted to connect with you. It worked a little too well, on my part. You were so . . ." He made a ragged, helpless sound. "I lost it a little, there at the end. I'm sorry."

She turned her head, searching his features. "I wanted you to lose control. I'm not talking about that," she said.

His forehead bunched in confusion.

"Never mind," she whispered, glancing away. "It doesn't matter."

He cradled the back of her head. She fit his palm perfectly.

"It matters."

She dropped her chin to her chest. "You overwhelm me."

"I apologize. I didn't mean to." He froze for a second after the words were out of his mouth. Was he lying? *Had* he meant to break down her defenses?

"You don't understand," she said so abruptly that he started. She glanced at him entreatingly. "There's nothing wrong with you. You're . . . wonderful. Perfect. I wouldn't want you to change anything."

"I'm not following you, Joy," he said slowly.

She shook her head. He sensed her frustration. He tamped down a strong desire to hold her; she looked so small sitting there, so lost. Instead, he stood. She'd told him he overwhelmed her. He couldn't push himself on her farther.

He reached for his trousers.

"You don't have to go," she said in a cracking voice.

He turned, his hand on the zipper of his fly.

"I think I better," he said. "Can I call you tomorrow?"

"Yes," she whispered.

He nodded and reached for his shirt. He was angry with himself for pushing her, but dammit, he had *wanted* to move her, to reach her, to touch her in more than the surface sense. That'd been the reason he'd made love to her the way he did. Joy clearly was a formidable fortress, but she wasn't entirely impregnable.

Tonight had shown him that.

He felt raw and confused. Irritated. The experience had rattled him as well as Joy. The only reason he was leaving was that she appeared to be even more exposed and bewildered by what had happened between them than he was.

Eight

Chad Thurman, the only male in Joy's class of ten, gave her a sympathetic glance when she checked the clock again above the blackboard.

"Do you want me to go out into the hallway and look around, Miss Hightower? Maybe he's lost. Their kind aren't always the sharpest tools in the shed."

"No, that's all right," Joy said, opening the drawer to her desk and digging in her purse for her cell phone. "I'll go out and have a look around and try to call him. Maybe he just got stuck in traffic or something."

"This is it. We're finally going to see what you look like with your shirt off, Chad," Chancy Orbus said, a teasing gleam in her dark brown eyes.

"You wish," Chad replied under his breath, the color in his cheeks belying his cocky negligence as he slumped in his chair. The rest of the girls in the class twittered. After spending six weeks with the talented, intelligent group of sixteen- and seventeen-year-olds, Joy still wasn't quite sure whether the experience of being the token male was an absolute torture or an utter delight for Chad; she daily saw evidence that argued for both.

"It's not going to come to that," Joy assured them, giving Chancy a wry, slightly repressive glance as she walked toward the hallway. "I'll be right back."

She grimaced when she opened the door and moved from the air-conditioned classroom to the stuffy, hot hallway. The Steadman School was located in a historical, enormous, Romanesque-style building on Chicago's west side. The arched hallways were either freezing in the winters or stifling in the summer. There wasn't a soul in sight. All the other classes being taught for summer school were located over in the academic wing of the building.

A wave of drowsiness hit her as she looked for the phone number, a combination of the sudden heat and a restless night. After Everett had left, sleep did not come easily. He probably thought she was a hysterical fool after the way she'd acted.

Why *had* she felt so shaken by the sexual experience—so vulnerable?

So what if it wasn't a position she'd ever before explored? It was just sex, and Everett was just a man. That's what she'd told herself repeatedly last night and this morning.

She was still waiting to actually convince herself it was true.

She suspected she knew what *Cosmo* would call the problem if a man were acting the way she was: *intimacy issues.* Joy would have called it *healthy caution.* Her life already existed on shifting sands. Falling for any guy at this point would be like adding an earthquake to her already shaky world. Falling for a man like Everett was like inviting a fiery, plunging meteor.

She forced her sluggish brain to its task. Her class schedule was going to be completely screwed up. She was going to have to use tomorrow for the final project versus today. She'd planned a casual checkout day in the classroom tomorrow, and then she was going to take the kids to an exhibit at the Art Institute and out for pizza. They would be so disappointed.

Frustration rose in her with every unanswered ring of her phone. Clearly, the young man she'd hired to model for the students' final project was blowing her off.

Chances were Everett would blow her off, too. Isn't that what usually happened after an awkward sexual moment with a new partner? A sharp pain of disappointment stabbed through her.

Surely it was all for the best.

She hung up when she heard the man's recorded greeting. *Strike his name from the eligible list of male models,* she thought as she hung up.

"Joy!"

For a split second, she thought it was the model she'd been trying to call. Relief swept through her. But that couldn't be right, she thought as she peered down the dim, empty hallway. She was sure she'd never mentioned her first name to him.

Once the man came closer, she immediately recognized his tall figure and confident gait. He passed beneath a window, and a ray of sunshine momentarily hit the blond hair beneath his hat.

"Everett," she said, thunderstruck when he approached her and stopped several feet away.

"Hi. I'm glad I caught you. I saw Max Weisman over in the other wing. He sent me this way."

He carried a supple leather duffle bag on his shoulder. In addition to his plaid newsboy cap, he wore a pair of well-worn drainpipes, gray canvas tennis shoes and a slightly wrinkled ivory T-shirt featuring three ducks flying across it. It was an awful combination.

Everett looked amazing in it.

"What are you doing here?" she asked, still stunned by his appearance in the familiar, mundane location of her workplace.

"My agent booked me on *The Shay Show* tonight," he said, referring to a popular late-night talk show. "The New York premiere of *Maritime* is tomorrow. I'm catching a plane in a few hours."

"Oh," she said.

He held her gaze for a second before he ducked his head. "I won't take up your time. I know you're busy. I couldn't leave town without telling you that I'm sorry about last night," he said.

"You shouldn't be," she rushed to say. "I had a wonderful time with you."

He glanced up. "You did?"

She nodded.

He let out a little puff of air and smiled. Her heart hitched.

"I thought maybe you thought I was a freak or something," he said under his breath.

"No. Not at all. I'm sorry if I didn't handle things well . . . That is . . ." Awkwardness swamped her, but she forced herself to meet his stare. "I'm just sorry."

"I hope not. I thought it was amazing."

Her cheeks blazed hot. A loud female hoot of laughter emanated from her classroom. She glanced back anxiously.

"I should probably go back in or they'll be hanging from the rafters soon."

He nodded. "I understand. I'm glad I caught you, even if was just for a few seconds."

Her bewilderment mounted. Was he here to say good-bye to a particularly pleasant but irrelevant fling before he left the city like a brilliant sunset?

"I'm glad you did, too," she said, searching his face and finding no answers to the dozens of questions buzzing like furious bees in her brain.

He nodded toward her classroom door. "What were you doing out here, anyway?"

Joy blinked. What *had* she been doing in the hallway? She stared blankly at her cell phone and got her clue.

"Oh. The male model I hired for the class's final drawing project blew me off. I'm going to have to try to find someone else for tomorrow. The Art Institute and pizza field trip I planned for the last day will have to be canceled."

He glanced toward the door, straining to see through the small rectangular window.

"You don't use nude models, do you?"

She smiled. "No. I'm afraid the school board won't allow it. We're just focusing on the torso and face."

"I'll do it for you, then, if it doesn't take much more than an hour. I left early for the airport."

Joy gave a soft bark of incredulous laughter. He'd sounded so matter-of-fact, like it was the simplest thing in the world for him to drop everything in his schedule and pose for a bunch of sixteen- and seventeen-year-old high school art students.

"I couldn't ask you to do that."

"I don't have the build you're looking for or something?"

"No, of course not," she said. His expression was impassive, but she sensed he was entirely serious. "I wanted someone who is lean and has good muscle definition. We've been focusing on accurate human anatomy. You'd be perfect, but surely—"

"I'd be happy to do it, if you think it'd be okay with my time limit."

She laughed again. He really was priceless. "Everett, it's a class full of teenage girls, save one. If you walked in that room, I'd probably have to reschedule their final project anyway, because they'd all faint from shock."

"They'd get over it. I get old pretty quick. Besides, artists are practical types."

She saw the tilt of his mouth and shook her head. "You clearly don't know that many artists. Especially of the teenage variety," she murmured, reaching for the door. "Are you really serious?"

"Yeah."

She inhaled deeply, trying to ground herself. "Okay, but I can't guarantee you'll come out unscathed."

"I like an adventure," she heard him say softly from behind her, his deep voice sounding just inches away from her right ear.

This was lunacy. *All* of it.

She led him into her classroom, her heartbeat starting to pound furiously in her ears. For a few seconds, the kids continued their typical self-involved teenage chatter. The first pair of eyes that moved, widened and stuck acted like a catalyst for the other nine.

"Okay. Move over to your sketch pads. Our model is here."

She could have heard a toothpick drop at the back of the room in the silence that followed. Joy clapped.

"Come on, you guys. If you don't move, we're going to have to cancel the field trip tomorrow and do your project then. *Now*," she added loudly when Everett continued to be the object of stunned, pale-faced incredulity. A few of them started to stand hesitantly, then the rest of them seemed to come out of their trances.

"Lacey, put that cell phone away, please. I've asked you to leave them in your backpack during class a dozen times," Joy said in a beleaguered tone as she set a high chair with a cushioned back before the students' drawing pads and easels.

"But . . . but, Miss Hightower . . . that's . . . isn't that . . ." Lacey trailed off, at a loss.

"It's Everett Hughes, yes," Joy said calmly. Everett gave the kids a friendly wave. "I don't want a lot of silliness. We're very lucky that he's volunteered to do this for us, but he only has so much time. If you guys waste too much of it gawking and trying to text your friends, you're going to flunk your final project. Not to mention miss the chance to own a personal sketch of Mr. Hughes," Joy added sharply when her previous threat had no effect whatsoever.

All ten of them sprang up like she'd set their seats on fire. "But . . . what's Everett Hughes . . . I mean"—Chad transferred his attention from Joy to Everett—"what are *you* doing here, dude?" Chad asked dubiously. The tension broke. The girls laughed nervously, and Everett smiled.

"He was here for his premiere of *Maritime* yesterday," Joy said innocuously as she moved the chair a little to get better light.

"I'm a friend of Miss Hightower's," Everett said. "I stopped by to see her just now, and she said the model she'd hired didn't show. I offered to fill in."

"Wow," Meg Brown said succinctly, staring from Everett to Joy and back to Everett again.

Everett approached Joy and the chair, his eyebrows raised in silent query. Joy silently mimed removing his cap and then pointed to his T-shirt.

She couldn't believe she was doing this.

She turned toward the clock on the wall, pretending to check it, not wanting Everett or the students to see her blush. Even her young art students were used to seeing partial nudity in the classroom. Learning to draw the human form was a crucial skill. She couldn't believe she was acting so ridiculous. She pretended to be searching for something on her desk, but glanced around when Chancy Orbus made a sound that sounded like *grrrgh*.

Everett had removed his shirt and sat in the chair. Chancy— with all her piercings and tattoos and nothing-can-touch-me teenage armor—was looking completely flattened.

"Can't we at least get a picture, Miss Hightower?" Shelby Ryan begged.

"Oh, *please*," Lacey whined.

Joy sighed. "This project is forty percent of your final grade. I suggest you try to focus. You have . . ." She glanced at Everett in query and wished she hadn't. His lean, golden six-pack obliques and negligent, somehow graceful pose were really something to see. "One hour?" she asked him, keeping her voice neutral.

"Works for me," Everett said.

"Can't he at least wear his hat, Miss Hightower? He's famous for his hats," one student said.

"And couldn't we at least have *one* picture?" Chancy persisted, entreating Everett directly.

He shrugged, smiling. "It's up to the boss," he said, glancing at Joy.

The kids looked to her hopefully. "Hair is a big part of your final project, so the hat stays off. As for a picture, there isn't going to be any time for one if you don't get to work. If there *should* be a minute at the end, you'll have to get Everett's permission."

"Fine by me," Everett replied pleasantly when ten pairs of eyes zoomed over to him. She normally would have arranged the model in the position she wanted in order to highlight certain muscle groups for her students to sharpen their skills, but she couldn't bring herself to instruct, let alone touch, Everett in front of all the rapt teenagers. Besides, she rather liked his pose.

"Begin now," she said. "You have until twelve o'clock. Just get done what you can with the time you have."

She had to hand it to her students: They went to work with a concentration she'd never before witnessed in them. Joy picked up her grade book and the half-empty coffee she'd picked up at Harry's that morning and walked to the back of the classroom, sitting in a desk where she could observe the students draw.

She could also observe Everett, and that made focusing difficult. Every once in a while, she'd feel his gaze on her like a tickle on her cheek. She'd glance up and see just the hint of a smile on his lips. It was more than likely some combination of her overactive imagination and libido when it came to him, but even at this distance, his eyes appeared warm . . . seductive. His nipples looked very erect. He must be getting chilly due to the air-conditioning. Why, then, did she feel so hot all of a sudden?

Joy shifted uncomfortably in the student desk and forced herself to concentrate on the task of entering the grades from a quiz last week in her book. After several minutes, she told the students to work on any corrections they might have while Everett took a break. Chad was the only one who worked during the next minute, however. Most of the girls were too busy gaping and drooling as they watched Everett stand up and flex and stretch his pectoral and arm muscles while he paced.

He was back in his chair almost immediately. The models she'd worked with in the past could take lessons from him.

Light seemed to love him, she thought as she distractedly moved her pen. It didn't seem to bounce off him like it did other people's skin. Instead, it seemed to mingle with his radiance. *Fascinating.* Could she ever catch that effect with her paints? Was it even conceivable to evoke that subtle, knowing expression in his eyes?

She blinked and stared down at the napkin that had been beneath her coffee cup. She hadn't been entirely conscious that she'd been sketching him. A flash of sad compassion went through her for her students. She'd given them an impossible task, trying to capture the essence of Everett.

She glanced at the clock.

"Please set down your pencils," Joy said, gathering her things and standing.

A few groans went up.

"I know, I know," she said, understanding completely the young artists' discontent with not being able to finish their task. "I'll be keeping the time constraint in mind when I grade your projects. I'm not expecting perfection," she soothed, walking among the students and easels. "You're free to get your things and go. I'll gather your sketches."

"But what about the pictures of Everett?" Shelby asked, her voice vibrating with excitement. Several of the students seconded this as they stood.

She gave Everett a pitying, amused glance. He'd just pulled his

T-shirt over his head. His arms were raised, pulling his abdomen
muscles especially taut. He grin seem to say, *Don't worry—it's
no big deal.* His easygoing grace amazed her.

"I've got a minute or two," he said, whipping his arms through
his sleeves.

"Get your phones, then," Joy told the students reluctantly. They
moved so rapidly to their desks and backpacks, it was like a teenage tidal wave.

"Do you mind if we post the photos on Facebook?" Chancy
asked Everett several minutes later. He'd patiently posed while they
all had taken pictures with him. The students were standing in a
ring around him now, their faces radiant at the idea of bantering
so casually with Everett Hughes.

"Okay by me. But thanks for asking, Chancy," Everett replied,
giving her a nod of respect. Chancy glowed with pride that she'd
asked the responsible question and been given permission above-
board to post Everett's picture publicly.

"Okay, time to go," Joy shooed, knowing the students would
hang around Everett for as long as they were allowed to. "Don't
forget to come a half hour early tomorrow for our field trip, and
don't bring any large backpacks or purses if you don't want to check
anything at the museum," she called loudly to their retreating backs.
The door shut behind the final student a few seconds later. Joy
turned to Everett and smiled.

"Thank you. Thank you so much. They'll remember that for
the rest of their lives."

"No problem. They're nice kids. They respect you a lot," he
said, walking toward her desk to pick up his leather duffle.

She shrugged. "That's one of the nice things about teaching
advanced students. They all plan to make art their careers. It's eas-
ier for teachers and students when they have that commonality."

He slung his bag on his shoulder and faced her. "Maybe, but

they respect you as a person, too. I could tell." He glanced at the clock on the wall. "I should be going."

Her heart seemed to stagger. With all the excitement and distraction of his staying to pose for her class, she'd completely forgotten he was leaving town . . . and that she might never see him again. She was at a loss as to what to say.

"I was going to call you about this, but I was wondering if you'd consider taking a little trip with me."

"What?" she asked stupidly.

"You mentioned that summer school is almost over, and I assume you have some time before the new semester starts?"

She nodded.

"Good, because Rill has asked your uncle Seth to visit Katie and him in Vulture's Canyon. Seth has definitely agreed to do makeup. He must have had a good night coming up with proof he's the guy for the job."

"Oh, I'm so glad," Joy said, pride for her uncle flooding her. "This is going to be a terrific experience for him, working with Rill."

"Yeah. Anyway, Rill wants to exchange some ideas for costume and makeup for *Razor Pass*. His costume designer is flying in on Sunday morning in order to meet with Seth. He wants me there, too, and Katie has invited you as well for a long weekend. It's Labor Day. When do you start school again?"

"Not until the week after Labor Day," Joy said. "We go on a quarter system here, so the kids have a bit of a break before the fall quarter begins."

"So this would work out great. Katie and Rill have built a little guesthouse on their grounds. It's nice—right in the middle of the Shawnee National Forest. Very relaxing. I thought it'd be a nice getaway for a couple days . . ." He faded off, and Joy realized he was studying her narrowly. "What do you think?" he asked.

A puff of air flew past her lips. She laughed raggedly. "I thought maybe I was never going to see you again after today," she said honestly.

"Why would you think that?"

She shook her head, avoiding his stare. "I don't know. This feels like unfamiliar territory to me, Everett." A strained silence ensued. She saw him shift on his feet.

"Unfamiliar territory? In what way?" he asked.

"I don't really know what . . . a person like you expects. *I* don't know what to expect," she admitted quietly.

"There is no 'person like me.' There's only me. And you."

His words throbbed in her ears. He could have said nothing truer. There was no one like him. He defied stereotypes. He was the most unique person she'd ever met. She noticed his eyebrows quirk up in a silent query.

Well . . . perhaps if she just framed the whole thing as a pleasant sexual encounter? No strings attached. It might not seem so intimidating then . . .

"What's this?" he asked.

He'd picked up her sketch of him on the napkin. He studied it, his brow slightly furrowed.

"It's just . . . I was doodling," she muttered. It had been a quick sketch, but she had successfully caught that expression he'd had in his eyes when he stared at her from across the room, that look that seemed to say, *When I get you alone, I'm going to make you scream.* Her cheeks burned. God, she'd never blushed so much in her life as she had in the past two days.

He glanced up, still holding the napkin, a strange expression on his face.

"Say you'll come with me to Vulture's Canyon."

"Yes," she replied in a choked voice.

He took three long steps and cupped her shoulders in her hands. He leaned down and kissed her—a quick yet total possession of her body and mind. It just wasn't fair, the amount of power he had over her.

"I'll call you tomorrow evening," he murmured. She glanced down when he carefully placed something in her hand. He strode out of the room, closing the door quietly behind him. The sketch of him looked up at her.

"No strings attached," she repeated under her breath.

But somehow, she knew that those comforting words and the expression she'd caught in Everett's eyes in the sketch were not going to be easily reconciled.

Nine

⌒∾⌒

Now that Joy had agreed to a long weekend with Everett Hughes, she wished it would happen sooner versus later. The nervous anticipation was starting to kill her. How many times a day could she ask herself if she was making a monumental mistake by agreeing to go? How many times could she lose herself in heated fantasies about being with him for so many long, glorious hours?

On Monday night, she'd been tempted to turn on *The Shay Show* to catch a glimpse of Everett. Perhaps fortunately—or perhaps not, Joy couldn't decide—Seth had asked to use the small studio in her apartment. He was there still by the time the show was set to air. Joy had been brainstorming some makeup concepts with him and been too self-conscious to excuse herself to watch the show. Seth probably would have thought she was acting like a breathless teenager, gaping at Everett as he charmed the nation on television.

Luckily, she had the field trip on Tuesday to keep her mind distracted. She returned home that night clutching a bag of groceries, tired but happy about how the day had gone. She bought the ingredients for a Cobb salad and a bottle of chardonnay. Her grand plan for celebrating the end of her summer semester was to eat dinner and watch television in bed—a rare, decadent indulgence she liked to treat herself to once in a while.

Her cell phone rang while she was in the process of frying up some low-fat turkey bacon. She glanced at the number and set her wineglass down on the counter a little too abruptly, causing the crystal to ring.

"Hello?"

"Hi. It's Everett," he added after a brief pause.

She smiled. "I know."

"How'd you know?"

Her brain froze for a moment. He hadn't given her his number. She didn't want to tell him she'd recognize his deep, resonant voice anywhere. "You have an L.A. prefix. I didn't recognize it as Seth's or any of my friends', though," she said lightly.

"Am I catching you at a bad time?"

"No, not at all. I was just making a little dinner to celebrate the last day of my summer semester."

"Is that a tradition?" In the background, she thought she heard the sound of springs giving way, as if he'd just fallen on a bed.

"To make a celebratory dinner for myself? Yeah, I guess so. It's nice to wrap things up."

"And give a little hurrah." She heard the smile in his voice. She wished she could see it.

"Yes. Exactly. Where are you?" she asked, picking up her glass of wine. "Are you still in New York?"

"No. Los Angeles, at my house in Laurel Canyon," he said, sounding less than thrilled. "My agent—a fine, upstanding woman who works way, way too hard at her job—saw fit to book me for some appearances on the west coast. I'm actually taking a break before I head out to tape an interview for . . . some show. I don't even know anymore."

"It must get crazy busy for you when you have a new movie come out," she sympathized.

"I'd hoped to be able to make it back to Chicago to see you again."

"Oh," she said, her wineglass halted halfway to her mouth. "Does that mean we're not doing the trip next weekend to your sister's?"

"No, that's definitely on. Neither wild horses nor my agent's bullwhip could keep me away."

Relief flooded through her. She took a sip of her wine and was suddenly glad that he couldn't see her grinning.

"Good, I'm glad," she said.

"I just meant that I wanted to see you before then. As things stand, I probably will have to just meet you at Katie and Rill's," he said regretfully. "Is that okay?"

"Of course. I'm flying down with Seth. That will work out fine."

"I'm looking forward to it."

She swallowed thickly. "I am, too."

For a moment, neither of them spoke. The silence swelled.

"So what's for dinner?" Everett finally asked.

"Cobb salad."

"Can I eat with you?"

She laughed and picked up a fork. "If you like. What are you going to have?"

"Your company," he murmured. "That's much, much better than anything I've got in the kitchen. Anything the best chefs in L.A. could offer, for that matter."

Joy paused in the action of flipping a piece of bacon. A prickling sensation had moved from her ear to her neck at the sound of his deep voice, causing her nipples to tighten. She shook her head as if to clear it.

She shouldn't have been surprised that Everett could seduce effortlessly, even through a phone line.

On Wednesday, she spent most of the afternoon helping Seth with his sketches. Afterward, Seth took her out for an early dinner and then had to rush back to his hotel for a conference call. Joy had just arrived back home and changed into a pair of yoga pants and a T-shirt when her cell phone rang. Her heart jumped when she recognized Everett's number.

"Hello?"

"I've already eaten tonight. We'll have to find something else to do together," he said, forgoing a greeting.

"And how do you know if I have eaten?" she asked amusedly.

"You're right. Rude of me. Have you eaten?"

"I have. Seth took me out to dinner. How was your day?" she asked as she filled a glass with ice.

"Given the state of technology today, I don't see why it's not possible for them to make a robot of me that goes around and repeats the same inane sentences over and over. It's no different from what I do for promotional appearances."

"What did you tape today?" she asked, filling her glass with water.

"*Entertainment Premiere.*"

"Oh, it's on right now. Shall I go and turn it on?"

"God, no," he groaned.

She laughed as she walked back to her bedroom. "I'm sure it's not that bad."

"It's not. It's worse. I have an idea. Let's watch TV together—just not *Entertainment Premiere.*"

"Okay. What?" she asked, finding her remote control on her dresser and flipping on the television.

"Um . . . *Hogan's Heroes*? Nah. CNN? Maybe. The Adult Channel?"

"I'm afraid I don't have it."

"Too bad. How about the Food Network? It's like golf. We can watch and talk at the same time."

"Okay," she said, flipping the channel, setting her water down on the bedside table and climbing onto her bed.

"Things are progressing really fast for us, aren't they?" Everett said.

She froze in the action of fluffing her pillow.

"What do you mean?" she asked warily.

"First dinner, tonight watching TV together; by tomorrow night we'll be having sex."

"Hah," she scoffed, finishing her fluffing. "We've already had sex."

"You don't have to remind me," he said quietly. "I think about it pretty much every minute I'm not sleeping."

She pressed her hand against her palpitating heart as if to muffle the pounding. "If you ask me what I'm wearing right now, I'm going to hang up."

She smiled when she heard him burst into uninhibited laughter. He had a great laugh.

"Black pepper–crusted pork tenderloin with a black cherry reduction. Yum," she murmured.

"I thought you said we weren't going to talk dirty to each other."

"Everett, watch the show," she scolded, smiling.

On Thursday night, she turned out the light for bed, admonishing herself the whole time for being disappointed that Everett hadn't called again. She'd see him tomorrow evening, after all, and she could hardly expect that he'd call her every day. She'd just drifted off to sleep when her phone rang.

"Hello?"

"Did I wake you up?" Everett asked. His voice sounded rough. Tired.

"No."

"Yes, I did. I'm sorry."

"It's okay," she murmured, rubbing her eyes. "How was your day?"

"Nuts. Busy. I can't wait to get out of this town tomorrow."

"You sound exhausted."

"I'm just done, that's all." She heard him yawn. "I can't wait to see you. Did you have a good day?"

After a while, their talk waned, and Joy had asked him if he wouldn't like to say good-bye so he could get some sleep.

"Would you mind very much if I stayed on?" he'd asked groggily. "We've never slept together, you know."

She opened her mouth to say something light and teasing, but then paused. "All right. If you like."

"Good. I like listening to you," he mumbled.

"Everett, I'm not saying anything," she admonished gently.

"I can hear you breathe."

"Are you suggesting I have a Darth Vader issue?"

He chuckled tiredly. "No, you're a *much* sexier breather than Darth."

Two minutes of silence later, she started to hang up when he didn't respond when she called his name. She stopped herself, though.

She listened to his slow, even breathing as he slept for longer then she'd care to admit.

Seth and Joy arrived in Vulture's Canyon at dusk the next day.

"Weird little town," Seth murmured, peering out the window

onto a deserted Main Street as he drove. She had the strangest feeling they'd just wandered onto a movie set as she stared at the ancient storefronts. Behind the shadow of the rickety porch overhang of the Dyer Creek Trading Company, she saw a sign painted in neon-bright bubble lettering: BODY AND SOUL—ART AND FOOD FOR LIFE.

If the road hadn't been paved, and if there hadn't been a sporadic car or truck parked along the side of the street, they might have been in a town built in the eighteen hundreds. The setting sun, the surrounding hills and the thick forest only added to the surreal feeling of having entered a time warp.

"Yeah. That's pretty much how Katie described Vulture's Canyon to me—*weird*," Joy said. "A lot of them work at a cooperative farm and use the produce to feed needy families in the Midwest and Appalachian region. It all sounds very free-spirited. There's quite a contingent of artists here, I understand. You'll fit right in." She smiled when she heard her uncle's doubtful grunt. "We're supposed to go straight through town, pass Dyer Creek, and take the first right we come to. It's called Eagle Perch Road," she said, squinting in the dim light to see the directions she'd written down. "Rill and Katie's place is at the top of the hill. According to Everett, we won't be able to miss it."

"Let's just hope Everett gives directions as well as he acts," Seth muttered.

Joy gave him a sideways glance. Was that a stab at Everett's questionable motives when it came to her, an allusion to the fact that Everett could be merely playing the role of an interested, persistent male? Seth and she had had a lot of opportunity to talk on the short flight from Chicago to St. Louis, and then the hour-long drive from St. Louis to Vulture's Canyon. She recalled again what her uncle had said about Everett while they waited for takeoff.

"Hughes has gone through women like tissues for the past fifteen years."

"That's not entirely fair," Joy had replied levelly. "It seems to me that I've read he's been in several serious relationships. Didn't he date Jennifer Turner for quite a long period of time? And Liv Arlo, as well?" Joy had asked, referring to a highly respected actress and a well-known Hollywood publicist. "I've never gotten the impression he has a Don Juan syndrome from the press, even if they do splash photos of him on every date he's ever been on. It can't be easy for him."

"Yeah, I feel real sorry for him," Seth had said dryly, trying to adjust his long frame in the tiny airplane seat. "It's rough having more money than you can possibly spend and knowing you can have any woman on the planet with a twitch of your finger."

"Careful. You're sounding jealous," Joy had teased, trying to lighten his grim mood. "You used to tell me you really liked Everett. When did you change your mind?"

"Since he started nosing around you," Seth had said, as if it were the most obvious thing in the world. Her expression had softened when she saw his stark concern.

"I just can't help but feel you're going to get hurt in this," Seth had said.

She'd said something similar to herself almost every time she'd gotten off the phone with Everett this week, but she didn't want Seth to know that.

"I'm not going to get hurt," she'd told Seth. "Because I'm not expecting anything besides the present moment."

Seth had looked doubtful. "I don't know if I like the sound of that any more than I'd like it if you said you were falling in love with the guy."

Joy had smiled. "Why is it that men can have casual affairs without anyone blinking twice, but if a woman says she's going to have one, everyone gets all concerned? I'm not that fragile, Seth."

"I never thought you were fragile. But you're not cold-hearted, either. You're like Alice," he'd said, referring to her mother. "You feel things deeply. It's not easy for you to feel just a *little bit*. We left that to your father," he'd mumbled bitterly.

"Maybe I have more of Dad in me than you think," Joy had said, staring out the plane window.

Seth had snorted at that.

In truth, Joy thought as they left the quirky little town of Vulture's Canyon behind them, she was worried herself. It alarmed her how much she looked forward to seeing Everett again. Just the thought of him touching her made her breathless. She had to ban herself from thinking about them making love—not that it worked.

Her nervous excitement mounted as Seth turned the car onto Eagle Perch Road. They began to ascend a steep hill as twilight fell. The sky was a golden fuchsia above the tops of the tall trees. She was glad Everett had suggested bringing some art supplies. The landscape was lovely.

It turned out that Everett was absolutely correct in saying they couldn't miss the Pierce house. The country road they were on narrowed to a private drive, which curved into a circular turnabout in front of a large, attractive white farmhouse with a wraparound porch and light glowing warmly in the windows.

"Seth?" Joy said when her uncle parked the car in a turnabout behind three other vehicles.

"Yeah?" he asked, twisting the key out of the ignition.

"Don't . . . don't mention anything to Everett about the cancer."

From her peripheral vision, she saw Seth glance at her sharply.

"Why not? It's nothing to be ashamed of."

"I know that. It's just personal, that's all. Oh . . . it's not a big deal," she said, completely contradicting herself. "*I'll* tell him if the topic should ever come up."

"If I know you, that'll be never. I'm shocked you brought it up just now."

"Seth, please." This conversation was entering territory she'd rather avoid.

"You never want to talk about it," he persisted. "You've closed in on yourself ever since you were diagnosed. You've moved thousands of miles away from me and from your friends. Remember? I was there with you with everything that happened to Alice."

"I know you were!" she said, stung. "How could I ever forget that?"

"I just mean that I know you're scared, honey. I know you were scared about the cancer, and I know you're terrified of it coming back. Why are you acting like I can't handle it when you know firsthand I can?" he said, his rugged face tight with frustration.

She saw a flicker of movement from the house. The front door swung open. She focused on Seth, entreating quietly. "You've been my rock since I was twelve years old. I *know* you can handle it. But so can I."

He shut his eyes briefly.

"Let's just put this on hold for now," Seth muttered. He gave her a small, apologetic smile, and she returned it. He squeezed her knee and turned to get out of the car. Katie stood on the front porch, waving at Seth and calling a greeting. A brown, doleful-looking basset hound sat just inches away from her ankle. Through the glass, Joy caught a glimpse through some curtains of a tall shadow moving toward the front door. It might be Rill . . .

Excitement shattered her anxiety when she saw Everett follow his sister onto the front porch. Joy got out of the car, breathless. She realized she was grinning like an idiot as she walked toward the house, but forgave herself when she saw Everett saunter down the front steps, smiling every bit as broadly as she was, his arms held out toward her.

*   *   *

Everett took a sip of his ginger ale—Katie had taken to making it herself. Much to his amusement, his cheeseburger-loving little sister had been converted by the hippy community of Vulture's Canyon into a health food nut. His attention veered for the twentieth time from Rill and Seth's discussion about setting, costume and makeup for *Razor Pass* to the hallway, where Joy had disappeared ten minutes ago with Katie. Dinner was over, and Everett sat with Rill and Seth at the enormous antique oak table in the kitchen. Seth's concept drawings for body art and makeup were sprawled out before them. Everett figured he'd hung out long enough at the big house to be polite. Seth and Rill clearly didn't need him.

He wanted to get Joy alone.

He'd wanted that ever since he'd reluctantly left her in her classroom earlier in the week. His desire to touch her had only grown exponentially since she had shown up earlier, looking fresh and sexy in a turquoise cotton skirt, a leather belt, a simple white tank top, a jacket and sandals. She'd taken off the jacket before dinner. The vision of the smooth, glowing skin of her shoulders and arms and the shape of her breasts in the snug top had left him distracted and vaguely irritable by the end of dinner. Not irritable at her or anyone in particular; he was agitated like a chained dog.

His cock twitched slightly and he sat up straighter when he heard female voices in the hallway. Rill did a double take, noticing his fractured attention. He glanced over his shoulder toward the hallway and gave Everett a patronizing, droll look. Everett scowled at his best friend.

Don't get all high-and-mighty with me, mate, when you turn to mush whenever my sister walks into the room.

Everett and Rill had been friends since they'd been eighteen and nineteen respectively. They'd worked with each other on several films. They were pretty good at reading each other, as witnessed by

Rill's slightly sheepish expression, as if Everett had spoken his thought out loud.

Everett had been dubious when Rill and Katie had gotten together a year and a half ago. They'd all been good friends before then, even if Katie'd had a silent, unrequited crush on Rill since she was a girl. Rill had been too busy building his career and marrying another woman to notice Katie's love for him, but when he'd discovered his wife's infidelity and ran wounded to the hills of Vulture's Canyon following her untimely death, it'd been Katie who had pulled him out from his dark hole and taught him the true meaning of loyalty and love. Now, like Rill, Everett couldn't imagine why he'd never noticed his closest friend and sister were perfect for each other. She was the light to his shadow. He was the depth and intensity that Katie craved to make her whole.

Rill leaned back when Katie came up behind him and put her arms around his neck. He leaned his head against her breasts and tilted his head up. Katie kissed his mouth.

"She's down," she murmured next to his lips, referring to their daughter. "If you all are okay out here, I think I'll try to get some sleep before she wakes up again."

"We're fine. I'll get Daisy the next time she wakes up. You get some sleep," Rill murmured.

"Wake me up when you come to bed," Everett heard his sister say softly.

Everett hadn't meant to overhear Rill and Katie's intimate exchange; it'd just filtered in like hushed background noise. He'd been staring at Joy. She smiled at him as she approached the head of the table.

"How are things going out here?" Joy asked.

"Great. Seth has come up with some terrific designs. He's really got a grasp of the look I'm going for," Rill said.

"Joy helped me out. I worked in her studio this week," Seth said, rolling up one of the drawings. "She'd taken her students to an exhibit on Genghis Khan at the Art Institute. She showed me the program, and it was the inspiration for some of these helmets I drew, the hairstyles and the body art."

"Mongol-chic. Brilliant," Rill muttered.

"Where's your studio?" Everett asked Joy, his chin resting in his palm as he studied her. The light from the chandelier hanging over the table made her skin the color of a golden peach.

"It's in my apartment—the room across from the bathroom," she explained. "It's small, but it gets good sunlight." She directed her attention toward Rill. "Seth and I brought our kits. If you'd like us to demonstrate any of the makeup or body art, we can do that."

"Thanks. What do you think? Up for a paint job?" Rill asked Everett.

Joy glanced at Everett and immediately dropped her gaze. He saw the subtle stain of pink on her cheeks. He hid a smile.

"Always," he murmured.

Apparently, Rill's word choice had brought the memory of the studio center stage to Joy as well. He stood. Everyone glanced around, startled, at the loud scraping of his chair on the tile.

"We'll be going to bed now." It took him a second to realize how abrupt he'd sounded. "I mean, if you're ready, Joy."

Rill smirked, Seth looked like he was considering beating him up, and Joy's cheeks turned a deeper shade of pink. He wondered if there was something he could say to disguise his overeagerness, but hell—that ship had sailed.

"Good night," Joy said to everyone when Everett took her hand and stalked to the front door.

"Sorry about that," he mumbled as they walked down the front porch steps, hand in hand.

"It's okay," she replied, her low voice tickling his nerves.

He cut into the yard, leading her through the still, pitch-black summer night. Clouds must have rolled in, because usually Everett never saw so many stars as he did on the top of this hill.

"I can't see a thing," she said when they cut around the corner of the big house.

"I've got you." He tightened his hand and she returned the gesture. His cock quickened like she'd squeezed it instead of his hand.

"I'm glad you're here," he said.

"So am I," she replied.

Had that been excitement vibrating in her voice? God, he hoped so. He hated the occasional uncertainty, the somberness he occasionally caught in her soulful eyes.

She rubbed her thumb between his knuckles. He felt the innocent caress along the root of his cock. "I left the light on in the guesthouse so that we could make it out when we came out tonight. There it is," he said, pointing to the golden glow of a lamp in the window, even though he knew Joy couldn't see his hand.

"Do you always stay in the guesthouse when you visit?" she asked.

"No. They just finished it last spring. I usually stay in the house, but Seth is staying in that room. Besides, I'd rather have some privacy, with you here."

She didn't reply, but he felt her warm hand in his, felt the brush of her hip against his thigh.

The guesthouse backed against the forest. The locusts and crickets had quieted their typical early evening cacophony to a low, lulling hum. He dropped Joy's hand to open the front door.

"It still smells new," Joy said when they'd entered the guesthouse and he'd shut and locked the door.

He turned in the small foyer and saw her standing there, the dim light from the living room showing him that small, mysterious smile. Was she so lovely to everyone as she was to him? What did it matter?

They remained standing like that for a moment, several feet separating them.

"Joy."

A shudder went through him when he stepped forward and took her into his arms, feeling the taut lines of her back and her firm breasts pressing against him. It hurt how much he wanted her. Her mouth tasted so good, like the very fount of sex. He dipped his tongue into it again and again, drinking from her, so thirsty for her sweetness. He felt desperate, like he thought she'd be inexplicably swept away from him at any moment and he'd be left empty-handed, the shock of hollow loss expanding in his gut.

She moaned softly when he backed her into the hallway and against the wall. He put his hands on her ass and lifted, needing to feel her pussy against his cock, requiring friction now, needing to press himself against her . . . into her. Her legs surrounded his hips, her thighs squeezing him tight.

Their tongues tangled in an almost angry dual. Apparently, he'd been wrong to think he was the only one who had suffered tonight, being forced to be staid and polite when all he'd wanted to do was climb all over her. She ripped at the opening of his shirt, sending a few buttons skittering across the wooden floor. Her hands made a frantic search of his shoulders, neck and head, her fingernails scratching his scalp. The evidence that she was just as wild with arousal as he was gave him tunnel vision . . . tunnel *sensation*.

The only thing he knew was Joy and a raging, howling need.

He rocked her against his cock. Lust slammed through him like a fist. It took him a moment to recognize that the rhythmic beating he heard wasn't just his heart. He'd been thrusting Joy against the wall as he flexed his hips. He broke their torrid kiss with a hissing sound, gritting his teeth at the abrupt absence of her taste. He was going to hurt her, rocking her against the wall like that. Her lips were immediately back on his, though, soft, warm, feverish, coaxing him back to her depths.

He kissed her like he wanted to fuck her, deep, demanding . . . like he wanted to leave a permanent, indelible mark on her.

He bent his knee and partially took her weight. His hand swept along her thigh, tugging up her skirt. Her skin flowed against his palm like silk. She shifted her hips, accommodating him. He shoved the fabric up around her waist and immediately went for her panties. If he didn't bury himself in her—and fast—he was going to spontaneously combust. He slid his hand beneath her underwear, his cock jerking at the sensation of the sweet curve of her ass. She reached between them, sinking her hands between the remaining buttons of his shirt. More buttons clattered and rolled on the floor. He growled like the chained animal he'd been all evening when he felt her anxious fingers at his groin.

He heard a ripping sound and the fabric between his clutching fingers melted away. It hadn't been his intention to tear her panties, but the caveman in him was rearing his head, apparently. He gave an anguished groan into her mouth when his hand brushed against wet, satin-soft flesh.

Later, he had no idea how he'd managed it. He got his cock out of his boxer-briefs by some miracle. His jeans were shoved just beneath his ass. He located a condom in his wallet in what must have been world-record-breaking time. He arrowed his cock into her, all of his desire and need made manifest into hard, swollen flesh.

She gasped and her head hit the wall with a thud. He flexed his hips, made savage by the feeling of carving into tight, warm, juicy flesh. His eyes sprang wide. Joy's breath struck his cheek in ragged gasps.

It felt like fucking nirvana.

Her fingernails bit into the naked skin of his shoulders hard enough to draw blood. He answered by tightening his grip on her ass and thrusting his hips, jerking her against the wall. She cried out sharply. He was buried in her to the root of his pulsing cock.

He groaned gutturally and began to fuck her. He knew he was probably bruising her, smashing her between the wall and his frantically bucking body. But this was a frenzy, and Joy seemed just as lost in the cyclone of it as he was. She was so small, but so soft, so

giving. He put his face into the hollow between her neck and shoulder and let her intoxicating scent send him further into a sexual berserk. He pounded into her, wondering distantly what excuse he'd make to Rill if they cracked the drywall in the brand-new guesthouse. His arm muscles screamed in pain when he lifted her slightly higher and spread her buttocks, but the sharp pleasure trumped the discomfort. He used his pelvis to give her clit a tight little jab on every downstroke of his cock, loving the surprised, gratified little yelp she made when he did.

"Evvverrreett," she keened a moment later, the vibrations from her call emanating into his lips.

He felt heat rush around him. His cock was so erect, so sensitive, so ready to explode, he could perfectly feel her vaginal muscles constricting around him as she started to come. She squeezed him, fisting him in an uncompromising grip. He didn't think he'd survive another minute of this torture.

"Fuck me," he said, his eyes crossing. Unfortunately, she took his muttered curse at face value. She started pumping her hips while she came, grinding her pussy against him. He growled in pleasure, felt that inevitable tingle deep in his balls. He roared in an agony of bliss as he erupted in orgasm.

"Aw, Jesus," he grated out. His face clenched tight as wave after wave of orgasm tightened his body.

They panted in ragged union. Joy slowly sagged down the wall like she was melting, her legs loosening around his hips. His muscles went lax as well, exhausted from the prolonged contraction he'd forced them to endure while he'd raced Joy to climax. Her feet finally touched the floor. It hurt to withdraw from her warm depths. He pulled her closer, his lips sliding in the smooth sheen of sweat on her fragrant neck. The scent of sex and her perfume filled his nose.

"Well . . . that was something else," he muttered.

She made a choking sound. He smiled when he heard her laughter and felt it vibrating next to his mouth. He lifted his head and kissed her curving lips. He caught her eye.

"I'm sorry. That was nuts."

"Yes," she whispered. He saw her throat contract. "But don't be. Sorry."

He swallowed and touched his mouth to hers. "Come on. Let's get cleaned up."

He took her hand and led her into the bedroom suite. After disposing of the condom, he turned on the large, luxurious shower and closed the glass door.

"You go ahead and get in," she said. "I'm just going to go and get a couple things from my suitcase."

Everett nodded. He had brought her suitcase out to the guesthouse earlier. He got into the shower and lathered up. His body felt good after that explosive release. Really good. He hadn't realized how tense he'd been . . . how anxious he'd been to see Joy . . .

How *desperate*, apparently.

The only thing that would be nicer after that mind-blowing quickie would be to have his hands running all over Joy's smooth, soft skin along with all the hot water from the shower, to show her he could savor as well as devour her. After a few minutes of her absence, however, he got out and toweled off, leaving the shower going.

"Joy?" he called, scraping his fingers through his wet hair. He tucked the towel around his hips and padded toward the closed bathroom door. It opened and Joy stepped in, still wearing her skirt and tank top.

"I'm sorry," she said. "I thought I hadn't packed one of my vitamins."

"Did you find them?" he asked, glancing down at the transparent bag she carried containing several bottles.

She nodded and walked over to the counter to set down the items.

"You must be a health nut, like Katie," he said, nodding toward her bag of vitamins. Her smile in the reflection of the mirror struck him as strained.

Whoa . . . What just happened? he wondered. He felt it again—that wall that seemed to fly up between them at times. She kept her face averted as she extricated her toothbrush and a few items from her bag. He opened his mouth to ask her what was the matter, but stopped himself.

"I'll give you some privacy," he said.

She glanced up. Their eyes met briefly in the mirror, but then she looked away.

He closed the door behind him, feeling a sense of defeat, not to mention confusion. She gave of herself so completely during sex. Why did she retreat into herself following physical intimacy?

He could tolerate many things when it came to new relationships, but something about the idea of Joy withdrawing the way she did spoke of loneliness . . . of suffering. And that was one thing, he thought as he dropped the towel to the floor, he wouldn't accept easily.

Ten

Joy felt awkward when she came out of the bathroom a short while later wearing her new lemon-colored silk nightgown, but Everett wasn't in the bedroom. Guilt washed through her. He'd obviously wanted to take a shower with her after they'd had sex. He'd known she'd avoided him. She'd seen it in the sober glance they'd exchanged in the mirror.

What was wrong with her? Why did she feel so raw every time he made love to her? She couldn't put the feeling into words. It felt almost unbearably good to give in to the elemental lust he inspired in her, but afterward she felt like a walking exposed nerve. For some stupid, inexplicable reason, it reminded her of making eye contact with other cancer patients she randomly encountered during her chemo. Usually, they dropped their gazes. Joy understood. She'd learned to do the same.

It was all she could take to manage her own survival. It was too painful to consider another's struggle . . . another's mortality.

She couldn't imagine why a similar feeling occurred with

Everett following their electric sexual encounters. She promised herself she'd stop being so weak, so idiotic. She set her clothes on top of her suitcase and started to go in search of him. The partially opened door widened before she got there.

Everett stepped into the bedroom carrying a champagne bucket. Two flutes were laced between his long fingers. His hair was a sexy mess of waves and wet spikes. He wore a pair of light blue cotton pajama pants that fell low on his narrow hips and nothing else.

He did a double take when he saw her standing there. "Hey. You look pretty," he said, his gaze running over her warmly.

"Thanks," she said. Bless his heart. He wasn't irritated at her for her momentary stupidity. She walked toward him as he set the glasses on the table and poured the sparkling fluid into them. "I bought it for this trip," she said, forcing herself to admit the little vulnerability as a lame apology for her earlier foolishness. When she saw his pleased expression, she was amply rewarded.

"You did?"

"Yes." She could smell the fresh scent of soap on his skin. She wanted to kiss the smooth, golden skin covering his pectoral muscle.

Then do it, idiot.

She stepped forward. His skin felt firm beneath her lips and still felt moist from his shower. He made a rough sound in his throat. She looked up when he touched the back of her head. His gaze on her was soft.

"I'm sorry," she whispered, not sure if he would understand her apology or not. His eyelids narrowed slightly. She sensed him studying her . . . considering. What had she been thinking? Of course he understood she was apologizing for her withdrawal following sex. What had Katie said? He was a creature of instinct. It was why he was such a great actor—he *felt* so much. He lived so deeply.

His life wasn't governed by fear, like hers was.

He turned and whipped the light blue, raw silk comforter back, folding it at the bottom of the mattress.

"Come here," he said quietly. He sat down on the bed, his back against the pillows, and beckoned to her with his free hand. Joy followed him, lying on her side and facing him. He held up his champagne glass. "To our little getaway. May it lead to a deeper understanding of each other."

She lightly touched the flute to his. The champagne was cold and dry and delicious. She made a sound of appreciation. "Did you buy this?" she murmured, studying the bold lines of his profile with appreciation. He nodded. "I suppose you're an expert. Let me guess— you took wine lessons from a world-renowned sommelier in his private chateau in the French Alps," she teased.

"No, I was smart enough to listen to my mother when I asked her advice on a nice champagne to offer you."

She paused in the action of bringing the flute to her lips. "Your mother? You told her about this weekend?"

"I told her about you," he corrected. "Why do you act so surprised?" His gaze was narrowed on her lips. A shiver went through her.

"I don't know," she said honestly.

"Because you wouldn't consider telling your mother about me, is that it?" he asked, eyebrows cocked. He put the glass to his lips.

"No, it's not that. I might have told her. If she were alive."

The champagne slid back into his flute before he'd drank it. "I didn't know," he said, staring at her. "How long has it been since she passed?"

"She died when I was almost eighteen."

"Do you have brothers and sisters?"

"No. It's just me . . . and Seth, of course," she said evenly, sipping her champagne. "What about you? Are there more out there like you and Katie?"

He shook his head. "No. Mom and Dad always say they had

their hands full with the two of us, and they couldn't imagine adding more chaos to the mix."

She laughed and pulled up her knees, cuddling closer to him. He put his hand on her hip and stroked her. She saw his eyebrow quirk up in male interest when he noticed she didn't wear any underwear under the gown. She smiled.

"Your parents are still together?" she murmured, resting her head on the pillow.

"Oh yeah. They're crazy about each other. It's embarrassing"— he caught her eye—"and great. Katie and I were very lucky growing up. I didn't realize what great parents Meg and Stan were until I was an adult myself."

"They must be the reason you've remained so grounded, despite all the fame."

"I've seen more people than you can imagine bottom out in this business. It seems like every time I've been on the edge of some Hollywood mind-fuckery, Dad was there to drag me out to the golf course and kick my ass, or I'd be bailing Katie out of some fiasco she'd gotten herself into with those crazy rich geezers she used to work for, or Mom would be calling, insisting I come over and help her get a hornets' nest out of the gutters, or yelling at me for not sending a thank-you card to Aunt Sherry for the fruitcake she gave me for Christmas, or Rill would be telling me the latest project I was working on was 'shite' and when was I going to do some *real* work for him, and there you have it—no matter what, I'm always Stan's and Meg's oldest kid, and Rill's oldest friend, and Katie's big brother. It's sort of hard to believe all the other crap you're fed in Hollywood when you have all those people seeing you so clearly."

"You're so lucky," she whispered.

His gaze sharpened on her. "Yeah. I am. So where was your dad when your mother died?" he asked so abruptly she didn't have time to put up her guard.

"He was on the national racing circuit. He left when I was sixteen."

"That must have been hard."

"It was and it wasn't," she said, running her hand over the swell of well-developed biceps and over his shoulder. She felt his skin pebble slightly beneath her touch. "He wasn't really there all that much, even when he was in residence, if you know what I mean. His job consumed him."

"Do you like him?" Everett asked quietly.

She blinked, his question surprising her. "Like him? Yes," she said, realizing what she said was true. "He's fun and charismatic. He has a zest for life I admire."

"So you're not mad at him? For not being there when your mom died?" he asked quietly.

Her gaze zoomed to his face. He watched her with the steady, focused calm she'd come to expect from him. "No," she said with pressured honesty. "I'm not angry with him at all."

He nodded slowly. "If you don't mind my asking, why did your mom pass? She couldn't have been very old, if you were only eighteen."

She studied the bubbles clinging to the side of her glass. "She had Hodgkin's lymphoma. It eventually spread to multiple organs. Her kidneys and liver shut down, at the end."

She glanced into his face when he didn't speak. He looked still and somber, the line of his mouth grim.

"She went back and forth between remissions and reoccurrences, a few months of health followed by another round of treatment, for more than five years before she died," Joy said. For a few seconds, she was scared he was going to mutter some kind of hollow platitude—one of the many reasons she typically didn't mention her mother's illness and death—but he didn't. He just took another sip of champagne and stroked her hip, the gesture striking her as bizarrely both reassuring and sexual.

"And you really hold no anger for your father whatsoever? He left not just your mother when she was suffering, but you," Everett said, his brows knitted together.

Joy turned and set down her champagne glass. "Have you ever had someone close to you die from cancer?" she asked when she turned back around.

"No."

"My dad isn't a monster, Everett. He had the guts to be honest in a situation he couldn't bear. He did what he could. It's all we can ever do in a heartbreaking situation—what we *can*."

He emptied his glass and reached around her, setting the flute on the table. She thought he didn't seem entirely convinced. He couldn't understand what she meant. His life had been graced, and she was glad of it. More glad than she could put into words. Everett deserved the life he led. In spades.

She leaned forward and kissed an erect nipple. It'd been tantalizing her, tempting her the entire time they talked. She felt his hand at the back of her head, cradling her against him. She closed her eyes and tested the turgid flesh with her tongue. He exhaled harshly. She felt him stiffen even more against her circling tongue.

"You're a closed book, aren't you?" she heard him mutter from above her.

She blinked and glanced up at him in surprise. Why did his features look so hard when his stare was so soft? "I don't mean to be."

"No?"

She swallowed thickly at the hint of sarcasm in his question. His eyes seemed to bore right into her. "Then why don't you let me restrain you before I make love to you again?"

The silence seemed to stretch tight and then slowly start to spin like a vortex, seemingly catching her thoughts and her very breath and swallowing them.

Had he really just said that?

It might have been something straight out of one of her overly zealous sexual fantasies in regard to him. His nostrils flared slightly as he studied her. "What's wrong? Does that idea turn you off?"

She swallowed thickly. "No," she said breathlessly. "I mean . . . I don't think it does. I don't have that much experience . . . considering it. Do you mean you want to tie me up?"

"I want to restrain you. I would have anyway—even not knowing you, I mean. It turns me on, in general. But in your case, I'm exponentially interested in the possibilities."

"Why?" she asked.

His mouth flattened into a straight line. He spoke quietly near her ear.

"Because you're one of the most tempting, beautiful women I've ever laid eyes on," he murmured, his deep, low voice making the hairs on her neck stand on end. He opened his hand wide at the small of her back and caressed her through the silk. "Because you're soft, and you're sweet, and because I want to give you as much pleasure as your mind and body can take." He leaned up and speared her with his clear-eyed gaze. "Because I think you want to do the same for me."

"I do," she said honestly.

He leaned down and kissed her softly. "I see the shadows in your eyes." She went still beneath his warm, moving lips. Shock reverberated through her flesh as she absorbed what he'd said. "I want to make them go away."

"You mean . . . through sex?" she asked, confused, thinking about how he'd expunged everything from her brain on that night in her apartment save raw lust.

He sat up. "I won't turn down the opportunity if it works."

She just lay there, bewildered by his grim expression. He swung a long leg around her and stood. She couldn't take her eyes off him as he got up from the bed, crossed the luxurious bedroom and opened a dresser drawer.

She turned and sat up slowly, her elbows bracing her upper body on the bed. He closed the drawer with a thud and faced her. He held several padded cuffs and a tangle of black straps in one hand. She felt the pulse at her throat start to throb and a pinch at her clit. He was always beautiful to behold, but seeing Everett stalk toward her holding those cuffs was a sexual sin in and of itself.

He stood at the side of the bed and started to unravel the straps.

"Four of them?" she whispered when he separated all the cuffs and set them on the bed.

"Yes. Is that all right?"

She met his stare. Her pulse now felt like it was trying to leap out of her throat.

His expression softened infinitesimally. "I'm not going to do anything you don't want me to do, Joy. All you have to do is tell me to stop and I will."

She swallowed and nodded. "Yes. Of course."

"Take off your gown."

She licked at her lower lip nervously as she sat up on the mattress. He stood watching her, his expression somber, his focus on her sharp. She lowered the straps of her nightgown and drew her arms through them. She began to draw the thin fabric down over her breasts.

"Slower," he said.

She paused, looking at his face, but his gaze was glued to her breasts. She watched him as she slowly lowered the gown over the upper swells of flesh. When her nipples peeked out behind the fabric, he shifted on his feet and his penis jumped behind the cotton pants he wore. Sensing his arousal joined her to him, despite the space that separated them. It fed her desire and quieted her anxiety. She opened her hand at the edge of the fabric, letting her palm cup the sensitive skin of her lower breasts and drag along her rib cage and caress the curves of her hips.

"Stop," he said abruptly when the silk lay like a yellow shimmering pool in her lap. "Stretch out on the bed."

Joy followed his instruction. Rill and Katie had furnished the guesthouse with comfortable luxury. The pale blue sheets felt sensual and cool next to her heated skin. She lifted her head, her heart racing when Everett touched her left ankle. The padded cuff slipped over her foot. She saw only the top of his head as he bent, tightening the cuff around her and somehow affixing it to the frame of the bed. He moved over to restrain her other ankle, and she pulled experimentally on her left leg. She could bend her knee, but only slightly. Everett lowered to tie her other ankle, and her thighs parted into a wide V.

"Does that hurt?" he asked, glancing up from where he knelt on the floor in front of the bed.

"No," she managed. She wasn't lying. It wasn't the stretch of her muscles that had made her eyes go wide.

A tiny smile tilted his mouth. She watched him, her breath growing increasingly choppy, as he moved to the head of the bed and restrained both of her wrists. Her head lay flat on the mattress, her arms stretched over her head toward both corners of the bed. The position seemed to constrict her breathing—or perhaps that was just her growing trepidation and excitement. If she weren't able to clearly see the fat, mushroom-cap-shape of the head of Everett's cock bob against the cloth of his pants, she might have considered telling him to stop. Everett had been right, though, when he'd said he thought she wanted to give him pleasure. Seeing how aroused he was becoming while he tied her up was her own aphrodisiac.

He finished and climbed onto the mattress, straddling her prone body on his hands and knees. His gaze lingered on her exposed belly and breasts.

"Try to relax," he murmured. She suspected he noticed her

erratic, shallow breathing. "Do you want me to tell you a joke?" he asked, smiling.

"This doesn't seem very funny," she whispered.

"No, but it's not supposed to be brain surgery, either." She met his stare. She laughed when she saw the heat and humor in his eyes. He chuckled and reached for one of the soft, decorative pillows and carefully lifted her head, leaning down and placing the cushion beneath her. "How's that?"

"Fine."

"Good," he said. He shifted his weight and came down next to her on his side, his elbow bent, his jaw in his hand. She turned her chin and looked at him.

"You like this, don't you?" she murmured, noticing his satisfied expression.

He reached across her and opened his hand along the side of her ribs, brushing the sensitive skin. Her nipples pinched tight.

"Why *wouldn't* I like this?" he asked, his gaze on her breasts. "I'm not stupid."

He continued to stroke the side of her from hip to waist, sending prickly tendrils of sensation across her breasts, belly and sex. He flickered his fingers between two ribs and then traced the taut skin over the bone. She gasped at the sharp sensation, something between a tickle and a jab of arousal. Her muscles tightened in the restraints. She saw his eyes on her torso, studying the effect of his caresses, seeing her pebbling flesh and tightening nipples. He glanced into her face.

"I noticed it before—how sensitive the side of your body is. It's amazing. I thought it might feel sharper for you if you were restrained."

She didn't respond. She couldn't, because his fingertips had trailed over her belly. He gently caressed the sensitive skin just above the draped silk of her gown, just inches away from her spread pussy. Warm liquid surged between her thighs.

"It's because your body is drawn so tight," Everett murmured next to her. She turned her chin to look at him, but he was watching his fingers enliven her flesh. Joy felt perspiration bead on her brow. "It stretches the nerves. Amplifies sensation. Here. I'll show you better what I mean."

She parted her lips to tell him she thought he was doing a fine job proving his point as it was, but was distracted when he shifted and straddled her again. His cock strained against the cloth over his left thigh. The bulbous head brushed against her as he reached for the pillow beneath her head.

"Tell me if I'm making you uncomfortable," he said. He shifted the silk pillow down behind her back, sliding it down to just above her waist, forcing her back into an arch. Before she understood his intent, he came down on his hands and bent his elbows, flexing his arm muscles, and licked her right nipple with a warm, laving tongue. She made a strangled sound, and then whimpered helplessly when he flicked at the sensitive morsel with the tip of his tongue.

"You have the prettiest breasts," he said, his warm breath striking her wet nipple. He gave the tip an openmouthed kiss and let the edge of his teeth graze her, finishing with a lusty smacking sound.

"Everett," she moaned.

"See what I mean?" he asked, giving her a smoky glance.

She swallowed with difficulty and nodded. Her entire body was stretched tight, her breasts thrust upward, easy targets for consumption. She saw what he meant, all right. Even his most innocent-seeming touches were making her burn.

"Say *yes*," he commanded quietly.

"Yes."

He leaned down and kissed her mouth. His firm, moving lips seemed to stroke her entire body—coaxing, molding, biting. She craned up for him, pulling the restraints tight.

It was as if she'd never experienced a kiss until that very moment.

She cracked her eyelids open a moment later when she felt the absence of his lips. The light from the bedside lamp gleamed in his narrowed eyes. He shifted suddenly. She twisted her chin to see what he was doing, but his stretching body blocked her vision. The sound of something clicking against metal reached her ears.

He came back over her. A shock went through her when he pressed a small cube of ice to her lips. He slid it against her lower lip, pressing, until she felt a trickle of cold water stream into her mouth. He made a gratified sound in his throat.

"You melt it in seconds, you're so hot."

He pressed another cube to her mouth and watched as he traced her spread lips with it. "I remember how hot it felt in your mouth," he murmured distractedly. "I thought you were going to melt my cock."

She made a desperate sound in her throat. His gaze flew to meet hers. The ice was now completely melted. Water wet her lips and trickled down her chin. He pressed his thumb to the center of her lower lip. "Where did you learn to suck cock like that, Joy?" he asked.

"I don't know. I don't remember ever being taught," she replied, her voice sounding garbled because of his thumb on her lip. He rubbed her chilled yet feverish lip again while he considered her somberly.

"No? Maybe I'll refresh your memory," he said.

Her eyes widened at the subtle threat she heard. He reached again and she heard the ice clanking against the side of the champagne bucket. This time when he returned to her, he held several cubes in his hand. He put his hand at the back of her head and lifted her before he raised his hand to her lips.

"Suck on it," he said tensely.

She stared up at him, confused, her lips automatically closing around the cubes he'd slid into her mouth.

"Go on. Let me see you melt it. Suck."

Her heart started to throb uncomfortably in her stretched rib cage, like there wasn't room for it anymore. She sucked on the ice, squeezing the water out of it like she might the juice out of cold fruit. Everett groaned as she watched her with a steady focus. She drew harder, her cheeks flexing inward, until the last of the slippery, hard, cold splinter in her mouth melted.

Everett slipped his finger into her mouth. He muttered something she couldn't catch before he gently placed the back of her head back on the mattress. Suddenly, he was coming down next to her on his back. Joy lifted her head. She saw his long legs fly up in the air as he tore his pajama bottoms off them with uncommon haste. Then he was back, straddling her, except this time he came higher, his knees tucking beneath her armpits. He reached again for the ice bucket. He lifted her head again.

Joy stopped breathing, spellbound by the vision of his long golden penis just inches from her face. It seemed to take up her entire field of vision. Her clit pinched so tight in longing, she grimaced.

"Open," he said gruffly.

But instead of his cock, he slipped more ice between her lips.

"Suck. It's the only thing that's going to keep me from fucking your beautiful face and coming in that hot little mouth, so you better chill it off," he said in a tight voice from above her.

Her eyes widened. What he'd said was raunchy and crude and so erotic, it short-circuited her brain for a second. "Suck," he prompted again, this time more gently.

Joy stared at the awesome sight of his erect cock and sucked for all she was worth. It was so beautifully shaped. The tapering, fat head; the long, straight shaft; the swollen, blue vein that ran from just below the defined rim beneath the head down the shaft—her tongue longed to taste all of it. His fingers moved, caressing the nape of her neck. His other hand lowered between his thighs. He grasped his cock, stroking the head and upper shaft with what looked like a tight grip.

Joy stilled.

"Suck," he ordered. "Melt all the ice."

He jerked on his cock. She saw the skin stretch tight from his squeezing stroke. The bulbous head took on a purplish tinge. Joy's cheeks hollowed out as she sucked furiously. He continued to stroke himself, sometimes with a loosened fist, sometimes yanking on himself in a manner that struck her as unbearably exciting. She watched, panting through her nose, as he used his thumb to rub a clear drop of ejaculate into the slit on the head.

A few splinters of ice still remained on her half-numb tongue, but she spread her lips wide in an invitation. He grunted and braced his upper body on the cloth headboard of the bed with one hand. Joy thought she'd shatter from the sharp anticipation that gripped her entire body as she watched him lean forward and guide his cock to her lips.

Hard flesh penetrated her mouth and stretched her lips wide. Joy closed her eyes, her entire focus on the sensation of his cock sliding against her tongue.

"Holy fuck." She heard his voice as if from a distance. "Your mouth is so cold." Joy's cheeks and jaw ached, she drew on him so hard. He groaned and thrust between her clamping lips. "And so damn hot."

She couldn't move toward him, restrained as she was and with his hand holding her head, but he must have sensed her eagerness, because he fucked her mouth for a moment, pulsing his hips and sliding in and out of her several inches. She wasn't hungry—she was ravenous. Crazed. Her entire world shrank, becoming the smell and the taste and the sensation of Everett's cock.

He paused, depriving her of a downstroke. Her nostrils flared for air and she clamped the head of his cock tighter between her lips. She laved at the taut flesh with a stiffened tongue, coaxing him to give her more. He grunted appreciatively.

"Open your eyes."

She did so sluggishly, light and vision splintering her dark, voluptuous world. He put his thumbs beneath her jaw and gently tilted her head back, thrusting his hips forward so that his cock remained lodged in her mouth. She stared up at the long, muscular length of him dazedly, feeling strange . . . drunk . . . drugged by desire.

"Enough."

He said it harshly at the same time that his cock slipped from between her lips. He laid her head back on the mattress. She murmured his name through numbed lips. Suddenly, his hands were on her breasts, plumping them in his palms, and one of her nipples was surrounded by his warm, wet mouth. He lashed at her with his tongue and drew on her until she cried out in anguished arousal. She wouldn't call his treatment rough, necessarily, but it was far, far from being the gentle, teasing awakening of her nerves he'd subjected her to earlier. He made a sound of satisfaction in his throat as he molded her breasts, sucking insistently on one tip. Her hips twisted on the bed in arousal. Her nightgown was still in her lap. The light, flimsy silk was inadequate pressure on her wet, wanting pussy. Everett transferred his mouth to her other nipple and gave it a similarly lusty, insistent treatment. She let out a groan of pure misery.

"Oh God, please."

He lifted his head and gently nipped at her nipple. Joy ground her pelvis down into the mattress and shifted her weight, desperate for friction.

"Please what?"

"Please touch my pussy," she panted. If he wanted her to beg, no problem. She had nothing else to do but lie here and twist and drown in excitement. "*Please*, Everett."

His mouth lowered. He dragged his teeth gently across her sensitive ribs, raising goose bumps on her skin, making her gasp loudly. She pressed down again on the mattress. Even her anus tingled with electric arousal. Everett's tongue touched her belly, making the muscles leap. She lifted her head, panting, seeing his back and shoulder muscles bunch as he held himself off her, his head lowering to the folds of yellow silk. She watched him through the mounds of her heaving breasts. She felt it in every cell of her body when he kissed her just above the silk. He lowered it slowly. She felt it sliding over her labia.

She dropped her head back on the mattress. She was having difficulty drawing adequate air into her lungs, the anticipation was so great.

"Oh, God," she muttered under her breath when she felt his fingers on her mons. She clamped her eyes shut when she felt him spread her labia. Wide. Had she ever been parted so wholly? She swore she felt his gaze on her exposed, wet flesh like a pressing weight. If nerves had mouths, hers would be screaming. The tip of his tongue flicked her clit.

Her entire body convulsed like she'd been lashed with a whip.

He made a rough sound. He kept her parted wide, making her clit entirely exposed for his rigid, rapid tongue. Joy just lay there, helpless under the ruthless flail. He pressed and agitated. It was patently lewd what he was doing to her—pressing, flicking, waggling his wet flesh against hers. He was going to make her come in seconds, his movements were so wickedly precise.

He covered her clit with his mouth and sucked. A curse flew out of her throat. She clenched her thigh and ass muscles so tight, she thought they'd break. Didn't they say the female anatomical equivalent of a cock was the clitoris? God, she thought wildly as she crested, she *so* wished she could swallow Everett whole and stimulate every single inch of him with a relentless tongue.

She did break—helplessly against the sharp edge of pleasure, her body shaking with release. He continued to lick and agitate and suck her as she came, seeming determined to milk every last shudder out of her quivering flesh. Her final cry segued into a shaky moan. Her body sagged into the mattress.

She felt like she'd been wrung dry.

She stared up at the ceiling sightlessly, trying to catch her breath. She tasted the sharp tang of her own sweat in her mouth. Through a haze of disorientation, she felt Everett move, and then the spring in the mattress when his weight came off it. She felt something flick against the arch of her foot and twitched, realizing her left foot was free. Everett was freeing her ankles from the restraints. For a few seconds, she heard nothing but her own ragged, soughing breath in her ears. Her body still buzzed, her nerves still zipped and sizzled. She was having a hard time calming following her explosive climax.

The mattress dipped and she lifted her head. Her breath caught, burning in her lungs for a moment, before she gasped again for air. Everett came toward her on his knees, naked, his already lean, defined muscles looking especially tight and hard. A condom stretched over his enormous erection. He looped his forearm beneath one of her knees and kept coming toward her on his knees until he paused between her thighs. She watched, her breath scoring her lungs, as he lowered his head and gently pushed back her thigh, rolling back her hips. His head lowered, he took his cock in his hand and pushed it into her slit. He flexed his hips, impaling her in one swift, shocking thrust.

Joy shouted out hoarsely. Her body tightened, her muscles rippling at the bold possession. He grunted thickly, gripping firmly on the thigh he held in the air. He lifted her hips several inches off the mattress and began to fuck her. She bit her lip to stop from screaming. The friction was nearly too much for her, but he was clearly enjoying it. No . . . relishing it.

Hadn't she thought just moments ago that she'd love to be able to swallow his cock and stimulate every inch of it at the same time? Maybe her mouth couldn't. But her pussy could. She ground her teeth together and bounced her hips in a counter rhythm to his pounding cock. The uncomfortable pressure deep inside her morphed to a burn . . . a delicious friction. She watched him, his glinting gaze, his rigid face, the long, golden stretch of flexing, pumping muscle.

"Harder," she managed between clenched teeth, even though part of her was screaming silently that she couldn't take it. "Fuck me harder."

His chest and arm muscle tightened. He drew her leg up higher and tauter at the same moment she spread her other thigh on the mattress. His hips turned his cock into a fluid, ruthless piston. He pounded into her until she screamed without drawing breath. She felt his cock jerk viciously high inside her. His pelvis crashed against hers with a loud *whap*. He lifted her, grinding himself against her exposed clit while his cock swelled.

Her scream of barraging sensation segued to a keen of climax. She shuddered in tight, delicious pleasure, but she lifted her head and opened her eyes, wanting to see him as he came, absorbing his primal growls, loving the way his sweat-gilded muscles tightened and loosened, went rigid and shuddered with each consecutive ejaculation . . .

With every beat of his wild, pumping heart.

She'd done that to him.

Savage triumph blazed through her at the thought. She let her head fall back on the mattress as she tried to catch her breath again. It was shocking, how accurately, how powerfully, he could give her pleasure.

But what was truly alarming—and definitely addicting—was how much she loved pleasing Everett in return.

Eleven

~⁓~

Joy's eyes opened the next morning in a room that had been transformed into a golden, light-filled globe. She remained still, her head resting on Everett's chest, spying a beam of sunlight escaping around the curtains to flicker across his biceps and reach its luminescent tendrils toward a nipple. His chest moved steadily up and down, teasing the little light fairy; the curtains shifted ever so slightly, and the beam danced along his shoulder.

Joy reached and gently mingled her fingers with the sunlight on his collarbone, making her touch nearly as ephemeral so as not to wake him. The light fairy had warmed his smooth skin. She snatched back her hand when Everett's facial muscles tightened and his even breathing halted, but he fell almost immediately back into a deep sleep. She carefully extricated herself from his hold and the bedclothes, smiling.

The light truly did love him.

She quietly removed some clothing from her bag and entered the bathroom. When she came out ten minutes later, dressed for a jog, the sunlight-speckled, mussed bed was empty. She found Everett in the cozy little kitchen of the guesthouse, wearing pajama bottoms and scooping coffee into a filter.

"Morning," she said when he glanced around and caught her eye.

"Hey." She liked the rough, early morning quality of his voice. He flipped the coffeemaker closed, set down the bag he was holding and switched on the power. He turned toward her, his arms outstretched and his gaze moving over her with appreciative warmth. She went to him, smiling as she put her arms around his neck. "You look like you're ready for some exercise," he murmured, his gaze on her mouth.

Her lips twitched. The way he was looking at her, she had a pretty good idea what kind of exercise he was thinking about.

"You have a one-track mind, Everett Hughes."

He grinned. "So I like to keep things simple. Is that a bad thing?" She laughed and he swept down to kiss her. He transferred his mouth to her neck after a moment, his whiskers and warm lips the ideal combination for making her shiver. She pressed her nose to a pectoral muscle and inhaled. He smelled delicious—lingering soap, a hint of sweet sweat and sex. His kisses on her neck were becoming lustier by the minute. She gave in to temptation and gently bit at dense muscle.

He lifted his head, looking vaguely irritated that she'd interrupted his breakfast on her neck.

"The kind of exercise I was thinking about was jogging," she said.

"Spoilsport."

She smiled. "Do you want to come or not?"

"I want to come, all right," he muttered. She snorted with laughter, not at all concerned about his beleaguered expression. He gave her a glance that assured her he knew he was being highly ill-used as he released her. "Just give me a second to get dressed," he said, leaving the kitchen.

Joy drank one of the high-protein shakes she'd brought along and made the bed while he was in the bathroom. While she was fluffing the pillows, she noticed the drawer that Everett had removed the cuffs and restraints from last night was slightly ajar. What other naughty things did he keep in that drawer?

She tossed down the pillow and edged toward the bureau. When she heard the shower door open, she fled the bedroom guiltily. By the time he came out to the kitchen again a few minutes later, she was pouring coffee into two cups.

"I don't know what you put in your coffee," Joy said.

"I take it black, thanks," he said, examining the label of her shake. Judging from his expression, Everett didn't put much stock in health food. Joy glanced down over him, her gaze sticking on his shoes.

"Everett . . . you're not wearing those jogging, are you?"

He looked down at himself dubiously. He was wearing an ancient-looking polo shirt that had once probably been black but had faded over many washes to a dingy gray, an Army-green pair of baggy cargo shorts that fell below his knees, white socks and a pair of black Converse high-tops with white laces. "What? It's comfortable," he said defensively. "The raccoons and squirrels aren't going to care how I'm dressed."

"I wasn't talking about your outfit, if that's what one actually calls an ensemble like that," she said wryly. "I'm referring to your shoes. You shouldn't be jogging in shoes like that."

"I always do," he said, taking a sip of his coffee unconcernedly.

"But, Everett—there's no support in those shoes whatsoever. Your arches are going to collapse."

He shrugged. "They haven't so far."

"That's not a good reason for you to keep doing it. My running shoes are the most expensive thing in my wardrobe. And here you have all that money, but you're wearing those pitiful shoes," she scolded as she walked over to the refrigerator. She opened the door and peered inside the nearly empty receptacle. "I can't believe no one in your family has guilted you into buying shoes that are good for your feet."

"I don't let people guilt me into anything. Are you looking for cream?"

"I can drink it black," she said, closing the door.

"We'll take our cups up to Katie and Rill's and sneak some."

"Okay. Wait!" she called when he started toward the front door. She reached for a spray bottle she'd put on the counter and held it up. "Sunblock and mosquito repellent."

His eyes glinted with interest as he walked toward her. "You want me to put it on you?"

"No. I already put it on. You should put some on, though."

He shrugged. "I never wear that stuff."

She shook her head, grinning when she caught his eye.

"You never worry about things like West Nile virus, Lyme disease, skin cancer?" she asked, amused, as they started out the door and across the large yard to Katie and Rill's house. The forest chirped, twittered and creaked behind them, cheerfully alive and hopping in the early morning light.

"I worry about stuff, but not about those things," Everett said.

"What things, then?" she couldn't help but ask as they crept up the front stairs. What *did* a man like Everett Hughes worry about?

He opened his mouth to answer but paused as he opened the screen door and tested the knob. It was locked.

"They're probably all still sleeping. I know Seth will be. He's usually up all hours working and sleeps until ten or eleven. It's only six thirty," Joy whispered guiltily as Everett used some keys he had in his pocket to unlock the door. They were both clutching their coffees. The summer day was already so balmy, hardly any steam rose from the hot liquid.

"We'll be the highest caliber cream thieves—get in, get the goods, get out," Everett whispered.

She rolled her eyes and followed him into the silent kitchen. Barnyard rose from his reclining position on the floor and trotted up to them on short legs, his doleful brown eyes slightly accusatory. He sniffed Everett's high-tops and waddled away.

"They must sleep so much more peacefully with a watchdog like that," Everett mumbled.

He was about to pour some cream into her proffered cup a moment later when he suddenly raised his hand in a *caution* gesture.

"What?" Joy whispered, eyes wide.

"Did you hear that? Daisy's awake."

Joy strained to hear, but the big old house was silent.

"I don't hear anything."

Everett hastily poured some cream into her coffee and set her cup on the kitchen island. He signaled for her to follow him. She really did feel like a thief tiptoeing down the long hallway after him. They crept into Daisy's confection of a little girl nursery, Everett several steps ahead of her. She saw him looking down into the white bassinet cradle. The next thing she knew, he was reaching in and lifting his niece into his arms.

He grinned at Joy and made a silent gesture toward the open door. Joy led them into the empty living room.

"Katie and Rill have both been sleep-deprived lately," Everett murmured as they sat on the couch. "Is it okay if we watch her for a little bit and give them a little more shut-eye?"

"Of course," Joy said, sliding over on the cushion so that she could look into the bundle tucked in the crook of Everett's arm. Daisy blinked sleepy-looking eyes and looked up at her uncle. She pursed perfect pink lips and made a wet burbling sound. Joy

grinned. Daisy had at first demonstrated some stranger anxiety toward her last night, but by the time the evening had been over, she'd
warmed up and allowed Joy to hold her. The little girl had inherited
Rill's dark hair and Katie's delicate features. As for her eyes, they
were a striking combination of Rill's blue and Katie's green.

"Her eyes remind me of yours," Joy told Everett, touching a
tiny hand. Daisy bobbed her fist and turned her sleepy eyes toward
her. "Hi, Daisy. Good morning, pretty girl."

Daisy went still and stared at her for a second as if spellbound.

"Yeah, that's how I feel when I look at her," Everett murmured.
Warmth flooded Joy at his casually spoken words. Daisy turned at
the sound of his deep voice. He leaned down and kissed her on a
smooth cheek, and Daisy pumped both of her fists at once, a definite sign of approval. Joy chuckled.

"She loves her uncle. You must spend a lot of time with her."

"Not as much as I'd like," Everett said quietly. "I can't believe
she's already been on this planet for almost half a year. Time flies,
doesn't it, Daisy-girl?"

He continued to talk to the baby in a low, confidential tone
about anything that crossed his mind. He asked her if the Dodgers
would make the play-offs this year, if she liked Joy's running shoes
better than his, and what was her opinion on Tinkerbell—minx or
misunderstood? Daisy stared up at him with a somber, adorable
focus. After a few minutes, Joy transferred her gaze to his face as
he charmed his niece. Her heart dipped in her chest. He looked
easily as happy and transfixed as Daisy did.

"You're going to get a big head, having a pretty girl look at you
that way," she murmured when Everett shifted Daisy to his lap.

"He already has one when it comes to Daisy. That's why he
comes up here and wakes her up, to puff himself up a little further," a sleepy, beleaguered voice said. Joy glanced up to see Katie
standing there, her long hair tumbling around her shoulders in a

wild, mussed tangle of curls and waves. She wore shorts, a tank top, slippers and a fluffy robe partially tied around her waist. "I can't believe you woke up my baby again, Everett."

"She was awake, wasn't she?" Everett asked, looking to Joy for confirmation.

"Yes, I mean—I think so," Joy said, hiding a smile. She'd never really had any independent confirmation of Everett's claim that his niece was awake.

"Morning, Joy," Katie said as she scuffed over in her slippers and peered down at Daisy.

"Good morning. Sorry if we woke you."

Katie smiled down at her daughter. "You didn't wake me. But I'm willing to bet mean old Uncle Everett got you up again, didn't he, Daisy?"

Daisy blew a raspberry and laughed at the sound. She hardly looked unhappy at the idea of being yanked out of bed by Everett. They all laughed along with her. Katie patted her diaper. "Here, I'll take her. I think she needs to be changed."

"I'll do it," Everett said, still smiling. He stood and walked out of the room, his tall male form and muscular arms a sweet contrast to the tiny, delicate female he carried. Joy shared a smile with Katie.

"He's impossible," Katie said, her fondness for her brother trumping her irritated act.

"He loves his niece," Joy said, standing.

"Yeah, he does. And of course Daisy worships him. One of the few women on the planet who can turn his head. Come on, I'll make us some coffee."

They ended up having a casual light breakfast of juice, coffee and toast with Katie and Daisy before they finally got off for their run, promising Katie on the way out the door they'd return for lunch.

"Aren't you going to stretch?" Joy asked Everett when they got toward the end of the Pierce driveway. She glanced up from a bent-over position, her palms touching the concrete.

"Why would I do that, when I can watch you do it?" he asked, his gaze on her making her feel warm.

She shook her head and stood, stretching her arms behind her back. "You're a mess, running around in beat-up tennis shoes, not wearing sunblock, not stretching before a jog," she murmured amusedly. "Someone ought to take care of you."

"You want the job?" he asked as she started to run and kept pace with her.

"Like you'd ever listen to anything I said," she said, keeping her tone as light as his.

"You might be surprised."

She gave him a wary sideways glance. He wore a devilish grin, but his eyes had that expression in them that she'd caught in the sketch. Her heart rate leapt up to an optimal cardiac exercise rate, and they'd barely cleared the driveway.

By the time they started to descend the hill road, Joy following Everett's lead, the sun was rising over the eastern tree line. It was going to be another summer scorcher. Joy was relieved when Everett suggested they get off the road and take one of the well-tended paths created by the forest preserve. Humidity clung heavily amidst all the tall trees, but the shade was a comfort and the scenery was lovely.

"How far do you usually jog?" Everett asked her fifteen minutes later. The path they were treading followed the course of a small stream. She gave him a sideways glance. He wasn't even a little out of breath. She had the impression he was slowing his pace to accommodate hers.

"About four or five miles?"

He nodded. "There's someplace I want you to see. I'll try to work it so we get there toward the end of our run."

Everett seemed perfectly capable of conversation while he jogged, but Joy found it more difficult to talk and maintain her rhythm. He must have noticed, because they jogged for a half hour in companionable silence. They began a slow, steady ascent up a hill. By the time they reached the summit, Joy was coated in a sheen of perspiration and breathing heavily.

"It's close by," Everett muttered next to her.

Joy didn't understand what he meant and didn't have the breath to ask him. They cleared a thick grove of trees and both of them came to a halt simultaneously.

"Oh, it's pretty," Joy murmured. She bent and placed her hands on her thighs, panting. They stood on the edge of a rippling, circular lake that nestled as if in the protective palm of the forest. The sun shone over the tops of the trees on the eastern side, casting a lengthened mirrored image of them nearly the length of the lake, making the water a shimmering green with patches of blue-reflected sky interspersed.

"Care for a swim?" Everett asked.

Joy gave him a dubious glance. "Is this a popular spot?"

"I've never seen anyone here. Even Rill and Katie don't know about it."

"You're keeping it a secret?" she asked, amused.

He shrugged. "It's my private place. I come here to think sometimes." He whipped off the ugly polo shirt, revealing his ripped, sweat-glistening torso as casually as he might flick at a fly. He kicked off his shoes, stripped off his socks and jerked down his shorts and boxer-briefs with as much ritual or thought.

"You coming?" he asked her when he finally stood there nude and more glorious than the rising sun.

"I'm just going to stretch a little to cool off," she said breathlessly.

He nodded and headed toward the lake, shoving aside some tall grass with his hand, heedless when it snapped back behind him, brushing his ass. Joy just stood there for a second, breathing hard, watching him with her mouth gaping open, a sense of unreality clouding her consciousness. How could he possibly be so sublimely beautiful and seem about as aware of it as the air he breathed? If there were a trace of disingenuousness in his actions, a hint of contrivance, it'd be one thing. But instead, he was all easy male grace and quick intelligence, good-natured humor interspersed with sudden, dark, smoldering sexuality. He was just . . .

Everett.

She blinked, rising out of her trance at the loud splashing sound of his body hitting the water. She did a few stretches and wandered over to a sycamore, using the minimal cover of the low-hanging branches while she carefully took off her clothes and set them on a flat rock. Unlike Everett, whose lack of self-consciousness was epic, she felt extremely exposed walking in the tall grass completely nude. Luckily, he wasn't there to watch her ungainly progress; he was swimming toward the middle of the lake.

The water was pleasantly cool when she stepped into the shallows, her feet encountering smooth stones and silt. She dove in when she reached thigh level, delighting in the cold rush of water over her heated body. She swam a ways, and when she surfaced, Everett's head poked out of the water ten feet in front of her.

"It's nice," she said, returning his grin and pushing her short, streaming hair off her forehead.

"I thought you might protest," he said, floating closer to her, both of them treading water.

"To the skinny-dipping?"

"No. To swimming in a lake with a bunch of fish and worms and mud and stuff. There's no such thing as fish and mud repellent."

She laughed. "Don't make me into a priss just because I don't want to be bitten by mosquitoes."

He came near enough that she could see the water droplets on his eyelashes and the green and blue dots of pigment in his irises.

His hand brushed along her side in a liquid glide. She shivered at his touch.

"Actually," she said breathlessly, "my father used to take us camping. I'm used to roughing it a little," she said.

"And did you like it? Camping?"

"More than my mother," Joy said, laughing at a memory. "She never slept when we went camping. Never. She was too scared to in the tent. She was convinced we were going to be murdered in our sleep by a mad axman or something."

His smile widened. "Well, those mad axmen need to work, too. They'd be in the unemployment line if it weren't for clueless campers." She chuckled and touched his shoulder, drawing herself closer. His legs tangled for a moment with hers as they tread water.

"Was your mother an artist?" he asked.

"I thought so, even if she didn't." She saw his eyebrows quirk up in a query. "She was a claims adjuster, but she was always a natural at drawing. Never had any formal education, but it was uncanny the way she could capture a fleeting expression on a person's face."

"Ah," he said, his hands touching the back of her rib cage. He brought her closer and brushed his chest against the tips of her breasts. His small smile made her think the action was completely intentional. "So you get the talent from her."

"I think so." She was having trouble catching her breath. Her nipples pressed fleetingly against his lower chest again. He pulled her gently in his hold, and their bodies came into contact, her right thigh curving over his hip, his cock sliding ever so briefly against her lower belly. He felt deliciously full. She bit her lip and forced her attention back to the topic of conversation. "I probably got it from my mother and from Seth's and Dad's mom. Grandma did beautiful pottery and watercolors."

"You prefer oils, don't you?" he asked.

Her breath caught when he touched her left breast with his right hand. He fondled her as they both continued to tread water. It felt wonderful; the water was cold and soft, and Everett was warm and hard.

"Yes," she replied distractedly.

"Exclusively?" He must have noticed her dazed expression as she focused on his fingertips circling her nipple, because he clarified. "You never use any other medium?"

"Well . . . sure, I like charcoal, and of course I use various things when I'm helping Seth with body art or makeup—"

She gasped when he lightly pinched her nipple. Everett brushed his long body against her, making his growing erection obvious.

"I just had this brilliant idea," he murmured next to her right ear.

"And does this idea possibly involve something that might get us arrested if we get caught?" she asked softly.

"What I'm thinking of might be illegal in a couple states," he mused as he shaped her breast to his palm and the head of his cock batted against her hip, "but I'm pretty sure we'll be okay here."

"Oh, well as long as you have all the legalities worked out."

His smile was the clincher. Joy didn't hesitate to follow him when he tilted his chin toward shore. She'd seriously reconsidered the allures of outdoor loving, however, by the time they climbed out of the water and she'd followed Everett through the prickly, itchy tall grass on muddy feet. She shivered despite the heat of the day when the breeze struck her wet skin. It was uncomfortable enough almost to distract her attention away from the sight of Everett walking in front of her nude, sunlight and shadow flickering across his strong back and golden buttocks.

Almost.

They walked beneath the shade of the sycamore tree where she'd placed her clothes. She started when Everett abruptly slapped the side of his ass. She looked at him, stunned, when he turned around.

"Mosquito," he said.

She snorted with laughter. "I thought you were trying to turn me on."

"Did it work?" He slapped at his elbow this time. Joy shifted on her filthy feet uncomfortably.

"Well, not really. Everett, let's go. This isn't . . . sexy," she mumbled, her avid gaze on his long, strong legs and cock belying her words. He didn't look quite as full as he'd felt while they were in the water, but as always, he was a sight to see, whether erect or not. She'd rather cavort with him in a nice, clean, bugless bed, but she had to admit, there was something erotic about seeing him naked in the woods.

"No?" he asked, his narrowed gaze on her wet, pebbled skin. Her nipples were stiff—from the breeze, she'd thought, until something shifted in her awareness as she stared at Everett, and he at her.

"Well . . . maybe," she whispered. She walked toward him, dropping her arms from where she'd wrapped them protectively around her breasts. She put her hands on his shoulders, and he put his arms around her waist. A shudder went through her when he brought her against him. Their skin slid together. He was wet and hard and warm. He felt wonderful.

"I don't know . . . how we can manage . . . anything without getting . . . filthy," she told him between kisses below his nipples and across his ribs.

He cradled her jaw in his hand and lifted her chin. "All the better."

He covered her mouth with his. His mouth felt hot and liquid— a delicious contrast to her chilled body. His cock swelled against her belly, and her sex answered with a rush of warmth. She moaned and pressed harder against him, twisting her torso slightly, dragging her nipples against his ribs. He responded by becoming the clear aggressor in their kiss, bowing her back against his forearm, leaning down over her and staking his claim with his agile tongue.

Perhaps sixty seconds had passed since she'd voiced her doubts about wilderness sex. Now she was arching against him, her skin prickly and feverish, her body softened, supple, eager to be possessed. He opened a hand over one of her buttocks, squeezing the flesh lightly, his fingers tracing the crack. Something about the size of his hand in comparison to her body, the teasing, playful way he touched her, caused another rush of liquid heat through her pussy. His cock lurched between them. He molded the flesh harder, shaping her to his palm. He swatted her.

She jumped in his arms and broke their kiss abruptly.

"Mosquito," he murmured, his eyes sultry.

"Liar."

"Okay. I've wanted to spank your ass ever since I first laid eyes on it; how's that for the truth?" he asked, his mouth twitching. He continued to look at her as his hand lowered between her legs. Her breath caught when he dipped the tip of a finger into her slit. Again, she felt his cock move.

"Well, isn't this a nice surprise?" he murmured. He removed his hand and quickly brought it around to the front of her.

"Ohhh," she muttered when he thrust his forefinger into her again. He watched her face while he slowly finger-fucked her. After a moment, the sound of him moving in wet flesh reached her ears. He grunted in satisfaction. Her cheeks flushed with heat, and she bit her lower lip.

"Do you always get this wet this fast?" he asked.

When it comes to you, yes, she thought. But she didn't say that. She felt vulnerable enough standing naked in the forest while Everett finger-fucked her and studied every nuance of her face.

"I don't know," she replied.

"Now you're the liar," he said, all remnants of playfulness gone from his voice and manner. His expression looked grim as he paused and bent, sliding his left forearm under her right thigh. He lifted so that she stood only on one foot. He slid his arm through her draped leg until her calf was braced on his shoulder. She clutched at him for balance.

"I've got you," he assured her, stabilizing her with his hand at the middle of her back. Now that she was spread with the back of her leg against his chest, her pussy was easy prey. He immediately sank a finger back into her, and then trailed the digit between her labia, stimulating her clit.

She moaned and quaked.

"You're very wet here, too," he said, playing with her clit in the juicy pocket between her outer lips. "Does that feel good?"

"God, yes," she whispered.

"Do you want to come like this?"

Her clit started to burn beneath his finger. She grimaced.

"Joy?"

Why did he have to make her say it?

"*Yes,*" she hissed.

He cupped her entire outer sex, the ridge of his finger pressing against her clitoris. His entire arm jerked as he stimulated her. Joy made a croaking sound of surprise. Her hips instinctively bobbed against his hand. It felt unholy good, but his actions were much more aggressive than he'd been with her before—than anyone had been with her. He was jacking her off, his movements unapologetically forceful and succinct. The burn in her clit became untenable. It reached all the way to the soles of her feet and her anus.

"Oh . . . Everett," she whimpered helplessly, her hips twitching as if he were a puppeteer and she were helpless to resist his hand's demand. Her ass muscles clenched tight, amplifying the burn.

He slid his middle finger into her slit, still palming her outer sex. He continued jerking his arm, up and down, up and down, until a vein started to pop in his rigid, flexing bicep. Her fingers clutched at his neck as she topped the crest of sensation. She tipped over, shuddering in orgasm.

"Oh . . . no . . . oh, God . . . awww," she muttered incoherently as he continued to stimulate her just as forcefully while she came. The waves of pleasurable release just kept coming. Every time she thought they'd ease, he jerked his arm, demanding more.

She gave it to him until she was left gasping and sweating, clinging to Everett like she thought there was a risk of drowning in all that sensation. She felt him shift his hips. His penis brushed against her lower belly, leaving a thin trail of pre-ejaculate on her skin. She knew he was testing to see if his cock could take the place of his finger.

He cursed. "You're too short."

"You're too tall," she corrected.

"I have an idea."

"Isn't that what got me here last time?" she asked dryly when he gently removed her calf from his shoulder and she stood again on two feet. For a few seconds, she just stood there dazedly. She realized he'd gone over to his cargo shorts and was hurriedly digging in one of the many pockets. He was in profile to her. His cock protruded from his body at a downward angle between his legs, the thick head reminding her of a fleshy, succulent arrow tip.

Her panting breath stuck in her lungs, her body perking up again in sensual awareness.

He returned, ripping open a condom package. She watched him avidly as he rolled the prophylactic onto his rigid member, his actions precise. Hasty.

"Here," he said, pointing toward the rock where she'd set her clothes. She glanced at him in surprise, realizing he wanted her to stand on the rock. She frowned and stepped up, wincing when her feet hit a rough ridge.

"Do you want to put your shoes on?" he asked, taking her hand to steady her.

"No . . . I mean, maybe," she said, flustered as she shifted on her feet, trying to find a smooth place on the rock. It seemed so strange to be discussing the mechanics of being screwed in the forest.

"What exactly did you have in mind?" she asked when he picked up one of her tennis shoes and started loosening the laces.

"Just like what we did there," he said, tilting his chin toward where she'd just stood on one foot while he'd made her come explosively.

"Everett," she protested, laughing. He bent over to slide her foot in her shoe. She stared at the length of his muscular back and the tops of his round, muscular ass cheeks. She shoved her filthy foot into her shoe. "I want you to know what I'm sacrificing. I love these tennis shoes."

"I'll buy you twenty more like them. And a couple cartons of bug repellent along with them," he muttered as he hurriedly helped her with her other shoe.

"That's not what I—" She swallowed thickly when he stood, steadied her with one arm and urged her to lift her leg again. A moment and some maneuvering later, she stood before him on the rock, the back of her leg resting on his shoulders.

She was damn well doing a split standing up, Joy realized.

Everett held her steady with one hand at her waist and pushed his cock into her widely spread slit with his other. He'd found the ideal angle for entry by standing her on the rock.

"Aw, Jesus," he muttered as he slid into her, his jaw clenched hard. His other hand shifted to her hips, balancing her in their precarious stance. "Don't ever let me make fun of you for stretching again." He thrust. They both groaned. The unusual position was making for a tight, highly stimulating ride. "I love your long, flexible legs," he muttered as their pelvises slapped together, the blows sending ripples of sensation through her flesh. She grasped his shoulders desperately, sensing the storm approaching in his hot eyes. She cried out sharply when he slid the length of his cock out of her and thrust it back into her with one long, swift stroke, their bodies smacking together, his hands on the back of her waist and hip, absorbing some of the blow. "I adore your nipples," he added, watching the way her breasts trembled at the impact each time he drove into her. Her vagina was stretched so tight, every time he withdrew she felt the drag of the thick ridge beneath the head of his cock. Her nerves protested and purred in pleasure at once. He powered into her again and groaned gutturally. "I *worship* your tight, wet little pussy," he grated out.

Dappled sunlight played across his rippling shoulder muscles and her clutching hands, a jay squawked loudly in the tree above them and Joy's senses swam in a rough, choppy sea of pleasure. The tight, wild expression on Everett's face as he fucked her was scored on her consciousness.

Had she ever given herself so completely as he did at that moment?

Was she even capable of it?

He drove into her, his teeth bared in primal pleasure, and met her stare. Their gazes remained locked, a steady lifeline in a barraging, surging sea of sensation.

It was fucking, pure and simple, two animals succumbing to the dictates of nature.

It was more—much more—and that knowledge burned her as much as Everett's pounding cock.

Come, she mouthed silently, a drop of sweat trickling between her lips. The angle wasn't ideal for her to reach climax, but she could tell from Everett's expression it was perfect for him.

His cock swelled large and high inside her. The muscle in his cheek jumped as he stared at her, his eyes like burning, gleaming crescents. He jerked his hips, his fingers digging into her waist and hip. She cried out sharply in a mixture of discomfort, pleasure and awe, feeling him spasm deep inside her, hearing his anguished groan of climax. It continued for several seconds until he drew breath sharply, flexing his hips, his moan coming to an abrupt halt. His muscles contracted in another seizure of bliss.

"Christ," he said a moment later when he withdrew from her,

grimacing, his gaze flickering over her face. "Shit. I'm always making you cry. Are you okay?" he whispered, his lips tenderly touching her damp cheek.

She whimpered when he took her into a one-armed hug, one hand slipping between her thighs. This time, his touch was gentle, soothing, but no less arousing.

"I'm not hurting, Everett," she whispered, her lips feverishly tracing his goatee, her hips moving in a subtle rhythm next to his pleasuring hand.

She couldn't tell him what had been the reason for her tears. She couldn't, because she herself didn't know the reason for their existence.

Twelve

A strange, wonderful bubble of euphoria seemed to surround Joy as she and Everett swam again after making love. They walked instead of running home, holding hands, enjoying the beautiful scenery of the forest and each other's company. The woods seemed brimful of energy, and Joy rejoiced in those moments that she was at one with the wildlife, exquisitely aware of the compelling man next to her and the wonder of being alive.

When they arrived back at the guest cottage, sticky and sweaty but smiling, it was late morning.

"Do you want to get in the shower first?" Everett asked.

Joy looked around from where she stood at the sink, filling a glass with water. There had been something in Everett's tone that had caught her attention. She couldn't read anything from his impassive expression, though.

"No, you go ahead. I need to take a couple vitamins with a protein bar," she said.

He merely nodded once and walked away. She shut off the water slowly. Had that been a flash of disappointment she'd seen on his face before he turned? She recalled their interaction last night, how that moment of awkwardness and discomfort had hit her after they'd made love so lustily and how she'd avoided getting in the shower with him.

A few minutes later, she walked into the bathroom naked. She rapped softly on the frosted glass door of the shower. Everett immediately opened it.

Warm steam billowed out around her. Everett looked out at her, his slick, naked torso covered with soapy lather.

"Can I join you?" she asked quietly.

"By all means," he said, looking pleased. He grabbed her hand and pulled her into the delicious heat with him. The spraying hot water felt wonderful on her lower back and bottom.

The sensation of Everett taking her into his arms and rubbing his lathered, smooth skin against her own felt even better.

"What are you doing?" she asked, giggling when he slid himself up and down more exuberantly against her.

"I'm all soaped up. I'm washing you," he teased, his mouth close to her ear. He leaned down and kissed her neck where it met her shoulder. She shivered despite the heat. "You're a sweaty mess," he told her, his gruff, sexy tone at odds with his words.

"You're such a flatterer," she murmured, twisting her chin to find his mouth. They fused in a kiss that was nearly as steamy as the shower. Their mouths clung for languorous, delicious moments while Everett used the soap in his hand to clean her back and ass and subtly twisted his lathered torso against her to clean her front.

She broke their kiss and stared up at him. Her lips parted when he slicked his fingers between the crack of her ass and then gently lathered her outer sex. He just pinned her with his laser-like stare as he lathered and then thoroughly rinsed her with water. It felt incredibly intimate . . . exceptionally good.

"Hmmm," he mused, his hand moving between her thighs. "Having some difficulty washing away all this cream."

Joy felt her cheeks heating from the inside instead of from the billowing steam. She was very wet, both from their former lovemaking and from his current stimulation on her pussy as he cleaned her.

He suddenly surprised her by sitting down on one of the benches at the side of the shower and pulling her toward him, his hands on her hips, her back facing him.

"What are you doing?" she asked.

"I've decided the last thing I want to do is wash away something so sweet," she heard him say. He urged her to move between his long, bent legs. "Bend over. Put your hands on your knees and arch your back. I want to suck on your pussy, but you have to put it up next to my mouth."

Pausing in the action of bending over, she glanced around in amazement at the rest of his instructions. She froze at the sight of his small, sexy smile and the gleam of arousal in his eyes.

"You asked to come into my shower. My territory. My rules," he teased.

"I'll remember that," she said wryly, bending over farther.

"I hope so."

He placed both hands on her ass, and she forgot to give him a repressive glance for his cockiness. Instead, she strove to do what he'd asked, looking over her shoulder to gauge approximately where his mouth was. She arched her back and sent her tailbone up higher. He gave a gratified grunt.

"Beautiful," he said, stroking her bottom. He parted her ass cheeks. Joy felt her delicate tissues being exposed to the warm air. Her clit burned.

"I can't wait to sink my tongue into you. But you're going to have to come just an inch closer . . ."

Suddenly desperate to have his mouth on her, she sent her tailbone higher, her thighs tensing hard. She imagined there was a string jerking her rear end up toward the ceiling.

"That's it. God, you're a sight to see," she heard him say thickly.

With no further ado, he sunk his tongue directly into her slit. It felt decadently erotic, standing there bent over, steam surrounding her and hot water splashing against her shoulder and back, while Everett tongue-fucked her. He squeezed her ass cheeks in his palms, spreading her wide for his consumption. She moaned uncontrollably. He lifted a hand, popping her bottom.

Her clit went from a burn to a sizzle.

As if Everett had known her response to his spanking, he swatted her again, the contact sounding brisk and volatile because of their wet skin. His tongue snaked between her thighs, lashing at her clit. He laved the sizzling flesh hard while he spanked her again and again, the sound of slapping flesh going off like gunfire in the closed-off space.

Joy wailed in pleasure. Her thighs began to tremor at the effort of holding the difficult position. The pain of tensing her muscles so rigidly spiked into her awareness, but nothing could compare with Everett's talented, lashing tongue. She sensed her release, tensing even harder, pressing against him, ignoring the protest of her muscles. Just when she was on the edge of climax, his mouth was suddenly gone.

She cried out in disorientation.

"Shh," Everett hushed from behind her, even though his voice sounded too tense to be really soothing. He pulled her down into his lap with a wet slapping noise. Her eyes sprang wide when she felt his rigid erection throbbing next to her ass, wedged between a buttock and his abdomen. "Lean over and touched your toes," he rasped. "Do it, Joy," he said, his voice breaking through the drugged haze of her arousal.

He held her bottom in his lap with one hand. She leaned forward so that her breasts crushed against her thighs and her fingers touched her feet. She sat in Everett's lap, her cheek pressed against her leg, wondering what in the world he was going to do, breathless in anticipation and excitement. He moved slightly behind her. She felt him slide his hand between her body and his. They were pressed so close that she knew he took his cock into his own hand.

"Everett," she moaned, suddenly wild with need. She tried to sit up. She wanted to see him touch himself, but he gently pushed her head back to her thighs.

"Stay still."

"I want to see you," she burst out.

"I'm lathering up my cock," he muttered. "Can't you feel it?"

Her clit twanged with arousal. She clenched her eyes shut. Yes, she could feel it perfectly; his hand moving between their bodies, sliding up and down the length of his erection. She ground her teeth together and backed up in his lap, desperate to feel more of the arousing sensation. He chuckled softly.

"Here. This will help you to feel it better."

Her eyes opened wide when he spread her bottom cheeks and slid his thick, throbbing member into the crack. He pushed her buttocks together and, for an electric minute, thrust between her ass cheeks. He grunted in pleasure. Joy began to tremble. His hold on her was absolute. It was too much, feeling his throbbing cock burrowing in and out of the crack of her bottom, sliding against her asshole. It was vaguely shameful the way he used her flesh for his enjoyment. It was lewd and salacious and so exciting, she began to wiggle in his lap, wild for just the tad bit more stimulation she needed to come.

He slapped her bottom. "Stop squirming," he demanded tensely. "Sit still. I'm going to come like this."

Tears mingled in the drops of water on her cheeks and thigh;

not sad tears, but ones of frustration and pure, undiluted excitement. He tightened his hold on her ass and began to thrust into the crevice more forcefully, groaning. She loved the sound of him taking his pleasure, of feeling him stroking her so intimately.

He thrust his hips hard and tightened his hold on her ass. She felt his cock swell until it felt enormous and rigid pressed against her asshole, the thick head pulsing against the base of her spine.

He muttered a blistering curse. At the same moment she felt warm semen spurt against her spine, he reached around her and wedged his hand between her thighs. He jerked his arm, stimulating her clit forcefully. Joy screamed in surprise as climax ripped through her. She knew she'd been unusually aroused, but hadn't realized she would ignite at first touch.

A minute later, she still leaned over, sitting in his lap, her breath finally slowing. Everett rinsed his semen from her back and continued to stroke her torso soothingly. Joy felt like her entire body could dissolve and swirl down the drain with the hot, rushing water.

"And to think . . . I thought showers were for getting clean," she murmured, her mouth moving against her thigh.

The sound of his laughter warmed her more than the steamy water. He leaned down and hugged her tightly in his arms. He kissed her ear.

"I have the feeling that just about anywhere is for getting dirty as long as you're there, Joy," he said quietly next to her ear.

Joy and Everett walked up to the big house for lunch. Rill, Seth, Daisy, Joy and Everett all convened around the large oak table in the kitchen while Katie prepared their meal and Seth placed his sketchbook on the table.

Rill smiled at Katie's reaction when she took a break from her cooking and looked at one of Seth's sketches.

"Oooh, it's amazing," Katie praised.

Curious as to what Seth, Katie and Rill were looking at, Joy gently passed Daisy, whom she had been holding, to Everett. Everett took the baby without missing a beat and immediately began to talk to his niece about nonsensical matters with utter seriousness.

Joy walked the length of the table, the smell of grilling sandwiches—fresh basil, spinach, mozzarella cheese and thinly sliced prosciutto—tickling her nose. She loved Katie and Rill's kitchen. They had a beautiful, obviously newly decorated dining room, but seemed to prefer to congregate in the cozy kitchen and eat at the large, weathered oak table. The comfortable, colorful, casual kitchen seemed the perfect symbol of the warmth and intimacy of Katie and Rill's marriage and home life.

Joy inspected her uncle's sketch for several seconds and looked up at Seth. "It *is* amazing."

Seth's lips flickered in a smile at her praise.

"How long were you up doing it?" Joy asked her uncle quietly, giving him a sympathetic glance.

"Not long," Seth replied laconically.

Rill flipped a few pages in the sketchbook, revealing several other eye-catching new drawings. Joy gave Seth a knowing glance.

He'd been up all night.

"They're completely fantastic," Rill enthused, staring at a sketch that integrated everything that he'd shown Seth last night, from drawings from the costume designer and some preliminary photos to drawings from the special effects and set departments. "Everett, you've got to see these. You aren't going to recognize yourself."

Everett stood, coming over to the rest of them holding Daisy. Rill took his daughter from his friend's arms and nodded significantly to the sketch currently on display.

Everett's face stared back at them, transformed into a brutal-looking warrior with a crude, S-shaped wooden helmet that curved up an inch at the neck, a bizarre, forked fringe of coal-black hair on his forehead, which was highlighted by upturned, sinister-looking eyebrows and a slick, highly stylized Fu Manchu.

"Badass," Everett said.

"The makeup is much less complicated than what we did for *Maritime*," Seth said. "It'll require a silicone prosthetic for that slight protrusion on your forehead, but the rest will be hair work and makeup application. Even though Slader is well-known for his unusual translucent, pale blue eyes," Seth continued, referring to the character Everett would be playing, "Rill has an idea leaving your own color might be just as effective. Your eyes are striking enough, and part of the importance is the contrast with the rest of the features, given Slader's complex heritage. Besides, Rill says that you have some trouble tolerating contacts."

"I do," Everett admitted, flipping a page in the sketchbook. "What would you decide about the contacts if you didn't know that?"

Seth hesitated. "Slader's eyes are the windows to his soul—or in his case, his lack of a soul. I know you're a fantastic actor, but I'm not so sure you can force your eyes into looking like windows onto a frigid day in hell."

"Seth's right," Everett said, meeting Rill's gaze. "I want to do the contacts."

Rill nodded once, respecting Everett's call.

"I'd like to do some sample runs with some different contact tints," Seth said. "We don't have to worry about that today, though."

"Can we see anything this afternoon?" Katie asked enthusiastically as she went over to the large griddle and flipped their sandwiches, which made a hissing sound.

Seth was studying Everett's face. "I can't make the prosthetic here, of course, but I brought some hair samples. We can do that

and makeup after lunch, if you're game. Joy can do his body tattoos. You'd have to shave your goatee for me to apply the hair."
Seth refocused his eyes, as if he was shifting between seeing Everett
as a human being and not an inanimate model for his art. Joy felt
a flicker of annoyance at her uncle and compassion for Everett. It
must be hard, having people look at you constantly like you were
an object. Guilt swooped through her when she recognized that she
routinely looked at models in precisely the same way.

"No problem. Can I use your stuff to shave, mate?" Everett
asked Rill at the same time he stole a piece of the yellow pepper
Katie was slicing, ignoring Katie's slap on his hand. Joy's heart
jumped. Everett planned to go and shave the goatee she happened
to love. *Right now.*

"Yeah. In the master bath," Rill muttered distractedly, not
glancing up as he smiled at his daughter's reaction to his jingling
some car keys.

"*Seth,*" Joy hissed irritably as Everett walked out of the kitchen.

"What?" Seth asked, looking at her with his dark brows
pinched together.

"Everett isn't one of your hired models," she whispered heatedly. Seth gave her a bewildered glance. Joy shook her head in
frustrated disgust. She stalked out of the kitchen down the hallway.

"Everett?" she called around the partially open door that she
knew led to Katie and Rill's bedroom.

"Joy?" he said. He stuck his head around an interior door. He
already had shaving cream spread on his chin. Joy hurried into the
bedroom. Like the rest of the house, it had obviously been recently
remodeled and was decorated in comfortable luxury.

"You don't have to shave right now. Not if you don't want to."

He blinked. She noticed the large smear of shaving cream still
in his right hand.

"What, did Katie say lunch was ready? Should I shave
afterward?"

"No . . . no, I mean . . ." She paused, flustered. "It was . . . it was just the way Seth said it to you, that's all."

He continued to look at her like she was speaking a language he hadn't yet mastered.

"Like you were an inanimate object. He said to shave off your goatee so he could experiment with makeup without even thinking twice about it."

Everett's expression shifted. "Why should Seth think twice about it? I didn't. It's just hair."

"Well, yeah, but—" She broke off and made a futile gesture with her hand. "It's *your* hair. I . . ."

"What?" Everett persisted when she faded off, his focus on her sharp.

"*I* happen to like your goatee," she burst out.

"You do?" He leaned his thigh against the marble countertop of the sink as if he was settling in for a nice, long conversation of interest. Joy experienced a need to backpedal.

"I just mean . . . he shouldn't have talked to you that way. Shave it off when production begins. You don't have to do it right this second just because Seth mentioned it."

He smiled slowly. Joy blushed and took a step back.

"Do whatever you want. I just thought—"

"You just thought you'd try to stop me from shaving because you've become partial to my goatee," he said, his eyes taking on that heated gleam to which she was also becoming partial.

"You are as bigheaded as Katie says," she mumbled. "I just didn't like the way Seth said it so flippantly. That's all."

Everett straightened and held out the hand that didn't have any shaving cream in it. He came closer and draped it around her shoulder, halting her exit.

"I'd prefer to think you've become partial to my goatee. Can I just go on believing that version of things?"

Her annoyed glance faded when she saw the humor in his eyes.

"If you like," she said quietly. "Everett, don't!" she cried when he started to kiss her, forgetting the shaving cream on his face.

"Oh, sorry," he said, although he didn't look it. He sobered when he met her stare. He smoothed her short hair and paused to caress the top of her ear with his fingertips. She'd had no idea the little fold of flesh was so sensitive, she thought as a shiver coursed down her spine.

"It really is just hair, Joy. I couldn't care less. If you don't want me to shave for a while, though, I won't."

"No. No, of course not. It's got nothing to do with me," she said, mortified now that she'd ever brought the whole thing up.

"I'll let you be the judge of that," he murmured soberly before he went back to his task.

Joy helped Rill clean up the lunch dishes while Katie fed Daisy and put her down for a nap and Everett and Seth got things ready for the makeup application in the back atrium. She'd discovered last night that while Rill had an intense intellect and unique ability to transform complex visions from his mind's eye to the big screen, he could also be warm, teasing and charming, most especially with his wife, daughter and Everett.

"Everett almost seems like a real brother to you," Joy observed as she took a platter he handed her and wiped it dry.

"He is. Katie was like a sister, too, until I wised up and realized a sibling was the last thing on earth I wanted her to be," Rill said with a sideways grin, which Joy returned. "Meg and Stan took me in when I came to California to go to school. The Hugheses have been far more of a family to me than I've ever had. I never even knew my real father, and my mother . . . well, she's impossible to know, even if you've lived with her for years—"

A phone started to ring, interrupting him. Rill wiped off his large, soapy hands with a dish towel and dug in his jeans pocket. He greeted whomever was calling warmly.

"No, this is perfect timing. We're setting up for makeup application right now. I don't think Seth has any sketches done for you yet, but this will give him a chance to size you up. You'll inspire him, no doubt. He'll be up all night working."

Joy speculated silently about whom it was on the phone. It sounded like someone associated with the film.

"Is John going to come with you?" Rill asked. He listened and nodded his head. "Great. We'll see you here in an hour or two."

"That was Jennifer Turner," Rill told her when he'd hung up his phone and replaced it in his back pocket. "She's going to be stopping by later this afternoon."

"Really? That's great," Joy said. "She's the other lead in *Razor Pass*, isn't she?"

Rill nodded as he plunged his hands back into the soapy water. Joy had noticed earlier that he cleaned with the gusto of a rugby player—which his stature and rugged good looks certainly called to mind. Apparently, Rill didn't believe in attacking even the smallest tasks in a small way. She'd watched in wonder as he'd given the kitchen a hearty once-over that any woman would have adored before he'd even begun the dishes.

"Yeah. She has a friend who lives nearby. He's having some renovations done on his place, and Jennifer came with him. She's a pretty regular visitor here."

"We can size her up for makeup," Joy said, her smile disguising a niggling worm of uncertainty that had started to squirm around in her belly. Jennifer Turner was one of the most beautiful, talented women in the world.

She was also one of Everett's old girlfriends. If the press had been even 10 percent correct about their hotly speculated two-year relationship, then the one-time couple had at least *considered* marriage.

It seemed like too much for Joy to wrap her mind around the idea of Jennifer Turner and her—Joy—on the same playing field when it came to a man. It definitely made something burn uncomfortably in her stomach to consider even the faint likelihood of them both vying for Everett's attention.

Stop being ridiculous, she lectured herself as she put away the large griddle in the cabinet that Rill indicated. It wasn't as if this thing with Everett was anything she should be getting worked up over. She'd just met him recently. If Everett truly did still have feelings for Jennifer, there was nothing she could do about it. He was an amazing guy. He deserved to be happy.

It wasn't as if Joy had any long-term influence on whether Everett found happiness or not.

Joy worked on Everett's arm tattoos while Seth did the meticulous hair application. Seth's sketches for the body art were still in the works, but she liked the preliminaries he'd done that incorporated a mixture of Native American, Chinese and ancient Mongol symbols melded and transformed by Seth's creative mind. It was a little weird working on Everett so closely while other people were around, especially given the history of their first sexual contact. Eventually, however, she managed to mostly lose herself in the art, only occasionally glancing up to admire her uncle's progress or to assist him when he requested it.

They worked in an atrium where the large surrounding windows could either be thrown open on a temperate day or shut and regulated during the winter and summer months. Given the hot, humid day outside, air-conditioning cooled the sunny room.

"Are you getting cold?" Joy asked Everett an hour or so after they'd started. He'd been holding his arm up for her as she drew on his inner biceps, twisting and flexing it at her request. With her head close to his chest, she'd noticed how hard his nipples had grown.

"I can turn down the AC," said Katie, who was sitting in a lounger, watching their progress while Rill checked on Daisy.

"No, that's okay. I'm not cold," Everett said, his gaze on Joy. She blinked when she saw how warm his eyes looked. It took her several minutes to get back in the groove of her drawing after that.

When they'd finished, Joy was amazed, and she could tell Seth was pleased by the result. Even though he'd only done a partial makeup job along with the hair application and Joy had only done the tattoos on Everett's arms, the transformation was stunning. Seth went to get his camera while Rill and Katie examined Everett. Rill glanced from Seth's tattoo drawings to Everett's arms.

"I like what you did in the application, Joy," Rill murmured. "You altered the tattoos to fit with the natural contours of Everett's muscle and bone. It gives it a living, organic effect."

"Thanks," Joy said, warmed by Rill's astute observation.

"She had me flex and move my arms so she could see the natural movement and use it to highlight the tattoos," Everett said.

Rill examined her with sharp blue eyes. "I know you're here as Everett's guest and you aren't an official part of Seth's makeup company, but will you consider doing Everett's tattoos personally when we go to production? Everett and Seth both say you did a fantastic job on the *Maritime* tattoo for promotional photos. Seth was upset he couldn't have you do it for the actual shoots."

"So was I," Everett said casually as he twisted his arms, examining them.

Joy blushed. "Oh, well, I doubt that—"

"Look who I found," Seth interrupted her as he joined them again, carrying his camera.

Joy paused, her mouth open, as she stared at the most beautiful woman she'd ever seen in her life following her uncle into the atrium. Jennifer's smile was like sunshine as she hugged Katie and received a kiss on the cheek from Rill. She turned her attention to Everett, her large, dark eyes going wide.

"I didn't recognize you at first!" She walked a few steps, her attention on Everett rapt. "Oh my God, you're going to be a perfect, totally intimidating Slader."

Joy's heart sank a little when the two of them shared a grin, Everett's charm breaking through the grim disguise. "I haven't seen you since the Toronto Film Festival," Everett said.

"I know. I've been so busy with—" Jennifer's attention was fractured when she noticed Joy standing there. "Hello," she said warmly, putting out her hand. "You must be Seth's niece. He told me about you just now. I'm Jennifer."

"Hello, I'm Joy," she said pleasantly, shaking Jennifer's hand. Jennifer's countenance was open and friendly. Her blond hair was almost as legendary as Everett's. It used to be longer, but she currently wore it at shoulder length. It fell in thick, lustrous waves around her delicate face. She wore not a hint of makeup. She didn't need it. Her expressive, dark brown eyes were soft and warm. It was almost impossible not to like her on first impression.

"I'm sorry for interrupting, but I was in the area, so I thought I'd stop by while John met with some contractors at the cabin."

"We're glad you did," Katie enthused. "There's been something I wanted to ask you." She waved Jennifer toward the living room. "We'll be right back," she told the rest of them.

"Joy, can you touch up Everett's fringe?" asked Seth, who was focusing his camera on Everett.

"Sure," Joy said, dragging her gaze off the doorway where Jennifer and Katie had just disappeared. She gave Everett a quick, furtive glance as she lifted a comb to the forked black bang on his forehead. What was he thinking upon seeing his old girlfriend—his nice, gorgeous, sexy former flame? His expression was calm and unreadable as he met her eyes. But then, Everett was an extremely good actor, wasn't he?

Jennifer stayed for about an hour, chatting with them all out in the atrium, asking about the various concepts Seth was having for the film, getting some clarification from Rill about the nuances of a line in the script and catching up with Everett. Joy noticed that Seth was quietly sketching her as she talked, the actress unaware of what he was doing.

"So what's this I hear about you falling into a hole?" Everett asked Jennifer as he returned from the kitchen carrying two glasses of iced tea. Seth had removed the hair and makeup after he'd taken pictures, but Joy's tattoos remained. She thought they looked quite eye-catching beneath the simple white T-shirt he wore. Everett handed one of the glasses to Joy and sat down next to her on the sofa.

Jennifer groaned and looked embarrassed. She gave Katie an accusing, amused glance. "You told Everett, huh? Well, what can I say? I was an idiot and fell into a sinkhole not eight miles from here and had to be rescued. It happened last spring."

"What?" Joy asked, pausing in the action of taking a sip of tea.

Jennifer laughed. "It's true. Twenty feet straight down into a sinkhole."

"There are lots of them in an area down south a few miles. Old abandoned mining area. It's why you shouldn't wander too far off the forest preserve paths. Let Jennifer be your lesson," Rill said.

Jennifer shook her head ruefully. "I'm a living lesson, all right. It would have been one of the worst days of my life if John hadn't fallen into that hole with me. But John has a habit of turning the darkest moment into the brightest."

"Now it does sound interesting," Everett said, sipping his tea.

"I'll introduce you to him," Jennifer told Everett warmly. "Speaking of John, I should probably get going," she said, checking

her watch. "We're going for dinner over in Carbondale." She gave
Joy and Seth a smile. "Joy, it was wonderful to meet you. Seth, I
look forward to working with you."

"You, too, Jennifer," Joy returned with genuine warmth.

"Same here," Seth said gruffly.

"Would you walk me out?" Jennifer asked Everett pointedly.

Everett nodded and stood, following Jennifer out of the atrium.
Jennifer had made the invitation so smoothly, and Joy had been
lulled by all this talk of a man who had made Jennifer's darkest
moments bright, it took a moment for that sick, ugly feeling to
creep back into her stomach. Joy couldn't decide if the feeling was
jealousy, inadequacy or some nasty combination of both.

"Joy?" Katie called anxiously later as Joy opened the front door.

"I'm going out for a drive," Joy explained pleasantly. "You've
said the scenery by the river is so pretty, and I have my sketch pad
in the car."

"Does Everett know you're going?" Katie asked, looking a little
confused as she walked toward her with Daisy in her arms.

"No," Joy said, avoiding Katie's gaze. She had an overwhelming
urge to flee. It was just making things worse to see the concern in
Katie's eyes. "He's out at the guesthouse, showering. It'll take him
a while to remove those tattoos."

"I know. I had the feeling he wanted you to help him," Katie
said wryly. "Joy, is everything okay?"

"Yes. Of course it is," she said quickly. "Will you please tell
Everett where I went? I'll be back in a few hours."

She didn't give Katie time to respond, but turned and plunged
out the front door, the rental car keys clutched in her hand. Unfortunately, she'd left her purse in the guesthouse. She hadn't wanted
to risk retrieving it and running into Everett, so when she'd asked
Seth for the keys, she also asked for some cash in case of an un-

likely emergency. He'd given her a concerned, questioning glance as he dug for his wallet in his pocket, but hadn't interrogated her in front of Rill and Katie, which she appreciated.

A lump had formed in her throat by the time she reached the spot where Everett and she had turned off the road earlier for their jog. What was wrong with her? she thought desperately when she suddenly had to blink to see through a film of tears.

She hardly knew Everett. This was supposed to be a fun, sexy weekend. It'd been a challenge for her, a risk to do something as crazy as have a fling with a man like Everett, but she'd taken that chance. She didn't want to blow it now by getting all . . . *involved*.

She had no interest in getting her hooks into Everett, any more than she wanted to allow him to return the favor. Joy didn't expect a serious relationship. She didn't want one. He could do whatever he wanted, including spending the better part of an hour talking to Jennifer Turner in private, serious conversation—and who knew what else—before Jennifer had finally left.

Joy irritably swiped at her eyes and put on Seth's sunglasses, which were sitting on the console.

The two of them had looked quite serious, talking while standing together in the shade of the front porch, Everett's feet planted on the first step of the stairs so that their bent blond heads were closer in height. Joy hadn't spied, of course. Katie and she had walked into the kitchen with empty glasses after Everett and Jennifer had been gone for twenty or so minutes, and Katie had wondered out loud what had happened to Everett. She'd flicked back the curtain on the front door to peer outside, and Joy had been unlucky enough to see the pair of them standing there in what appeared to be intimate, intense conversation. She'd caught a fleeting image of Everett's eyes on Jennifer's face, his expression solemn. Katie had quickly released the curtain.

"Oh, they're still talking." Joy had suspected Katie's tone and smile were a little too cheery given the circumstances. Her need to flee had started to build at about that point. She'd been thankful when Everett finally came back inside and told her he planned to go and shower off his tattoos.

This way, she had a clear path to the car and temporary escape from the source of her bewildered longing.

Thirteen

Joy came to a halt at the turnoff at the base of the hill. Which way was the Ohio River? Seeing no signs, she turned left toward town.

The diner appeared to be the only open establishment in the woefully dilapidated Main Street of Vulture's Canyon. It was as if the hot, oppressive summer day had cast a spell on the tiny town, Joy thought as she parked and approached the restaurant. Maybe everyone took a siesta in the afternoon? There was seemingly little else to do around here but sleep when the sun was at its most fierce.

Bells tinkled above her head as Joy walked into the blessedly cool diner. An older, gray-haired woman stood behind the counter wearing a flowery kurta and colorful beads around her neck. The only other occupant of the restaurant—a wiry man in his thirties wearing a grimy-looking baseball hat and sitting on one of the counter stools—didn't look up from whatever he was examining in his hand.

"Hello," Joy greeted the waitress, walking up to the counter.

"Hello," the woman said in a mellow voice, closing her book. Joy had just been going to ask for directions to the river, but found herself examining the chalkboard menu with interest. In addition to traditional diner fare, there were some tempting vegan and vegetarian dishes and sandwiches. "Too bad I had such a big lunch," she said. "Your menu looks terrific. Do you get a lot of your ingredients from the local communal farm's co-op?"

"Yes," the woman said, approaching her. "One hundred percent organic, guaranteed fresh. You visiting Rill and Katie Pierce?"

The man wearing the hat looked up. Joy noticed his ears stuck out from the side of his head beneath the sides of the cap.

"Yes. How did you know?" Joy asked.

"You're a stranger. Chances are, if you're a stranger in Vulture's Canyon, you're visiting the Pierces." The woman smiled, and Joy instantly liked her. "Besides, Katie told me she was expecting guests this weekend when she was in on Friday morning."

"Do you know Katie?" the man asked her abruptly.

"Yes," Joy replied. The man set what appeared to be a toy model car on the counter.

"I'm Olive Fanatoon and this is Errol," she explained, nodding toward the man.

"I'm Joy Hightower," Joy said, shaking the woman's hand. "I've heard Katie mention you. You help her watch Daisy, don't you?"

"That's right," Olive said, smiling widely.

"I was hoping to get directions to the river. I'd like to do some sketching, and I heard from Katie the view is lovely."

"I live on the river," Errol said. He alighted from the counter stool and came toward her, his hand outstretched. At first she thought he was coming to shake her hand, but he kept his hand in a fist. Joy glanced at the woman behind the bar dubiously, but extended her hand. The man dropped a piece of metal into it.

"It's nice," Joy said after a moment of examining the model race car.

"Ferrari 150° Italia," Errol said bluntly.

"Katie's got him hooked on cars now," Olive said. "He used to just focus on model airplanes."

"Katie's uncle is Howard Hughes, the famous pilot," Errol stated.

"Not an uncle, just a distant relative," Olive said with a rehearsed air that gave Joy the impression it was a familiar correction.

Joy smiled and handed the car back to Errol. "They use that kind of car on the Formula 1 circuit."

Errol's brown eyes went wide at that. "You know about Formula 1 racing? Do you know Michael Schumacher? Sixty-eight pole positions, ninety-one Grand Prix wins, seven world championships," he said in a pressured rush. "He's Katie's and my favorite driver. Katie took Derek and me to see him drive once in St. Louis, and—"

"Errol, that's enough. Remember what we talked about. Not everyone loves cars and planes as much as you do."

Joy smiled. "You and Katie sound like very good friends."

"Katie ran me over with her car—a Maserati GranTurismo," Errol said matter-of-factly before he returned to his stool and continued to study the model.

Olive's eyes twinkled with amusement when she noticed Joy's stunned expression. "Katie accidentally hit Errol on her first night in Vulture's Canyon," she explained under her breath. "Errol had to have knee surgery. They've been friends ever since."

"I can show you the way to the river," Errol mumbled, his head lowered as he turned the car in his hands.

Olive pursed her lips, considering. "That's not a bad idea. Can Ms. Hightower sketch out on your dock, Errol?"

"Yeah, okay," Errol said.

"It's up to you," Olive said, glancing at Joy. "Errol can show you the way if you give him a ride. He walks into town every day. He's got a beautiful view off his dock. That's probably the view Katie was referring to when she mentioned the river."

Joy hesitated only for a split second. The proposal was unusual, granted, but there was something so innocent about Errol and Olive's familiar, protective attitude toward him, it didn't strike Joy as anything but a kind and well-intentioned offer.

"That'd be wonderful. If you're sure it's okay, Errol?" Joy asked.

Errol's shrug seemed to convey he'd be content either way.

"Errol, Jamie is going to come in for the dinner crowd to replace me. I'll be out to your house when she gets here," Olive said. "Here's a loaf of seven-grain bread. You can make some toast if you get hungry. And offer Ms. Hightower a glass of something cold when you get there. It'll be hot out on that dock," Olive instructed when Joy and Errol stood up to leave the diner. Errol grabbed the bread, his gaze still glued to the model car, and trailed after Joy out of the diner.

Katie glanced up from where she was sitting on the living room floor when Everett walked in.

"Where is everyone?" Everett asked, his gaze running over Rill, who was looking up something on his laptop and lazily stroking Barnyard's neck.

"Seth is sketching out in the atrium, and Joy took off about twenty minutes ago," Rill said gruffly, his attention returning to his computer screen.

"What do you mean Joy took off?" Everett asked, stunned.

Daisy gave a happy little shout from her baby swing. Katie imitated the sound, smiling, and stood up.

"I'm going to talk to Everett in the kitchen; can you watch Daisy?" Katie asked Rill.

"Yep." Rill set down his computer and lowered himself to the floor on all fours, acting like a lion on the prowl. Everett saw his niece's eyes pop wide as she stared at her dad, and then heard a giggle before he followed Katie into the kitchen.

"Where did Joy go?" he asked Katie impatiently. He'd been in such a hurry to shower and remove the tattoos that he hadn't followed Joy's careful instructions or used the solvent she'd given him, utilizing an abrasive loofah instead. All that rush and the sacrifice of a layer of skin, and she wasn't even here.

"She said something about going to the river to sketch. I told her it was a pretty view."

"Oh," Everett said, disappointment flickering through him. He'd have liked to have gone with her, but supposed he'd just have been in the way.

"Sit down for a second," Katie said, nodding at one of the kitchen island stools.

Wariness prickled through him. "Why?" he asked suspiciously.

"*Everett,*" she said, rolling her eyes.

"What's this about? Is it about Joy?" he asked cautiously, sitting on the edge of the stool.

"Yes," Katie admitted, standing with her hands on the counter.

"Well, spit it out," he demanded, concern giving his tone an edge.

"Everett, was it absolutely necessary for you to spend all that time with Jennifer?"

His mouth dropped open. He glanced toward the front door and the porch.

"Wait . . . are you telling me that Joy left because she was upset about my talking to Jennifer? Did she tell you that?" he demanded.

"No, she did not tell me that," Katie said succinctly. "She told me that everything was fine. But I—unlike you—am sensitive to what she was probably experiencing."

"Jennifer was telling me about that guy, John Corcoran, for

God's sake," he blurted out. "She's in love with him. She's crazy about him! She wants to marry him. He had some hang-ups about being blind and being able to take care of her, but they've worked through all that. But that's not the point—you know as well as I do that Jennifer and I are just friends. We broke up because we realized our relationship wasn't going to grow any further than it had."

"I know that. Joy doesn't, though."

"Well, why didn't you tell her, then?" Everett asked loudly. Daisy gave a little shriek in the distance. Katie gave him an admonishing look. "Sorry," he mumbled, contrite, but still irritated. "Why didn't you stick up for me?"

"I tried to, but Joy was too busy running out the door," Katie insisted.

"But all I did was talk to a friend."

Katie rolled her eyes. "It looked like a pretty intense talk."

He cursed under his breath.

"Everett, when are you going to wake up and acknowledge the rest of the world—you know, the majority of the planet, the people who only know about you from multi-billion-dollar movie productions and *Entertainment Premiere* and headlines on tabloids at the grocery store checkout? What do you think it's like for Joy to be asked out by Everett Hughes, and suddenly have his ex-girlfriend— one of the most stunning women in the world—show up here? How many times do you think Joy has stood in the checkout line and looked at photos of you and Jennifer cavorting on a beach and supposedly making plans for having a baby—"

"Don't you dare quote that particular pile of horseshit to me. It has nothing to do with reality, and you know it," he interrupted sharply.

"But does Joy?"

"But there's nothing between Jennifer and me. Nothing like *that*."

"Try to see things from Joy's point of view, Everett. I'm your sister. I know you and Jennifer don't consider yourself a god and goddess walking on earth, but practically the entire rest of the population of the world does."

"That's crap," he said, sick of the familiar refrain coming from Katie. "Joy isn't like that. She's very down-to-earth."

"I know she's down-to-earth. That doesn't mean she doesn't have a few insecurities, just like most people."

Everett winced. "You think she was really upset?"

"I'm sure it's nothing that can't be repaired." His gaze sharpened on his sister when she hesitated. "You seem to really like Joy, Everett."

"I do."

Katie nodded. "She's not a Hollywood player, but she's also not like one of those women from that dating agency you tried—that one that features nice, normal women that are difficult for a movie star to meet."

"*Supposedly* nice, normal women," Everett said darkly. The dating service Katie referred to was called Corner International. Its clients included the Hollywood elite and wealthy, individuals who were fed up with being surrounded by sharks of their own kind and wanted to meet the girl or boy next door. Everett knew of a few friends in the business who had liked the service and ended up marrying quite happily. Everett's experience had been less than ideal, however, and he'd ended up swearing off any kind of dating service years ago.

"Well, whatever," Katie said. "My point is, at least those women knew what they were signing up for. Joy hasn't signed up for anything."

"You don't need to remind me, Katie."

"Everett, I just mean—"

"I know what you mean," he said abruptly. He met Katie's concerned glance and added more restrainedly. "I do."

He knew she was right, but it frustrated the hell out of him nevertheless. He was a man whose job happened to hurtle him into the limelight. He loved acting, relished in perfecting his craft, savored the challenge of conquering a new role. If he'd ended up on the local stage, or as a film character actor with small, rewarding parts, he would have still been an actor. He would still have loved his job. As a matter of fact, he routinely took roles in independent, low-budget films that spurred his growth and creativity because he *did* love acting so much. It just so happened that his career trajectory had hurtled him into the living rooms and consciousness of millions of people. He couldn't say he regretted the opportunities fame had provided him, because that would be a lie. But he identified most with acting, not being a movie star. And there were times—like right now—he would have gladly chucked the whole thing if it meant being seen clearly by a woman like Joy.

"Everett?" Katie called to him when he shoved back the stool.

"I'll be back in a little while," he said before he walked out the front door.

Joy's hand moved rapidly over the page. The view from Errol's dock was beautiful. The trees on the riverbank behind her cast her in shadow, while the sun shone full-out on the opposite shore. She'd never seen so many shades of green and gold. She wished she had her paints, although the heat would have given her poor consistency.

She'd calmed quite a bit since settling down in the rickety lawn chair, surrounded by the sylvan glory of the forest and the fast-flowing, wide river. Having a pencil or a paintbrush in her hand always went a long way to grounding her. She'd been being ridiculous by allowing herself to become upset because Everett had spent all that time talking to Jennifer.

Errol lived in a tiny gray-shingled house nestled amongst the river-bottom trees. The house needed some repairs, but the view made up for its shabbiness. She paused in her sketching, using her forearm to blot the perspiration accumulating on her upper lip before she took a sip of ice water. Errol had dutifully supplied the cold beverage when they arrived before he'd sat down in his kitchen and fixed his entire attention on a black and white rerun of *McHale's Navy*.

It was shady where she sat, but the humidity and heat were still quite bad. In the distance, she heard a car door slam, and looked around distractedly. She did a double take when she saw Everett striding down the path.

"Hi," she said, sounding breathless at the unexpected sight of him. She set down the glass of water on the dock and started to stand.

"Don't let me interrupt you," he murmured, his gaze on her sketchbook. He looked out at the river. She studied his classic profile from beneath her lashes. He wore a dark green T-shirt and a pair of cargo shorts that showed off his muscular, well-shaped calves. His wavy hair looked like it was still damp in the back from his shower. She was still getting used to him clean shaven. She'd thought she was partial to his goatee and sexy whiskers, but of course, with his face, Everett could pull off just about any look.

"They came off okay," she said, nodding at his arm, referring to the tattoos.

"With a little work."

An uncomfortable feeling settled on her. Everett seemed strained . . . subdued. Was he angry?

"I hope you don't mind that I came out to sketch," she said, setting down her pencil on the dock and closing her sketch pad.

"Of course not," he said quietly. "I'd mind if you were upset for any reason, though."

"I'm not upset."

He peered at her through narrowed eyelids. "I'm not interested romantically in Jennifer Turner."

She swallowed thickly and studied her bare thighs. "It wouldn't be any of my business if you were, Everett."

She looked up when he muttered a restrained, but nevertheless blistering, curse. She was once again staring at his profile.

"I just meant . . ."

"What? What did you just mean?" he demanded when she faded off, his eyes blazing.

"We hardly know each other. I know you have a life that has absolutely nothing to do with me," she explained, her words coming fast now that she'd gotten started. "I know you have a life that I probably couldn't even comprehend, for that matter."

"It's not that hard to comprehend," he said, his manner just as pressured. "I'm a guy; you're a girl; we're both straight. I like you. I like you a lot. I haven't been this interested in a woman for . . . for . . . *ever*. If you don't feel the same way, fine, but at least give me the courtesy of not repeatedly shoving it in my face how we hardly know each other. It's like you're throwing up the Great Wall of China between us every time you say that."

Her mouth fell open in amazement at his intensity. He rolled his eyes in what appeared to be exasperation.

"Every time you say you hardly know me, it frustrates the hell out of me," he said.

"But we've only been out a few times," she said, still stunned by what he'd said. *I haven't been this interested in a woman for . . . for . . . ever.* "We talked on the phone for hours, true, and we've had sex," she finished under her breath.

"How well you know someone isn't always measured by a clock or a calendar . . . or the number of times you've done it, for that matter."

"I know that," she said, anger rising in her.

"So while you might concede that to be true in some cases, you can't accept it with me. Because you can't trust what you're feeling because of all the movie-star shit. You believe I have some kind of standards and values that are completely foreign in comparison to yours. You actually think that I live in some kind of world where I would ask you here for a getaway because I'm crazy to spend time with you, but have no problem whatsoever in going off to flirt with another woman right in front of your face."

"I never said that."

"No, but you were thinking it," he bit out, his words and glance striking her like a fiery whip.

She started to protest heatedly, but then caught herself. If she were being honest, she'd have to admit that what he'd said was true. Her caution when it came to Everett went beyond the whole enigma of fame, however.

"I just think it can't be . . . accurate," she said after a pregnant pause.

"What can't be accurate?"

"The way I feel about you."

She watched the fast-flowing, gray river in the tense silence that followed.

"Why not?" he eventually asked.

She felt her courage slithering away like a cowardly snake. "It's an infatuation. It's . . . sexual." When he didn't respond, she glanced up at him anxiously.

A rigid, fierce expression had come over his face. "A sexual infatuation," he repeated, his tone oddly flat. "That's what you think is going on here?"

She didn't know what to say. It was hard to look straight into his eyes and be dishonest.

It was harder to meet his stare and tell the truth.

"I don't know, Everett," she finally said lamely.

He leaned down and took her hand in his, pulling her into a standing position. She set her sketch pad on the seat of the lawn chair before she faced him. She had to suppress an urge to step back. Forget the tousled blond hair and a face that had graced thousands of glossy magazine covers; Everett was just a man in that moment . . . an intimidating, elemental, virile man. He took her into his arms, his presence striking her like a precise, focused flame—a determined blowtorch.

That was Everett.

"You know what they say," he said softly, bending his neck until his face was just inches from hers. His body felt hard and unwavering next to her own. His scent filtered into her nose: clean male skin, spices . . . sex.

"About what?" she wondered, dazed.

"About the best way to get over a sexual infatuation. Just give in to it. Hard. It's bound to burn itself out in the end."

He bent and picked up her pencils and sketchbook. He took her hand and led her off the dock.

Joy followed him, nervousness and anticipation warring for room in her consciousness. She'd been the one to goad him, even if she'd done so unintentionally. She'd been the one to ignite that fierce blaze in Everett's eyes.

Now there was nothing left but to see if she could survive the heat unscathed.

Fourteen

It was almost five o'clock by the time they reached the guest-house, but the sun still felt intense. The interior of the little house was dim and cool. Joy tried to get a full inhale of the chilled air when they entered and Everett shut the door behind them, but her lungs didn't seem to be working adequately. She was breathless. She glanced back at him, her nervousness only amplifying when she saw him locking the door. She experienced an overwhelming urge to run, but stilled herself with effort. It wasn't as if they'd never had sex before.

She lifted her chin and stared at him with what she hoped was a calm expression when he turned and leaned against the door.

"What am I going to do with you, Joy?"

She bristled and crossed her arms beneath her breasts, ignoring the shiver caused by his quiet, husky question. "I suppose you're suggesting it's a challenge to put up with me?"

"No," he said, pushing himself off the door and stalking toward her. "I was just asking myself what I planned to do to you."

Her heart stalled and then resumed beating in double time. She
looked up at him, her arms still crossed beneath her breasts, when
he came within inches of her. He put out his arm in a silent, ironic
invitation and challenge. Joy turned, keeping her gaze defiantly
latched to his, and walked ahead of him into the bedroom.

She stood by the edge of the bed, watching him warily as he
entered behind her.

"I'd like to tie you up again," he said.

She flinched slightly—not in hurt or fear, but in a quick, surprising shock of excitement.

"Take off your clothes," Everett said.

For a few seconds, she didn't move. She wasn't being defiant;
she was just temporarily unable to interpret the flood of feeling she
experienced at that moment, the bewildering urge to surrender herself to a surging, unnameable need.

The silence seemed to swell against her eardrums as she began
to undress. Finally, she stood before him, naked. It was much more
difficult to meet his stare this time, but she did. He looked his fill
at her, his expression unreadable. After a moment, he stepped toward the bed and whipped back the comforter.

"Lie down please," he said.

The sheets felt cool and soft next to her naked skin.

"No, not like that. On your belly," Everett said.

Her gaze shot up to his. He returned her stare calmly. Wondering if she was completely losing her mind, Joy slowly lay facedown
on the mattress. She heard a drawer opening and closing through
the drum of her heartbeat, but couldn't see what he was doing with
her cheek pressed against the sheets. A moment later, she knew he'd
been retrieving the cuffs he'd used on her the previous night. Neither of them spoke as he restrained her ankles and wrists to the
bed. When he'd finished, he drew the comforter over her bare legs,
leaving everything from her ass up bare. Joy appreciated the gesture; it was chilly in the air-conditioned room.

Everett sat on the mattress next to her and smoothed back her hair. She watched him through one wide eye as he held up a package and began to open it.

"These are disposable finger vibrators. They've never been used," he said quietly.

"What . . . what do you mean?" she asked, confused.

"Don't you own a vibrator?" he asked, withdrawing a couple blue, two-inch-long tubes with little nubs along the surface from the package.

"No," she said honestly. She'd considered buying one a couple years back, but had never gotten around to it. She studied the little objects with interest. The package Everett had opened contained two of the tubular objects, but he opened another one. He pushed a button and one of them began to vibrate subtly. Much to her amazement, he slipped the little device over his forefinger, where it buzzed next to his fingertip. He did the same thing with the remaining devices over three other fingers.

He was going to touch her with those blue, vibrating fingertips, Joy realized in growing excitement. Her pussy started to buzz in tandem with the little devices.

Everett gave her an assessing glance.

"I bought these specially for you. They're unique. Each one heats up and gets nice and warm in addition to vibrating. I've noticed how sensitive your body is. I'm going to find all your sweet spots," he said, as though he were clarifying a simple mission.

And with that, he began. He brushed the surface of one of the vibrators against the shell of her ear. The tiny, soft silicone nubbins caused a tingling sensation to course down her neck. She instinctively turned her face into the mattress, hiding herself—and exposing more of herself to his sensual assault. He continued to stimulate her ear softly even as he ran both vibrating and firm, warm, flesh fingertips over her neck, as if he wanted to capture the shivers he was causing. He experimented with her other ear and the tender skin behind it. The tiny hairs on her neck stood on end as he tickled them almost playfully. Joy'd had no idea the area was so sensitive. Prickly spikes of sensation tore through her, tightening her nipples, belly and buttocks.

He detailed the slope of both of her shoulders at once, then returned to the top of her spine, stimulating her teasingly before he pressed with all the vibrators at once against the first several inches of her backbone.

"Oh," she whimpered into the sheets, feeling her flesh melt beneath his touch. The vibrators had started to warm. He lifted one hand, leaving two of the vibrators at her neck, and placed the other two at the base of her tailbone. One finger massaged the skin just above her ass while the other pressed between the top of her buttocks.

Joy gasped as pleasure zipped down her spine and then mellowed to a sweet burn. Her buttocks clenched tight against the tingling pleasure at her anus and all along her perineum, ending in a sizzle at her sex. He kept the vibrators at the incendiary spot at the base of her spine and ran the others all along the length of her backbone. Goose bumps popped out all over her skin.

She heard Everett grunt in approval.

The vibrating fingertips made a study of her shoulder blades. He spent considerable time running them over the sides of her ribs— so much so, in fact, that Joy decided they were instruments of torture. He charted out every little nook and cranny of sensitive skin between her ribs, until Joy let out a frustrated, muffled moan into the mattress.

"You've got more nerves along your sides than most people do in their whole bodies," she heard Everett observe. "I love the curve of your hip," he said a moment later as he trailed it. She whimpered when he ran flesh fingertips and the vibrators over the skin just above her ass. She yelped when he put two fingers between the crack of her ass again and tapped her tailbone in an erotic rhythm.

"Everett, stop it," she said shakily. Over the past twenty minutes of his teasing and massaging her flesh, she'd made a patch of the sheet beneath her mouth damp with the vapor from her panting and perspiration from her upper lip. She pressed her cheek against the warm spot and gritted her teeth together in deprivation when he did what she'd asked.

"You don't like it?"

"No, I do," she said in a strangled voice. Her pussy was wet and spread. She couldn't stand him touching other places when she was so ravenous to feel his caresses between her thighs. She also loved his sensual exploration. Adored it. "I just want . . . need . . ."

"What?"

"To come," she whispered between pants for air.

"Let it build," he replied.

If it built any further, Joy thought, she was going to burst. He deliberately folded back the comforter and ran his fingertips at the very tops of her thighs, just beneath the curves of her ass. She could tell by the smooth glide of the vibrators over her flesh that a coat of sweat had gathered there.

She let out a groan when the vibrators came less than an inch from the wet tissues of her pussy.

"Shh," he whispered gruffly at the same time he used one hand to explore the back of her right thigh. He ran the fingertips of his other hand between her buttocks in a brushing caress that hardly calmed her. He tickled and stroked the sensitive skin behind her knee and repeated the quick, elusive caress down the crack between her buttocks. She tightened her ass muscles and ground her pussy against the mattress.

"Okay, okay," he said soothingly.

She felt the mattress shift around her and thought he must have come down on his hands and knees over her. She saw him reach above her. Joy jerked her chin up, desperate for information about what he was doing. The way she was restrained, her head was a foot below the bedside table. She went still when she saw what he grabbed. It was a bottle of lubricant.

She opened her mouth to protest. It wasn't as if she was completely unfamiliar with anal play, but she'd never experienced it before while she was lying in a prone position, restrained and utterly, completely vulnerable. Her words stalled in her throat when she heard the click of the flip top on the lubricant bottle. Her vagina clenched tight in arousal.

"Everett," she said. "I don't think—"

"Don't think," he said starkly. "Just feel."

"But—"

"It's just sex, Joy," he said. "Isn't that what you told me on the dock?"

She panted through lips that felt swollen from sustained arousal. He didn't wait for her answer, but pressed one of the now lubricated vibrators to her anus, where it buzzed warmly.

"Push back against it," he said quietly.

Joy did, gasping when the silicone sheath penetrated her. She just stared blankly at the opened door to the bedroom, seeing nothing, just feeling the erotic vibrations pulse in her anus, enlivening nerves she didn't even know she possessed. He'd removed the vibrator from his finger, she realized, and was pushing the little device about an inch into her anus.

"How's that feel?" he asked, his voice sounding subdued and rough.

"I . . . I . . . good," she admitted, unable to say anything but the truth, she was so overwhelmed.

"Good," he grunted. "You have an amazing ass," he said at the same time he cupped one of her cheeks, his fingertips sliding toward her sex.

"Oh, no," she exclaimed loudly when he slid one of the vibrators into her spread pussy.

"Oh, yeah," he refuted thickly at the same moment that he pressed one of his vibrating fingertips against her clit. Joy knew it was just pleasantly warm, but to her it felt like being touched by a red-hot poker. For a few seconds, she just keened desperately while nerves sizzled in her anus, sex and clitoris, sending jolts of sensation up her spine. She couldn't stop the tsunami of sensation when it rolled over her. She fisted the straps that restrained her, her fingernails biting into her palms, and detonated.

Her lungs heaved for air in the aftermath. She wasn't sure when Everett had removed those instruments of agonizing pleasure, but as she struggled for air, she became aware of him touching her with naked fingers. He stroked her from hip to waist, his large, open hand seeming to shout a message of how much power he held over her, a scream inside her head that if he did hold the reins over her frantically pounding heart, it was Joy's own fault for giving him that power . . .

. . . her own fault for being helpless to halt her surrender to his touch.

"You're so beautiful," she heard him murmur as his open hand caressed the side of her body and she quivered like a live wire. "You shine so brightly in my eyes."

She clamped her eyes shut and felt a burn behind the lids.

"Say it's just sex now, Joy."

Anger flickered into the swirl of her satiation.

Was it anger? Or was it fear?

"Your silence is a dare. Don't dare me," he said, his voice deceptively soft.

She clenched her eyes shut tighter. Her anguish had lowered to her throat, tightening it. It was like a hand squeezed it, halting the brewing volcano of emotion in her chest. She felt as if his touch were putting her in direct contact with life—with joy and laughter and light and passion unlike anything she'd ever known or dreamt.

She *hated* him for making her feel this much.

She turned her face into the mattress, hiding her anguished longing.

The mattress shifted beneath her as Everett moved. She held her breath, hearing the subtle sounds of him disrobing—the rustle of fabric, the metallic sound of the buttons on his fly being tugged through the holes. The mattress sank again as he came back onto the bed.

"I'm going to fuck you here," he said, gently palming her ass, his fingertips just beneath the cheeks, the heel of his palm just below her tailbone. She held her breath, waiting for his next gruffly spoken words like her life depended on them. "I know how raw that is. I know how intimate it is—at least it will be for me, Joy. I want you to know that. If you don't want it, just say the word right now."

She inhaled raggedly.

"Joy?" he asked, concern edging his tone. "Say something if you want me to stop."

She bit her lip. She couldn't swallow. Nothing would go down. No words could come out the other direction. It shocked her to the core, to realize her need was bigger than her fear. His hand cradled the back of her head. Funny, how perfectly it fit his palm. She turned her chin and looked up at him reluctantly with one eye. He was on his hands and knees over her, his gaze hot but compassionate.

"Go on," she whispered, and she herself didn't know if it was a plea or a defiant dare.

His expression hardened. He loosened her wrist restraints, giving her some slack, and grabbed two of the unused pillows. She said nothing when he propped them beneath her hips, raising her ass. She waited for several agonizing seconds. Nothing happened. Then he was spreading one ass cheek and pressing something flexible but hard next to her anus. It wasn't warm like the little finger vibrators, but cool and slippery. He applied pressure and it slid into her body. She gasped softly and pressed her forehead into the mattress.

"Okay?" he asked, pushing the dildo back into her ass when her muscles resisted the invasion and expelled it.

"Yes," she said quickly.

"Have you done this before?" he asked.

It was on the edge of her tongue to tell him it was none of his business—why must she reveal such private things when he was doing something so personal to her? She didn't want to make this whole ordeal bigger than it deserved to be, though.

"What you're doing now—yes. Once," she managed. He was pushing the dildo deeper now. "Not . . . not with a man, though. I mean, it was with a man, but—"

"Not with a man's cock," he finished for her, his voice sounding rough, edgy.

"Yes. Is that what you're going to do?"

"Yes." He withdrew the slippery dildo, and her eyes sprang wide. Apparently, he meant *yes* as in *yes, right now*. He shifted again behind her. The anticipation of not knowing what he was doing was killing her. She tried to peer over her shoulder, but only caught a glimpse of his right arm, leg and a bit of his golden torso as he knelt between her thighs. He edged forward on his knees. She felt his lower thighs nudge her legs and spread them a tad wider. The cool air licked and tickled her wet, warm outer sex.

"Oh," she mumbled, dropping her forehead back to the bed. He'd just spread her buttocks and pressed the tapered head of his cock against her asshole. It was considerably larger than the dildo.

"I'm going to go slowly. Just tell me if the pressure is too much."

She nodded.

"Press back against me," Everett said tightly.

She did, groaning when his cock slid into her ass. It felt odd. Joy wasn't sure she liked it, but it didn't hurt as much as she'd thought it would.

"Press again."

She tightened her muscles and pushed up on his cock. He slid farther into her, and this time, sharp pain did spike through her.

"Ouch," she said before she could stop herself. He paused, and the pain almost immediately faded. She felt his cock throb in that overly sensitive channel. So strange to have something so vibrant there, so teeming with life. Suddenly, the nerves began to burn. Her clit pinched in excitement. What Everett was doing to her struck her as not only highly intimate, but lewd. Raunchy.

Dirty.

She pushed up on his cock. He was the one to groan loudly this time.

"Aw, God, you're so tight. Your ass is on fire," he muttered. For the first time, he thrust. She felt his balls and pelvis press against her ass. She hissed and he gave a low, animalistic growl that made her a little crazy. He was completely submersed in her. He grasped her hips, his thumbs sinking into the soft flesh of her buttocks, and began to fuck her.

Joy bit her bottom lip to prevent herself from crying out. There was pleasure in it, but she couldn't compare it to vaginal sex. It was a dark, primitive, elemental thing. Her arousal mounted with every downstroke, her discomfort fading. Everett's grunts and growls of pleasure rang in her ears. He'd fucked her harder before—she had the impression he was being careful of her—but even so, she also had the impression he'd abandoned himself to the rich eroticism of the moment.

As he took his pleasure, the burn in her clit grew, spreading to her belly and making her nipples prickle with arousal. The soles of her feet grew hot, as if the nerves Everett agitated with his plunging cock were somehow connected to them. She moaned feverishly, writhing slightly on the mattress, trying to get friction on her aching nipples and clit. Everett grunted gutturally and gave her a slap on the bottom.

"Don't wiggle around," he said in a strained tone. "Does this feel good? Do you want to come?"

"Yes," she moaned, her voice sounding muffled since her forehead was pressed to the mattress. He withdrew his cock and thrust it back into her, his pelvis striking her ass with a whapping sound. She cried out. He continued to fuck her with small, controlled, rapid strokes.

"You like having your ass fucked," he said as he flexed his hips in rapid, firm movements.

"Yes," she admitted, gritting her teeth. The pressure was both nearly unbearable and delicious at once. She twisted her torso slightly, rubbing her nipples against the sheets, desperate.

"It's all right," he muttered. "I've got you."

He paused, his cock high and throbbing in her ass. She felt him work his hand between her hip and the pillow. Then he was rubbing her clit in that masterful, Everett way, and she was keening and bucking her hips against his spearing cock. He gave a wild growl and began to pump his hips in short, hard movements, fucking her even as he was making her come.

"Oh, God," she cried as orgasm shuddered through her. She ground down against his hand and then bobbed her ass, stroking him, lost in a crazed blur of pounding pleasure and release. After a moment, he firmed his hold on her ass and began to fuck her with long, thorough strokes, holding nothing back, slamming into her again and again. Joy screamed and gripped the wrist restraints like she was flailing for her survival. Her brain seemed to short-circuit. She couldn't hold on to reason, or fear, or anxiety. Instead, she hung on to the vibrant energy pulsing and pounding in her flesh. It was the only thing that was real.

The only thing that mattered.

* * *

Afterward, Everett released her from the restraints and took her hand. Joy followed him into the bathroom, where he turned on the shower. This time, she entered the large stall with him, all of her awkwardness and discomfort about doing the same thing the previous night having vanished. They didn't speak, but they didn't need to. Everett's bluish green eyes gleamed with emotion as he gently washed her body, taking his time. While he was busy lathering her belly, Joy slipped her hand into his. He looked up, moisture beading on his lips and brow. She took the soap from him, and he returned her small smile.

She smoothed the lather over dense muscle and soft skin, wondering at his beauty, the differences between her body and his own. Men really were a different race—not just a different sex. How could his biceps be so steely, his chest so wide, the oblique muscles like a plate of ridged armor?

She recalled how Everett had been so lackadaisical about shaving, seeming to consider his appearance almost as a tool of his trade, nothing more, nothing less. He took care of his body as a carpenter might keep his tools well maintained. As Joy washed him, however, she sensed the nerves just beneath the surface, felt the patches of skin that sent ripples of pleasure through him, knew on some deep level that her touch moved *him*—Everett, the man beneath the body and face of a careless god.

Is that what he'd been trying to tell her all this time? That she held this power over him, and that it wasn't a common, everyday thing?

She looked up at him, awe tingeing her expression. He watched her with a tight focus, and then leaned down, covering her mouth with his. Joy stood there beneath the steaming, jetting water, surrounded by all his heat and hardness, and experienced his kiss like an affirmation . . .

. . . a benediction.

The bedroom felt blessedly cool when they walked back into it.

They lay down on the bed, both of them on their sides, her back to his front. Everett spooned her and stroked her body with long, languorous caresses. Desire mingled with drowsy comfort. There was no moment of clear delineation between cuddling and making love.

When he lifted her leg and entered her, Joy closed her eyes, inundated with the sweet sublimity of the moment.

"That's my cell phone. It's probably Katie, wondering if we're coming for supper."

She opened her eyes. Much to her surprise, she'd drifted into a warm cocoon of sleep after they'd finished making love. Everett stroked her hip. She turned and looked at him. His smile made something flutter in her chest.

"Did you fall asleep?"

"Yes."

His smile faded as his gaze ran over her face. "You're tired. I'll call Katie and tell her not to expect us. I'd rather stay here with you anyway."

"No," Joy said, swiping her hand over her face as if she could remove the cobwebby tendrils of sleepiness that draped her consciousness. "Seth will worry about me. More than he probably already is, I mean. He seemed concerned when I left the house so abruptly earlier."

"I'm sorry again about that."

She blinked and brought him into focus. It seemed like weeks ago instead of hours that she'd grown so discombobulated by Everett's talking to Jennifer for so long.

"No," she said softly. She cupped his jaw and stroked his newly shaven chin. "I'm the one who's sorry. I can't even imagine all the stunning women you interact with on your job, day in and day out."

He grunted. "It couldn't have helped that you probably were aware that I'd dated Jennifer before. You knew that?"

She nodded.

He sighed and sprawled back on the pillows. Joy turned on her other side to face him. "Jennifer's one in a million when it comes to the Hollywood crowd. She's genuinely a nice lady—a class act." Joy stilled. He met her stare. "But she and I both knew our relationship was doomed to go only so far. That's just the kind of thing you know in your bones. It was sad to break things off with her, but I know it was the right thing to do. Now I know it for a fact. So does she," Everett murmured. "She's met the love of her life—a guy by the name of John Corcoran. That's what she was telling me about on the front porch this afternoon."

"Oh. I see," Joy said, glancing away abashedly.

"Don't be embarrassed," Everett murmured, stroking her arm. He really could read her mind. "I'd rather inspire a little jealousy than nothing at all. Are you sure you want to go up to the big house for dinner?"

Joy nodded earnestly. She really wanted to make sure Seth knew she was all right after she'd behaved so erratically earlier.

"Okay," Everett said, popping up out of bed. She blinked heavy eyelids and smiled.

"Do you have to be quite so energetic?" she asked, moving much more slowly.

He hesitated at the side of the bed. "You really are tired. Let's skip it."

"No," she said resolutely, willing her fatigue to fade. She stood, letting the sheet slip off her nude body. "I want to go."

Fifteen

Katie and Rill outdid themselves for dinner. Katie prepared several salads from fresh ingredients she'd purchased at the Vulture's Canyon communal farm and co-op, and Rill made juicy, flavorful ribs on the grill. Everett could hardly keep his eyes off Joy for the entire meal, so much so that Katie, who was sitting on his right, kept having to bump the dishes she was passing against his arm to get his attention.

He'd sensed the shift earlier in Joy, felt her rigid defenses soften and bend during their tumultuous, challenging lovemaking, and later, during their quiet, soulful communion. Her face had always struck him as sublime—peaceful, mysterious, achingly lovely. Tonight, however, she looked even more compelling to him. Her lips and cheeks were flushed. A soft sort of luminosity seemed to cling to her.

As dinner and energetic conversation drew to a close, however, and Everett noticed how little she'd actually eaten off her plate, he started to wonder if her enigmatic glow wasn't more from her being unwell versus being the result of any blossoming attachment to him.

Daisy started to get fussy, so Rill took her for a little stroll. Seth stood to help Katie clear. Everett and Joy were the only ones left at the table.

"Are you all right?" he asked her quietly.

"Yes," she said, giving him a brilliant smile. Her striking, large eyes looked glassy, even though she'd barely drunk half a glass of wine with dinner. Everett's gaze dropped to her mostly filled plate. She noticed. "I just don't have an appetite, for some reason."

"I think we should go," he said, wiping his mouth off with his napkin. "You might be coming down with something."

"Everett." He met her stare. She gave him a warm, amused look that felt somehow personal to him, familiar and fond. "I'm fine," she said succinctly.

"If you say so," he replied doubtfully.

"I do."

They all went onto the front porch after the dishes were in the dishwasher, each of them sipping lemonade and observing night's silent creep into the forest. The tree frogs' cacophony slowly muted to a low, lulling buzz.

"It's nice, seeing all those stars," Seth said quietly as he rocked back and forth contentedly in a chaise lounge. "Reminds me of where I grew up."

"Where was that?" Rill asked in a mellow tone. Daisy had fallen asleep in his arms, and so everyone's voice had grown hushed.

"Albuquerque. The Isleta Indian reservation."

"How many brothers and sisters do you have, Seth?" Katie asked.

"Just Joy's dad, Jake," Seth said shortly.

"He must be older than you. You and Joy aren't that far apart in age, are you?" Everett asked.

"Jake's older, by quite a bit. Not that you'd ever guess it." Everett tightened his hand around Joy's when he heard the subtle hint of bitterness in Seth's voice.

"Where does your father live?" Katie asked Joy.

"He has a mailbox in Italy, but he travels all over Europe. He manages the European Formula 1 racing team," Joy replied.

"Oh my gosh, did you tell Errol that?" Katie asked, wide-eyed.

Joy shook her head.

"If you do, you will have an adoring friend for life," Katie assured her.

Joy laughed. "He's a very sweet man, Errol," Joy said.

"He's so comfortable in his own skin," Katie mused, staring out into the dark night. "More so than anyone I know. Besides Everett."

"Where'd that come from?" Everett mumbled, scowling.

Rill chuckled. Everett glanced at Joy and saw her looking at him with a knowing smile. Out of the corner of his eye, he noticed Seth watching his niece.

After a while, Rill and Katie went inside to put Daisy to bed. Joy collected their glasses and went inside to clean them. Barnyard must have had enough of the humid night, because he trotted after Joy. Seth watched the front door close behind the basset hound's waddling rear and turned to address Everett.

"Joy told me that you visited her classroom earlier in the week."

"Yeah, I did."

"Did she seem to like it? The new job?" Seth asked.

Everett nodded. "Yeah. I actually went into class for a while, saw her work. The kids really like her . . . respect her. She's very comfortable teaching."

Seth nodded, seeming to consider.

"Are you worried about her moving to Chicago?" Everett asked after a pause.

"A little. She doesn't know anyone there."

"I met two of her friends—the Weismans. They're a couple. Joy teaches with them."

Seth gave a doubtful grunt. He opened his mouth, closed it again, and then said abruptly, "I'm going to ask her to be a partner in Hightower Special Effects."

"You are?" Everett asked, leaning forward. "Do you think she'll accept?"

"I don't know. Joy's a law unto herself. To call her independent is an understatement."

"Yeah. I've noticed," Everett said dryly.

Seth speared him with his stare. "You're not just stringing her along, are you," he stated more than asked.

"No. I'm not. Joy is . . . special."

Seth turned his gaze back to the black night, his profile unreadable.

"I'm glad to hear you think so. Because Joy isn't weak, by any means. But she's vulnerable. She didn't just watch her mother go through five years of hell; Joy walked with her. Every step of the way. And then her father—my stupid-ass brother—abandoned both Alice and Joy when they needed him most." He paused. Everett sat there, trying to absorb the idea of a teenage girl enduring all of that grief and pain and fear. Not any girl—*Joy*—the stunning, gifted woman he strongly suspected he was falling in love with.

"If you were to hurt her in any way, I wouldn't take it lightly," Seth said starkly.

Everett arched his eyebrows at the subtle challenge. He wasn't offended. Not in the slightest.

"I can understand that. I wouldn't take it lightly, either. I don't take *Joy* lightly. Just the opposite, in fact," Everett replied evenly.

Seth and he settled into a silence that wasn't companionable, necessarily, but comfortable. They'd both had their say, and they both knew it.

* * *

Joy was in the process of drying off the glasses they'd used for lemonade and putting them into the cabinet when Katie walked into the kitchen.

"You don't have to do that, Joy. You're a guest," Katie protested.

"I'm glad to have something to do. It makes me feel like I'm earning my stay. Is Daisy all tucked in?"

"Snug as a bug. For a few hours, anyway," Katie said, drying off the clean lemonade pitcher. "Are you having a nice time? With Everett, I mean?"

"Oh, yes," Joy replied, shutting the cabinet. She carefully folded the dish towel and set it on the counter. "He's . . . very unique, isn't he?"

"I can't tell if you're being sarcastic or polite," Katie said with wry amusement.

"No, I mean it in the best kind of way," Joy said in a burst of honesty. "I've never met anyone like him."

Katie smiled and tossed her dish towel on the counter. "He's one of a kind, that's for sure. Mom jokes that light poured out of her womb before Everett popped his head into the world."

Joy laughed. "Too funny. But you know, I can see what she means." She made a face. "Was it hard for you? Being his little sister?"

"You mean always walking around in the shadow of his brilliance?"

"I think you're pretty brilliant yourself," Joy said quietly. "I just meant—"

"I know what you meant. And the fact of the matter is, if I didn't adore Everett so much, if he weren't genuinely one of the most awesome people I'd ever met, I would have had an inferiority complex the size of Mount Everest. Everett has never been secretive about his own vulnerabilities, though. It helps to know he bleeds just like we all do."

"Maybe I'm a poor observer of character, but I couldn't begin to guess what Everett's vulnerabilities are. It's like you said out there on the porch—he doesn't seem to know how to feel awkward or question himself."

Katie gave her a quick, assessing glance before she opened a cabinet and placed the pitcher inside.

"You may not have recognized it yet about him, but Everett is all about family and close friends. He'd do anything for Mom and Dad. He would—and has—dropped everything on a dime and flown to my side when I needed him. He'd open a vein for Rill or Daisy."

"That's wonderful," Joy murmured. She'd already guessed that about Everett, but hearing his sister say it brought it home.

"It is wonderful," Katie agreed. "The thing of it is, though, Everett worries he'll never have that. Not for himself."

"You mean his own family?"

Katie nodded.

"But . . . surely he's had his pick of available women."

"Of course. Unfortunately, he hasn't found the one he wants to spend his life with. He never has said it in so many words, but I think he sort of worries he's . . . cursed in that department."

"What?" Joy asked, confused.

"Not cursed, exactly. But he's very aware of his blessings. Never think otherwise. He doesn't take for granted his influence or his money or his luck. He's incredibly charitable with his time and his money. He knows he won some kind of colossal cosmic lottery."

"But . . ." Joy said slowly, sensing there was more.

"The only thing that hasn't come to him easily is love, partnership . . . a family," Katie said quietly, leaning her hip against the counter.

Joy frowned. "It's got to be so hard for him. He probably questions other people's motives all the time, wonders if they're just using him."

Katie shook her head. "That's not the problem. Everett has an instinct for users. No, I think he's just worried fate gave him so much, that it'd be *too* much for him to find love."

"You mean like it'd be unfair in a karmic sense?"

"Yeah."

"He envies you. I see the way he looks at you and Rill and Daisy sometimes," Joy said quietly.

"I see the way he looks at you."

Joy looked up quickly. Katie's expression was unusually somber. Was it worry she saw etched on Everett's sister's face? She swallowed. Her throat felt tight.

"I . . . I don't know what's happening," she admitted to Katie in a burst of honesty.

"It's pretty clear to me. Everett's falling in love with you," Katie said in a quiet, matter-of-fact tone.

Joy put her hand over her heart.

"Joy? Are you all right?" Katie asked after a moment.

"Yes. I'm fine, I just—"

"Maybe you'd better sit down," she heard Katie say. Joy sat dazedly in the chair Katie pulled out from the oak table. Had that sudden pain and tightness in her chest been the result of Katie telling Joy that Everett was falling in love with her? It must have been. But it'd felt so sharp. So real.

"Everett, Seth," she heard Katie call.

She blinked and looked up as Everett and Seth trooped into the kitchen, both of them seeming to tower over her. She felt as if she were seeing them through a heat haze.

"There's something wrong," Katie said. "Joy's ill."

"No, I'm not," Joy muttered, even as she blinked to try to bring Everett into focus when he stepped in front of her. He touched her forehead.

"She has a fever," he said. "Katie? Do you have a thermometer?"

"I should take her to the doctor," Seth said.

"No," Joy said heatedly, standing. "I'm fine."

"I'll get the thermometer," Katie said, eyeing Joy worriedly.

Joy met Seth's gaze and noticed a flicker of fear in his dark eyes. Her heart started pounding uncomfortably in her chest, almost as if it were struggling to do its task.

"The kids in my class have been passing around a bug," Joy said. "I probably got it. That's all." She looked at Everett. "We should go out to the guesthouse. I wouldn't want Daisy to catch anything."

"I'm going to take you to the hospital," Seth declared.

"She probably just needs some Tylenol and some R & R," Everett said, watching her with concern etched on his features.

"Here's the thermometer," Katie said, bustling into the kitchen, Rill on her heels. "Sit down, Joy."

Joy felt extremely foolish and vulnerable with four people—three of whom were well over six feet tall—staring down at her while Katie took her temperature using the temporal artery thermometer.

"One hundred and one, almost a hundred and two," Katie said a moment later.

"If you give me the directions to the closest hospital, I'll take her now," Seth said, his tone brooking no argument.

Joy sat there, feeling miserable. She didn't want to make such a fuss, but perhaps Seth was right. Her heart was back to throbbing uncomfortably. Joy suspected it was purely an anxious response. Everett was studying her face closely.

"I'll drive both of you over to Prairie Lakes," he said. He glanced at Rill for confirmation. "That's the closest facility with an emergency room, right?"

"Well, I don't know if I'd call it an emergency room, exactly. It's a pretty tiny hospital. Most serious cases go to Carbondale or St.

Louis. But they do have a twenty-four-hour doctor on call. Joy will be seen."

"Okay. Let's go then," Everett said, taking Joy's hand.

Joy despised the smell of hospitals. She'd had no idea until she was treated for her own cancer how much it had been grafted into her brain during her teenage years—the smell of impersonal, sterile care, of helplessness, of death.

She sat fully dressed in the examination room. The physician had just left after his consultation. Joy had made a request that Seth be called from the waiting room to speak with her.

She smiled at her uncle when he knocked and peeked around the door. He entered, looking entirely too large for the tiny exam room.

"Is everything okay?" He'd asked the question lightly, but Joy saw the lines of dread and worry on his face.

"Yes," she assured. "Sit down."

He sat awkwardly in the only other plastic chair in the room. "What did the doctor say?"

"That I have all the symptoms of a viral infection," Joy replied.

Seth closed his eyes briefly. "Thank God."

Joy smiled. "I know. I'm relieved, too."

Seth exhaled. "So what—you just need to rest and take an antibiotic or something?" She nodded. Seth's expression shifted as he studied her. "What is it? You're not telling me everything. You didn't call me back here to tell me you have the flu, did you?"

"The chances are, that's precisely what I have. I am going to get sick at times, you know. I'm not any different from anyone else," she said, smiling ruefully. "The thing of it is, though, my glands are swollen."

Seth stiffened.

"Which is completely normal if I have a viral infection," Joy assured him quickly. "But given my history, and the fact that I'm having some chest pain and fever—both of which are also consistent with a flu bug in addition to early lymphoma signs—the doctor thinks I should get a biopsy on a lymph gland, just to be sure."

"Okay," Seth said quickly. He glanced around the room. "So they're going to admit you?"

"I'd rather have it done in Chicago. I put a lot of time and research into choosing Dr. Chen," she said, referring to her oncologist. "It'd make me feel more secure doing it there."

"We'll leave first thing in the morning, then?"

"I will."

Seth flinched. "We both will. Of course we both will."

"Listen to me," she said firmly. "The chances are that this is nothing. I want you to understand that. I'm just playing it safe. Rill's costume designer is flying in tomorrow specifically to consult with you about *Razor Pass*. Both Rill and she would be disappointed if you weren't there."

"I don't care if Rill's disappointed," Seth said, looking insulted.

"I do. This is a wonderful opportunity for Hightower Special Effects. I won't allow you to compromise anything by leaving Vulture's Canyon early when there's no need for it."

"No, absolutely—"

"Do you have any idea of how guilty I'd feel if you abandoned this job because I have the flu?" Joy interrupted fiercely.

Seth hesitated, seeming torn.

"It's not a big deal, Seth. Please don't make any more of it than it is. I really need your cooperation on this."

"What about Everett?" Seth asked slowly. "Are you planning on telling him why you have to leave early?"

"No," Joy said, holding Seth's gaze. "And I'm asking you, as a personal favor, to please not say anything to the Pierces or to Everett. I've had a wonderful weekend here so far. I'd rather leave it at that."

A pained expression crossed Seth's face. "Joy, I'm not so sure Everett is going to accept that. I think he really cares about you."

Joy swallowed. She told herself the soreness in her throat was from her swollen glands. "You and I both know this thing between Everett and me was just a blip on the radar. What else could it be, really? Him being who he is. Me being who I am."

"Does that mean you don't care about him?"

"It doesn't matter, does it? In the end?" she asked quietly.

"What's that supposed to mean?" Seth demanded. The edge to his tone made anger rise in her, a sort of desperate fury.

"It means that even if my cancer hasn't returned today, it may tomorrow, or next month, or next year!"

Seth's mouth fell open in surprise. "That's what you're worried about? So what—you think Hughes wouldn't be able to handle something like that?"

"It means I don't *want* him to handle it," she said so forcefully that Seth blinked. She hadn't meant for any of this to come out now, but she didn't seem able to stop the deluge of honesty. Something about these circumstances, about the terrifying possibility—no matter how remote—that her cancer had returned, about the fact that Everett was sitting out in the waiting room, wondering and worrying, seemed to have blown the cap off her restraint. "God, Seth, don't you get it? I wouldn't wish what we had to go through with Mom, what you had to go through with me, on my *worst enemy*." She shook her head, fighting back unwanted tears. "You and Mom were always so angry at Dad for leaving, but I never was. Don't you get why?"

"I guess not," Seth said, stunned.

"Because I completely understand him," she burst out. Tears skittered down her cheek. "Because if I'd been an adult and could make my own decisions, *I* might have chosen to leave, too. Who would want to witness all that suffering, all that pain? Who would *choose* to sit by and watch someone they love slowly waste away, eaten alive by a foul, meaningless disease?"

"You don't mean that, Joy," Seth said grimly. "You're sick. You're not thinking straight."

"I know precisely what I'm thinking!"

"You were old enough to choose not to be at Alice's side as much as you were."

"I had no choice," she bit out.

"If you had no choice, it was because you loved her so much," he said sternly. "That's not the same thing as being forced into something."

A convulsion of emotion shuddered through her. God, had all the pain and grief associated with her mother really been just beneath the surface all along, fresh and sharp? Seth stood and grabbed a box of Kleenex. She sobbed, taking one of the tissues when he offered it.

"It doesn't matter. None of that has to do with what's happening right now," she managed in a more subdued tone, wiping her cheeks.

"The hell it doesn't."

She looked up at Seth. He stood next to her, his expression a mixture of compassion and concern.

"I'm so sorry," she whispered, wishing she could make him understand what she meant by those three words, all the love she had for him, all the regret and guilt she felt for adding to his suffering.

A muscle rippled in his cheek.

"Don't you know how much you mean to me? You're my family. I'd do anything for you," he said.

Joy shut her eyes and took a deep breath.

"Thank you," she said quietly. "Thank you so much."

"I think Everett would want to know. I had some words with

him. I was wrong to doubt his intentions in regard to you. They seem genuine. I think you should tell him. He deserves the opportunity to choose, as well."

She wiped her eyes dry and threw the tissues into a waste can. She stood and faced her uncle.

"No," she said. Seth opened his mouth to argue, she was sure, but she halted him. "Please respect me in this. Please don't take away whatever control I have in this situation."

His stony countenance crumpled for a brief second.

"Just follow my lead in whatever I tell him is my reason for leaving," she pleaded.

"Jesus, Joy," he muttered, sounding pained.

"It'll all be fine. You'll see," she said.

After a moment, he nodded once. "But you'll call me and tell me as soon as you get into Chicago and tell me when you plan to go to the hospital? I'll meet you there as soon as I finish up here on Monday."

"I'll have to take the car."

"Not a problem. I'll drive into St. Louis with Rill when he goes to pick up Amanda Garcia," he said, referring to the costume designer arriving tomorrow. "I'll pick up another rental car then."

She gave him a thankful glance. "I have one other favor to ask of you while you're in St. Louis tomorrow," she said as she picked up a notepad and pen that were sitting on the little desk. After she'd jotted down a note, she tore the paper off the pad and handed it to a bemused-looking Seth. His bewilderment faded to a solemn expression as she told him what she wanted.

A few minutes later she led him out of the exam room, steeling herself for the task of seeing Everett and convincing him that all was well during their last night together.

Sixteen

~~~

Joy dropped her hands from her neck when Everett rapped on the bathroom door. Her glands really were quite swollen.

"Come in," she called. She'd left the door open a crack. He stuck his head into the opening.

"You doing okay?" he asked.

"Yes. I was just getting ready for bed."

He walked into the large bathroom. He wore nothing but a pair of dark blue pajama bottoms, the drawstring tightened low on his hips. She glanced over him, not hiding her appreciation, not guarding against her desire.

Not tonight.

His gaze dropped over her. "Another new gown?" he asked, touching the black lace strap on her shoulder and caressing her skin in the process. "I like this one even better."

"Thanks," she said softly. Their gazes clung before something caught his attention on the counter.

"So this is the medication the doctor prescribed?" he asked, picking up a bottle.

"Yes, it's not much of anything. Just something to help soothe my throat. The Tylenol has already brought down the fever," she said. A prickle of wariness went through her when she noticed his narrowed gaze on her.

"And that's why you called Seth from the waiting room," he clarified. "Because you wanted him to go and pick up throat spray at the pharmacy."

Joy nodded, forcing a smile. "I thought it'd make things go quicker to have him do that while I got dressed and checked out."

"It's probably just my imagination, but Seth seemed awfully tense tonight."

"Really?" Joy asked, busying herself by pumping some scented lotion into her palm and rubbing it into her skin. "I told you how much he worries about me."

"Yeah," Everett said thoughtfully. "Almost as if he thinks there's something significant to worry about."

She paused in the action of rubbing the lotion on her arm. She met his gaze in the mirror.

"He's like a father and brother to me. Don't tell me you wouldn't worry if Katie got sick."

He said nothing. Joy resumed applying the lotion, working her way up to her shoulder. She felt his sharp observation the entire time.

"Let me," he said after a moment. He pumped some of the lotion into his hand. "Lower your straps."

A shiver coursed down her neck at the sound of his low, rough voice. She brushed the straps off her shoulders, watching him in the mirror as he lifted his hands. He began to massage the lotion into her shoulders and upper back, squeezing her muscles, using his fingers to knead away the tension that had grown there over the course of the evening.

"Feel good?" he asked when she gave a muffled groan of appreciation.

"Fantastic," she said, letting her eyelids flutter closed. His hands felt warm and strong; her flesh seemed to melt beneath them. He touched the side of her neck with a long, questing finger. Her eyes opened. She met his stare in the mirror.

"Sore?" he asked.

She nodded. He moved his fingers in a gentle quest, watching himself touch her.

"Your glands are swollen," he murmured.

She nodded. "Yes. The doctor noticed."

He looked at her again in the mirror. Joy stared back at him unblinkingly. Slowly, his massaging hands moved back to the slope of her shoulders.

"How do you feel right now?"

"I feel fine, now that the Tylenol has taken down the fever."

He nodded. His thumbs dug pleasurably around her shoulder blades, loosening tense muscles. Suddenly, he put his hands on the drooping straps on her black negligee and slid them down her arms, lowering the garment. The fitted silk dragged across the upper slope of her breasts until her nipples popped out from beneath the fabric. She lifted her hands free of the straps. Everett pushed the gown several inches beneath her breasts.

Her nipples stiffened as she watched him pump more lotion and rub the emollient between his hands, warming it. Liquid warmth surged between her thighs when he cupped her breasts and tenderly began to rub the lotion into her skin.

"It's hard to believe that skin can be this soft," he murmured from behind her. He cradled both breasts in his hand, lifting them, gliding his warm fingers along the lower swell of flesh. Her nipples darkened to the color of ripened raspberries. His fingertips touched the reddened crests. She stifled a whimper as he circled the beading tips. "Look at that," he muttered, a hint of awe in his tone. "So amazing. So beautiful."

Something volatile tightened in her throat. For a panicked moment, she thought she was going to burst into tears like she had earlier with Seth. Instead, she spun around, facing him.

"I want to be the one to touch you."

He blinked. Joy realized she'd sounded quite fierce. His small shrug and slightly stunned expression seemed to say, *By all means, don't let me stop you.* She smiled when she saw it.

"I'm sorry," she murmured, her head down as she pumped some of the lotion into her hands. "I just meant—you're always making love to me, taking control of the situation." She put her palms together in preparation to warm the lotion and looked up at him, her hands in a partial praying position. "I want to make love to you tonight."

She laid her hands flat on his abdomen. His muscles leapt beneath her touch. She paused, feeling all the life and vibrancy contained in his flesh. She'd never seen a more beautiful man in her life.

She never would again.

Slowly, meticulously, she made a study of his body, rubbing the lotion into his narrow, lean waist and his ribs, feeling his chest rise and fall more erratically beneath her palms as she stimulated his small, erect nipples with her fingertips. Her arms rose as she moved to his shoulders. She glanced up into his face as she massaged dense deltoid muscles. His lips parted when their gazes met. He moved forward, as if to kiss her, but she moved her head back slightly and continued her exploration, rubbing the cords between his shoulders and neck. His nostrils flared slightly, his expression telling her loud and clear he did not like to be deprived when he saw what he wanted.

She arched her eyebrows and gave him a small smile. Tonight she would not be hurried in the process of touching him . . . of loving him. She massaged his rigid arm muscles, feeling his gaze on her movements the entire time. Looking down, she saw the pillar of his stiffened penis pressing against the cotton fabric of his pants. When she'd finished his arms, she gently urged him closer to the mirror so that he was watching her touch him. She moved behind him, one arm snaking around his waist where she touched his ridged belly, the other massaging corded back muscles. Little lotion remained, but she didn't want to stop touching him. The skin covering his shoulder blades was so smooth, so thick, that she gave in to an urge to feel it against her cheek, and then against her lips. She pressed her naked breasts against his back.

He started to turn to take her into his arms.

"Don't move." She spoke softly next to his skin. She reached around and pulled on the drawstring of his pants. He froze. Both of her hands slipped beneath the waistband, her palms sliding against the sides of his firm, powerful buttocks. She released the fabric and it gathered around his thighs.

Joy moved her head around his arm and gazed in the mirror. His cock hung like some type of glorious, fertile fruit between his thighs, the tapering, fat head pinker than the light gold, straight shaft. Holding her breath, she reached around his hip and took the heavy member into her palm, wrapping her fingers around the stalk. He throbbed into her hand, the weight of the firm flesh thrilling her. She moved her fist, stroking him. When she reached the head, she squeezed it between the constricted ring of her fingers.

"Joy," Everett groaned.

Her gaze flashed up to meet his in the mirror. He wasn't watching her hand on his cock, but her face as she touched him. Keeping his penis in her hand, she moved to the side of him. She ran her hand along his length to the base, where she cupped his heavy balls and gave them a gentle squeeze.

"Let's go to bed," he said roughly.

"Wait," she whispered, her hold on him making her demand

difficult to ignore. She fisted him again and gave a good jerk. She recalled how forceful he'd been when he'd stroked his cock while she sucked on the head last night. It had been exciting to see him treat his own flesh almost aggressively. She gave him a few more lusty yanks. His guttural moan told her she'd been right. Everett didn't like his cock to be treated with kid gloves. She beat at the tumescent member for a taut moment, watching in fascination as the veins popped on the surface and the shapely head took on a purple hue.

"I think they call that abuse," Everett mumbled. She glanced up at him, pausing with her fist at midstaff. His jaw was rigid.

"What do you call it?"

"Heaven."

She smiled. He grunted in irritation when she released her hold, but held his tongue when she grabbed the vanity stool beneath the countertop and pulled it toward him. She sat, her profile to the mirror. Without any preamble, she put her hands on his hips and turned him toward her. She wanted him to be able to watch in the mirror, if doing so would bring him pleasure. His pants slid to his knees. She took his penis into her hand, and for a moment just stared, absorbing the sight. She wanted to be mindful. She wanted to remember this moment.

Everett hissed something unintelligible when she lifted his cock and slid the head into her mouth. The firm, warm flesh stretched her lips. His flavor spread on her tongue. She closed her eyes and sucked. His musky, salty taste filled her consciousness; his turgid penis became her whole world. Her jaw ached and her lips screamed for a reprieve, but she wouldn't stop. It was as if his pleasure had been mainlined into her veins, as if his gratification had become her own. When the head of his cock slid into her throat and her body jerked in a reflex to expel him, she overcame even that, sacrificing herself to his bliss.

"Joy," he said sharply.

She blinked open her eyes dazedly. Had he been calling her name repeatedly, and only the last exclamation had fractured her focus? Tears were running down her cheeks. She leaned back, Everett's stiff member sliding from her mouth. She looked up the length of his naked body and froze when she saw his expression. His nostrils flared; his eyes looked wild.

"How can you give yourself like that and claim this thing between us is meaningless?"

She swallowed thickly. Her throat hurt badly. Perhaps he noticed her grimace, because his intense, almost angry expression softened. He kicked off the pants that had pooled around his ankles and grabbed her hand. He led her to the bedside table where he picked up a bottle of water.

"Drink some," he said.

The cool water felt delicious sliding down her tender, raw throat.

"Your cheeks are flushed again." He touched her forehead. "I think your fever is back," he said grimly. He tossed back the comforter and sheet. "Go on. Get into bed," he said when she just stood there. He sighed and drew up her negligee over her breasts. "You need to sleep. I shouldn't have let that happen."

"Don't be ridiculous. My cheeks aren't flushed because of a fever," she rasped.

"It sounds like you've swallowed sandpaper," he said, his brow furrowed with worry. "Get into bed, Joy. Please?"

Instead of following his demand, however, she opened the bedside table. She'd observed that Everett kept some condoms in there. She withdrew one and tore it open.

"What do you think you're doing?" he asked, grabbing her wrist when she moved to roll it on his penis.

"I told you. I want to make love to you," she said, glancing up. "Please."

She saw his throat convulse. His hold on her loosened. Joy

rolled on the prophylactic. When she'd finished, she waved toward the bed. "Sit down with your back against the headboard. Please," she added softly when he gave her a blazing glance. He said nothing, but did as she asked.

"What are you planning on doing?" he asked when she lifted her gown and straddled his thighs. She took his cock into her hand and arrowed it into her pussy. She was wet—very wet—but at first, her vagina seemed to resist the intrusion of a thick, hard cock. She gritted her teeth and clung on to Everett's shoulders. He grasped her hips. Her cry segued to a shaky whimper as she applied a solid pressure and his cock carved into her body.

"Jesus, Joy," Everett mumbled. His head fell back against the padded headboard. He looked as if he'd just had a workout at the gym. Every muscle on his torso was defined, tensed and glazed with a sheen of sweat. She sat in his lap, her body harboring the length of his penis.

"Do you remember that night of the premiere, when we made love and you said you'd wanted to connect to me?" she whispered throatily.

"Of course."

"I want to do something similar now. Let's talk."

"Talk?" he asked, looking disbelieving.

"Yes. That's a tantric sex thing, isn't it? We're supposed to keep ourselves on the edge of arousal for as long as possible. Talk. Commune. Share ourselves, and when . . ."

She swallowed thickly when her voice broke.

"Joy?"

She continued more firmly. "When the end finally comes, it will be all that much more special."

She met Everett's stare determinedly. "It's what I want. I'm not afraid to feel close to you, like I was on that night. I'm not afraid of your honesty."

"You said I overwhelmed you."

"Tonight, I want to be overwhelmed."

He moved his hands on her hips. His cock swelled inside her.

"What should we talk about?"

"Anything. What was the happiest day of your life?"

He blinked. "I'd like to think it hasn't happened yet," he said slowly. He gripped her hips and moved them in a subtle circular motion. She gasped. He grimaced. "This isn't going to work, Joy. Your fever—it's making you so hot. It's like being buried in a tight fire."

"Focus," she whispered. His gaze flickered over her face.

"Well, if it weren't for you getting upset about Jenny and getting sick, I'd say today was pretty damn awesome."

She smiled.

"What about you?" he asked.

She closed her eyes briefly, willfully resisting an almost overwhelming urge to ground her pussy down in his lap to get pressure on her throbbing clit.

"When I got my full scholarship to art school, that was pretty special. For a while there, I was concerned I wasn't going to be able to go to VCU's program. It was my first choice for art school, and it's not easy to get in. My mother was so happy I'd been accepted, but she died not realizing we really wouldn't have been able to cover the finances. When I found out about the scholarship, it was like someone lifted the door on my cage," she said.

"And the dove flew free."

She gave him a shaky smile. "What's your favorite movie of all time?"

He grimaced and clutched at her hips, tilting her forward slightly on his cock.

"Everett?" she gasped, feeling him press erotically against the front wall of her vagina.

"Hard to say," he said tightly. "Probably *On the Waterfront*."

"I can see that," she murmured. "You have all the ragged passion of Brando, somehow stabilized."

He grimaced, and she knew it had nothing to do with what she'd said. "What's yours?"

"*Casablanca.*"

"I can see that."

"Why?" she asked, finding it difficult to focus. The pressure in her genitals was becoming unbearable.

"You and Ilsa both have that elusive thing going on that drives a guy crazy," he mumbled, referring to Ingrid Bergman's character.

"I do not!"

"Have you ever been in love?" he asked her, abruptly changing the topic.

She couldn't resist any longer. She pressed down in his lap, getting friction on her clit. A ripple of pleasure shuddered through her. "I . . . don't know," she gasped.

"How can you not know?"

"I can't be sure." She nervously licked at the perspiration gathering on her upper lip. "Have you?"

His fingers dug into her hips. He seemed to realize what he was doing and smoothed the silk over her skin as if to apologize for his forcefulness.

"Yeah." Was that uncertainty she heard in his tone or some other emotion?

"But you don't know for sure?" she whispered, scanning his features.

"No. I know," he said grimly after a moment.

Her heart throbbed against her breastbone. Her vaginal muscles tightened around him without conscious instruction on her part. *Change the subject,* she thought desperately.

"When I was talking to Errol down in the diner earlier today, he said something about Katie being related to Howard Hughes. Is that true?"

"*What?*" Everett said, his gaze narrowed on her.

"Are you related to Howard Hughes?" she asked.

"Oh. Um . . . yeah," he said as if he were trying to dredge for inconsequential information in a murky area of his brain. "He's some kind of sixteenth cousin removed on my father's side or something."

His hands shifted. He lowered her nightgown back down beneath her breasts. She felt his cock lurch inside her as he stared at her chest.

"How much longer do we have to do this?" he asked, his gaze glittering . . . ravenous.

"Much longer."

He exhaled exasperatedly. "Why did I know you were going to say that?" He stroked the tender skin at the sides of her body, making her shiver and her nipples tighten. Again, her vagina tightened around him. She shot him a repressive glance. He knew how sensitive she was there. "Okay, how about the worst day of your life?" he asked.

"The day my mother died," she said without thinking. He caressed her bare back with warm hands. This time, she found his touch comforting as well as arousing. "I had thought for sure when the end came, when her suffering finally ceased, I would be relieved . . . glad that her pain was finally over. I was wrong. It was exponentially worse, knowing I'd never hear her speak again, never feel her touch," she whispered. He regarded her silently for a moment. "What about you?" she asked.

He grimaced. "I'd rather not say."

"Why?"

"Because compared to your worst day, I'd sound like a spoiled, shallow jerk."

"Don't say that, Everett," she said, caressing his shoulders. She had to move. She must. She lifted herself a few inches off his cock and settled again. They both gave restrained groans.

"One person's suffering doesn't compare to another's," she said once she'd caught her breath. "We're not in a contest. It's a completely private, personal experience. What you would say is your worst day is about you, no one else."

He hesitated, his gaze lowering to her breasts. She held her breath when he ran the tip of his forefinger along the sensitive skin on the lower swell of flesh.

"Okay, but don't say I didn't warn you. It might have been when I took my parents to the director's screening for *Stardust*. Maybe you saw it—it was my first major motion picture and a colossal flop. When I looked at the expression on my father's face when he saw me on that screen wearing tight silver pants and spouting the most moronic lines ever spoken by a human being, including during the Neolithic era, I thought I'd die of humiliation. I knew the screenplay was bad, and had a pretty good idea it was going to tank, but until I saw myself up there through my parents' eyes, I didn't get just how horrible it was. I was too young to tell my agent to go screw herself when she insisted the project was revolutionary and cutting-edge. I was too stupid to understand that the magic fairy dust of filmmaking is completely ineffective on a crap screenplay." Her heart squeezed in compassion when she saw the vivid discomfort on his face. It still bothered him, even now. "After that experience, I didn't act for nine months. I was twenty-three years old and totally pissed at myself for agreeing to be a part of such a shit project. I was convinced I was a total sellout."

"I never saw *Stardust*."

His eyes sprung wide. "Will you marry me?"

She suppressed a smile at his earnestness. "It changed your life, that day. After that, you always were extremely careful of the parts you chose. You only wanted best, and that often wasn't roles in the highest-budget films. You challenged yourself on independent films and foreign projects. You became the opposite of a Hollywood sellout."

"Only because I'd prostituted myself to begin with," he mumbled. He put his hands on her hips and flexed his arms, lifting her up on his cock. His facial muscles convulsed as he lowered her again and she sunk onto his erection. "*God* that feels good."

"I think your worst day became your best. That says a lot about you."

His eyes turned lambent as he stared at her. Sweat glazed both of their faces now. A slight sheen of it gleamed on his chiseled torso. "Thanks. That was a nice way of reframing it. I'm not so sure I deserve it, but it sure sounds better that way."

She smiled. "You deserve it." She circled her hips, watching his reaction. His head banged against the headboard.

"Have we talked enough?" he asked in a choked voice.

"I don't think so."

His hands shifted to the tops of her thighs. His long thumbs inched toward her outer sex.

"Can I make you come, then?"

"No, Everett," she said shakily. Her body would like nothing better, but her brain wanted to stretch this moment with him . . . make it last.

He frowned. "Then tell me something really sexy. Something you've never told anyone before."

She licked her upper lip nervously and tasted salt. "After you left my apartment on that day of the rainstorm," she began quietly, "I . . . I masturbated while thinking about you fucking me."

He stilled. A sharp glint entered his eyes, reminding Joy of a predator sighting prey. "How did you think about me fucking you?"

"Hard," she said on a puff of exhaled air. His cock lurched inside her. She stared at his parted lips, entranced. Her clit burned. She stroked him with her pussy—quick and firm, landing back in his lap with a sharp smacking sound. "Like you were making me take it," she grated out, "all of your cock . . . all of you."

"Joy," he rasped, firming his hold on her hips.

"No, Everett. No. Don't make it end yet," she pleaded.

He stared at her, panting. He was like a coiled spring beneath her, a receptacle of incipient energy, a keg of dynamite about to explode at the smallest provocation.

"What's a moment you'll remember for the rest of your life?" she asked in a rush.

"This one."

She clamped her eyelids shut and ground down in his lap.

"Another one," she whispered. Was his cock growing larger inside of her? It seemed to be stroking her inner walls, firing her nerves, but he wasn't moving.

"At the studio when you asked me if *I minded*. The way you looked when you turned around in that doorway and saw me running to you in the rain—"

"*Don't*, Everett," she moaned. "Don't say those things."

"Why not? It's true. You said you weren't afraid of my honesty. That's all I'm doing—telling the truth. The moment when I saw that sketch you made of me on that napkin," he continued relentlessly, "and you somehow managed to capture something I was just beginning to realize."

She lifted herself off him and ground her pussy back in his lap, her eyelids clenched tightly as if it could make her stop hearing him—or make her hear him more clearly. His hold on her tightened and he lifted.

"That I was falling in love with you," he said as he drove her back on his cock.

The stroke—or perhaps his volatile words—ignited something in her. Hot, spiking pleasure cascaded like a beating waterfall in her flesh. She gripped his shoulders. They began to move as one, both of them submersed in the same pure pool of electric delight. She heard their skin slapping together and the headboard thudding against the wall as if through a dense, heavy fog. Sharp pain shot through her buttock and she cried out. Her eyelids popped open and Everett spanked her again, squeezing both her ass cheeks and jerking her back down on his cock. The burn of pain was the subtle spice to her boiling pleasure.

He spanked her again and again as they mated frantically, as if he truly was bent on creating a fire in her flesh. It worked. Her fingernails sunk into his shoulders and she began to climax. His cock lurched inside her. He roared.

Joy continued to bob desperately in his lap, increasingly wild to stretch those fleeting, exquisite moments.

Seventeen

In the dead of night Everett awoke to the sensation of cool, air-conditioned air on his skin and a warm, wet mouth on his thigh. He shivered at the sensation of sweet, skimming kisses.

"Joy?" he whispered, slightly disoriented in the darkness.

"Everett," she whispered against a damp spot on his thigh. Her voice sounded thick with drowsiness. Goose bumps broke over his body. He felt the edge of her front teeth scrape gently over his skin.

"Come here," he mumbled, clumsily reaching for her.

She came—warm, decadent silk sliding next to his chilled skin. His arms went around her. She brought the comforter with her and settled it around them. She laid her cheek and palm on his chest. One moment, he had been cold and naked; the next he was co-cooned in Joy's fragrant warmth.

"Joy?" he whispered after a moment, confused by her utter stillness. Had she wanted to make love again? He wasn't quite sure he was up for the deed after such an active day and night, but he'd be more than happy to bring her pleasure. He palmed the back of her head, the sensation causing a surge of tenderness, wonder and passion to go through him, a heretofore unknown, powerful combination of emotion. He ran his fingers through her silky hair.

"Joy," he repeated, this time with no expectation of a reply. She must have been enacting her dreams. Her even, soft breath on his chest told him she was fast asleep.

Golden sunlight leaked into his awareness when he pried open his eyelids the next morning. Not yet prepared for the intrusive brilliance, he clamped his eyes shut again. He flopped his hand onto his abdomen, frowning as he absentmindedly scratched himself. Something was missing in the crook of his arm.

He opened his eyes and glanced around the bed without moving his head off the pillow. He was alone. It didn't surprise him; Joy had awakened earlier than he had yesterday. He'd always thought he was a morning person, but Joy seemed to rise with the dawn. He rubbed his eyes and thought about the previous night.

"Joy?" he called, his vivid memories making it suddenly imperative he see her right that moment . . . touch her. How was she feeling? Better or worse?

No answer came. The guesthouse seemed silent. Maybe she'd already gone for her morning jog? Surely it wasn't a good idea for her to be exercising when she was ill.

Of course that didn't prevent you from letting her make love to you last night, did it, Mr. Nice Guy?

He tossed the sheet off him and sat up, swinging his feet to the floor. He noticed the folded piece of paper while he was scraping back his hair with his fingers. It had been set against the bedside table lamp and had his name written across the front.

He picked it up and opened it slowly. Surely the sharp sense of dread he was experiencing was uncalled for. It was probably just a note telling him that she'd run down to the Legion Diner for some coffee or something.

He read the note rapidly.

It wasn't just a note telling him she'd run into town for coffee.

He stood abruptly and for the first time noticed Joy's suitcase was gone.

Five minutes later, he entered the big house's kitchen, Joy's note clutched in his hand. Katie sat at the oak table near a window, sunlight spilling around her as she bottle-fed a hungry-looking Daisy.

"Did you see Joy leave?"

Katie did a double take when she noticed his tense expression. "No. The car was gone when I got up. I thought maybe you two had gone to the diner for Sunday breakfast or something."

"She's gone," he said starkly, staring around the sunlit kitchen as if he thought it'd provide him some vital clue that would explain Joy's inexplicable absence. "Where's Seth?"

"He's sleeping, of course." Her green eyes looked bewildered. "Everett, what's that you're holding?"

He paused and glanced at his hand in rising irritation. "It's a note. From Joy."

"What's it say?"

"It's a Dear John, that's what it is. It says this whole thing between us would never work, and she thinks she'd better end it before one or both of us gets hurt. Some kind of crap like that," he said bitterly. He started to walk determinedly toward the staircase that led to the dormer bedroom where Seth was staying.

"Everett, what are you doing?" Katie called, standing. Daisy made a muffled sound of protest and then started to cry.

"I'm going to ask Seth what he knows about this!"

"Why would Seth know something that you don't?"

"He's got to understand *something* better than I do, because this"—he snapped Joy's note in the air—"completely blindsided me."

"Everett, stop it."

Katie's sharp tone brought him to a halt as he reached for the door that led to the stairs.

"Come back over here. Please," she added more softly. "Let's try to sort this out."

He rolled his eyes in exasperation, but gave in to her request, although he refused to sit. He was too worked up. Adrenaline was pumping through his veins. He experienced an almost imperative mandate to get in his car and chase after Joy. It was torture to just stand there.

Katie sat and murmured to an agitated Daisy, reinserting the nipple into her mouth. The baby almost immediately began to suck again with gusto. Katie turned her attention to him.

"When you called last night on the way home from the hospital, you said Joy was going to be fine. Seth didn't indicate anything different when he came in. Did something happen between you and Joy that could explain this?" She nodded at the letter he still gripped in his hand like a bloody knife discovered next to a dead body.

For a second, he just stared at his sister, dumbfounded. Had something happened? *Hell yes*, something had happened. They'd had a mind-blowing, life-altering, intimate sexual and emotional exchange, and for the first time in his life, he'd told a woman he loved her and meant it in the way he'd always worried he never would.

"Did you fight or disagree on something?" Katie prompted when he just continued to stand there.

"No. We—" A puff of air popped out of his throat. "Talked."

"You talked?"

Everett stared at Katie, his mouth hanging open. He felt like he was still disoriented from a sucker punch. "I told her I was falling in love with her."

For a few seconds, only the wet, sucking sound of Daisy break-fasting could be heard in the tense silence.

"You've fallen in love with Joy?" Katie asked slowly.

"You don't have to look at me like I just said I'd cured cancer while I slept. I do have the capability to love someone, you know," he said, annoyance creeping into his shock at seeing Katie's amazement.

"Of course you do. And I'd been hoping it was true, watching you with Joy this weekend. It's just that . . . it's awfully big news, isn't it?"

"What's big news?"

Everett turned to see Seth walking into the kitchen. He looked like he'd already showered and dressed for the day in jeans, a white shirt and a leather belt with a tooled silver buckle. A flicker of sus-picion went through Everett. Hadn't Seth woken up midmorning yesterday, and hadn't Joy once referred to the fact that he was a night owl who often slept until ten or eleven? Joy's uncle had cer-tainly risen early, almost as if he'd been preparing for something.

He held up the letter. "Joy has left."

Seth's features looked even more classically Native American than usual as he gave Everett an impassive, cold stare.

"Yes. I know."

"You *knew*? Did she come in here and talk to you before she left this morning?"

"No. She told me she planned to leave last night."

Everett realized he was gawking. His heartbeat started to pound in his ears. How could this be possible? How could Joy have told Seth that she planned to break things off with Everett this morning, then return here and share such a soulful, intimate night with him?

"What the hell is going on here?" Everett demanded.

Seth blinked. Everett realized the question had cracked out of his throat like a blistering whip.

"What did Joy say in the letter?" Seth asked, nodding toward it.

"That she doesn't think things would work out between us." He lifted the piece of paper and read a portion word for word. "'In the end, our lives are just too different. I would disappear in the largeness of your world, and you'd be suffocated by the smallness of mine. I think after I go away, you'll see the truth of that quickly enough.'" Everett dropped the letter abruptly, where it crumpled next to his thigh. "Well?" he prodded Seth.

Seth shrugged, his expression unmoving. "Isn't your answer right there?" A frown flickered across his stoic features when he saw Everett's disbelief. "I'm sorry, Everett. If it helps any to know it, I told Joy that I thought you really cared about her. But it's her choice, in the end. I can't stop her from doing what she wants. I never could," he added quietly under his breath.

Everett glanced, aghast, from Seth to a somber-looking Katie. They didn't understand. They didn't know what had passed between Joy and him last night. They had no idea how singular their initial attraction was, how unique their growing feelings toward each other were.

Sadness crossed Katie's face. Or was it pity? He felt a twisting sensation, like someone had just reached into his gut and rung his intestines. He'd been kidding himself. Deluding himself. This intense attraction he had for Joy . . . this incredible, swelling feeling . . . this growing love . . .

It was all on *his* part. Or mostly, anyway.

Christ. He really was cursed when it came to this business.

"Everett," Katie said in a strained voice, but he could tell by her hopeless tone she didn't really expect him to halt in his exit out the front door.

*   *   *

"Shit," Katie cursed succinctly when the door shut after Everett with a thud.

For a few seconds, Seth and she stared at each other. Did he feel as helpless as she did?

"He's never really fallen for a woman before like he has Joy," she said. She examined her daughter, whose energetic sucking had slowed as her delicate eyelids started to close. She sighed and removed the bottle, setting it on the table.

"Do you really believe that?"

Katie looked up at the stark question. Seth stood on the other side of the table.

"I don't believe it. I know it. Everett and I are very close. He hasn't been all that . . . lucky in the romance department."

Seth gave a small derisive grunt.

"Shame on you," Katie said.

"What?" Seth asked, incredulous.

She frowned and studied her daughter's peaceful face. "You seem like a smart man. You work in the land of make-believe, just like Rill and Everett. Surely you aren't silly enough to fall for all the smoke and shadows. You're one of the people responsible for *making* the fantasy. Surely *you* know there are real people behind the screen of illusion."

"But Everett—*Everett Hughes*"—Seth specified, waving toward the door—"has never fallen for a woman like he has my niece?"

"I don't understand why that's so shocking," said Katie, firing up. "Lots of people don't fall in love until they're in their thirties or forties. Have you found the woman you'd sacrifice just about anything for?" She studied his stunned, blank expression. "I didn't think so. Why should Everett be any different from you? And by the way, you sound awfully cynical in regard to your niece. If you haven't noticed, Joy's gorgeous and kind and amazingly modest, considering all her talent and gifts. To be honest, I'm not surprised at all Everett has fallen for her. He hates artifice, even though he thrives in the midst of it. Joy is fresh and understated and . . . and . . ."

"What?" Seth prompted, no longer looking taken aback by her outburst, but interested.

"Well, sort of haunted, to be honest," Katie said regretfully. "It's the kind of combination a man like my brother would find irresistible."

"He would think her being haunted was *irresistible*?" Seth asked, sounding mildly offended.

"No," Katie said. "He'd find the idea of bringing her peace and happiness irresistible."

For a moment, neither of them spoke as Katie watched her sleeping child. "She has reason to—look haunted, I mean. Doesn't she?"

She looked up when he didn't immediately answer, stilling when she saw his face. It no longer was shrouded.

"Yes," Seth said. "Joy lives with many ghosts. Many fears. She fights them fiercely, guards herself against them."

"Does that have anything to do with why she left this morning?"

Seth exhaled slowly. "Yes. Unlike your brother, she doesn't believe the haunting will ever end."

Joy's oncologist was concerned enough about her reported symptoms that he examined her immediately upon her return to Chicago. As he finished giving her the results of some diagnostics, he told her he planned to admit her to the hospital first thing the following morning. He had scheduled a mediastinoscopy with biopsy.

Fear settled in Joy's gut like cold lead when she'd heard a mediastinoscopy was warranted instead of a mere needle biopsy of a lymph node. They could do a lymph node biopsy outpatient with a local anesthetic, while the mediastinoscopy required general anesthesia. An instrument called a mediastinoscope would be inserted into a cut in her neck so that tissue samples could be taken from lymph nodes in her chest region. It wasn't so much the procedure that bothered her. Ever since her first round of treatments, she had gained an illogical paranoia about general anesthesia, a nameless fear that she'd never wake up.

Dr. Chen noticed her discomfort.

"I'm just playing things safe, Joy," he said comfortingly as he put away her X-rays. "The procedure will take a half hour, tops. Your family member can pick you up on Tuesday morning, if all goes well."

A childish loneliness surged through her at the thought of taking a taxicab to her empty apartment.

"Can't we do the procedure outpatient?"

"No. The incision we'll make is small, but I'd still prefer a night of observation afterward, just to make sure."

Joy sighed. "I hate staying in the hospital."

He put his hand on her shoulder. She looked into his kind, round face. "Most cancer survivors do. If I didn't think it was for the best, I wouldn't push the issue. You'll be groggy after the procedure. Tuesday morning will be here before you have a chance to grow a worthy aversion to the hospital food."

Joy attempted a smile. "When will I get the results from the biopsy?"

"I'll insist on a rush job. I know how hard it is to wait for these things. I'll try to get you results before I discharge you on Tuesday."

That afternoon after she'd packed a bag for the hospital, she called Seth. He listened patiently while she explained about the biopsy, downplaying the fact that it would be an inpatient surgery versus an outpatient procedure.

"Dr. Chen agreed with the doctor at Prairie Lakes. He doesn't think it's a return of cancer. He thinks it's a regular old everyday infection. I wish I could get the flu like a regular person," she added ruefully to lighten the moment.

"When will you have the biopsy?"

"Early Tuesday," she lied smoothly. "It only takes ten minutes. I'll be home later that morning."

"I'll come to the hospital to get you," Seth said.

"No," Joy said abruptly. If he arrived at the hospital, he'd know she'd lied about the outpatient procedure. "You're due back in L.A. Tuesday morning. You're supposed to be meeting with your staff about *Razor Pass*."

"It'll wait," Seth said bluntly.

"I won't have you ruining any of your plans to pick me up for a stupid little outpatient procedure. I'll call you as soon as I get home, if you like. Where . . . where are you right now?" she asked, curious, but also wanting to change the subject.

"I'm standing on Katie and Rill's front porch."

"Did you . . . did you already pick up Amanda from the airport?"

"Yeah. I got back early this afternoon."

"Do you like her?"

"Yes, I think we'll work well together."

How did Everett respond to my letter? Was he upset? Did Rill and Katie find my abrupt departure rude? What is Everett doing right this second?

Her unspoken questions screamed into the silence.

"I . . . er . . . suppose Everett got my letter?"

"He got it. He wasn't at all pleased. I can't say I blame him."

Joy dipped her head and stared blankly at the overnight bag resting on her bed.

"Is he all right?" she asked quietly.

"No one knows. We haven't seen him since he stormed out this morning after he confronted me over what I knew about your letter and departure."

The back of her neck prickled with uneasiness. "Did he leave in his car?"

"No. The car is still in the driveway. Rill went out to the guest-house to have a word with him before we left this morning, and Katie tried this afternoon. He's not in there, though."

"And he seemed upset when he left this morning?"

There was a pause before Seth responded quietly. "He was blindsided by your letter, Joy."

Joy clenched her eyes shut, an ache throbbing beneath her breast at the knowledge she had caused him pain. She knew it was for the best in the long run, but it hurt almost unbearably.

He'd said he loved her . . .

Don't think about that. He didn't mean it. It happened in a heated moment during sex.

"Joy?" Seth prompted when she was silent for a stretched moment.

"I might know where he is," she said huskily. "He has a private place where he likes to go in the woods. If I give you directions, will you tell Rill or Katie how to get there? Someone should go to him." She quickly explained about how to access the forest lake.

"If all of this stuff with the biopsy is truly insignificant, why did you feel the need to break things off with Everett?" Seth asked, taking her by surprise.

"One has nothing to do with the other. Everett and I just aren't . . . suited. It'd never work."

"Joy—"

"Are you going to tell Rill and Katie about the spot in the woods?"

"I'll make sure someone looks for him," Seth said grimly.

She paused, misery temporarily strangling her throat. She hated feeling at odds with Seth.

"I'm sorry for what I said in the exam room last night. I realized on the flight home how it must have sounded to you. I want you to know, I'd never leave your side if something bad ever happened—"

"You don't have to tell me that. I know it," he interrupted.

"I was just trying to explain—"

"I understand what you were getting at. You were trying to tell me something I've been too stupid to see myself. You were trying to tell me that part of you envied your father's being able to pick up and leave during all those years of waiting and hoping and stress and misery."

"Yes," she said, her voice cracking.

"Joy, that's not the same thing as saying you'd do the same as Jake. It's normal that you would have had fantasies about being able to run away."

She couldn't respond at first, her throat felt too tight. She'd never been so confused about how she felt about her mother's cancer; her cancer; her father's leaving. It'd all become a cyclone of emotion brewing inside of her for the past week and a half.

She sat down on the edge of her bed. "Do you really believe that?" she asked in a small voice.

"How could you not have thought things like that once in a while, given how much Alice suffered and for how long? But I know you, Joy. You don't have to assure me you would be there for me, or anyone you love, if they were going through a trial. I *know* that."

She moved the receiver away from her mouth so he wouldn't hear her muffled sobs. Perhaps Seth sensed her emotional state, because he cleared his throat gruffly and changed the subject.

"There was something I planned to talk to you about while we were in Vulture's Canyon, but given the way things turned out, I never got the chance."

"What?" Joy asked, wiping a damp cheek.

"I want to ask you to become a partner in Hightower Special Effects."

Joy's mouth fell open in surprise. It'd been one of the last things she'd expected him to say.

"It's got nothing to do with the fact that you're my niece," Seth said hurriedly, as if he was expecting her to turn him down flat. "I respect your talent more than I do anyone else's in the business. I'm always one hundred percent confident in any project you undertake. I think we work really well together."

"Thank you," she said, still stunned. Seth had worked so relentlessly to make his company the success that it was today. She was deeply moved at his offer to share it with her. "Thank you so much. I . . . I don't know what to say."

"Take some time to think about it, then. I know how much teaching means to you. Maybe we could figure something out? Maybe you could teach a few art classes at a junior college here in the Los Angeles area or something?"

Joy closed her eyes. "Seth, does this offer have anything to do with the fact that you want me to move back to the west coast?"

"No. Absolutely not."

She let out a ragged sigh. She wasn't quite so sure she believed him. Six months ago, she might have resented it. Now, she wasn't so certain it was such a bad thing, even if Seth *was* trying to subtly manipulate her into moving closer to him.

"I'll think about it," she said quietly. "And I am extremely flattered by the offer. Thank you. I'll call you as soon as I get home on Tuesday?"

"Do you promise?"

"I promise."

Eighteen

Joy had been right about the mosquito repellent, Everett thought dully as yet another red welt was raised, this one on his chest. The little buggers had been making a feast of him since his last swim in the lake. He'd grown so numb as he sat there beneath the sycamore tree that he'd stopped slapping at them when he felt them bite.

He'd been down before. He knew what it was like to pick yourself up after you'd been body-slammed hard on the pavement, figuratively speaking. In the past, he'd taken enough time to lick his wounds and recover. Then he'd thrown himself right back into the fray and gotten what he wanted. If not that time, then the next. Persistence had always been his guiding principle. A half hour after he'd left Katie's kitchen this morning, he'd been convinced that personal value would see him through this rough spot with Joy. He'd go after her. He'd convince her that they weren't as different as she suspected. They could make it work.

Now that the sun was dipping in the western sky, however, he found himself doubting. Perhaps persistence didn't work in this murky area of romance and love? He didn't really have enough experience with caring about someone this much to know for sure. It wasn't Joy he doubted, it was himself—his ability to convince her he was the real thing and not some insubstantial caricature of a film star. There had been so many times when he'd looked into her eyes in the past several days that he was sure she'd been seeing him accurately, appreciating who he was as a person. In truth, he'd believed he'd seen that in her gaze since that very first time at the studio.

Obviously he'd been kidding himself in a very large way.

He forced himself to stand from the rock where Joy had perched while they'd made love—masochistic of him to come here, he knew. He pulled on his shorts, socks and tennis shoes and was in the process of shrugging on his T-shirt when he heard a quiet tread on the path. Seth Hightower's head appeared over the rise. He paused, taking in the scene of the hilltop lake. Everett remained quiet. The sycamore branches protected him from sight. He wasn't sure he wanted to be found.

Seth took several more steps toward the lake. Curiosity overcame Everett's need for privacy.

"Seth."

Seth's head swung around. Everett walked out from beneath the shade of the sycamore, the rays of sun immediately scorching his face.

"Were you looking for me?" Everett asked.

Seth nodded. Without speaking, he dug in the leg pocket of his cargo shorts and retrieved a bottle of water. Everett took it, unscrewed the cap and chugged three quarters of the contents in seconds flat. He'd become dehydrated sitting up here all day. He grunted in appreciation and wiped his mouth. Seth was staring at the tree-rimmed lake.

"It's pretty," he said gruffly.

"How did you know I'd be here?" Everett asked.

"Joy told me where to look."

He stilled. "You spoke with her, then?"

"Yes."

"Is she all right?" Seth didn't immediately respond, just stared silently at the rippling lake. "Seth? Is Joy all right?" Everett repeated, taking a step toward the other man.

"Is there somewhere we could sit and talk out of the sun?" Seth wondered aloud.

Everett swallowed uneasily. Something about Seth's manner was setting off a tiny alarm bell in the back of his head.

"Yeah. Over here," Everett directed.

He led the other man beneath the shade of the sycamore—not to where Joy and he had made love, but to a thick fallen limb from a tree that was nearer to the lake. He nodded at the branch in an invitation for Seth to sit if he liked. Seth gave him a questioning glance, and Everett said, "I've been sitting all day, in between swims to cool off. You go ahead."

Seth sat, the tree branch squeaking but holding beneath the solid weight of his body.

"You asked me if Joy is all right," Seth began, his hands on his thighs. "I didn't answer right away because I wasn't certain how I should."

A prickle of wariness went down Everett's neck. "What's that mean?"

Seth exhaled. His face was set in its typical impassive expression, but Everett sensed that he was torn about something.

"Seth? Is Joy okay?" he asked sharply, taking a step toward him.

"She says she's fine."

"But you don't believe her?"

Another pause. Everett sensed he had to give Seth time to sort through whatever was bothering him, but he'd never experienced such a pressure to demand answers more.

"Has Joy told you about how her mother died?" Seth asked suddenly.

"Yes."

Seth regarded him with a dark-eyed stare. "She told you about how brutal Alice's cancer was? How long it lingered? How her father left them when she was sixteen?"

Everett nodded, his focus on the other man intent.

"Did Joy tell you how she feels about her father?" Seth asked, once again staring out at the lake.

"She told me that she doesn't hold his leaving against him. She said she isn't particularly close to him, but that she doesn't hate him. I gather you feel differently about your brother?"

"I think he's a spineless degenerate for abandoning Joy and Alice like he did," he said, the acid in his tone indicating the depth of his derision for Jake Hightower. He turned his stare once again onto Everett. "What do you think about Jake's leaving like that?"

"Joy insisted I shouldn't judge him, not ever having been in a situation like that myself." Everett gave a rueful shrug. "But personally, I'd say your brother sounds like a real louse. Who could leave their wife under those circumstances? Who could possibly leave their daughter to cope with it, when he couldn't even do it?"

He noticed Seth's narrowed gaze on him. "What has this got to do with how Joy is doing right at this moment?" Everett demanded.

"So you've never been close to anyone who had cancer?"

"No. How is that relevant?" Everett asked, not confrontationally. He just wanted to know why it was meaningful to Joy, because he was starting to realize more and more that this part of Joy's history was crucial.

"How do you know that you wouldn't want to avoid that situation, like my brother did, when you've never been in his shoes?"

"That's what Joy said," he said, exasperated. Why couldn't Seth just tell him whether Joy was all right or not?

"Well? I'm still asking the question."

"If I loved someone, I would never, *ever* walk out on them while they were suffering. I wouldn't even consider it. I wouldn't even know *how*," Everett stated heatedly. "Just because I've never been close to anyone who's battled cancer doesn't mean I'm incapable of compassion and loyalty."

"You have been close to someone."

Everett blinked. "What?" he asked, not sure he'd understood Seth.

"Joy."

A whip-poor-will called in the distance. It was like a heavy, dark cloth was being draped over him slowly from head to toe. He blinked away the dark spots that appeared before his eyes.

"Joy has cancer?" he asked hollowly.

"She's in remission. At least I hope she is."

Everett sat heavily on the thick branch, making it creak loudly with their combined weight. It held, however, which was good. He suddenly wasn't certain his legs would have.

"What does that mean, at least you *hope* she's in remission?" he asked Seth hoarsely.

"She's been doing well since her treatment, which ended last winter. Chances are, she's still doing well. But with this fever and the swollen glands, the doctors want her to have a biopsy, just to make sure everything is all right."

"When will she have the biopsy done?" he asked tensely.

"Tuesday morning, at Northwestern Memorial in Chicago."

Everett sprang up from the branch as a surge of adrenaline went through him.

"Why didn't she tell me?"

Seth shook his head, and Everett paused in his pacing in the weeds.

"She didn't tell anyone about her cancer. None of her friends. If she and I weren't so close and she could have avoided it, she probably wouldn't have told me. After her chemotherapy and radiation were finished, she made plans to move to Chicago. I couldn't talk her out of it," Seth said, sounding desolate.

Everett stared at the ground sightlessly. Seth was usually so controlled in how he expressed emotion. He typically gave the impression of being a very powerful man. Even though there had hardly been any inflection in his tone as he spoke just now, Everett sensed his profound desperation and helplessness when it came to Joy.

"Why?" Everett asked. "Why is she withdrawing so much?"

"At first, I thought it was just because she felt guilty for forcing me to watch her suffer. I assumed she felt wretched that I had to endure the whole thing with Alice, and then had to re-experience it over again, this time with her."

"That makes sense," Everett said, his mind a whirlwind of thoughts and emotions. He began pacing again. "Not that I'm agreeing with her logic, but I can understand her emotional need to protect you. What sort of cancer was she diagnosed with?"

"Lymphoma."

Everett grimaced and came to a halt in the weeds. "Isn't that the type of cancer her mom had?"

"They were both lymphomas, but Alice's was Hodgkin's. Joy's type actually has a much better prognosis and treatment success than Alice's did."

His heart leapt. "That's good, isn't it?"

He wished Seth's nod were a little more reassuring.

"When was she diagnosed?"

"Last summer. I remember it was while we were working on *Maritime*."

Everett stared out at the sun-dappled lake. Pieces of memory barraged his consciousness like sharp fragments. Joy's panic after their sexual experience in the studio, her large, tear-filled eyes looking up at him as he'd told her everything was going to be all right.

No. No, it's not, she'd said, her frantic tone slicing him to the quick. He'd be willing to bet she'd known about her diagnosis on that day. Maybe that's why she'd behaved so uncharacteristically in regard to their sexual encounter. He should have recognized the depth of her desperation. He heard himself teasing her lightly—cluelessly— about all her pill bottles and how she must be a health nut, and then her solemn stare back at him in the mirror.

A pain unlike anything he'd ever experienced before pierced him. God, it hurt, to think of Joy being afraid . . . being alone. He covered his face with one hand. After a moment, he slowly low- ered it.

"That's why she left, isn't it? She's afraid to get too close to anyone. She's afraid she'll subject them to potential pain and . . ."

"Loss," Seth said when he faded off. Everett turned and saw Seth's gaze on him, cold and flinty. He felt the judgment in the other man's stare. He returned the look unflinchingly.

"I'm in love with her," Everett said.

"Jake was in love with Alice. Or so he said. Once."

"Well, I'm not Jake," Everett snarled. He started toward the path.

"Where are you going?" Seth asked.

"To Chicago."

"Everett, wait."

Everett almost didn't stop—why should he? Seth had almost as much faith in him as Joy, but he wasn't the one he had to convince. It was Joy to whom he wanted to prove himself. It was Joy he *needed* to see. At the last moment, however, he thought of how much Seth had endured and how much he loved Joy. He thought of how much Joy adored her uncle, and his feet came to an abrupt halt.

"What?" he said, not turning around.

"Joy begged me not to tell you any of this. I've broken my vow to her."

Everett turned around slowly. Seth had stood and faced him. "Why?"

"Because I don't have complete faith that she's telling the truth about this procedure she's having done in Chicago. I think things could be worse than she's letting on."

"What makes you say that?"

Seth inhaled slowly and released it. "Because after she decided to move to Chicago and separate herself from me, I started to suspect that if she ever had a return of her cancer, if she ever had to go through treatment again, she would keep it from me."

"You think it's the main reason she moved to Chicago, don't you?"

"So that she could live her life privately. Alone. Yes."

"I won't accept that," Everett said. "Even if she doesn't feel the same way about me as I do her, I won't let someone I care about suffer alone like that."

"I admire your steadfastness."

"But you thinking I'm blowing hot air?" Everett challenged, taking a step toward Seth. A cool breeze caused the trees to quake and sigh and the water to ripple along the shore behind them.

"No, it's not that," Seth finally replied. "The fact is, there's something about Joy that I didn't understand until last night when we spoke after her exam."

"What?" Everett demanded.

"It's about Jake—Joy's father. I always knew that Joy didn't share my contempt for his leaving, or her mother's heartbreak. Until last night, I'd just assumed Joy's attitude toward her father was the understandable loyalty a child feels toward both of their parents."

"She's amazingly forgiving about the fact that her father abandoned them when her mom was so sick. It really struck me, her attitude."

Seth nodded. "Last night, she got really emotional when I encouraged her to tell you about her history of cancer and why she was leaving Vulture's Canyon."

Everett stilled, realizing Seth was getting to the meat of things. "What did she say? Seth?" he prodded when the other man hesitated. Dread filled him. "Did she tell you she thought I couldn't handle dealing with her being ill? She thinks I'm like her father, doesn't she? A glory hound who only cares about himself?"

"No," Seth said in a ringing tone that brought him up short. "A little part of her—the scared kid in her—is afraid that *she's* like Jake."

Everett blinked. "I don't understand. How could she think that? You told me she walked every step of the way with her mother during her treatments . . . all the way until the end."

Seth nodded. "Yes, and like all people, especially a child, she occasionally had fantasies about what it would be like to run . . . to flee all the hurt and fear. A part of her envied her father for being able to walk away from all that heartache. Because she had those natural longings once in a while, a small part of her identified with him."

Everett's throat tightened. He shut his eyes. It wasn't fair. How could such a unique, lovely woman like Joy be forced to struggle and suffer so much?

"Joy doesn't believe that you can't handle things, Everett," Seth said quietly. "She doesn't want you to *have* to handle it. In her own words, she wouldn't wish what she endured on her worst enemy, let alone you."

Everett cursed softly.

"She feels she never had a choice in the matter. She was a child, a dependent, while Alice was sick for all those years. She's afraid that if the choice had ever been given to her as an adult, like it was her father, she'd choose as he did. She wouldn't, of course. Not in a million years. Joy loves very deeply. There were plenty of times I had to pull her away from her mother's bedside because she was half dead with exhaustion. It's her self-doubt, her fears, that are at the heart of things."

"And so she keeps people away. She's taking away the necessity for people like me or you to choose to be with her, in health or in suffering," Everett said starkly, understanding bringing a heavy wave of sadness along with it.

Seth nodded. "I think it's both—she feels guilty for subjecting others to her condition. She also, in her own way, is protecting the people she cares about from having to make the choice of being with her or not."

Everett closed his eyes and felt the burn. "Part of her hates herself for understanding Jake's need to escape."

"Yes," Seth said heavily.

"Why are you telling me all this, Seth?" Everett asked after a long pause.

"Because Joy only opened up to me, she only told me what's been in her heart all these years, when I suggested that she speak to you about her cancer. I saw how passionate she was—how desperate—for you not to know. She wanted to protect you at all costs."

"How will I convince her that I would choose to be with her, no matter what happens?"

"I don't know. I don't even know if it's possible."

Everett looked at him incredulously.

"The only thing I know is that I haven't been able to get through to her so far. Perhaps it takes the type of feelings she has for you, versus those for an uncle, to truly break through to her."

His heart started to thud loudly in his ears. "You think she really cares about me?"

"If I didn't, I wouldn't be here talking to you right now."

Everett inhaled slowly. "I should go," he said, gazing toward the path.

"I'll stay here for a while, but here," Seth said, stepping toward him. Everett gave him a dubious glance when he handed him the keys to his rental car.

"I already have a car," Everett said.

"No. There's something in the trunk for you. From Joy."

Everett glanced up in surprise.

"She gave me some money and a note for you last night, and made a request that I purchase something while I was in St. Louis this morning. It's in the trunk of the car."

"Thanks," Everett said, accepting the keys.

"Everett?" Seth called.

"Yeah?" he asked, turning only his chin, impatient to be gone.

"Good luck."

Everett nodded once and strode toward the path with a hasty determination.

When he reached the circular turnabout in front of Rill and Katie's house, he immediately approached Seth's rental car. He popped the trunk. It was empty save for a square box. He drew off the lid and immediately saw a folded note with his name on it in Joy's handwriting. He picked it up. The notepaper had the insignia and address for Prairie Lakes Hospital on it. Beneath it, he read:

Everett,

I have never met another person who lived life with so much passion and grace. I count myself lucky to have known you. Please, please . . . take good care of yourself?

Always,
Joy

He flipped back the paper and saw a brand-new pair of men's high-end running shoes.

He stared, thinking of how he'd said he'd be the one to buy her all the shoes she wanted. Here, she'd done it for him, and the gesture meant so much more than his hollow offer because Joy didn't have the financial means to go around buying expensive running shoes.

Bitterness rose in him when he thought of how she must have considered his condescending, cavalier attitude toward his health and good fortune, how he never questioned it, like he was some kind of fucking self-righteous prince of the realm.

He slammed the trunk so hard, it rocked the car.

"Everett?" Katie called a few seconds later. He glanced up to where she stood on the front porch, the box clutched against his chest. "Where have you been?"

"It doesn't matter," he said as he strode toward the guesthouse. He'd get in the shower, pack a few things and be on the road in three minutes flat.

"Then what *does* matter?" Rill called.

Everett paused. Rill had walked out onto the porch after Katie and stood next to her. He tossed Seth's car keys to his friend. Rill caught them without ever taking his gaze off Everett.

"Joy. I'm going after her," Everett said.

The last thing he saw was Rill raise his eyebrows at his adamancy, and then nod as if Everett had just uttered the most reasonable thing on earth.

Nineteen

Joy paused in the action of flipping the channel with her remote control in her hospital room when she saw Everett's face on the screen. She tried desperately to find the volume control on the device while not removing her gaze from his image. He was talking soberly to a famous daytime talk show diva. His goatee was in place, so Joy knew it couldn't have been a live interview. It must have been recorded last week when he'd been doing all those rounds of publicity appearances.

"Do you think you'll ever settle down and get married?" the talk show host asked in the friendly, confidential tone for which she was known.

"Oh yeah. Family is very important to me."

"So what's holding you back?"

"Finding the right woman."

"You have a studio full of women right here who would be

happy to audition for the part," the host joked. The camera panned to the small arena filled almost exclusively with cheering, whistling women before it cut back to Everett. Now that Joy had grown to know him, she noticed that his smile didn't reach his eyes.

"It's not a *part*. But thanks, I'm flattered," he said, softening the edge in his tone and smiling at the audience. "Actually, I think I'm doing okay with my own search."

The host's eyebrows shot up with interest. "I'm sensing there's a story here."

"No, no story," Everett said, shaking his head. "Just someone special."

"Can you tell us something about her?" the host coaxed.

"Sure. She's very private," Everett replied unblinkingly.

For a split second, the host looked taken aback at his subtle remonstrance for her prying. Then Everett grinned—full out and brilliant—and of course he was forgiven. Both the audience and the host broke into laughter.

"Joy?" A voice penetrated her intense focus on the television screen and the sound of her pumping heart in her ears. She blinked and turned her head, seeing Dr. Chen standing next to her bed.

"Dr. Chen," she said breathlessly, fumbling with the remote control. She turned the TV off. "I'm sorry, I was just—"

"Everett Hughes. I saw," he said, grinning knowingly.

She gave a hollow laugh.

Had Everett been talking about *her* on that talk show?

She felt a little sick all of a sudden. Disoriented.

Heartsore.

"Can we do the procedure now?" she asked Dr. Chen, forcing her mind into the world of the mundane versus the flash of Everett's smile.

Unfortunately, after she'd been admitted, the surgery had been delayed due to the fact that her temperature had gone up again and was over one hundred. Dr. Chen didn't want her to undergo general anesthesia until it at least dipped below ninety-nine degrees. Joy had been forced to wait for three hours now, willing her fever to go down the whole time.

"The nurse is about to come and do your vitals. If your fever has gone down, we'll take you to the OR right away. I just heard from the anesthesiologist that she's got an opening."

Joy held her breath in anticipation as the nurse took her temperature. She hated the fact that she'd already been in there longer than she'd expected.

"Ninety-eight point eight," the nurse said.

Joy glanced triumphantly at Dr. Chen, and he gave her a thumbs-up.

"I'll send over some transporters to transfer you," Dr. Chen said before he left.

Joy set aside the remote control and lay back on the flat, uncomfortable hospital pillows. Why had she been so eager to get the procedure underway? she wondered as her familiar dread for the general anesthesia rose like an encroaching shadow ready to pounce. She started to panic.

What if she never woke up? Why hadn't she asked Seth to be here with her?

Had she done the stupidest thing she'd ever done in her life by telling Everett good-bye? She had an overwhelming desire to call him. She sprang up and fumbled with the phone on the bedside table. A young man dressed in white knocked on her door and rolled a gurney into the room.

Slowly, Joy set down the receiver.

Everett saw a meter maid writing out parking tickets a half a block away. Crap. He couldn't believe they gave out tickets at night. He glanced at the sign posted at the side of Joy's street. Apparently, vehicles were supposed to have a neighborhood sticker to park here legally.

For the two hundredth time since he'd arrived in Chicago that evening, he looked at the brownstone where Joy lived. Her apartment remained dark. She wasn't answering when he buzzed her intercom. She wouldn't pick up her cell phone.

Where the hell was she? What if she was up there in her apartment, sick and fevered? His thoughts about picking the locks to get into her place fractured when he heard a tap on the windshield of his rental car. He glanced up and saw the meter maid—a short, light brown–skinned woman of about fifty—squinting at him. She waved her hand toward the street as if to say *Get going and I won't ticket you.*

Everett shrugged and gave her a sheepish glance, wishing she'd just give him the ticket and leave him alone. Joy's street was lined on both sides with bumper-to-bumper cars. He wasn't going to give up his prized spot. Instead of ignoring him, however, the meter maid shone a flashlight in his eyes and indicated she wanted him to roll down his window. He pulled down the bill on his cap and followed her instructions with a resigned sigh.

"What're you doing?" she asked bluntly.

"I was waiting for a friend," he said, tilting his chin toward Joy's brownstone. A thought occurred to him. "Hey, have you passed this street earlier today? You haven't seen her coming in or out, have you? The woman who lives in that brownstone? Real pretty, short brown hair, great legs—"

"Joy," the meter maid stated rather than asked.

"Yeah," Everett said, leaning forward eagerly. "Have you seen her by chance?" He squinted when she shone the flashlight full in his face. He ducked his head.

"You could pass as a double for that guy—Everett Hughes," the woman said, peering at him.

He slunk back into the shadows. "That's what I've been told a time or two. Hear it more when I have a goatee," he mumbled, wondering belatedly why he hadn't thought to do a foreign accent to further disguise himself. "Have you seen Joy or not?"

"Are you going to move this car, or do you want a ticket?"

"I'll take the ticket," Everett said. He started to roll up his window, but the meter maid tapped on it lightly with her flashlight, glaring at him. He waited resignedly while she filled out the ticket and handed it to him.

"Gee, thanks," he said with tired sarcasm.

"My pleasure. And I did see Joy today when I was ticketing early this morning. She caught a cab up at the corner. She had a bag on her shoulder, like she was going somewhere," the woman said, giving him a significant glance.

"Thanks," he said, meaning it this time.

"You're welcome, Mr. Hughes," the woman said.

Everett watched her while she moved on to leave her cheerful little greeting on the windshield of the next car. He'd already called Seth a half hour ago to clarify what he'd told him earlier: Joy wasn't supposed to go in for her procedure until tomorrow morning. Why wasn't she at home? He replayed his conversation earlier by the lake with Seth.

I don't have complete faith that she's telling the truth about this procedure she's having done in Chicago. I think things could be worse than she's letting on.

The meter maid glanced up, watching him as he backed up the car a foot, swung it into a tight U-turn and accelerated down the dark street.

A half hour later, he leaned against the circular information desk at Northwestern Memorial Hospital. The security guard behind the desk was elderly, his snowy white hair a bright contrast to his dark brown skin. Everett had learned that his name was Nathan.

"We got some of the spillover from the traffic from that premiere of yours over here by the hospital the other night," Nathan said, giving Everett a condemning glance.

"That's terrible," Everett said. "They should control traffic flow better around a hospital."

"Especially when we've got the busiest ER in the city," Nathan added pointedly. "Imagine how bad you'd feel if all those crowds got in the way of your sister—what's her name? Joy Hightower?—getting treatment as quick as she needed it."

"Yeah. All because of a stupid movie."

"It wasn't stupid, though," Nathan said, his sudden amiability suggesting he'd admonished Everett sufficiently for being inconsiderate enough to plan his premiere near a hospital. "The missus and I saw it the other night. She wants to see it again."

"I'll send some tickets here to the hospital. Which theater would you like to see it at?" he asked, resisting a strong impulse to check his watch out of impatience.

"That'd be mighty nice of you! Margaret will be over the moon when I tell her about meeting you."

Everett jotted down the name of the theater along with the security guard's name.

"It's a real shame about your plane getting in late and your missing out on visitors' hours," Nathan said offhandedly as he plucked at his computer keyboard.

"Yeah. Rotten luck," Everett said, gazing longingly at the bank of elevators behind the security desk.

"I saw you in the spy movie—*Killer Instinct*. You reckon you learned anything about being sneaky in that movie?"

Everett blinked. "Tons. I may look clueless, but that's just an act."

Nathan hid a grin. "You'd have to be slick to avoid the night nurse on the eighth floor. Name's Edna Shanoy, and she'd scare the daylights out of a *real* CIA agent if she ever caught him on her floor past visiting hours."

"Thanks, Nathan," Everett said earnestly.

"For what?" Nathan asked mildly, turning his attention to his monitors.

Everett took the stairs instead of the elevators, not having ever learned enough skills while playing a spy to know how to muffle the sound of an elevator door opening. He was glad he had, because the hall he stepped into on the eighth floor was amazingly hushed, dim and inactive at midnight. He saw no one as he hurried down the hall, peering into several doors and realizing he wasn't on the medical unit proper. These weren't patient rooms. He stayed in the shadows of a door recess and stuck his head out. Ahead, he saw a bright light and a young nurse with a sweet, round face and short auburn hair rise from her seat at the nursing station and walk into a room behind it. This close, Everett could see the patient rooms were straight ahead of the nursing station.

Ideal location for a nurse to see her patients' rooms; less than perfect for an interloper.

He plunged down the hallway before the young nurse returned, dipping into the first patient room on the right. Four times, he struck out miserably, his only saving grace that all of the patients were sleeping when he snuck up to look at them. He checked the nursing station before he reentered the hallway again and held a curse. The nurse had returned. He waited until her back was to him as she returned a chart to the cart and darted into the room directly to the right of him.

The bed closer to the door was empty, the bed neatly made. The privacy curtain had been partially pulled, making it impossible for him to see the identity of who was in the other bed. He pushed the door closer to the "shut" position, but still left it open enough not to raise suspicion. How was it that hospital patients were granted no privacy whatsoever? he wondered irritably.

He knew he'd found Joy. He had no idea how. Maybe her singular scent somehow lingered in the air. Maybe he knew because of the way his already pounding heart started to do a battle-like drumbeat in his ears.

He stood by the side of her bed, looking down at her. They'd left on the light just above her head. The fierce beating against his eardrums seemed to wane and almost stop. She lay fast asleep, her face very pale, an IV inserted into her arm. He realized he was holding his breath, waiting to see her chest rise and fall. He couldn't see the subtle movement in the loose-fitting hospital gown, and so, desperate, he moved closer to her and placed his hand over the top swell of her left breast.

He felt her warmth and the precious beat of her heart next to his palm. His pulse began to throb again at his throat.

There was a white bandage at the side of her neck. Was that from the biopsy? Had there been some complication with the procedure? Is that why she'd had to stay overnight and required an IV?

He looked around anxiously for a medical chart, but recalled they were kept behind the nursing station. Joy's hospital room seemed barren. Only a plastic glass and pitcher of water, some Chapstick, a napkin and a book lay on the bedside table. In some of the other patient rooms he'd sneaked into, he'd seen flowers around the beds, cards from family members, he realized, a pain going through him.

He picked up the book and saw it was a worn copy of *Razor Pass*. He set it down and almost turned away before he halted. He picked up the napkin that had been partially covered by the book. His face looked back at him. Once again, he marveled at how Joy had managed to capture so perfectly in his gaze what he felt as he looked at her in that classroom—the essence of what he was only beginning to comprehend.

He set the sketch on the table.

He walked over to the far side of Joy's bed and carefully lowered the metal rail, wincing at the squeaky metallic sound the hinges made. Hadn't this thing ever been lowered? She stirred almost imperceptibly at the noise.

"Joy?" he said quietly, sitting on the edge of her bed.

She didn't budge, but he thought he saw her eyelids flicker.

"You didn't want anyone here, but I'm here anyway," he said gruffly.

He touched her cheek, and then came down in the bed next to her. He curled on his side, trying to make his large body as innocuous as possible on the narrow bed. With his arm just above her waist and his hand opened along the side of her rib cage, he could feel her slow, even breathing more easily. Through the sanitized, slightly chemical odor that clung in hospitals, he inhaled her floral scent.

Her facial muscles tightened. She moved her mouth, speaking with no sound. Her head jerked slightly, and she tilted her chin in his direction. Her lips were dry. He reached across her, mindful not to disturb the IV tube, and grabbed the Chapstick. He rubbed some of the emollient onto his fingertip and carefully outlined her lips with it. Again, her mouth moved.

"Shh," he soothed, slicking the emollient along her lower lip.

"Everett," she said with what appeared to be great effort.

A muscle leapt in his cheek at the sound of her saying his name in a rough, hoarse whisper.

"I'm here. Go back to sleep," he murmured, although he wasn't sure she'd ever really awakened. Her facial muscles slackened, and once again her breathing grew even.

He recalled how she'd kissed his thigh and said his name before she'd come so sweetly back into his arms. *Was that really just last night?* he wondered, amazed. That memory of her saying his name while she dreamt had been what he'd clung to after he'd gotten the letter where she'd said everything was over. Joy might be convinced it was best for her to be alone during the waking hours, but her sleeping self thought differently.

He just lay there, alert and unmoving, looking his fill of her face.

When her mom had first been hospitalized, Joy had been twelve. When she sat next to her mother's bed, gazing at her while she slept, she was small enough that she did so through the metal guardrails. They had reminded her of the bars of a prison cell.

Suddenly, someone stepped forward and lowered the rail, the metal hinges squawking. She could see her mother clearly now, sleeping peacefully. She glanced up to thank her uncle Seth, but instead saw Everett standing there, wearing his ragged plaid cap, his jaw no longer clean shaven, but darkened with whiskers.

He smiled at her—that flash of pure brilliance. Her heart began to beat erratically. Why did her eyelids feel so heavy? She wanted to see him, more than anything.

But she *was* seeing him. Wasn't she?

"I know how much you cherish your privacy," he said, suddenly sober.

"I know," she said. Her throat was so sore, it was laborious to talk. "You said so—on that talk show."

"You saw that? You knew I was talking about you?"

To nod took all of her effort, and she still wasn't quite sure she'd managed it.

"It was the only real part of the interview," he said confidentially as he sat on the edge of her bed—for suddenly it was she who was lying there, not her mother. Everett's body was a welcome weight on the mattress. She wanted desperately to tell him how glad she was he was there, but it felt like her larynx had been tied in a painful knot. Her mouth felt so dry.

She drifted.

Everett touched her upper lip. Her body responded to his touch and scent: her breath quickened, her nerves tingled, her nipples tightened against the cloth covering them. He slid his fingertip along her lower lip. She wanted so much to thank him for lowering her prison bars and freeing her, but her eyelids and her throat and her voice were failing her. Then she couldn't remember what she'd meant by *prison bars* and she had to narrow the focus of her will-power even more in order to utter the name of her desire.

She did so with terrific effort.

"Everett."

"I'm here. Go back to sleep," she heard his gruff voice say. But was it real? Or was she dreaming?

She felt the weight of his head on the pillow next to her. He covered her breast softly with his hand, and she felt her nipple press against his warm palm. He was here.

He was real.

She relaxed, surrendering her struggle, and sank back into the dark, peaceful realm of sleep.

"What the hell do you think you're doing?"

Everett started at the sound of the harsh female voice. His eye-lids popped open. He stared at the blue-and-white print on the hospital gown Joy wore. He'd fallen asleep with his head on the pillow next to her. He immediately looked into her face, concerned, but Joy continued to sleep.

"Get your damn hand off that girl!" the scandalized voice said.

Everett blinked and gazed first at the large shadow looming on the other side of Joy's bed. *Edna Shanoy,* he thought with a sense of dread, remembering what Nathan had called the fearsome eighth-floor night nurse. He glanced to where she was glaring with large, protuberant eyes. His hand lay on Joy's breast.

He removed it hastily. "If you could just keep your voice down," he said groggily. "I don't want to wake her."

"You know . . . I think that's . . . I would swear that's Everett—"

"I don't care if it's Everett *Hughes*!" Edna hissed, interrupting the soft, incredulous female voice. Her square jaw quivered with indignation. "No one sneaks onto my unit and paws at my patients."

Everett clambered out of the bed, snatching his cap from where it'd fallen behind Joy's pillow. Behind the boulder-like body of Edna Shanoy, he saw the slight figure of the young, auburn-haired nurse staring at him with wide eyes.

"All right, I'm going," he said in a hushed tone, clapping his hat on his head. Edna bared her teeth at him menacingly as he rounded the bed. "I'm not some kind of degenerate," he snapped. "I happen to be in love with her."

"You can tell the officer about it," Edna said, tilting her head smugly toward the hallway.

"But Miss Shanoy, I think it really is him. I saw that sketch next to the patient's book when I was pouring her water earlier and I thought it looked like Everett Hughes," the young nurse said breathlessly, "and now here he is—"

"Shut up, Cheryl," Edna Shanoy growled.

Cheryl's spine stiffened angrily, but she didn't retort. Everett looked past both of them, hoping to see Nathan's kindly face in the hallway. Instead, he saw a tall, burly outline dressed in black. His gaze skimmed the letters on the bulletproof vest.

Shit. Chicago PD.

"Our night duty officer from the ER, here to take care of you, pervert," Edna said, giving him a beady, triumphant glance.

"Twisted cow," he muttered. He ignored Edna's snort of disbelieving fury and glanced back at Joy. Her eyes didn't open, but her head moved on the pillow and her expression was anxious. He shot an annoyed glance at Edna and stalked out of the room. He didn't want the woman shouting any more accusations and waking her. He rolled his eyes when the cop grabbed his elbow.

Could this night get any worse?

"You're under arrest," the police officer said.

Apparently, it could.

Twenty

❧

Joy entered her apartment on Tuesday evening feeling like she'd just gone a couple rounds in the ring with a prizefighter. Except for the soreness at her throat, her aches had nothing to do with the procedure. Her fever had flared again this morning, delaying her discharge and causing her muscles to throb in protest. She felt like an eighty-year-old woman as she entered her bathroom and removed her clothing, the Band-Aid that covered where the IV had been and the bandage on her neck.

She hesitated before she stepped into the steaming water. Part of her wanted nothing more than to wash off the clinging remnants of the hospital from her skin, yet there was that other fragrance that she caught sporadically when she tilted her head to the right—spicy and complex, male and delicious.

How could it be that she kept catching *Everett's* scent on her?

She blinked heavily, fatigue weighing her down. She wasn't thinking properly. The lingering effects of the anesthesia, the fever, or both were making her have strange experiences and memories. Like how she could have sworn she'd woken up in the middle of the night and opened her eyes with extreme effort, only to see the oddest sight—men's white-and-silver running shoes with orange stripes stacked one on top the other and pressing against the footrest of her hospital bed. She strained to recall what was attached to those shoes, but nothing came.

Very odd. Why should that unlikely memory make her want to weep? Was it because she'd seen how many times not only Seth but Everett had tried to call her between last evening and when she'd checked her cell phone on the cab ride home? She couldn't find the energy to listen to the messages Everett had left her. It'd make her sad. It'd fill her up with more longing than she knew what to do with in her moment of weakness.

She'd barely had sufficient energy to call Seth, who was at the St. Louis airport. He'd been so frantic with worry that she hadn't called him earlier that he'd been in the process of changing his flight from Los Angeles to Chicago. She'd assured him that she was fine and explained about the fever delaying her discharge. By the time she'd gotten off the phone with him, he seemed mollified.

She willed her exhaustion and ragged emotional state to the periphery of her consciousness and gingerly stepped into the hot spray. It was a blessed thing. She showered mechanically, taking special care in regard to the small incision on her neck, cleaning it as the discharge nurse had instructed. After she'd stepped out, she affixed another bandage, ran a comb through her hair, took her medication and brushed her teeth, her legs growing weaker and weaker by the second.

She dressed in a tank top and sleeping shorts, padded to her cool bedroom and threw back the comforter. It'd been after five o'clock by the time she'd finally been discharged. It was past six now. Pale evening light peeked around the closed drapes. She sagged into the mattress with a sigh of relief. Despite her exhaustion, she couldn't

immediately sleep. It was as if she was forgetting something . . .
some important detail.

She kept searching through her sluggish brain, anxious for
some clue. Sleep claimed her before she could locate the crucial,
elusive thread.

She swam languidly in the in-between world between sleep and
wakefulness. Someone touched her lower lip, stroking her. She
opened her mouth wider, granting permission for the intimate
caress.

"Everett," she whispered.

"Your lips can actually read fingerprints, can they? I shouldn't
be surprised; they're so sensitive. They're still chapped, though.
Poor thing."

A memory trickled into her sleepy awareness of someone gently
applying an emollient to her lips while she lay in the hospital bed.

Her eyes popped open.

Her bedroom was almost completely bathed in darkness, save
a dim light emanating from above the kitchen sink in the far distance. It cast enough glow for her to see the shadow of a man leaning over where she lay. She saw the bill of a cap.

"Everett," she said through a raw throat.

"Shh," he soothed.

Pressured-stored emotion frothed and boiled in her breast,
threatening to erupt—fear, regret, shame, longing . . . love.

Love, most of all.

He cupped her jaw with his hand and put his cheek next to hers,
his forehead next to her on her pillow. Did his tears mingle with
her own? She wasn't sure, because when he next spoke, his voice
sounded sure and even.

"Let me get you some water. Can you use any throat spray or
anything?" he asked quietly.

She nodded and croaked the word *bathroom*. She was over-whelmed. Everett was here. It wasn't a dream. She touched the side of his rib cage and felt his lean, warm torso through his T-shirt as he sat up. He paused at her caress, sitting on the edge of the bed. He leaned down and kissed her on the lips very gently.

"I told you in that letter I didn't think we should see each other again," she said miserably when he lifted his mouth.

"I decided that really meant you were falling in love with me and running scared."

She smiled despite the fact that her cheeks were soaked with tears. "That was a bold interpretation," she whispered, wincing at the effort.

"Accurate, though?"

The familiar anxiety pressed on her chest, but Everett's hand gently stroking her arm seemed to ease it.

"Yes." A few more tears fell silently down her cheeks.

He kissed her again, quick and heartfelt. She watched his loom-ing shadow recede as he left the room.

"You were there . . . in . . . in the hospital?" she managed when he returned just seconds later. Her throat felt like it'd undergone a pounding with a meat tenderizer. It had already been sore, but the insertion of the breathing tube during the surgical procedure had worsened matters. He sat on the edge of the bed as she pushed herself up on the pillows. He found her hand in the darkness and placed a cool glass into it. The icy fluid felt heavenly sliding down her throat.

"I was there. Fat lot of good I did you. That witch nurse Edna Shanoy had me arrested when she found me in bed with you."

"*What?*" Joy asked, spilling some ice water on her chest.

"Why do you think I wasn't there this morning?" he murmured. "Thanks to Edna, I was sharing a luxury suite in a communal holding cell with nine of Chicago's finest citizens. Edna made me out to be a prime pervert for lying in bed with you after visiting hours. Of course, her interpretation might have had something to do with the fact that I fell asleep with my hand on your breast, but—"

"Oh, no," Joy muttered, her voice a little stronger. She actually remembered that—his hand on her breast. How could she have forgotten it? Strange, the effects anesthesia had on the mind. She set the glass of water down on the bedside table and reached for a box of tissues. She wiped her cheeks dry. "Why didn't they wake me up and ask me if I wanted you there?"

"I didn't want them to wake you. Besides, Edna ended up not pressing charges. The other nurse she worked with finally talked her out of it, according to the officer. Of course, Edna wasn't entirely convinced I wasn't the Crazed Groper of Northwestern Hospital until she'd forced me to sit in that holding cell for the night and most of the day. Jimmy K., Mad Louis and that lot were pretty nice guys, but they didn't really smell too great. Neither did I, by the time they finally let me go this afternoon, come to think of it."

She'd caught a whiff of him earlier when he'd lain by her side and hugged her. "You smell wonderful."

"After I found out you had already been discharged from the hospital, I checked into a hotel and showered before I came over. Didn't want to make you sicker with my smell. Here," he said, giving her the throat spray. Joy used it, thankful for the numbing sensation. She set down the bottle next to the glass of water.

"Better?" he asked, his voice like a rough caress in the darkness.

"Yes, thank you." She blinked, the reality of his presence finally fully penetrating her consciousness. "How did you get in my apartment?"

"Picked the locks," he said matter-of-factly. "I had one of the most notorious cat burglars in Europe teach me for *Cat*. He's completely reformed now," he added, as if he thought Joy was worried about his morals.

"Everett, there's something I want to tell you," she said.

He came down next to her on the bed, lying on his hip, his front pressed against her side. He put his arm around her waist and caressed the exposed skin between her shorts and tank top. She shivered, not knowing if the reaction was from anxiety or his touch.

"Then tell me. I'm ready to hear whatever it is. I'm not going anywhere," he said quietly.

Her throat swelled, making her pause for a moment before she continued. She took comfort from his stroking hand at her waist.

"Last year, I was diagnosed with PMBL. That's a type of lymphoma," she said in a rush. She'd only said these words once before—to Seth. This time it felt even more difficult. "It's cancer," she added, not sure how much sense she was making.

"I know," he said, his hand not faltering as he caressed her.

"Oh, okay. So, well . . . anyway, I went through treatment— chemotherapy and radiation. I was told last winter I was in remission. I've been okay until last weekend, when I got sick. And I got the swollen glands and the fever, and . . . and those are possible signs of a reoccurrence of the cancer."

His hand continued to stroke her, and the words just kept spilling out of her mouth.

"And the doctor in Prairie Lakes said I should have a lymph node resection done. He thought it was just a virus, but he wanted to make sure. So I came up here to see my oncologist, Dr. Chen, and he wanted to make sure, too. I had to do the surgery inpatient, though, instead of an outpatient biopsy."

"How come?" Everett asked.

"They had to do this kind of procedure where they can resect a lymph node near my lungs. They have to cut my throat and insert this instrument down in between my lungs. I'm sorry. I don't mean to gross you out," she said apologetically.

"You're not grossing me out," he said evenly. "Go on."

"Well, it requires general anesthesia, so I had to spend the night."

"That's why you weren't here. I waited out on the street for hours. Seth said you weren't supposed to go in until Tuesday morning."

"I sort of—"

"Told him it was an in-and-out procedure so he wouldn't worry. I know," Everett finished for her, his matter-of-fact tone easing her embarrassment. He opened his hand along the side of her waist and grasped her gently. She could feel the pulse at his wrist next to her naked skin. Why was his heart beating so fast when he sounded so calm?

"Joy?"

"Yes?"

"Before you go on, I think it's only fair to tell you that Seth already told me about your cancer diagnosis." He must have felt her stiffen. "Please don't be angry with him. He was desperate. He didn't know how to break through to you."

"Break through to me about what?"

"He wants you to know that he knows you're scared. He's worried about you. He doesn't want you to suffer alone. He feels as if you've shut him out, and he turned to me with some thin, crazy hope that you'd hear my plea when you wouldn't—or couldn't—hear his."

The silence seemed to swell and press against her eardrums. Anger at Seth's betrayal of her trust mingled with a profound sense of shame. She wanted to hide . . . to run. Yet she couldn't bear the thought of leaving Everett again. She felt like she stood at the edge of a cliff while a terrifying monster quickly approached from behind, her heartbeat racing as if she truly believed it was taking its last beats.

"I won't let you go through this alone," he said. "I will *not*. Even if you decided you just want to be friends instead of lovers, even if we hear that your cancer has returned and you have to go through another round of treatment, even if it reoccurs five times or ten times."

A shudder of emotion went through her. She'd never felt so naked, so exposed. She covered her face in her hands, but Everett gently removed them, kissing her cheek and then her clenched eyelids. Bitter tears escaped, scattering down her cheek. He pressed closer against her, his body absorbing her anguish.

"I will be here. Right *here*." He firmed his hold on the side of her body and shook her slightly for emphasis. "I've fallen in love with you, Joy. No one and nothing will keep me from you if you need me. Not thousands of miles, or some cow like Nurse Shanoy, not God himself. But the thing of it is," he added in a low, pressured whisper, "you have to say you need me. There's no sin in needing another human being. Not when that person wants more than anything to be at your side, offering support, offering love."

She shook, trying to keep the avalanche of emotion from freefalling out of control, straining so hard to contain it—to keep herself safe. It'd been so long, though, that she'd held it down. She didn't know until that moment how hard she'd worked to protect herself from feeling.

Everett came down over her, his lips pressed against the swell of her left breast, both of his arms encircling her.

"It's okay," he whispered gruffly, his breath warm next to her skin. "Don't fight it. I've got you."

Everything hurt. She couldn't stand the pressure a moment longer. An anguished cry erupted from her throat, the harbinger to a rush of terror, confusion, helplessness and love.

She couldn't stand the thought of Everett suffering because of her.

"I wouldn't *want* it for you." Caught in a ruthless, grinding grip of emotion, she only distantly realized what she'd said.

"I wouldn't want you to suffer," he said with calm deliberation.

"Who would ever want that for someone they care about? We can't choose our fates, though. We can only choose how we respond to them. I would choose to be with you. I want to celebrate your existence, Joy. Every day that's available to me, I want it. I'll cherish it."

She felt like she wanted to howl as the tidal wave of emotion rushed over her. She wept and shuddered for—she didn't know for how long. When her sobs finally slowed, Everett still held her fast, his cheek against her breast, his hands moving soothingly at her waist and back. She felt like a hollow, spent vessel.

Lighter.

Everett lifted his head.

"Here, drink some water," he said quietly, and she took the glass he offered, swallowing the cool fluid between hiccups.

"Oh my God," she rasped, spilling water on her chest for the second time. "I just realized I didn't say—I already got the results. Everett, the biopsy came back negative for cancer," she said, her words coming with the rapidity of machine gun fire.

She heard him breathing in the silence that followed. "I'm so sorry," she moaned. "I was so caught up in everything . . . shocked you were here . . . Oh, Jesus . . . I should have said sooner."

He made a sort of choking sound and suddenly his arms were around her again. Joy held up the water, trying to keep it from spilling on him while he hugged the daylights out of her.

"Dr. Chen says I have a really bad virus, and that's all. No cancer whatsoever," she managed to get out through Everett's tight squeeze.

"I'm so glad," he muttered.

She laughed. "Everett, I can't breathe."

He released her immediately. "I'm sorry."

"It's okay," she said, smiling. His hand touched her chin. Her fingers skimmed his lips. He was smiling, but she couldn't see it. Why hadn't they turned on the light? Suddenly, she wanted nothing

more than to drink in the sight of his face. She leaned over and
switched on the bedside lamp. She immediately put both of her
hands on his jaw.

For a stretched moment, they just stared at each other, both of
them smiling. She had the strangest impression their hearts were
joined, both of them pounding and near to bursting, they were so
full. She studied every detail of his face. How could she have ever
thought it was the property of an adoring public? The face of the
man she saw right now with the expression of indescribable desire
and love in his eyes—that face was *hers*, and hers alone.

Slowly, realization dawned on her. He must have noticed her
incredulous expression.

"Oh, Everett—you *didn't*," she cried. She removed his cap; her
eyes sprung wide. She touched the smooth skin of his skull, needing
another sense to back up her eyes. Every bit of his blond, tousled,
movie-star hair—*gone*.

"I shaved at the hotel," he said matter-of-factly.

"Why?" she gasped.

"As a show of support. In case your cancer had returned," he
said. He touched her short hair. Regret flickered across his handsome face. "I was so clueless. I thought you'd cut it short for a fashion statement." He lightly caressed the port scar on her chest, the
reminder of her chemotherapy. He met her stunned gaze. "Please
forgive me for being so clueless."

"Everett," she finally managed to say. "I can't believe you did
that." She would have sworn it was impossible for her eyes to man-
ufacture more tears, but that was before she'd seen Everett's
smooth, bald head.

He flashed his grin at her. "It's just hair, Joy. It's not a big deal."

She shook her head disbelievingly, a bark of laughter erupting
from her throat. "No. No, it's the stupidest . . . sweetest, most incredible thing . . ." she said brokenly.

She halted, once again overwhelmed. This time, it was she who squeezed the daylights out of him. She kissed his neck feverishly, transferred to his jaw and finally settled on his mouth. She parted his lips with her tongue, so desperate, so eager to celebrate his existence. He made a gruff, appreciative sound in his throat and ran his hands along her sides, pausing to cradle the sides of her breasts in his palms. Joy hugged him to her, kissing him like she thought his lungs held the last oxygen on earth. She felt his body respond to their embrace and made a sound of confused protest when he broke their kiss. He looked down at her, his nostrils flaring slightly. She read the question and concern in his blue-green eyes.

"It's just the flu," she reminded him hoarsely. "But even if the cancer were back, I'd want you inside of me right now. I want to assure myself that you're real, because from where I'm sitting, you look like the most amazing thing I've ever seen."

"Remind me never to let you switch positions, then," he said wryly as he grabbed the bottom of her tank top and peeled it off her.

She loved the small smile that flickered across his lips. She loved the blazing heat in his eyes as he touched her breast. She loved the fact that he'd cut off all his glorious hair to remind her of what she should have known.

Everett was the real deal.

"I love you," she gasped when he pushed his cock into her a moment later. "I *need* you."

His face tightened with emotion. He touched his lips to hers and then lifted his head, watching her face as he thrust.

He paused with his cock high inside of her.

"Put your legs together," he muttered.

"What?" she murmured, her hands moving anxiously over his hips and buttocks.

"I want to feel every nuance of you. I want to feel as close to you as I can."

She moaned as she tried to do what he'd suggested. The pressure in her sex grew intense.

"Touch your feet together," he encouraged. She heard the hard edge to his voice and knew he, too, was being affected as she squeezed his cock tighter within her body. "Now cross your ankles," he demanded.

It wasn't easy. Everett was not small, and nor was the thick, throbbing flesh embedded inside her. But the position definitely had its advantages. She had never felt his cock so clearly while it was harbored in her body—the shape, the heat, the throb of his heartbeat along the shaft.

She gritted her teeth, sweat gathering on her upper lip, and crossed her ankles. They groaned in unison. The pressure bordered on pain.

Everett slid out several inches and sank back into her, and Joy realized it also bordered on pure, intense pleasure. She saw a spark ignite in his eyes. Excitement zipped through her, because she knew what that feral gleam in his eyes signified.

He began to plunge into her again and again, their skin smacking together rhythmically. She could feel the thick rim beneath the head perfectly as he pulled his cock out of her. She'd never felt so inundated by a man, so possessed . . . so cherished.

"When I come, I'm going to leave a part of myself in you," Everett said solemnly as he fucked her.

"Yes," she moaned, for what else was he doing right now but pounding himself so entirely into her being that she would never—could never—let fear rule her again? That was what he was showing her, that love was the master of fear.

Emotion and sensation blended until the pleasure was too much to bear. She exploded with it. Everett was there with her, though, mixing with her, sharing with her, helping her to endure the sweet, shattering bliss.

Epilogue

"Joy?" Everett called as he closed the front door.

"I'm here—in the studio," he heard her call in the distance. He smiled and set the mail, a small box and the overnight bag he'd been carrying on the bench in the foyer so he could take off his jacket. He slipped his hand into his back pocket, his grin widening when he felt what he was searching for.

He was still celebrating his good fortune at finally having Joy in his house. She'd decided late last summer to become partners with Seth at Hightower Special Effects, but had insisted that she had to teach the fall term at the Steadman School. The administration wouldn't have had the time or opportunity to hire a new art teacher, and she hadn't wanted to leave her students hanging. As such, Everett and she had endured a long-distance romance for much longer than he preferred. He'd grown so impatient for her to join him in Los Angeles that Rill had hollowly threatened on a few occasions to ban him from the production studio for *Razor Pass* because of his surly mood.

Joy had just moved into his Laurel Canyon home two days ago. Unfortunately, no sooner had Everett helped her settle in than he had to take a prearranged visit to Death Valley with Rill, where they'd be moving production of the film to onsite location next week. Norman Cassavita, the author of the novel *Razor Pass*, was dead. For whatever reason, Rill considered Everett to have a better grip on the setting and nuances of the novel than anyone he knew— probably because Everett had been obsessed with the book since he'd first read it when he was sixteen years old. Everett had agreed to take the scouting trip with him to Death Valley before he knew that Joy would be moving in just days before.

This was his first time returning home to find Joy in the house, and it was a sweet experience indeed.

"Hi," he greeted her as he walked into the large bedroom they'd converted into studio space for Joy. She stood before a half-finished canvas and was in the process of hastily rinsing off her paint-brushes. She dropped the brushes in a jar when she saw him and turned toward him, her face glowing.

"Welcome home," she said before she flew into his arms. He lifted her feet off the ground, hugging her tight with his face pressed at the juncture of her neck and shoulder. He inhaled the smell of her floral shampoo, the singular fragrance of her skin and the slight hint of her paints—a scent combination he'd come to treasure as uniquely Joy's.

"I like the sound of that," he murmured as he lifted his head. He studied her face for a moment, gratified to see happiness in every nuance of her expression. He kissed her soundly.

"Did Rill finalize the set locations in Death Valley?" she asked when he lifted his head a moment later.

"Yeah. It's going to be a brutal schedule. Rill wants to finish in ten weeks in order to keep down costs," Everett murmured, touching her cheek softly. It'd grown pink and warm following their kiss. Her hazel eyes grew smoky at his caress.

"At least we'll be together," she murmured, turning her head and kissing his palm. Joy would be at the onsite shoot in her new capacity as partner of Hightower Special Effects. "It'll be the first time we've worked together . . . officially, anyway."

"What about the *Vanity Fair* cover?" Everett muttered distractedly as she pressed another kiss to his palm, and then tasted his skin with a warm, red tongue. He referred to a magazine cover they'd collaborated on several months ago. Joy had done a nude body painting of Everett that was already becoming a collector's item. Joy had posed him in front of a background mural depicting a sunlit field of grapes. Everett stood in front of a trellis where ripe fruit hung, his body paint of sun-soaked leaves, vines and the weave of the trellis precisely matching the background so that he blended perfectly into the scene. She'd made him into a fucking God with that painting—a fertile Dionysus coaxed by her paintbrush into springing right out of the canvas.

The painting had been a private affair between Everett and Joy. The result had been stunning, Joy having caught his rising desire for her as she tortured him with her tickling paintbrush just as she had done that first day in the studio. His tense, rigid muscles, the flame of arousal in his eyes as he stared at her, a painful erection that didn't entirely dissipate for three solid hours while she worked—all of it had been captured in the painting. When they'd finally made love afterward, it'd been like an inferno tearing through a fireworks storehouse.

All of it had ended up in the final photograph except his actual cock. For the cover photo, Joy had inserted a lush, large, juicy-looking bunch of grapes between his thighs in place of his raging erection.

"The *Vanity Fair* cover was hardly work," Joy said before she slipped one of his fingers between her lips.

"You know, I never really got you back for that," Everett mused as he watched her suck on his finger. His cock twitched when she began to slide it in and out of her warm mouth. He threaded the fingers of his other hand through her soft hair. It'd grown a few inches in the past few months. She wore it in a short bob that emphasized her cheekbones and large eyes. He'd been relieved and beyond grateful that Joy had been pronounced perfectly healthy at her last checkup. In the future, she'd only have to return every six months.

"You've gotten me back plenty of times," she murmured around his finger, giving him a bewitching smile before she bit the tip of his finger gently and released him.

"Not in the exact same way."

"Do you want to paint me?" she asked, amused.

"Yes."

She blinked.

"Of course I won't be able to do it with a thousandth of your skill, but my body paint will have its advantages."

She arched her eyebrows, looking bemused but interested. He grinned and walked out of the room, only to return a few minutes later with the box that had been delivered with the mail.

"I ordered this for you," he said, ripping open the box. "Well, for me, too."

Joy read the label on the package.

"'Erotic edible body paints—chocolate, strawberry, blueberry, peach and sweet cream.'"

Everett pumped his eyebrows. "Do you have any unused brushes?"

She laughed. "Yes." She walked over to a large bureau and opened a drawer. "Here," she said, handing him several brushes.

"Take off your clothes, little girl."

She gave him a droll glance, but began to unbutton her cotton blouse.

He watched her fixedly while he tore off several sheets of the white paper Joy used to protect the carpeting while she painted, the result being that he didn't make the paper long enough and had to start all over. When he'd laid several layers of the paper on the floor, he said, "Be right back." He hastened to Joy's and his bedroom and retrieved their favorite pair of padded leather cuffs from the bedside table. He grabbed a pillow from the hall closet.

"I didn't handcuff you for the Dionysus painting," she chastised amusedly when he reentered the room.

"Yeah, but I almost always cuff you. No reason to alter the tradition just because of a paint job," he murmured silkily, approaching her. She looked extremely beautiful standing there wearing nothing but a tiny pair of pale pink panties. Her breasts looked firm, full and tender, contrasting markedly with her delicate, narrow rib cage. He caressed one of the soft globes, molding her to his palm. Her nipple stiffened so quickly, he leaned down and pressed his lips to it, so grateful for her responsiveness . . . her sweetness.

"Lie down on your back on the paper," he said. He whipped his shirt off as she followed his instructions, and then removed his shoes and socks. A moment later, he came down on his hands and knees over her, the paints, brushes and cuffs in hand. He dragged the pillow beneath her head. "Stretch your arms over your head. Straighten them as best you can," he murmured.

He cuffed her wrists together, and then pocketed the key in his jeans with a satisfied smile. As always, the sight of the black leather cuffs next to her smooth skin, the knowledge that she would be helpless in the face of desire, sent a jolt of excitement through him.

"You're a sick, sick man, Everett Hughes," Joy said with wry amusement.

"And you love me for it."

"True," she conceded.

He grinned and opened the package of blue paint. He dipped the paintbrush into the thick liquid, stirring it, before he withdrew it and set the container next to Joy's hip.

"Let's see. Where to begin," he mused, studying his breathtaking human canvas. "Spread your legs so I can make an informed decision."

She did so slowly. She had trimmed her pubic hair very short. His pulse quickened at the sight of her pink, feminine folds. Unable to resist the lure, he lowered his head between her thighs and inhaled her subtle, sweet perfume. His cock responded to the smell of her sex instantly, swelling and lurching against the fabric of his jeans.

"So lovely," he murmured, kissing her once on her labia and evoking a small whimper from her throat before he crawled higher over her. "I may not have artistic talent," he said, "but I have the instinct of a lover. And it's telling me to start on Joy's sensitive ribs."

She jumped slightly when he touched the wet brush between two ribs and painted a stripe as far around her as he could go. He used the blue paint for the skin between her ribs and the peach-colored paint for the bones themselves. By the time he'd finished covering her ribs, he noticed that goose bumps had risen on her skin and that her nipples looked like hard, red berries.

"Cold?" he asked, gazing at his work appreciatively.

"No," she said in a strained voice. His gaze leapt to her face. Her cheeks were flushed, and her eyes had taken on the glassy sheen of arousal he so prized. He held her stare as he leaned down and tongued off a blue stripe slowly.

"Hmmm. Not bad. Blueberry." And then, a moment later, "Peaches and blueberries taste awesome together." He felt her shiver beneath his tongue as he licked along her tender sides. It never ceased to amaze—and arouse—him how sensitive she was there.

"I'm so glad you're enjoying it," she said breathlessly. She moaned and wiggled when his tongue dragged just below the lower curve of her left breast.

"You'd like it, I think. Want a taste?" he asked, lifting his head minutes later.

The sight of her lips parting made a stab of arousal go through him.

"Okay," she said, seeming a little dazed.

He grabbed the dark pink paint along with a fresh brush. He straddled her, his knees at either side of her chest, and dipped the brush into the liquid.

"Keep your lips parted. Just like that," he said as he began to trace her lips with the pink paint. The color looked vivid and a bit lewd on Joy's sweet, lush mouth. It excited him. His cock grew so stiff that his jeans were increasingly becoming too confining. He set aside the paint and brush and hastily unbuttoned his fly. He reached down his pant leg, grimacing as he drew his erection over the waistband. The fabric of his boxer-briefs and jeans bunched around his balls. His cock fell heavily, but his clothing propped it up so that it stuck out of his fly at a downward angle.

He glanced up when Joy moaned. She was staring at his penis avidly, the tip of her tongue slicking along her graphically pink lower lip.

"Uh-uh," he chastised lightly. "No dessert before supper."

He gently lifted her head and used the tip of his penis to trace her smile. His cockhead now thoroughly covered with the pink paint, he thrust it between her lips into the warm, wet cavern of her mouth. A shudder of pleasure went through him as she eagerly sucked away the paint.

"Ah, that's good," he muttered tensely, thrusting into her mouth several times. He felt a tingle deep within his balls. "A little too good, in fact," he muttered regretfully, pulling his cock out of her mouth and setting her head back on the floor. She looked up at him, her eyes glazed with desire, and licked off the remaining sugar from her lips. His cock bobbed in the air.

"I might have to spank you for that later," he told her.

She grinned like the Cheshire cat.

He chuckled and scooted backward.

"Hmmm, let's see. What flavors for the prettiest breasts in existence? Peaches and cream, I think."

He went to work, using the largest brush available to him to coat the curves of her breasts in the peach paint, carefully painting around the crests, leaving the nipples naked. He paused after he'd picked up a smaller brush and the white paint. "It seems a shame to cover your nipples," he said. "They're a work of art all on their own. Guess I'll just have to lick it off immediately," he said with a decisive shrug.

He dipped the brush into the creamy liquid. He painted one nipple, and then the other, and then set aside the paint and brush. Joy's breathing was becoming heavy. He came down over her on his hands and knees, elbows bent, and inserted just the tip of her breast between his lips. He listened to her moan softly as he first licked the sweet, cream-flavored, pebbled flesh and then sucked it greedily. She called his name sharply when he took a gentle bite of the sensitive flesh.

By the time he'd finished with both her breasts, her chest heaved as she panted. The firm globes of flesh were clean, damp and gleaming from his tongue. He was becoming unbearably aroused. There was something important he had to do before he lost his head in the heat of lust.

"Lower your hands to your belly," he said. "I'm going to paint your fingers."

She did so. He spent the next several minutes painting her fingers and one by one, laving off the paint with his searching tongue. A shudder went through her when he dragged his front teeth along the length of her last paint-covered digit—her ring finger.

"There's something missing here," he said gruffly, sucking the digit back into his mouth.

"The paint? It's running down your throat," she teased, watching him warmly.

"No, not the paint. This," he said, reaching into the back pocket of his jeans.

He slipped the ring onto her finger.

"Maybe it's not fair asking you while I have you at my mercy, but the truth is, I'll take whatever advantage I can get." He kissed her knuckles. "Will you marry me, Joy?"

He could tell by her flat, stunned expression that she hadn't entirely absorbed what was happening. Finally, she blinked. He saw her eyes narrow as she stared at the flashing diamond solitaire he'd just placed on her finger. He waited on tenterhooks.

"I hope you like it. I picked it out, but Katie helped me. If you don't like it, we can exchange it for another—"

She stared at him with an amazed expression.

"I *love* it."

"Does that mean the answer is yes?" he asked hopefully.

Her smile was incredulous, but radiant. "Yes," she said in a pressured whisper.

"Good. I guess that means I can uncuff you then, seeing as how you've agreed and all," he joked. She laughed as he dug for the key for the leather cuffs.

"I can't believe it," she said after he removed the cuffs. A tear had fallen down her cheek. She lifted her left hand and gazed at the ring and then his face in dawning wonder.

"Why can't you believe it? Did you really think I wasn't going to make an honest woman of you?"

"No. I can't believe it's possible to be this happy," she said simply.

His eyes smarted a little when he blinked. She started to sit up, one hand outstretched as if to embrace him, but he gently lowered her back so that her head again rested on the pillow.

"I want to finish." He ran his hand over her belly, his fingers skimming the strip of skin above her pubic hair. "I want to thank you for letting me into your world. I know it wasn't easy for you. I'm always going to be there for you, Joy."

"I know," she said in a choked voice, several more tears skittering down her cheek. "Thank you for not giving up on me, Everett. I'm always going to be there for you, as well."

He smiled and picked up the little container of chocolate paint. "I saved the best for last."

She whimpered and sighed as he carefully painted the liquid onto the lips of her outer sex and clit. She watched him with a tight focus, so much love in her eyes, as he set aside the paint and knelt between her thighs. He slid the tip of his tongue between the tender folds and agitated her clit. The taste of Joy's sweet musk mingling with the chocolate made him a little wild. He tongued off her labia carefully and then spread the lips wide, making her swollen clit his captive target. He stiffened his tongue and agitated the sensitive kernel of flesh ruthlessly, his actions unapologetically lewd and demanding.

He became so lost in his desire, he barely noticed her tense pleas or the sensation of her fingers tangling in his short hair or even her nails scraping his scalp. He opened his hand over her hip, the fingers of his other hand keeping her lips spread, making her immobile, insisting she take all the pleasure he could give her.

By the time he felt her shudder in release, there wasn't a trace of chocolate left. Only Joy's sweet cream coated his tongue and throat.

His breathing sounded harsh to his own ears as he clawed at his jeans and underwear, desperate to be rid of his clothing. He stifled a curse when he entered her tight, warm embrace. He leaned over her, his arms holding him off her, his naked cock buried deep inside her. A spasm of pleasure rippled through him as he stared down at Joy's perspiration-dampened face and rapt expression.

"You're going to be my wife," he said, feeling a savage sense of pride and possession.

"And you my husband," she said, awe crossing her features as she caressed his bunched arm muscles. She met his stare. "For better and for worse."

"And every blessed thing in between," Everett said before he began to move.